CRIES FROM THE LOST ISLAND

KATHLEEN O'NEAL GEAR

DAW BOOKS, INC.
DONALD A. WOLLHEIM FOUNDER
1745 Broadway, New York, NY 10019
ELIZABETH R. WOLLHEIM
SHEILA E. GILBERT
PUBLISHERS
www.dawbooks.com

First Printing, March 2020
1　2　3　4　5　6　7　8　9

TO DARLEEN BAKER

THANK YOU FOR TWENTY-FIVE YEARS OF FRIENDSHIP.

ACKNOWLEDGMENTS

I owe special thanks to William Michael Gear who is the joy in my heart and light of my world.

My editor, Sheila Gilbert, is simply the best in the business, and the incredibly talented people at DAW Books are amazing professionals.

Thanks hugely to Betsy Wollheim who continues to publish innovative and thought-provoking science fiction and fantasy. Some of my favorite books of all time have been published by DAW Books. It is an honor that my books are part of that legendary publishing house.

Lastly, Matt Bialer has been a friend for twenty-eight years, and he is the finest literary agent on the planet.

Thanks to you all. Literature is richer because of you.

CHAPTER ONE

By the time I was thirteen, I knew that the girl of my dreams was not what anyone would call a sane child. My first hint came on a bright autumn afternoon when Cleopatra Mallawi was helping me rake up mountains of fallen maple leaves from our front yard in Georgetown, Colorado.

At around two o'clock, Cleo took a break to lean on her rake and stare up at the mountain peaks visible through the branches that spread across the blue sky. Straight coal-black hair hung to her shoulders.

"Look, Halloran. A demon."

My full name is Halloran Justin Stevens, but pretty much everyone, except Cleo, calls me Hal.

After I'd combed blond hair away from my blue eyes, I glanced around the leaf-filled yard. I've always been overweight, and exertion really gets to me. My hooked nose was dripping sweat down the front of my denim shirt, so I wiped it on my sleeve. All I saw was another two hours of work.

"I don't see anything."

"Oh." She sounded disappointed. "That's okay."

She quietly returned to raking leaves, but I couldn't take my eyes off the place near the maple where she'd been looking. After a couple of minutes of examining every pile of leaves for hidden claws or fangs, I shrugged and started raking again.

Cleo was definitely the most interesting person in Georgetown. She'd been born in Macedonia, but grew up in Egypt, was fluent in nine languages, and had been orphaned during the revolution that rocked Egypt a few years before. She'd studied ancient Egyptian history—claimed she'd been Queen Cleopatra in a former life—and said she'd personally met a variety of Egyptian gods and demons. Not only that, Cleo had supposedly shot a demon with her father's pistol at the age of ten. Right after her parents' deaths, the demons had invaded her home, wearing gas masks, and she'd barely escaped with her life.

Hypnotized by the idea that a demon might be standing there—a demon only Cleo could see—I stopped raking, and asked, "Which demon?"

I've won the Colorado Classics Award three times—which is the state record. It's an award for young ancient history scholars, so I take this stuff seriously.

Cleo turned toward the maple. "A huge one with the head of a crocodile, the front legs of a lion and the hindquarters of a hippopotamus. She is known as Ammut, the Devourer of the Damned. Today she has turquoise skin. She and her earthly priests have kept me from reaching the Island of the Two Flames for over two thousand years."

The Island of the Two Flames was one version of the ancient Egyptian land of the dead. There were several versions. After all, Ptolemaic Egyptians were way more creative than modern people.

"Where do you see her exactly? Where's she standing?"

As though the famed demon from the Egyptian Book of the Dead was right there, only a few feet away, dread filled Cleo's eyes. "She's leaning against the maple with her arms crossed. Don't you see her at all, Halloran? Not even her shadow?"

I looked. "No."

"Well, she sees you. She's watching you."

Naturally, my blood had turned to ice.

You have to understand, I'm a true fear fanatic. I'm the happiest when I'm scared to the point of filling my Levis, which was one of the reasons I found Cleo so fascinating. Every time she talked about the demons that chased her, I had spectacular nightmares where I found myself running headlong down the streets of ancient Alexandria with giant lion-headed beasts bounding after me. The honking of horns on the Colorado street outside would metamorphose into court trumpets, the traffic on the Interstate became the roar of cheering crowds, and the shadows of tree branches cast upon my bedroom wall by the moonlight became gnarly demonic arms reaching out for me. Cool stuff.

Even more wonderful for my overactive adolescent imagination were the stories she told about plucking the lyre of Orpheus with her own hands or traveling to Sparta to smooth her fingers over the egg from which Helen of Troy had hatched. Since I was a voracious reader of historical tomes and considered myself to be the future world expert on ancient Rome and Egypt, being around Cleo was as exotic as seeing an alien spaceship land on the football field at Georgetown High. I plagued her to tell me stories about her life, which she did in a quiet dignified voice, only slightly accented. Such stunning wonders filled her long-gone world that I felt this modern age was but a pale reflection, tepid and boring beyond endurance. Which is probably why I play so many ancient world video games.

How she'd gotten to Georgetown was mostly a mystery, though I knew she'd come to live with her aunt and uncle. Apparently, her aunt was the only family she had left in the world. On the fateful day that Aunt Sophia had learned Cleo survived the riots, and her parents were dead, she'd immediately flown to Egypt to pick Cleo up and bring her back to America. Cleo's uncle, Dr. James Moriarity, taught Egyptian archaeology at Colorado State University in Fort Collins during the school year, but in the summers he excavated sites abroad. That's where he'd met Cleo's Aunt Sophia, a woman twenty years his junior, digging in Egypt.

By the time I was sixteen, I was five-nine, weighed two-ten, and was desperately in love with Cleo. We were inseparable. Often, we would lie together on the floor of my bedroom—as we were on this sunny May afternoon—studying maps of Ptolemaic Egypt and role-playing. She was my Cleopatra, and I was her Marcus Antonius.

The most famous lovers in history, their doomed romance was brilliant and passionate, and far more tragic than *Romeo and Juliet*, because Cleopatra and Antonius were not theatrical inventions. They had lived. And each had died by his or her own hand in 30 BC. Their rulership of ancient Egypt and their battle against Octavian was also one of the most glorious war stories of all time. The fact that Cleopatra and Antonius had suffered a spectacular defeat made them even more interesting to me. Especially Cleopatra. A queen at eighteen, for twenty-two years she ruled the last great Egyptian empire, lost it once, regained it, and—finally—heartbroken and alone, she lost everything.

"Who's that?" I tapped the image. The map was ringed with artistic sketches of notable people, most of whom I recognized, but not this one.

Cleo tilted her head to study the figure. "That's Cicero. He was a member of the Roman Senate and a detestable man." She added, "Antonius despised him as much as I did. He called Cicero the greatest boaster alive."

In the process of becoming scrupulous intellectuals, we insisted upon historical accuracy, so we refused to say things like Marc Antony or Beirut. It was Marcus Antonius and Berytus. We read aloud the works of Lucan, Plutarch, Appian, Josephus, and Dio, and discovered that none of those ancient authors could be trusted. In fact, when it came to the truth about the lives of Cleopatra and Antonius, there was obviously a secret historical conspiracy to destroy the evidence. Not one authoritative painting or sculpture of Cleopatra existed. Even Cicero's letters from 44 BC when Julius Caesar and Cleopatra had been together in Rome, were mysteriously missing. Dellius, who'd betrayed Antonius and Cleopatra at the Battle of Actium in 31 BC, had also written a chronicle. But it, too, had vanished. And though Appian had promised to tell more about Cleopatra and Caesar in his vast four-volume history of Egypt, none of those books existed today.

While Cleo could not say why (because she'd died before those things had happened), I concluded that Octavian had purposely purged the archives of all references to his dead enemies. He would later become known as the legendary Augustus Caesar, first Emperor of Rome. In fact, Octavian's own account of the Battle of Actium, where he'd defeated Antonius and Cleopatra, left out all references to them. To make matters worse, after their deaths, Octavian convinced the Roman Senate to issue a decree that the names "Marcus" and "Antonius" could never again be conjoined. It made perfect sense that the new Roman Emperor would leave no stone unturned when it came to conquering his enemies, including erasing their very existences.

Therefore—in the absence of facts—I turned to Cleo for information and sat rapt, listening to her extol the history she had supposedly lived. It was all mythic, larger-than-life, and utterly amazing. I so longed to step into her memories that I only felt truly alive when her soft lilting voice was guiding me into the past to walk the streets of Alexandria—a vision of gleaming white marble with the famed lighthouse soaring four hundred feet above the ocean waves in the distance.

Someday, we're going to Egypt together. To prepare me, she's been teaching me Egyptian, as well as ancient Greek and Latin, and she's promised to show me where Antonius is buried. That's really important, because no one knows where either of them is buried. Their true graves have never been found.

I rolled to my side and propped my head on my hand. "But Cicero was one of the greatest orators in history."

Cleo reached out to gently touch my cheek and stare into my eyes. Her smile melted my heart. "He was, Hal, that's what made him so dangerous. People listened to him."

"People like Octavian?"

"I knew no one of that name." She lowered her hand, and examined the bust of young Octavian on the map. Her delicate black brows drew together. "After the death of my lover, Julius Caesar, the man you call Octavian was called Gaius Julius Caesar, because Julius had adopted him in his will. I knew him as little Gaius." Venom filled her voice.

I protested, "But all my history books call him Octavian."

"Yes. They're wrong." It was a calm statement of fact.

Determined to prove her wrong, I got up and went to my bookshelf to pull down my encyclopedia, whereupon I discovered she was right. Octavian came from his name, Gaius Julius Caesar Octavianus. "Octavian" was actually . . .

There was a sharp knock on my closed door. "Hal? I need to speak to you," my father called.

"Just a minute, Dad."

My parents were experts at keeping me and Cleo apart. They constantly pushed me to date other girls, but I refused. Who needed to date when the reincarnated Queen of Egypt was in my bedroom staring at me with adoring green eyes?

Not only that, I had dirty blond hair, was overweight, and had a hooked nose that resembled an oversize eagle's beak. Plus, I was completely incapable of "small talk." I didn't know the latest movies, music, or celebrities, and I routinely bored girls to tears talking about dead people they'd never heard of. Not exactly the kind of boy that girls line up to date.

Quietly, Cleo said, "Your father wants me to leave, Hal. I'll be waiting on our bench. Come soon?"

"See you in fifteen." Our bench was in front of the local Starbucks.

"Excuse me," My father said as he rudely shoved open my door. "Cleo, I'm sorry, but it's time for you to leave. Hal has other obligations today."

I said, "What?"

Cleo grabbed her canvas shoulder bag and hurried toward him, politely saying, "I had a lovely time today, Mr. Stevens. Thank you for letting me come over. Goodbye."

She veered wide around my father, and her hurt expression broke my heart.

I glared at him. "What is it, Dad?"

Despite the fact that it was a weekend, my father was dressed in a starched white shirt and tan trousers, his blond hair greased and combed with the precision of a Greek statue. He was a high school English teacher, and looked it.

"Please, come into the kitchen, son. We need to talk." He turned and disappeared.

I didn't follow him because I was seething.

Ten minutes later, when I finally deigned to enter the kitchen, I found my father sitting erect at the table with his hands folded neatly in his lap. Trim and athletic, he had an annoyed look on his face. In clipped tones, he said, "You are aware, I assume, that there's no such thing as former lives?"

"Really? How do you know?"

"Don't use that tone with me, Hal. I'm on your side, but we need to have a realistic conversation about Cleo. I know you like her—"

"I love her, Dad."

He gave me one of those narrow-eyed looks. "Look, hands down, you are the best thing that's ever happened to Cleo, and we want her to get well, but she is not mentally stable. It worries us that you spend every free moment with her."

"I'm fine, Dad. Now, I got to go. I got plans." I started for the front door.

"Come back here. Please, sit down?" he asked. "Let me finish."

"I promised Roberto I'd be at his house at three! He has the second edition of 'The Ghost of Cleopatra,' where the ghost follows you through the whole video game, and I've only played it once so far. I'm going to be late!"

"*Sit.*" He stabbed a finger at the chair beside him, and his blond eyebrows plunged down over his slightly hooked nose.

I walked back and slumped into the chair. "What is it?"

Leaning toward me, he held out a hand as though to calm me down. "Hal, do you realize that Cleo's mental illness is one of the reasons you are ostracized at school? Isn't it bad enough that you're the smart kid? No wonder nobody wants to be your friend—"

"I have friends."

"Who?"

"Roberto—"

"Roberto the Biker Witch is completely pathetic and probably just as mentally unstable as Cleo. Do you really want to fit into *that* group?"

"Yeah, I do."

Dad ground his teeth for a couple of seconds. "Okay, look, your mother says that Cleo feeds your unnatural obsession with ancient cultures. You eat, sleep, and breathe ancient Rome and Egypt. That's all you talk about. You don't even go to movies, or try out for sports, or—"

"I thought you detested sports when you were in high school?"

"I did." Dad's mouth pressed into a tight white line. "But at least I tried out for football and basket—"

"Does my 'unnatural' obsession embarrass you? Is that the problem?"

Dad propped his elbows on the table and massaged his temples. "No, son. I love you, and I'm proud of you for being a scholar of the ancient world. But you need some time away from Cleo. You don't realize the depths of her illness. Just—"

"She's the best thing that's ever happened to *me*, Dad."

He took a breath as though girding himself for my response. "I know you believe that, Hal. Your mother and I have been talking about this for weeks. For your own good, we've decided to ban Cleo from visiting here for one week. Just to give you time to—"

I lurched to my feet. "You can't do that! I love her."

"Listen, Hal, you do not really know Cleo." He was speaking in slow precise words, as though explaining to a ten-year-old. "She has real problems. Under the right circumstances, your mother thinks she could even be dangerous. I mean it."

"I don't care. I love her, and she's the best historian I know."

Dad sagged back against his chair and gave me a pained look. "I don't get it. Why can't you find any good friends? I think you refuse to associate with quality people because you like being an outcast—"

"Nobody likes being an outcast, Dad. It's awful."

Dad squeezed his eyes closed for a long moment, and when he opened them, he said, "Hal, I'm trying to help you. I don't want you to have to go through what I went through. Believe me, I know what it's like to be the smartest kid in school. When I was your age—"

"No, you don't! You have no idea how it feels to be chased down the hallways with people throwing things at you, and all the girls cheering for the bad guys to kill you."

"Stop exaggerating. That's never happened. You're just trying to—"

"Yeah, right. I'm a liar."

"Now, son, I never said . . ."

He continued, but I blocked his voice and thought about Cleo. A tiny part of me reluctantly suspected Dad was right. Cleo was not mentally stable. My mom, a psychiatrist, had treated Cleo right after she came to America. And while Mom was adamant about doctor-patient confidentiality, I remember her saying once that Cleo's "memories" of ancient Egypt were really longings for a better Egypt; a homeland she still missed. And the demons that filled Cleo's waking nightmares were actually fanciful representations of the men in crisp uniforms, wearing gas masks, who had destroyed her world six years ago.

While I was gritting my teeth, my phone chimed in my pocket. I pulled it out and read Cleo's text: *R U okay? Please, come soon.* She always signed off with the Greek word *Ginest-hoi*, which meant "Let it be done."

Much to my father's dismay, I texted back: *There in 5.*

His mouth puckered like he'd just bitten into a sour lemon. "Was that her? Was that Cleo?"

"No, it was Roberto. I'm late. He wants to know if I'm still coming."

"Give me your phone. I want to see the number." He stuck out his hand.

"No way. It's none of your business."

"As long as you're under the age of eighteen, you're still a child, and it is my business. Now, please, give me your phone." Thrusting his hand closer to me, he snapped his fingers. "Right now!"

I stuffed the phone in my shirt pocket and threw down the proverbial gauntlet. "You'll just have to beat it out of me when I get home, I guess. I'm leaving, Dad. I'll be at Roberto's."

With that, I shoved out of the chair and started for the door.

"Hal, wait." Dad's stern expression transformed into serious worry. "Are kids really chasing you down the halls at school? You didn't get beat up again, did you? Is that why you're so surly today?"

Unfortunately, I did get beat up a lot. Nobody liked me much, which meant they enjoyed ganging up on me. Just last week my obsession with history became an issue when my archenemy, Alexander the Gross, got me in a headlock at lunch. Alex was studying demonology with the local whacko cult in Denver. While he wrung my neck, he announced to the other boys at the table that I was the reincarnated Julius Caesar, and he needed three of my pubic hairs to use in a magical warding-off ceremony against some other Satanists in San Francisco who were psychically attacking him. Two football players jumped on me to hold me down. What a fight that was. For five endless minutes, I got the holy crap knocked out of me while I fought to keep my pants on. There was no question in my mind but that if I lost the fight the nickname "Pubic-hair Hal" would be all over the Internet before I could escape the cafeteria.

When I finally knew I was doomed, I screamed, "KARNAK! KARNAK!" at the top of my lungs. Only two people in the world know my secret emergency code.

Fortunately, my best friend, Roberto, was standing in the food line when he heard it.

Roberto came crashing through the crowd with something in his hand, yelling, "Out of the way! Out of the way! *Corpse powder!*" When he blew the red powder from his hand into the Gross' face, Alex shrieked and ran off crying. Turned out to be chili powder, but—

"Did you hear me, son? I asked if you'd been fighting at school."

"Nothing major, Dad. Now, please, I just want to go over to Roberto's. I'm late, okay?"

"No, it's not okay. You're grounded for today. When your mother gets home, maybe she can explain to you why you can't spend all your time . . ."

Stamping to the front door, I threw it open and slammed it closed behind me with enough force to shake the house, and then I ran hard for the street before he could get outside. I only glanced over my shoulder when I was far enough away that I knew he wouldn't chase me. He was standing in the open door frowning at me as I blasted around the corner and out of sight.

CHAPTER TWO

I found Cleo in our usual meeting place in front of Starbucks. Clouds had moved in, as they often did on May afternoons in the Colorado high country. The muted light gave her white T-shirt a bluish tint that complemented her jeans. She'd tucked her shoulder-length black hair behind her ears and was biting her lip.

When I trotted up breathing hard, my phone chimed. I pulled it from my pocket and read Dad's text: *Sorry, son. I know you're at Starbucks. Come home. Let's talk.* Shoving it back in my pocket, I sat down next to Cleo. Years ago, my parents had installed an app on my phone that allowed them to find me no matter where I was, just in case I was abducted by a crazed pedophile.

"What happened, Halloran? Did you get another lecture about me?"

"Yeah, Dad pulled me aside to tell me you were totally insane, and I was crazy to believe any of your stories, and, oh-by-the-way, 'For your own good, your mother and I have decided to ban Cleo from visiting here for one week'."

Cleo blinked and looked away. "What did you say?"

"I told him I loved you."

For several long moments she stared up at the mountains with a sad expression. Finally, in a faint voice, she said, "I love you, too."

"You okay?"

"I just . . . it hurts. I know I'm not always . . . here . . . but your mom really helped me. I—"

"Doesn't matter. I don't care what my parents think."

Cleo clutched her canvas bag in her lap and stared at me with tormented green eyes. I could tell she was trying to work up the courage to tell me something. Her face was tense with the struggle.

"Hal, I've never told you . . . what it was like right after I came to America. I was really sick. I didn't speak for months. I ran away and hid from my aunt and uncle several times. No matter where I went, I felt the demons seeking me in my dreams. Even after the police found me and dragged me home, I stole knives from the kitchen and slept with them in my hand. It wasn't safe to be around me."

Her beautiful voice gave me a glimpse of the terrified ten-year-old child she had been, trying to hide from the demons, never able to rest. Knowing no one in this world could protect her from the evil that stalked her, waking or sleeping. It brought back my own childhood fears that monsters lurked under my bed or were hiding in the back of my closet. The difference was that Cleo had stood face-to-face with her monsters. They'd killed her parents.

"But you're well now, Cleo."

"I—I think I'm well, but maybe not. Maybe you shouldn't be around me. I could be danger—"

"Honestly, I don't think it's about you, Cleo," I said soothingly. "I think it's actually about me. They want me to be normal, whatever that is. Dad said the problem is that you feed my obsession with the ancient world. Instead of studying Greek and Latin, they want me to go to movies, date other girls, and try out for the football team. God forbid," I groaned. "When it comes to me, I think my parents want two and two not to equal four."

Cleo gently touched my cheek and smiled up at me with all the love in the world in her eyes. "I've prayed that before. Haven't you?"

That made me smile. "Often."

She held her canvas bag tightly for a moment, then she unzipped it. For a while, though, she just sat there. "I have a favor to ask. I should have asked earlier, but your father interrupted before I'd actually decided . . ." She paused.

"Anything. You know that."

Glancing down the street at the tourists dragging children by the hands, she halfway pulled a golden medallion from her bag—just enough that I could really see it. About the size of my palm, it had a hole in the top, as though it had been worn as a stunning pendant. The gold was crusted with what appeared to be rubies, sapphires, and emeralds. Greek letters encircled the rim of the medallion.

"My God, that looks real! Where did you get it? Is that something your uncle found on an excavation?"

I reached for it, but she carefully hid it in her bag again. "My father found it in the desert near Port Said, Egypt. He gave it to me just before the Rebellion. He said the medallion had belonged to me in 30 BC."

"In the desert? You mean on an archaeological excavation?"

Cleo nodded. "At the site of Per Amun. I'm not exactly sure where in the ruins he found it. I think he was afraid to tell me. All I know for certain is that he dug it up along the Great Horus Road, which runs through the site."

"But I thought Per Amun was gone, erased by the sands of time?"

"Some of the ruins still exist. Today, archaeologists call the site Pelusium, but locals call it Tell el-Farama." She slipped her hand into her bag and seemed to be holding the medallion for protection. "My aunt and uncle tried to take the medallion away from me this morning."

"They can't do that. Your dead father gave it to you. Why would they want to take it away?"

Cleo looked frightened. "They didn't know I had it until today. I've kept it hidden for years. My father told me to never show it to anyone."

"Then how did your aunt and uncle find it?"

"I've started sleeping with it under my pillow. I forgot it was there, and my aunt found it on wash day."

I took a moment to suck in a deep breath while I considered that news, then I reached out and took her free hand to squeeze it gently. "Why are you sleeping with it? What are you afraid of?"

She whispered, "A few nights ago I—I saw something. A demon, I think. But it might have been a real man. It was really dark; it stood at the foot of my bed wearing an Egyptian Army uniform. It wants the medallion."

The hair at the nape of my neck stood on end. The vision didn't surprise me. Not really. In her mind, ancient Egyptian demons served in the national army. And why wouldn't they? At the age of ten her parents had locked her in their apartment with a loaded pistol and gone down into the streets to participate in a peaceful demonstration against the government thugs that ruled Egypt. She'd never seen them again. Instead, her door had been broken down by men in blood-soaked uniforms, shouting orders. Her demons wore gas masks and carried guns.

I matched her whisper: "Will the medallion protect you from the demon?"

"I don't know. Father said . . ."

A small herd of tourists shuffled by carrying brightly colored plastic bags. We went silent. I could hear the steam engine chuffing up the Georgetown Loop railroad, and smell the scent of pines that carried on the wind.

After the herd passed, Cleo said, "Father said I had to give this medallion to his old friend Samael, a legendary Egyptian archaeologist."

"Why?"

"I think it was some kind of secret bargain. Father said that when I was old enough I had to give this to Samael. In return, he would give me the sacred dagger that will allow my soul to climb out of the netherworld of *Duat* and travel to the Island of the Two Flames."

"How can a dagger get your soul out of Duat?"

"It opens a channel of light that leads to the island. All I have to do is follow it. But I must have the dagger in my hand."

All ancient Egyptian beings, gods, demons, the dead, inhabited the afterlife, called Duat. But at certain times the boundary between life and death weakened and allowed the living to visit the dead. It also allowed supernatural intruders, like gods and demons, to cross over into the world of the living. Apparently, the dagger facilitated such otherworldly events.

"Why would a demon want the medallion?"

"To keep me here in this world, I think."

"I don't understand."

"They want me to live forever, Halloran. To be reborn over and over again. It's punishment."

"Punishment? For what?"

As though she did not wish to remember, she quietly said, "Do you know that Antonius offered to kill himself to save me? Many times before that last day. I—I betrayed him. Before Actium. Not to save myself. I did it to save our children and Egypt, but he deserved my loyalty. He had sacrificed so much for me. Even on that last day, he forgave me, he . . ." She couldn't finish. Tears filled her eyes and she looked away.

Just now Cleo seemed much older than her sixteen years, more like a grown woman who had witnessed the worst that life could throw at anyone.

She wiped her wet eyes with her hand. "Father gave me the medallion at the same time he handed me the pistol. That was moments before he and my mother went down to the demonstration where they were murdered. He said that if the sacred dagger had been buried with me over two thousand years ago, I would never have been reborn."

"Why wasn't it buried with you?"

"I don't remember. Maybe my servants couldn't find it. It was so hectic on August tenth of 30 BC. Anyway . . ." She zipped the bag closed and handed it to me. "Please guard the medallion for me? You're the only one I trust. Please, please, don't tell anyone you have it."

Though I'd often heard Cleo talk about the demons that accompanied her through life, I'd never heard such despair in her voice. Giving her a solemn nod, I slipped the long strap over my shoulder. "I won't."

Cleo exhaled the word, "Thank you," and leaned her head against my shoulder as though in relief. Her black hair fell down the front of my denim shirt like a silken ebony mantle.

Putting my arm across her shoulders, I pulled her close and kissed the top of her head. "Don't worry now, Cleo. Everything's all right."

Thunder rumbled across the peaks, and I saw lightning flash to the north. In another half hour or so it was going to be raining. "I'm headed to Roberto's to play video games. Want to come?"

Cleo looked up at me and smiled. "Thanks, but I have to study for the geometry final exam."

So did I, of course, but I wasn't going to. Geometry was second nature to me, as easy as breathing. "Want me to walk you home?"

Cleo's house stood in a grove of pine trees just outside of town. It was about a twenty-minute walk.

"No, but . . . ." She lifted her head and looked up at me. "Halloran? Can you . . . Don't panic, okay? It's finals week in Fort Collins. My aunt and uncle are teaching late classes tonight. They won't be home until after ten. Can you come over and stay with me until they get home? Maybe . . . maybe even spend the night with me? That's the only way I'll feel safe."

The invitation sent a little jolt of fear and . . . well, other things, through me. *Spend the night* with her? I contemplated all the horrors my parents would heap upon me if I didn't come home tonight, but after today, they deserved it. I'd have to ditch my phone somewhere, of course, or they'd know exactly where I was.

"Yes, of course, I will."

CHAPTER THREE

B y the time I'd walked halfway to Roberto's house in the historic heart of town, a misty rain drifted down around me. Clouds hung like gauzy scarves on the mountains, and I could see a few of the resident bighorn sheep grazing on the steepest slopes.

Turning onto Roberto's street, I trotted toward the green-and-yellow historical home with the giant cottonwood in the front yard. The house had been designed by some renowned architect in the 1890s and had a broad porch supported by carved posts and a cupola. My mother, who hated all buildings over the age of three, called it a "gingerbread nightmare."

I rang the doorbell and waited, listening to the neighborhood dogs bark at each other.

When Roberto opened the front door, he gave me a quick once-over. "Christ, you've gained another five pounds since I saw you yesterday. Are you ever going on a diet, fat boy?"

"Just as soon as you stop blowing priests for communion wine."

Roberto rolled his eyes. "My father's a sommelier at the Holiday Inn. I don't drink cheap shit."

Robert Dally, who preferred to be called "Roberto" always dressed like a bad-ass biker, which is how he saw himself. After all, he had a Honda 125. To project this image, he wore a scruffy leather jacket and torn faded jeans. He was rail thin, or as my mother said, "Pathologically emaciated." Four pentagrams dangled from his left ear to tell everyone he was a witch, although the local coven had denied him entrance on the grounds that he was just too weird. His brown hair hadn't been washed in at least a week, which he considered very cool, and hung around his freckled face in greasy chin-length locks.

Roberto said his witchcraft powers had come at the age of four, after he'd died. Really. Dead as a doornail. He'd fallen into a river while his family was on a hunting trip, and when his father dragged him out, he'd had no heartbeat. Ten minutes of artificial respiration had brought him back to life, but he'd been a little bizarre ever since. For one thing, he spent weekends target practicing with pistols and rifles, which is why everybody at school thought he was a latent serial murderer.

I followed him across the room and flopped down on the blue couch in front of the big-screen TV that took up half the wall, while Roberto sorted through the games on the bookshelf. "Where's your parents?"

"Out."

"Doing what?"

With a shrug, he answered, "Rolling drunks for food stamps. How do I know? They don't tell me where they're going. It's like every Saturday is their own personal screw-fest. They rent a room so I can't hear them."

"No joke? At the Holiday Inn?"

He shook his head and frowned at a game before shoving it back on the shelf. "Naw, a fleabag down the mountain called The Garden Plot. Seventeen bucks an hour."

My brows lifted in admiration. He knew the price. Roberto prided himself on being the 007 biker witch of Georgetown. Spying on people wasn't a hobby with him; it was defense intelligence work.

"You followed your parents to their love nest? And asked the desk clerk how much it cost?" I asked in disbelief.

"Sure. After they forced a bottle of ammonia into my hands and made me wipe my greasy ear prints off their bedroom door, they stomped out of the house. I wanted to know where they were going."

He tossed a couple of games aside, and finally turned around to squint at me. "Want a beer before we play?"

"Okay."

When Roberto slouched toward the kitchen, I slid Cleo's bag from my shoulder and turned my attention to the twenty or so smutty paperbacks that covered the coffee table. Used bookstores had been his salvation since the age of eleven when he'd first discovered Internet porn, and his parents had first discovered "parental locks."

I fanned through the pages of a couple of books. Most were sizzling romances with lurid covers, but a few "adult" westerns sprinkled the mix. Usually these hid under Roberto's bed. He must be absolutely certain his parents weren't coming back for a while, or they wouldn't be out here in clear sight. Roberto had never actually read the books, of course, just the dog-eared pages.

While Roberto clattered around the kitchen, I used the books to build a pretty respectable replica of the Giza pyramid. A short time later, Roberto returned with two Buds stuffed in his jacket pockets and a plate mounded with cold hot dogs and Velveeta slices. He pulled one beer from his pocket and used it to demolish my engineering marvel, before he tossed me the can and set the plate in the middle of Giza's ruins.

"You're a freak, you know that?" He gestured to the paperbacks. "Hot throbbing thighs and pulsing manhoods stare you in the face, and all you can think of is the Sphinx? You need help, bro."

It wouldn't do any good to explain to Roberto the difference between a pyramid and a sphinx, so I just said, "I tried to read a couple, but all the dog-eared pages were stuck together."

Popping the top, I downed a long satisfying drink of Bud. My mother only drank wine, and Dad didn't approve of any beer unless it resembled crankcase drippings. By my standards, the total lack of flavor was a gourmet treat.

Roberto dropped onto the couch beside me and cracked open his beer. "So, how's your day been? Holed Cleo yet?"

I shook my head. "Bad day. Dad had a heart-to-heart with me. Told me they were banning Cleo from coming over for a week."

"No way." Roberto looked truly concerned. He knew I was madly in love with Cleo, and he liked her, too. Mostly because she was strange and shunned at school. Roberto was a loyal sort who figured all of us outcasts had to stick together.

"Yeah. In the middle of the lecture Cleo texted me, and Dad started climbing the walls, told me to give him my phone and go to my room, because I was grounded for the day."

Roberto leaned back and draped one arm over the couch back to stare at me. "Yet here you sit. How'd that happen?"

"I shoved the phone in my pocket and told him he could beat it out of me when I got home."

Roberto took a long swallow of beer, belched loudly, and said. "You're my hero. So, you're going to stop at the pharmacy on the way home to stock up on bandages, right? Your dad lifts weights."

I upended my beer, expertly drained the can, and set the empty on the coffee table. "Not going home."

Roberto stared incomprehensibly at me for a second, then a broad grin split his face. "Yeah? Headed to LA to become a movie star? I always wanted to become a street beggar in New York. You know how much those shysters make in a day? There was a PBS special on it."

I thought about it before I lied, "I'm going to hide out in the forest behind Cleo's house for a few days. Can you take care of my phone for me? Otherwise, they'll track me down like a rabid dog."

"Yeah, sure, but if you're going camping for a week, you'll need a shitload of toilet paper, my man. Remember last year when Mom and Dad shipped me off to that summer conservation institute? Two or three days of leaves and rocks and you'll run home screaming."

I'd actually scoped out the forest before, thinking that if I ever had to make a run for it the old, boarded-up gold mine shaft that sank into the mountainside behind Cleo's house would make a reasonable hideout. Providing that no idiot miner a hundred years ago had left a crate of crystallized dynamite down there, I figured I could survive for at least a week.

"So, bring me a four-pack of toilet paper."

"Jesus! Four rolls in a week? I'd barely use one, if that. You really are full of shit."

"Okay, *one* roll. I'll make do."

Roberto took another drink, and gave me a sideways grin. "Can do. Be there tomorrow."

That was the thing about Roberto. Despite his quirky personality, I could depend on him. I suspect if my life was in danger, Roberto would throw himself in front of a bullet to protect me.

"Okay, I've got two new games: 'The Ghost of Cleopatra II' or 'The Gangster Cyclops from Centaurus.' Your choice. "

"'The Ghost—'"

"Yeah, I knew it. You get orgasmic when Cleopatra's ghost starts following you through the ruins of Karnak."

Roberto chuckled, finished his beer in four swallows, and walked to the bookshelf to pull down the TV remote, but before he could get there, my phone vibrated.

Digging it out of my pocket, I checked the number, and said, "Hi, Cleo. What's hap—"

"Halloran, *help!*" she shouted into my ear loud enough that Roberto heard her. *"Oh, my God. They. . . !"*

He spun around. "She sounds freaked. What's wrong?"

"Cleo, what's wrong?" I leaped to my feet, grabbed her bag, and slung it over my shoulder. "What . . ."

The phone went dead.

"Cleo? Cleo?" Like an idiot, I held the phone out in front of me and stared at it.

Roberto's blue eyes widened. "What was that about?"

"I don't know, but we have to get there fast!"

"Let's take my bike!"

I followed him at a run through the house and into the garage where I jumped on the rear of his 1973 rust-bucket Honda SL 125. It took Roberto four tries to kick it to life, and then we whined off down the street in the middle of a downpour so heavy we couldn't see thirty feet ahead of us. Old Man Jackson, standing in his window next door, stared at us as we sped by. Soon, the mountains disappeared in the onslaught. All I could see from the back was a gray lightning-slashed haze.

"Faster, Roberto! *Faster!*"

CHAPTER FOUR

The tires slipped as Roberto swerved around the corner and we wobbled onto the dirt road that led to Cleo's house. When we hit the potholes, the Honda bounced and rattled as though about to fall apart. I clung to Roberto's middle and tried to see anything through the rain. Finally, her small log house appeared, and the first thing I noticed was that the front door was wide open.

"Come on! Come on, Roberto!"

He gunned the throttle and almost lost the bike in the mud, but managed to keep it upright long enough to slide to a stop in front of the house.

I leaped off the back and ran through the open door.

The house looked as though a bomb had exploded inside. The refrigerator and kitchen stove lay on their sides, heaped with splintered wood. It took me a minute to figure out that the wood had been chairs. The couch. The dining room table. Thousands of torn pages fluttered in the storm winds that whipped through the front door. They were all that was left of the books that had stuffed the bookcases.

I stood there gasping for air for way too long before I raced through the house, calling, "Cleo? Cleo, where are you?"

"Oh, dear God," Roberto said as he entered the house, but by that time I was up the stairs searching the two demolished bedrooms. There was almost nothing left of Cleo's room. Her dresser, bed, and beloved history book collection were little more than piles of debris.

"Roberto!" I yelled down. "She's not here!"

"Okay, I'm going outside to search for her!"

Roberto's boots hammered across the wood floor, and then I heard him shout, "There are footprints in the mud out here, but they're getting washed away fast!"

I lurched down the stairs and found Roberto kneeling, looking at the mud.

They were Cleo's tracks, all right. I knew the tread of her Nikes better than my own.

"Somebody tore this place apart, Hal. Looks like she ran away."

Cupping a hand to my mouth, I shouted into the storm, *"Cleo?* Where are you?"

The deluge eased slightly, becoming a normal rainstorm rather than a downpour, and I could finally see her trail heading toward the old boarded-up gold mine. She must have been trying to reach it. It took three or four seconds for it to occur to me that if I could still make out her tread, it had only been moments since she'd burst through the front door. I unzipped the shoulder bag and pulled out the ancient medallion. I didn't have anything else to protect myself.

"What in holy hell is that thing?" Roberto asked. "Where'd you get it?"

My heart almost stopped when two rifle shots rang out.

From up in the trees.

Then screams.

Another shot.

I roared, *"Cleo?"* and lurched toward the sounds with my feet slipping and sliding in the mud.

"Hal! Dude, we're running *into* gunfire. You crazy?"

I didn't have the time to answer. To his credit, Roberto kept following, panting right behind me. I knew he was scared stiff. So was I. But that's how you know a true friend. When you're in trouble, he gives himself up for dead and follows you into gunfire.

"Look!" Roberto said. "She veered off before she got to the mine, and ran up the slope into those trees."

Jerking around, I saw where he was pointing, saw her trail curve sharply right, and head for the towering pines. I charged up the hill. When I entered the trees, the wind picked up, flailing the branches and shrieking around the trunks. The water-soaked needles shook rain down on me. Her trail had vanished in the springy forest duff.

"I don't see her, Roberto. Do you?"

"No. I don't see her or her trail!"

With my heart in my throat, I ran blindly up the slope. A hunting rifle lay about thirty feet into the trees. Her uncle's. I almost stumbled over it. Even before Roberto picked it up, I knew it must be the weapon she'd used to try and protect herself.

"It's been fired. I can smell the gunpowder," Roberto said. He drew back the bolt to check the magazine for bullets and then stared through the barrel. He was an expert rifle and pistol shot. "Empty. She fired until she ran out of ammo." He started to put the rifle down.

"Keep the rifle," I ordered. "You can use it as a club, if nothing else."

"Should have thought of that myself." Roberto cradled it across his chest. "You think the guy who attacked her is still here?"

"Could be. Be careful!"

I trudged higher up the slope with my gaze moving across the forest, expecting to see men with guns everywhere. But all I saw were smoke-colored wet trees dripping rain and an occasional squirrel leaping through the branches.

"No . . ." Roberto said. "Is that her?"

Roberto swept by me, his legs pumping, struggling up the mountain, heading for what appeared to be a white T-shirt visible between two dark tree trunks.

Suddenly, I couldn't get air into my lungs. What had she been running from? Something terrible.

Roberto dropped the rifle and fell to the ground beside her.

"Hal, get up here!"

Each step I took, my heart pounded more forcefully. It became a hammer in my chest, battering my ribs. Light-headed, I could no longer feel my feet striking the ground. What had happened? Why would anyone hurt Cleo? She was just a troubled sixteen-year-old girl.

When I arrived, Roberto was quietly sobbing. On the ground before him, Cleo lay on her back with her hair spreading like a black halo around her pretty face. The coppery scent of blood filled the air. Standing there with the medallion clutched in my fist, I didn't realize I was shaking until I dropped it. Slashes, like knife wounds, split her arms and legs. *Or ... claw marks?*

"Cleo?"

I was crying when I sat down and cradled her head against my chest. Rocking her back and forth, I said, "I'm sorry. I'm sorry I didn't walk you home."

No answer, but an agonizing second later, I realized she was breathing. I sucked in a surprised breath. "She's alive. Roberto, she's alive! Call the police."

Roberto stumbled to his feet and pulled his phone from his jacket pocket. While he gave the police the details, I smoothed Cleo's silken hair with my hand and whispered to her, "Everything is going to be okay. I promise. Help is coming. Can you hear me? I'm right here, Cleo. I'm not leaving you."

She stirred weakly, and her eyes fluttered open. I saw our whole life together reflected in those green depths. All the smiles and laughter, all the serious discussions. I saw how much she loved me.

"Medallion," she whispered.

"It's right here, Cleo?" I picked it up and held it in front of her so she could see it.

"Don't . . . don't let . . . My aunt and uncle can't get their hands on it."

A suffocating feeling closed my throat. I reached down to twine my fingers with hers. "You are not going to die, Cleo. Help is coming, I can hear sirens—"

"If they find it, they . . . they'll . . . ."

"Roberto," I said as I tossed the medallion to him. "Start thinking crime scene, and hide this somewhere nobody will find it."

"Got it!" He plunged down the hill and into a big briar of currant bushes.

"Did your uncle do this, Cleo? Did he hurt you?"

She gave me a sleepy look. As though it took too much strength to keep her eyes open, she blinked a few times and closed them.

Roberto yelled, "Cops coming!" and ran stumbling farther down the slope, waving his arms at the two sheriff's cruisers, shouting, "Here! We're up here!"

"Halloran."

Her voice had grown so faint I had to place my ear almost over her lips to hear her. "What is it, Cleo?"

"I . . . I don't want to live forever. Need to . . . to get to the island."

My throat had gone so tight I could barely answer: "I know, Cleo."

Cleo was fading away, slipping into oblivion before my very eyes. As her blood soaked through my pants, her eyes seemed to sink into her skull. I almost couldn't feel it, but she weakly squeezed my hand, then her fingers relaxed, and Cleo went limp in my arms.

"Cleo?"

My soul was dying. I could feel it draining from my body, along with every ounce of strength I had left. The scent of pines seemed suddenly stronger, as though the storm winds had collected the fragrance from all across the mountains just to blow it down upon us.

That's when I heard a crackle.

Twigs snapping.

Through a blur of tears, out in the forest, I saw something . . . Turquoise. An Egyptian uniform. Red hair. For one blinding instant, it leaned out from behind the spruce to stare at me.

It was a face straight out of the Egyptian Book of the Dead.

As though stepping back into Duat, I saw a burst of light. Then it vanished.

CHAPTER FIVE

I was sitting in the interrogation room at the local sheriff's office, shaking, when the officer came in. Roberto sat slumped in his chair beside me. I kept staring at my right fist. I couldn't seem to unclench my fingers. My hand was covered with Cleo's blood. I was holding onto a part of her, the only part I had left, and I couldn't let her go. It didn't matter that I'd held her as she'd died. I knew she still needed me to protect her.

"You boys okay?" the officer asked as he closed the door behind him and walked over to sit on the other side of the table, opposite us. He had wiry gray eyebrows and buzz-cut gray hair.

"Yeah, sure," Roberto said. "We just found our best friend murdered. We're fine, thanks. You?"

"All right, I know you're both in shock. Try to relax." Every time the man looked at me, I felt like a stiletto had been plunged into my chest. "I'm Officer Sackett. Can you tell me what happened?"

My brain had stopped working. I swear. I was having trouble remembering anything. In a small stunned voice, I stammered, "I-I didn't walk her home. I should have walked her home."

Officer Sackett leaned forward. "What time was that? Where were you when she asked you to walk her home?"

I forced myself to try and recall. "She . . . she didn't. Ask. But I should have. We were at the Starbucks. Around three."

Since the officer was not taking notes, I assumed the entire session was being recorded, and instinctively looked around the little room for cameras. If we were being recorded, we were probably also being filmed.

"I called your parents. They're on the way. Your father said you were surly this afternoon, Mr. Stevens. Said you had a violent argument with him, stamped out of the house, and ran off. That true?"

I opened my mouth, but for a few awful instants no words came out. "I went to meet Cleo."

"But you told your father you were going over to Mr. Dally's to play video games."

"I met Cleo at Starbucks first."

He leaned back in his chair. "Uh-huh. What games did you play when you got to Mr. Dally's?"

"What?"

"Games. What did you play?"

I shrugged and shook my head at the same time. "I . . . I don't think we played any. Did we?" My memory had huge gaps. I turned to Roberto. "Did we play any games?"

The officer turned to Roberto and squinted one eye at him.

Roberto said, "We didn't have time to play. While we were sitting around talking, Cleo called and said she needed help, so we took my bike to her house."

"Your next-door neighbor, Mr. Jackson, said you both jumped on the Honda and left in a hurry at approximately 3:45 pm. Your parents also said they found empty beer cans on the living room table. Had you been drinking?" His gray brows lowered as though he thought we were the worst sort of juvenile delinquents.

Roberto seemed to be coming back to himself. He crossed his arms over his chest and announced, "Nobody's read us our rights, you know that? I want an attorney."

In a threatening manner, Officer Sackett leaned across the table toward us. "Listen, boys, you're in trouble. Real trouble. You realize you're both suspects in a murder case? You could help yourselves by being cooperative."

Roberto shook his head. "Not a chance. And I want to see my parents. Right now. Are they out there in the waiting room?"

Officer Sackett's voice dropped to a low threatening growl. "All right, Mr. Dally. My assistant will escort you to your parents."

Instantly, another officer came in and took Roberto away. Before Roberto left, he gave me one of those "don't say a word" looks.

But I wanted to tell someone. I had to. Maybe if I told the police everything, they could find the killer.

For several moments, Officer Sackett ground his teeth with an ugly look on his face.

"Are m-my parents out there, too?" I stammered.

"No. I told you the truth. They're on their way."

Finally, he lifted his eyes. His stern gaze went through me like a lance. "I need you to tell me exactly what happened."

Tears filled my eyes. "I don't remember much."

"Just start at the beginning. Tell me what you do remember."

"Well, I mean . . . I don't . . ." Taking a deep breath, I spoke in a rush of words that came out so fast I almost choked on them: "Cleo was Queen Cleopatra in a former life, but the demon Ammut won't let her go to the Island of the Two Flames, so she keeps being reborn in new bodies. I think it has something to do with the fact that she betrayed Marcus Antonius in 30 BC. Or maybe 31 BC at the Battle of Actium. I—I'm not sure."

Officer Sackett blinked a couple of times. "I'm asking about the murder. Do you have any idea who did this? Did you see anyone else out there at the scene?"

The conversation went straight downhill after that.

CHAPTER SIX

Six days later when I followed my parents out to the cemetery for the funeral, it was raining.

A green canopy roofed the chairs in front of the freshly dug grave. Only a few people had come. Roberto and his family sat in the second row, behind Cleo's aunt and uncle. Three of our teachers were there. One man I didn't know sat in the very back. Short and stocky, he had black hair and a carefully clipped mustache. Late fifties, probably, he was around five feet five inches tall. He looked Egyptian, and I wondered if he was a close relative of Cleo's. When he fixed his blue eyes on me, I had the urge to flinch.

As I looked around, it was stunning to me that Roberto and I were the only friends her age that she had in the entire world.

As we walked forward, Cleo's uncle, Dr. Moriarity, stood up. A tall muscular man with graying brown hair and black eyes, he was fifty-eight and looked like he'd spent all those years in bright sunlight. Deep wrinkles cut across his weathered face. Black-rimmed glasses and a thick beard gave him a sinister appearance. He gestured to the front row. "Please, sit with us. You're family."

Lowering myself onto the chair beside him, I nodded politely to Cleo's Aunt Sophia. The black-haired woman gave me a weak smile. She looked so sad. Her eyes were badly swollen and bloodshot. She reached across Dr. Moriarity's chest to clasp my hand, and say, "Thank you, Hal, for being her friend. She loved you so much."

Tears tightened my throat when I replied, "I loved her, too."

"I know you did."

My mother and father sat down to my left. The closed coffin rested on the stand next to the grave. It was polished steel. A bouquet of her favorite flowers, lilacs, spread across on top. I stared at it and listened to the blood pulsing in my ears, a slow dull rhythm. This was a nightmare. . . .

It couldn't be real.

Cleo couldn't be dead. I could still feel her presence and hear her voice talking inside me. *I'm right here, Halloran.*

Father Josephs stepped up to the podium and opened a Bible. A short white-haired old man, he had gentle eyes and a deep voice. I barely heard anything he said. Something about how much we'd all loved Cleo, what an excellent student she'd been, how much she had suffered in her life, and how it was over now because she was with God in heaven.

After a while, I couldn't stand it. I closed my eyes and pretended I was walking the magnificent streets of ancient Alexandria with Cleo. Hand in hand, we strolled past Doric tombs decorated with crocodile gods in Roman garb, Ionic marble columns, and gigantic sphinxes and falcons, which lined the pathways to Greek temples. Down the street ahead of us, the awe-inspiring lighthouse stood on the western side of the harbor entrance to Pharos Island and was connected to the city by a long man-made causeway. Soaring into the sky, the lighthouse was not merely an engineering marvel; like all Ptolemaic monuments, it was a work of artistic brilliance that glittered in the sunlight reflecting from the vast blue Mediterranean Sea. Life-size paintings of Egyptian gods and goddesses covered the structure. The magnificent turquoise image of Set stared down upon me, which made me feel very small. Though, oddly, I was different in the daydream, taller, more muscular, and dark-haired. Obviously, I was playing Antonius in my daydreams. Cleo was older. In her thirties, maybe, and stunningly beautiful. Cleopatra had been thirty-nine when she'd committed suicide.

As we stared at the lighthouse, she took my arm and leaned her head against my shoulder. I bent down to kiss her and breathed deeply of her lemon-scented hair. "All will be well, my love. Stop worrying."

"He's coming. You know he is. By withholding the wheat, we've given him no choice. Rome is starving. There will be war."

"And we will defeat him. We just have to force him to fight on land. Sea battles are not my strength—"

Dr. Moriarity leaned sideways to whisper, "Did she give you the medallion before this happened? We can't find it anywhere."

Like a slap in the face, the words brought me back to the funeral, and I found myself staring at a steel coffin adorned with lilacs. The scent of wet earth rode the wind that swept the graveyard. Losing Cleo and Egypt was almost unbearable. It took me a few moments to gather my wits, before I could say, "What medallion?"

Dr. Moriarity glared at me through his thick glasses. Barely audible, he said, "You're the only person she would have given it to. I want it. It doesn't belong to you."

"What can you tell me about the Island of the Two Flames? How do you find it?"

His black eyes flared. "Did she tell you to ask me that? Is she trying to get there?"

"I've been researching it. It's in the middle of the Nile, right? Where exactly?"

Moriarity lifted a finger and pointed it at me, as though about to make a threat, when my father bent forward to hiss, "What's the problem, Moriarity?"

The professor shook his head and sat back in his seat, but for the rest of the funeral, he kept turning to glower at me.

When the ghastly ordeal was finally over, and the workmen were lowering the coffin into the grave, I walked a short distance away to stare up at the mountains. I couldn't watch them shovel dirt over the top of my Cleo. My whole body hurt. I didn't want to feel anything. Not ever again. Since the mountains had always filled me with a sense of peace, I tried to will myself into their cold stone hearts.

Roberto walked up beside me. He'd washed his brown hair, but still wore his black leather jacket and jeans with the knees out. Casting a glance back over his shoulder, he said, "What did Dr. Who want? I saw him whispering to you in the middle of the ceremony."

Roberto had never much liked Cleo's uncle. He said the archaeologist was a spooky know-it-all.

"He asked if I had the medallion."

Roberto's eyes went wide. "Holy shit. If he wants it, we'd better go get it *pronto*."

I looked around to make sure no one could overhear us. The unknown Egyptian man who'd sat in the rear was standing alone, off to the side, pretending he wasn't monitoring me, but I knew he was. He had cold, ice-blue eyes, so he was either a cop or a mass murderer. "They're watching me like hawks. There's always a sheriff's car or police car outside our house. I think they're taking turns. They follow me everywhere I go. Can you get it?"

"*No problemo*. The cops have pretty much decided I was an innocent bystander. Nobody's watching our house, but I'll use an invisibility spell anyway. I'll go tonight. Hide it in my gym bag."

"With your dirty underwear?"

"Sure. Who'd brave the smell to search for it?"

I considered the possibility. "Be careful, Roberto. The thing that killed her might still be out there."

"Hal, listen . . ." he said in a soft voice.

I stared at him with despair in my eyes. The tone in his voice brought home the fact that we had just lived through true horror together. We were both different people now.

Roberto licked his lips. "We need to talk. Alone, and I mean *alone*. You didn't tell the police about the—"

"No, of course not. I haven't told anyone about the medallion except you."

He expelled a relieved breath. "Okay, that's good. Did you meet the Egyptian cop?"

"He's a cop?" My eyes moved to the man still sitting in his chair in the rear. Bronze-skinned and dressed in a crisply ironed green shirt and pants, no one would ever mistake him for a man to be taken lightly. He was in charge. No doubt about it. "Who is he?"

"Name's Colonel Sattin. He came over to talk to me when we first got here. Says he's trying to recover a stolen Egyptian antiquity that he suspects Cleo had."

A hard swallow bobbed in my throat. "You don't think—"

"No doubt, bro. But I don't—"

"Robert?" his mother called.

Roberto swung around, scowled at her, and said, "Give me a second, for God's sake." Then he turned back to me. "Gotta go, Hal. See you at school tomorrow?"

"I . . . yeah, I don't know. Maybe. Don't know if I can stomach the questions from the morons."

"There's only three days of school left. Why don't you blow 'em off? You've already earned an A in every class. Besides, the sympathy factor will kick in with the teachers. They'll probably give you A-pluses if you're home grieving."

I shrugged. "Yeah, but if school's open, my parents will force me to go. Mom always says you have to 'stand up to your worst fears' or you end up being a bed wetter when you're forty."

Roberto's brows lifted. "Want me to curse the school so it's closed tomorrow?" He drew a lopsided pentagram in the air, as though it was a secret signal. Like I was the only person present who knew he was a witch, even though he made a point of telling every person he passed.

"That'd be great. Thanks." I didn't actually believe his spells worked, but what harm could it do?

Roberto saluted and trotted off to get in his parents' car. I watched them drive off and felt lonely beyond words.

CHAPTER SEVEN

T he night of the funeral, the dreams started.

A rush of air filled my bedroom. Hot, sweltering air. That's why it roused me. I curled onto my side and gazed at the back of my closed eyelids where little white sparks shot around. I felt hollow. I kept reliving the nightmare, but not her death. Instead, I clung to that last conversation on the bench outside of Starbucks, repeating it over and over in my dreams.

Slowly, as I climbed out of sleep, I heard things.

Jewelry clinked.

The air smelled of lime-laden dust and sunbaked stones running with water.

Then, footsteps. Almost not there.

They came across the room, and I felt the side of my bed sink as someone sat down beside me.

"Halloran? Don't be afraid. It's just me."

I longed to weep. "Oh, my God, I'm so glad you're here. I dreamed that you were dead."

"I'm here. I'm not leaving you. I came to help you."

A warm hand touched my face.

"Hal? Hal, wake up!"

My father's panicked voice made me sit bolt upright in bed, gasping for air. Through my window, I could see the blizzard and hear the wind shrieking as it hurled snow at the house. "What? What's wrong?" I asked. Adrenaline was shooting through my veins like fire.

While Mom stood like a black silhouette in the doorway, Dad ran to me, sat down on the bedside, and wrapped his arms tightly around me. His blond hair was a mass of tangles. Clearly, they'd leaped from their bed to charge to my room.

"You were sobbing in your sleep, Hal. Are you all right?" Dad asked in a worried voice.

I was still sort of locked in the dream. Cleo's voice echoed in the back of my mind. "Yeah. I'm okay, Dad. Just a dream. Sorry I woke you."

"Was it about Cleo?"

Before I could answer, Mom said, "Of course, it was about Cleo, John. How could you even ask?" As a psychiatrist, Mom had perfected the art of making people feel stupid. Oh, I loved her. But I'd never liked her much.

Dad shouted, "Let him answer, will you?"

"It was Cleo," I said. "She was . . . was here . . . in the room."

Mom leaned against the doorframe. "Hal, you have to stop blaming yourself. It wasn't your fault."

I rubbed a hand over my numb face, and my eyes drifted to the window to watch the whirling snow that glittered in the gleam of the streetlights outside.

It *was* strange, wasn't it? For the moment, I'd blocked Cleo's death. Instead, every night I returned to Starbucks. Maybe because she was still alive there, not dying in my arms, not dead in a coffin beneath six feet of dirt. At Starbucks, I could still hold her. I could still love her. And she loved me. Loved me with all her heart. But this latest addition to the Starbucks dream was new and strange. It didn't feel like a dream at all. It felt like some ancient doorway had creaked open, and Cleo had walked out of Duat into my bedroom, carrying the scents of ancient civilizations with her.

Dad turned to the window. "This is a bad blizzard. They're sure to cancel school today. That will give us more time together. We need to talk with you, Hal. Will that be okay?"

"I just want to sleep, Dad. I'm so tired."

I stretched out on my back and closed my eyes. Mom and Dad whispered, then one of them quietly closed my door. Their bare feet tapped the stairs. A little while later, the kitchen lights came on, which created a yellow square around my door.

Had Roberto found the medallion? The murder scene was roped off with yellow tape and being searched for more clues every day. The cops hadn't staked it out, had they? Would they catch him? Surely, the cops weren't out there in this kind of blizzard. But I knew Roberto would be. He'd be digging through the snow, trying to find it. I prayed he'd be okay. Every year people died in Colorado blizzards.

Wind whistled outside. I opened my eyes and stared at the snow flying beyond my window. Dad was right. Terrible storm. Georgetown would be buried beneath three feet of wet snow tomorrow morning. School would definitely be closed.

Roberto would be so proud of himself.

CHAPTER EIGHT

The next morning my parents poured themselves cups of coffee, put on their reading glasses, and boxed me in at the breakfast table. I felt like a rat in a cage being studied by scientists with magnifying glasses. Between them lay copies of the police reports. The police had interviewed me twice and the sheriff's office four times. They'd also interviewed lots of students at high school, as well as my teachers. My normal life was gone forever. I'd tried to give the cops every detail I could remember to help them find the thing that had killed Cleo.

Every interview had been agonizing. As the days passed, I blamed myself more and more for her death. Why hadn't I insisted upon walking her home and guarding her until morning? After she'd told me about the demon at the foot of her bed, how could I have gone off to play video games with Roberto?

Mom loudly flipped over a couple of pages, then started tiptoeing around the subject she really wanted to discuss. "Hal, this report says that after you found the body you saw someone in the trees. Who was it? Did he run away?"

The body. Not Cleo.

All morning long, my parents had refused to say her name, probably on Mom's advice. After all, the kid might go berserk and shoot up a post office if he heard Cleo's name too often.

"I don't know what it was. It was wearing a uniform and had a turquoise face and red hair."

Mom said, "A turquoise face? You mean . . . it wasn't human?"

She was evaluating me with her professional eyes, blank, just listening. I'd observed a long time ago that she was a curious character—even though she was my mother. Because her clients wore colorful clothes, she only dressed in black. Because her clients shopped at Walmart and Barnes and Noble, she wouldn't be caught dead carrying a bag from a big chain store. In fact, she wouldn't go anywhere that she might cross paths with one of the deviants she counseled, which meant she didn't go out much. When Dad got pissed at her, he called her a "spoiled trust fund baby, paranoid beyond endurance." The only evidence of the trust fund that I could tell, however, was the vast wine collection in the basement. Maybe they did have money, but I never saw any of it, so I just assumed they'd spent the bucks long before I was born.

"Hal," Mom's voice had turned edgy. "Was it human?"

"No."

I suspected Dad had probably told Mom she couldn't yell at me or tell me I was full of crap, which she ordinarily would have. Instead, she continued in a placating voice: "We're just trying to understand. Your dad and I can't help you unless we know what really happened. We—"

"What *really* happened? I told you what happened. And those reports tell you what happened. You saying you don't believe me? My own parents don't believe me?"

"Well, Hal . . ." Mom shoved short blonde hair behind one ear. "Some of the stuff in these reports is pretty bizarre."

"Like what?" It was a rhetorical question, of course. By now I knew where this was going.

Mom took a sip of her coffee. When she set her cup down again, she looked at me over the tops of her reading glasses. "Do you really believe in demons?"

Answering would not have improved my situation, so I clamped my jaws together and didn't say a word.

She continued: "It says here that you described the man as being a giant." Her finger tapped the police report. "Is that correct?"

"It was a giant. And it may have had a crocodile head. I didn't get a very good look at it, but it could have been Ammut."

"What's an Ammut?" Mom asked.

"Ancient Egyptian demon. The Devourer of the Damned."

As though they'd synchronized their movements, my parents leaned back in their chairs at exactly the same moment and started drinking coffee like nothing was wrong. It was just another dull ordinary Wednesday. They blinked at the ceiling and out the window. I knew I was in trouble when Dad started cleaning his fingernails on the corner of the police report, absently brushing the black detritus onto the kitchen table, and Mom said nothing.

"Hal." Mom spread her hands. "I want you to listen to me. Finding a friend murdered is a powerful and traumatic experience that can result in dissociative episodes. It can, well, unhinge a person's mind."

"You think I'm unhinged?"

Mom braced her elbows on the tabletop. Her voice became authoritative, deep and a little dark. "Of course, you are. Who wouldn't be? Dissociation is a coping mechanism. There are two basic human instincts: fight and flight. When a person undergoes a traumatic experience, as you did when you found your best friend murdered, his mind either has to fight against the unbearable stress or flee from it. You've chosen the latter. You're not suffering from blackouts yet, are you? Passages of time that you can't account for, or—"

"No, Mom, no blackouts." I tried to defend myself, even though I knew it was hopeless. When Mom had made her diagnosis, there was no escape. A person just had to endure "the cure."

She pointed a stern finger at me. "You have to be very careful now, Hal. In the worst cases of dissociation the victim develops DID, Dissociative Identity Disorder, which we used to call multiple personality disorder. To protect himself, the victim creates surrogates, different personalities to help him survive or to blame for the incident. Once the victim has created the other personalities, he can go hide somewhere inside and let the fabricated personalities take the blame." Now her words became precise, spoken one at a time, for effect: "Despite what you say, I know you are overwhelmed with guilt. You believe that her death was your fault, don't you?"

Mom had not moved a muscle, apart from those that controlled her mouth. Her finger was still pointed at me like a stiletto. Since I'd been playing this psychiatric game of baseball my whole life, I sort of knew when to catch and when to throw hard at the pitcher's head. "Of course, I know it's not my fault that an ancient demon killed her. But I also know it killed her because she was Queen Cleopatra in a former life, and the demon refuses to allow her to get to the afterlife, which is the only place Cleo will ever find peace. My 'unbearable stress' comes not from guilt, but from the fact that I don't know how to find the Island of the Two Flames."

Mom didn't say anything while she prepared her next salvo. After a deep breath, she said, "Listen carefully, Hal. The demon is the personality you've created so you have someone to blame. You have to let go of that surrogate personality. Let me help you. I—"

"No, thanks."

"All right, then, not me. But you need someone's help. You have to kill that demonic personality before it leads you headlong into the mythic underworld of the unconscious where your soul will be trapped forever in darkness. This isn't a game, Hal. It's serious business. You must—"

Dad threw up his hands in frustration, and shouted, "For God's sake, Jenna, give it a rest! He just needs to grieve for a while. On this score, Moriarity is right. Hal needs a chance to live his fantasies. We should let him go—"

"Moriarity?" I asked a little breathless. A powerful jolt of fear had gone through me. "You talked to Cleo's uncle about me?"

And Marcus Antonius thought Ahenobarbus' betrayal at the Battle of Actium was bad? It had devastated Antonius when his old friend had taken a small boat and defected to Octavian—carrying Antonius' battle plans—in 31 BC. If Antonius had been forced to endure my traitorous parents, he'd have slit his wrists at the age of sixteen and avoided all that. Then, again, given what happened later, Antonius might have seen an early death as a blessing.

Keeping his voice low and steady, Dad said, "Yes, Hal. Of course, we did. After we read the police reports, we went to see him. You and Cleo were completely absorbed by this ancient Egypt stuff, and Dr. Moriarity is an expert in that field. We just needed to hear his opinion. We weren't trying to invade your privac—"

"What did he say?"

Mom and Dad exchanged one of those looks, like now they were really walking on eggshells, and if they said a single wrong word, I'd shatter into a thousand tiny pieces that no one would ever be able to glue back together.

Mom spoke in the same chilling professional tone that I figured she used with the paranoid schizophrenics she treated. "The simple truth is that you're suffering from delusions brought on by the event and the intense role-playing that you and Cleo used to do. Do you understand? I'm telling you the bald truth because I know you're old enough to get it."

When I just sat there with my arms folded, Dad gave Mom an I-told-you-not-to-say-that look.

I said, "I see. I'm crazy. So, what are you planning to do about it? I'm sure you've already figured out how to solve my problem for me. After all, there was no need to discuss it with me before coming to your decision. Who else you been talking to?"

"Now, Hal, that's not fair," Dad said. "We're worried sick, son. We're just trying to help—"

Mom interrupted him: "For your information, I consulted with several of my Denver colleagues to get their advice, and they agreed with Moriarity that perhaps living out your fantasies would be therapeu—"

"I was there, Mom! I saw the demon!"

"I'm sure you think you saw it, Hal, but you didn't. There's no such thing as demons. Now, let's talk about Egypt . . ."

My phone rang. I pulled it out of my pocket, checked the number and hit "talk," knowing how it would drive my parents to the basement for a bottle of wine.

I said, "Hey, Roberto."

"Cool storm, huh?"

"Yeah, thanks. Appreciate it."

"No problem. I got to get out of this house, bro. Is your Internet up? Our dish is full of snow, and the lack of service has my parents barking at each other like mad dogs locked in a kennel. They just told me they were going to arrange a lovely summer vacation for me at the Juvenile Detention Center. If your Internet is working, we can play online games for a few hours while discussing how much the world sucks."

"Yeah, come over. I could use the company."

"Okay. See you in ten."

I clicked off, tucked my phone in my pocket, and looked up to find my parents scowling at me.

"We are not finished with this discussion, Hal," Mom said in her most dire voice. "We have much more to say to you."

"Well, can you stop all the shit and get to the point?"

"Do not curse in my presence," Mom said and started to lay into me, but Dad put a restraining hand on her arm.

Mom gave him a sidelong look, and calmly said, "Here's the upshot. Your father and I had decided to send you to a psychiatrist we know in Denver, a professional colleague of mine who specializes in adolescent psychoses, but Dr. Moriarity—"

"I won't go, and you can't make me!"

"If you'd just listen . . ."

Out the kitchen window, I saw a dark-haired girl hiking through the blizzard. She was only faintly visible in the wavering white curtain, but her movements were somehow familiar. My attention fixed on her. She struggled through the drifts to get to our sidewalk, and then started slogging toward the front door. Three paces away, she lifted her head and looked straight at me. The snow stopped dead, the flakes caught in mid-fall. It was surreal. I could see her face clearly. She gave me a sad smile.

A wave of heat flushed my body. *This isn't real.*

Her lips formed two unmistakable words:

Don't go.

Then the snow started falling again, and her image melted into the snowfall and was gone.

My parents' panicked voices were only faintly audible beneath the rush of blood in my ears.

"Hal? Hal are you all right?" Dad called.

Both of my parents were on their feet rushing toward me. By the time they reached me, I was shaking so hard I just barely managed to stumble out of my chair.

Shoving past their grasping hands, I sprinted for the front door, threw it wide open, and screamed, "Cleo? Cleo, come back!"

Less than a pace behind me, I could hear my parents whispering to one another.

Mom's voice was low and ominous: "He *sees* her. Dear God."

"What should we do?" Dad pleaded.

"Let me discuss this with my colleagues before we consider commitment."

CHAPTER NINE

By the time Roberto arrived, I was back in the safety of my room, lying on the bed and staring at the ceiling with my heart thundering in my chest. I heard the doorbell ring. Then voices. Finally, Roberto's boots thumped up the stairs, and he flung open my door. He had on the same black leather jacket and torn Levis he'd been wearing five days ago, but it looked like he'd changed his white T-shirt.

As he slipped out of his backpack, he said, "Jesus, your parents are *intense*. Your dad told me you are prostate with grief, and I can only stay for half an hour. I thought the prostate was in your dick?"

I sat up, and the room spun for a second. "Probably said prostrate not prostate. It means 'overcome.' Overcome with grief."

Roberto shook his head. "Oh. Okay. Christ, English teachers are so obsessed with adverbs and commas and shit." He dug around in his pack and handed me the golden medallion.

I grabbed it and clutched it to my chest. "Did they follow you?"

"Naw, once I cast my invisibility spell, they couldn't see me. And the snow wasn't that deep when I got there."

"Thanks, Roberto. Really."

"Yeah, of course, I—"

"If Dad's only giving you a half hour, I don't have much time, and there's something I have to ask you."

Roberto shoved greasy brown hair out of his eyes and gave me a concerned look. "You're not going to quiz me about the demon again, are you? I'm telling you, I didn't see a demon out there or even a non-demon."

"Not about that. I believe you. Can you sit down?"

Roberto pulled my desk chair over to my bed and sat down. Leaning the chair back on two legs, he propped his dripping hiking boots on my blue bedspread. "Bad day?"

"My parents are insane. Mom psychoanalyzed me at the breakfast table."

"Figured it was bad. On the phone, you sounded like you were trying to choke down a big one."

I had no idea what that meant, and wasn't about to ask. "My parents think I'm delusional."

"Oh, dude." Roberto shook his head. "You remember that time your mom cornered me in the grocery store and told me she knew I tortured kittens? God, I was horrified. I love cats. The worst part was the eerie *I'm-Hannibal-Lector-and-I-know-more-than-God* glow in her eyes. Scared the holy sh—"

"They may have me committed to an asylum."

"Are you fucking kidding me?" he half shouted.

"Shh. Keep your voice down!"

Roberto thoughtfully looked around my bedroom. "Okay. Look, give me a few seconds to process this shit. There's got to be a way to work this. I just need to figure the angle."

"Angle?"

"Sure. You have at least a couple of options. You can either play along or hire your own attorney."

"How would I ever pay for a lawyer?"

"I'll give you the three hundred bucks in my sock drawer. That ought to buy you an hour."

"Thanks, but . . ." I felt really tired. Muted white light, filtered through the snowfall, was streaming through the window, sheathing everything in a liquid pearl gleam: My desk, Roberto, the pale blue carpet. "Roberto, I have to tell you something. But you can't *ever* tell anyone. You understand?"

"I'm no Judas Icarus. What?"

No point in telling him it was actually "Iscariot." My mouth had suddenly gone dust dry. I licked my lips. "When you were running down the slope to meet the sheriff's cars, Cleo said something. I'm sorry I haven't told you before, but . . ."

The front two legs of his chair banged down on the floor as he leaned forward. "Wait a minute. Have you told anybody this?"

"No. I was afraid to."

Roberto pulled his wet boots off my bed, planted them on the floor, and propped his elbows on his knees. In a grave voice, he said, "What'd she say?"

I massaged my forehead. I had a headache coming on. "Have I ever told you about the Island of the Two Flames? It's mentioned in a number of papyrus texts—"

"Get to the point, Hal. I don't want a lecture about moldy Greek or Roman gods."

"It's the ancient Egyptian island of the dead. Supposedly it sits in the middle of the Nile, but I don't know exactly where. I'm not sure anyone today does."

He looked slightly confused. "And?"

"Cleo told me she needs to get there."

"But if it's the island where the dead live . . ." Roberto straightened in his chair. A dreadful tone entered his voice. "Wait a minute. You're not, like, planning to dig up her body and take it to Egypt, are you? Jesus, don't ask me to help you do that. I really liked her. I don't think I could force myself—"

"No, no, my God, I couldn't either. How could you even think that?"

"Well, how else can Cleo get there?"

Silently, I lifted the golden medallion and turned it my hands. The emeralds shimmered like the tears in Cleo's eyes that last day at Starbucks. Strangely, the medallion started feeling really heavy, as though pulling me toward the center of the earth. Before I could stop myself, I started shaking again. The medallion slipped from my fingers and thudded softly on the bed. Cleo was close by. I could feel her. Watching. Listening. And very worried about me.

"Hey! What's wrong?" Roberto reached out to me. "You okay? Did I say some—"

"I saw her today, Roberto."

His mouth was still hanging open from the sentence he hadn't finished. Slowly, he closed it and swallowed hard. "Like . . . *really* saw her?"

That sentence felt like the sword of Damocles about to fall and spear down through my head. Truly. That's exactly what it felt like. A life-or-death moment. Either my friend believed me, or he told me I had completely lost it and needed to be locked up with all the other crazies in Colorado.

"She was here, Roberto. Just outside my front door."

Roberto gave me the most adult look I've ever seen on his face. "You didn't tell your parents, right?"

I shrugged helplessly. "I couldn't help it! They were right there when I saw her walk up the path to the front door. I'm not sure what I said aloud, but they at least heard me shout her name."

Roberto leaned his chair back on two legs again and rocked it back and forth while he stared across the room to consider that fact. "Okay, I hear you. No wonder your mom thinks you're delusional. This could be the luckiest break of your life, dude."

"What makes you think that?"

"Oh, come on. If you play along and go see the shrink, you can make them give you anything you want."

"I don't want anything. Except maybe a first-class ticket to—"

"You're not thinking right. Don't you remember last fall when Dwight Hornsby ran through math class stark naked screaming his dead grandmother was loping after him on all fours? His parents bought him a freaking Porsche to soothe his nerves. You should start making out your Christmas list. How about a red Ducati?"

"I don't want a red Ducati."

Roberto looked more stunned by that than by my revelation that I'd seen Cleo standing just outside my front door. "Well, if it bothers your conscience, you can sign it over to me." He paused, and then returned to the subject at hand. "So, what did Cleo look like? Was she a ghost, or—"

"Just like she did that last day at Starbucks." I wrapped my arms around myself and tried to force my muscles to stop shaking. The day she died an earthquake had been born inside me, and it wouldn't stop.

Roberto got to his feet, wiped his sweaty hands on his jeans, and sat on the bed beside me. "When you shouted her name, did she answer?"

"No. But before I ran to the door, I was watching through the kitchen window. I saw her mouth the words *don't go*."

"What'd she mean?"

"How would I know?" I cried in frustration.

Roberto extended his hands and made a calming motion. "Chill, bro. We just need to stay calm and figure this out. Maybe she didn't want you to go see the shrink?"

I dropped my head into my hands and massaged my throbbing temples. "Yeah. That must be what she meant."

"Sure. What else could it be?" He gave me a quizzical look, as though he knew there was something I wasn't telling him.

"I don't know. God, I'm glad you came over today. I really needed to talk to somebody who can think straight."

"You may be the only person who's ever concluded that after talking to me. So, what aren't you telling—"

From downstairs, my mother called, *"Robert? Isn't it time you headed home?"*

Roberto made a disgusted sound. "My half hour must be up. I should probably leave before she comes up to throw me out, like usual. You going to be okay?"

"I'm a little better now." Actually, I felt a ray of hope for the first time in days. "Thanks. I mean it. You're a good friend. My . . . my best friend." I would have never said that if Cleo was still alive, and Roberto knew it.

The sound of my mother's shoes pounded the stairs.

Roberto got to his feet and straightened his bad-ass-biker jacket as he reached down for his backpack. "Yeah, well, don't start thinking you can bombard me with stories of Hector or Plato or other boring shit like you used to do Cleo. I still have my pride."

Tears filled my eyes, but I actually smiled. "I won't."

I tucked the medallion beneath my blanket and watched him walk across the room.

Roberto stood in front of my door, listening to my mother's steps, then jerked open the door at the exactly the instant Mom was about to knock.

"Jesus, Robert, you scared me!" She threw a hand up to her heart.

"Oh, hey, Mrs. Stevens. Sorry about that. Take care."

Roberto shouldered past Mom and trotted down the stairs. I heard the front door open and close. If I knew Roberto, right now he was searching for Cleo's tracks in the snow.

Mom stood in my doorway looking in at me through her reading glasses. Suspiciously, she asked, "What did you two talk about?"

There was an unpleasant accusation hidden in her voice, but I wasn't sure what I was being accused of, so I said, "Oh, nothing. His mom has been sending naked pictures of herself to fifteen-year-olds. Close my door, please?"

Mom got a slightly horrified look on her face. Apparently, she wasn't sure I was joking. When she opened her mouth to ask a question, I said:

"I'm suffering from DID, Mom. I need to sleep."

"Right. Okay." She pulled my door closed.

Flopping onto my back, I stared at the ceiling.

It had just occurred to me for the first time that I would never again lie on my bedroom floor beside Cleo, reading Plato and Plutarch aloud, laughing, mesmerized by her knowledge and the sheer wonder of her presence. I felt empty. Just so empty, as though losing her had torn my soul loose and cast it out into the storm. Deep aching cold settled in my bones.

Reaching for the medallion, I clutched it against my heart and rolled up in my bedspread to try and sleep. If I could just sleep long enough, maybe I'd wake to discover this was all a bad dream. Maybe she'd still be alive, smiling at me with love in her eyes.

"The blood! The blood!"

I sat bolt upright in bed screaming, holding my shaking fists out in front of me. It was evening. Stars glittered outside my window. The air in my bedroom smelled of pines and wet earth.

"Hal!" My father cried, and I heard his feet climbing the stairs. "Hal, I'm coming!"

He threw open my door and lurched toward my bedside. "What happened? You all right?"

"Sorry. I'm sorry, Dad."

He sat down on the bed and gathered me in his arms, rocking me like a child. "Don't be sorry. Everything's going to be okay."

I sagged against him. "Is she really dead? Is she dead, Dad? Did I just dream that?"

"She's dead, Hal. But you're all right. No one's going to hurt you, not while I'm alive. You hear me?"

Cleo's dead....

He kept rocking me in his arms while I cried.

CHAPTER TEN

At 2:00 the next afternoon, I was coming back from the library, slogging through the snowdrifts, when I saw the Starbucks ahead. My steps faltered. I really needed to warm up, but Starbucks had been "our" place. Girding myself, I tried not to look as I passed the bench where I'd always sat talking and smiling with Cleo. Shoving open the door, I hurried inside.

The place was empty except for the gray-haired woman behind the counter. I'd never seen her here before, but in small mountain towns businesses went through employees fast.

"I'll have a coffee. Grande, please," I said as I dug in my pocket for money.

"Coming right up."

While I waited, I wandered around the store, picking up logo cups, examining them, putting them down, smelling the bags of coffee and tea in the displays. For some reason, the Darjeeling smelled especially good.

"Here you go," she said at last and set my cup on the counter.

I took my coffee over to one of the tables on the opposite side of the store where I could stare out the window at the quiet street. The mountains beyond the glass gleamed with fresh snow. They looked pretty, though I felt sorry for the trees. Because of the weight of the snow, the boughs sagged mournfully. I suspected there would be a wealth of broken limbs when the snow disappeared.

For a while, I just held my hot cup in both hands. The warmth felt good on my icy fingers.

Two of the girls in my history class walked by outside. Bundled in down coats and mufflers, they briefly stopped to stare in at me, as though surprised to see me having a coffee by myself. Neither waved. They hated me. The one dressed in the red coat was Stef Brown. She was best known around school for having two rows of needle-sharp teeth in her jaw. I'd asked Stef out on a date once when I was thirteen. She'd humiliated me in front of everybody by laughing in my face. The girls whispered furiously to each other for a few seconds, then continued on their way.

I felt awkward. Having a coffee alone was a bad experience. Every time I'd ever been here, I'd been with a friend. Usually Cleo. What wonderful times those had been. If only I'd cherished them more, but I never thought they'd end. Closing my eyes, I tried to live in those moments, tried really hard, but grief was a strange thing. I could remember the happiness of being with Cleo, but not actually feel it. It was as though an ocean of emptiness had dragged me far out to sea, and I couldn't find my way back to shore.

And I wondered if Marcus Antonius had felt this way? He must have known that by losing the Battle of Actium, he'd signed Cleopatra's death warrant. Did her impending death become his life? Just as Cleo's death had become mine?

Pulling the lid off my coffee, I took a sip. It was just barely cool enough to drink, so I nursed the cup, taking small sips, enjoying the flavor and the warmth while I thought about history and demons. Everyone kept telling me that the thing I'd seen in the forest was a figment of my imagination. Was it? Had I been so traumatized by her last words, by watching her die, that my mind had invented the "demon"? After all, though the moment had seemed endless, I'd only seen it for a second. Maybe less than that. Even in my memory the experience had a sparkling dreamlike quality.

Brought on by the intense role-playing you and Cleo used to do.

"No," I whispered aloud to myself and glanced around to make sure the barista hadn't heard me. "I saw it. *I saw it.*"

When I started fiddling with my empty cup, using it to trace the circles of old coffee rings on the dirty table, I figured it was time to leave.

Halfway across the floor, the strangest feeling hit me. As though my body knew something my brain refused to believe, every nerve ending suddenly tingled to life with fiery intensity. My brain said *panic attack*. My body said *run!*

"Stop this!" I hissed to myself, barely audible. "Look around. There's nothing to be afraid of in Starbucks."

The woman behind the counter called, "Did you say something to me?"

Turning, I smiled. "Just trying to remember what I was supposed to do this afternoon. You know how sometimes just asking yourself about it jogs your memory?"

"Oh, yeah, sweetie. I do that all the time." She smiled back and returned to wiping off the counter.

My heart rate had slowed a bit, enough that I could get a full breath into my lungs, so I continued to the door and pushed it open. Cold air hit me in the face as I stepped outside and headed home.

I hadn't taken four steps before I froze.

Sitting on the bench with her back to me was a girl with shoulder-length black hair. A girl I would have known anywhere: asleep, dead, walking the lonely road to heaven.

Overwhelming relief rushed through my veins, and I longed to run to her, to throw my arms around her, but to do so would be to leap over the fragile cliff of sanity and plunge into the depths of madness. *She's not there*. She couldn't be. I'd seen her die. I'd gone to her funeral.

The girl rose to her feet, and walked away, heading west down the snowy street.

I couldn't stop myself, I shouted, "Cleo?"

At the sound of my voice, she broke into a desperate run, slogging through the drifts. I could hear her panting as though terrified. As she swerved to run around the street corner, she cast a glance over her shoulder. I couldn't see her face, but it was as though she saw something—something I did not see—following her. Then she vanished around the corner.

Moments later, two rifle shots rang out.

Then.

Screams.

Another shot.

I spontaneously cried out and almost started to run after her.

But I knew . . . I knew . . .

Dear God, I'm reliving the day of her death when I'm awake.

As of this instant, the imagination game had been elevated to a whole new level.

Before my knees gave out, I walked to the bench where she'd been sitting and eased down to try and pull myself together. I really was falling apart. No doubt about it. My parents were right. Maybe I should be institutionalized for my own good.

"What's happening to me?" I asked through gritted teeth. "I have to figure this out. If I can't control . . ."

The realization seeped in slowly, shutting down my voice.

The bench was still warm.

CHAPTER ELEVEN

A cry formed behind my lips, and without my own volition, my head turned to stare at the street corner where she'd vanished.

Striding around that corner, as though without a care in the world, was Dr. Moriarity. He had the hood of his navy-blue coat pulled up, but I could see his distinctive black-rimmed glasses and graying brown beard.

He'd made the turn and started up the walk to go into the Starbucks before he noticed me and did a double take. My face must have been ashen or something, because he quickly detoured and walked to the bench to sit beside me. "Are you okay, Hal? You don't look well."

"Fine. You?"

"Still struggling, as I'm sure you are."

We sat in silence, each staring out at the snowy town. The historic buildings struck me as oddly alien, as though I was seeing them through someone else's eyes.

Trying to strike up a conversation, he said, "You know I'm meeting with your parents and the police this afternoon. Is there anything you want me to tell them?"

My head slowly turned. "Meeting? About what?"

Moriarity blanched, as though he suddenly realized that it was supposed to be a secret meeting. "I should let your parents tell you, but . . . I really want you to think about going to Egypt with me. When I spoke with your mother yesterday, she said you were hesitating. May I ask why? I know you and Cleo always talked about going to Egypt together."

My nerves were still jangling. I whispered, "What are you talking about?"

"Oh. My God," he said as though shocked. "Sorry. I didn't know they hadn't spoken to you about it. That's unfortunate."

"You want me to go to Egypt with you?"

"Well, yes. I have a dig starting there in a couple of weeks, and I thought, you know, if you spent some time in the land she loved, it might help you get over—"

"I'm not going to get over it! Not any time soon. It doesn't matter whether I go to Egypt on your dig or not, I'm still going to be sad and lonely for a long, long time."

"Well . . . sure," he said sympathetically. "We all know that. You're human just like everybody else. The horror of what happened—"

"Is tearing me apart, okay? Can you leave it at that?" I was shouting and didn't realize it until my voice echoed from the buildings across the street. I glanced around, expecting to see Cleo appear at any moment and give me that sad heartbreaking look.

Dr. Moriarity squinted at the rivers of melted snow running down the gutter. After a few moments, he shoved his hood back and used a hand to ruffle up his hair. "Hal, let me explain why I think it's important that you come to Egypt with me. I know you have the medallion—no, don't try to deny it—but I also suspect that you don't know why it's important."

Only my eyes seemed capable of moving. They slid to the side to look at him. If I asked what it was for, it would verify that I had the medallion. If I did not ask, I'd explode.

Moriarity continued, "Did Cleo explain that her father had found it in my excavation along the Great Horus Road?"

Mildly, I asked, "What's the Great Horus Road?"

"An old military road. I know it was found there, but I don't know exactly where. Cleo's father never told me. However, I know a man who was excavating with him at the time, so I'm fairly sure I can find out. The problem is that Samael Saqqara is sort of a demented hermit."

Samael . . . secret bargain . . . the medallion for the dagger.

"Why didn't Cleo's father tell you where he'd found it? What was he afraid of?"

Moriarity's eyes glinted just for an instant, before the professional mask came back to his face. "I suspect he found more than the medallion, and didn't want me to know about it, because he feared I'd take some action."

I paused. "What does that have to do with me?"

"Hal, I want to be your friend. You and I have the same passion for ancient history. We should be friends." He gave me one of those have-to-humor-the-psychotic-kid looks, which I found totally insulting. "Would that be all right?"

"Where's your dig in Egypt?"

Moriarity frowned, probably because I hadn't answered his question. "A site called Pelusium. That's why I pleaded with Cleo to give me the medallion, so I could take it back and try to reconstruct exactly where her father had found it. You see, Hal, I'm fairly sure he stole it from a grave."

"Whose grave?"

He looked like he didn't want to tell me, but finally said, "All right. Here's the story in a nutshell: No one knows where Cleopatra or Marc Antony are buried. Local legend says it was either at Per Usiri or Per Amun. Today, Per Amun is the archaeological site called Pelusium. Finding their grave would be the archaeological discovery of the century. Do you realize that? The archaeologist who found it would become a legend."

"You want to become a legend?"

"And have my name spoken with the same reverence as Howard Carter and Lord Carnarvon, who discovered King Tut's tomb? I wouldn't mind that a bit."

Ignoring him, I considered what he'd told me.

Per Usiri meant "House of Osiris," and Per Amun was "House of Amun." Two very different gods with vastly different functions in ancient Egyptian society. Osiris was the god of death. Amun was the life-giver, the creator, sometimes invisible, like air.

To ancient Egyptians, then, the two sites would have been symbolic opposites, one representing death and the other life.

"What does your mysterious medallion have to do with all this?"

An almost smug look crossed the professor's face. "Oh, it isn't just any medallion, Hal. It's part of a magical formula. It was found on top of a 'bagsu,' a ceremonial dagger that signified the mastery of dangerous power. The medallion was like a name tag. It identified the bagsu as belonging to Cleopatra VII. The bagsu created a supernatural doorway—"

"So you think the medallion verifies it was found in her grave?"

"That's the first possibility." He gave me a knowing smile. "Keep in mind that Queen Cleopatra always wore a dagger at her hip, inserted into her belt. Scholars have assumed it was for self-protection, but also in the event that she needed to end her life in an honorable way. I disagree. Which brings us to the second possibility. It may have come from the grave of her Sem priest."

"Her Sem priest?"

He leaned forward to brace his elbows on his knees and stare out at the mountains. "The 'Opening of the Mouth' ritual."

"The Opening of the Mouth ritual," I repeated, astonished. I was eleven when I'd first come across a reference to that ritual. A bagsu had been found in the tomb of Tutankhamun. I'd seen pictures of the magnificent artifact. "Then that particular bagsu would have been associated with Amun, correct? Not Osiris?"

He gave me a nod of approval. "Correct. That's why it makes more sense that Antony and Cleopatra were buried in Per Amun. She was, after all, believed to be the reincarnation of the goddess Isis, and the city of Per Amun was dedicated to Isis. At the very end, Cleopatra ordered her loyal servants to hide her body and secretly bury her with Antony. You remember Plutarch's words, of course." He left the question dangling as though this were a classroom test.

In the back of my mind I could hear Cleo's voice reading Plutarch's version of Cleopatra's agonizing last days. Plutarch had written that Cleopatra had wept over Antonius' dead body and begged her servants to hide and then bury her body in secret with Antonius.

. . . since out of all my innumerable afflictions not one is so great and dreadful as this short time that I have lived apart from you.

I had often asked Cleo which of many versions of the story were true, but she'd only gotten tears in her eyes and answered that she could not speak of it, except to say that she couldn't bear to enter the afterlife without him. I'd spent years researching the different versions to try and decipher why the subject was so agonizing for her.

"I remember. But didn't her servants, Iras and Charmion, die with her?"

"She had many servants, Hal. Probably hundreds of them. And a select few would have been responsible for secretly burying Antony."

"What does that have to do with the Opening of the Mouth ritual?"

He lowered his voice to just above a whisper. "Every ancient Egyptian ruler, including Cleopatra, carried a bagsu for his or her Sem priest. After death, the priest was expected to take the bagsu and perform the Opening of the Mouth ceremony that created a doorway that allowed the soul of the dead to enter a living body in this world."

Which was way different from what Cleo had told me. She'd said the dagger opened a channel of light that led the soul out of Duat and to the Island of the Two Flames. But maybe it could be used for both. How did I know?

I lifted my eyes to stare up at the icicles hanging from the roofs down the street.

Moriarity leaned closer. "Listen very closely. Cleo's father either pulled the medallion and dagger from Cleopatra's hand or her Sem priest's hand. If so, the dagger must be returned. Her Sem priest had vowed on his life to make sure she was reincarnated in a new body."

Despite the hot cup of coffee I'd just finished, I was starting to get cold. Really cold. A sense of impending doom was forming inside me: If my Cleo was the reincarnated Queen Cleopatra, then her Sem priest had succeeded, perhaps against Cleopatra's will. But in any case, the priest no longer needed the dagger. Unless . . .

I turned to Moriarity. "Then, if the Sem priest holds the dagger in his hand, Cleopatra will be reincarnated forever? Over and over?"

"Yes. Do you understand now? She can *live* again." Moriarity stared at me with the strangest eyes—eyes that seemed to suck my soul down into a bottomless whirlpool of darkness. Very softly, as though talking to himself, he said, "Will you help me?"

In the back of my mind, I heard Cleo telling me that the dagger had to be in her hand for the channel of light to open. She didn't want to live forever. She wanted to die forever. My responsibility was clear. No matter what happened, I could not allow Moriarity to give the dagger back to the Sem priest.

"I need to think about it."

"All right, but if you decide to go to Egypt, you're going to have to be in better shape. Archaeological fieldwork is not for the faint-hearted. You're going to have to lose—"

"My dad has an exercise room. Weights, stair-step, treadmill. I'll work out, okay?"

Moriarity sighed and gazed up at the snow blowing across the slopes in the distance. "All right. In the meantime, the sheriff's report said you saw a turquoise-colored creature with a crocodile head and red hair in the forest. Are you sure it was turquoise?"

My skin crawled. It had been a matter-of-fact question. No patronizing bullshit intended. "That's what I'd call it."

"The color is very important. Ancient Egyptians had five different shades of blue. While it may have been Ammut—by the way, there's an Ammut cult in Denver, a real bunch of lunatics—the only major supernatural figure with turquoise-colored skin is Set."

"Set?"

"Yes, he's very old, one of the oldest and most powerful of Egyptian gods. Six thousand years ago he was portrayed as a crocodile-headed god. He's the brother of Isis. So perhaps he came to guide Cleo's soul to Duat."

"If it was Set, why would he be dressed in an Egyptian Army uniform?"

Moriarity shrugged. "He was the god of war. Maybe he wanted to adopt a more modern look."

"The god of war is interested in fashion?"

I had no idea where this conversation was going.

He continued, "But if the color is more azure, it might be Horus. Personally, I hope it was Set. On a cosmic level, since Cleo was the reincarnated Isis, he would be her brother and protector."

I felt like I was floating, as though my soul were drifting out of my body.

His eyes had a bizarre glitter now. "Don't you want to come to Egypt with me?"

I shifted on the bench to face him.

"Would you mind if my friend, Roberto, comes, too? He's my only friend now. I don't want to be alone in a foreign country."

Moriarity straightened. He looked away from me while he considered the ramifications. He did not look happy. "You won't be alone, Hal. Both Sophia and I will be there."

"I don't know you very well. I want to have a friend along. If you don't mind, sir."

"Is that your condition for going with me? Roberto has to come along?"

"Yeah, it is."

Moriarity bowed his head for several moments, and his cheeks vibrated as he ground his teeth. "Will his parents agree?"

"Pretty sure."

If I knew Roberto, he'd torment them until they did. Which probably wouldn't take that much effort. They definitely wanted him out of the house, and a trip to Egypt would be far more socially acceptable than shipping their son off for a lovely vacation at the Juvenile Detention Center.

Moriarity bent forward and braced his elbows on his knees. He seemed to be scowling at the mountains. As the sunlight shifted, the fine haze of snow blazed and drifted down the slope like gold dust. "One last thing."

I braced myself. "Yes?"

"If nothing else convinces you, think about this: I suspect Cleo was attacked by someone trying to find that medallion. Which means, if you have it, they will come for you next. You're far better off out of the country for a while."

Time seemed to stop between two heartbeats. Nothing moved.

"I don't have the medallion, Professor. Really."

Moriarity scanned my face, trying to tell if I was lying. "Well . . ." he said as he rose to his feet. "If you don't, Cleopatra is doomed. Right now her soul hovers in the nether regions of Duat. Do you want to condemn her to that fate? Or get that dagger to put in the grave of her Sem priest so he can bring her back to the light and warmth of this world?"

He gave me a long hard stare, flipped up his blue hood, and walked away down the street.

If Plutarch was right, Queen Cleopatra had been desperate to join Marcus Antonius in the afterlife. But someone had stopped her by reincarnating her soul in a new body. Someone had kept the greatest lovers in history apart for over two thousand years.

Cleo told me that Ammut and her priests were responsible.

Far down the street, I heard feet crunching in snow and children laughing. Moriarity turned the corner and was gone.

When I knew he couldn't hear me, I whispered, "I want to help her get to the Island of the Two Flames."

I sat there for a long time, just watching my breath frost in the air.

I'm going to Egypt. . . .

CHAPTER TWELVE

Thirty minutes later, Roberto trotted up to my house and rang the doorbell. When I opened the door, he said, "You scared the holy shit out of me. That was some bizarre phone message you left. What's going on?"

"Come in." I walked into the kitchen where I started pacing in front the plate glass window.

My parents liked their lines clean and sharp, the corners empty, blinds, no curtains. Everything was a perfectly orchestrated painting of vanilla and peach, my mother's favorite colors. And because they hated artificial lighting, the large window that overlooked the street allowed natural light to fall across the waxed oak floors during the summer months when the sun cleared the high peaks.

Roberto looked around. "Your parents out?"

"Yeah. A meeting with Moriarity and the police. I'm not invited because it's about me."

Removing his leather jacket, Roberto hung it on the back of the chair and sat down. As he propped his elbows on the table, stringy brown hair fell around his freckled face. "You okay?"

"God, no. I'm starting to think I really am crazy."

"Is that what you meant in your message? When you said your nightmares had stepped into your waking world."

I tried to choose my words carefully. "I . . . I stopped by Starbucks on the way home. She was there, Roberto. Sitting on our bench, as though waiting for me to come out of the shop."

Roberto tried to look calm, but I saw the hard swallow go down his throat. "Tell me exactly what you saw."

"A girl with shoulder-length black hair sitting on the bench. I couldn't see her face because she had her back to me."

"Well . . . What did she want?"

See, that's what a good friend does. He doesn't tell you you're suffering from a dissociative episode. He asks what the figment of your imagination wanted.

"I don't know!" I shouted. "She didn't tell me."

"Did she say anything?"

Walking back and forth through the slanting window light, I was creating a kind of strobe effect across the kitchen, but my nerves were so shot I couldn't sit down. "Not a word."

"If she had her back to you, and she didn't say anything, how do you know it was her?"

"I *know* her, Roberto. I know the way she moves!"

He folded his arms across his chest. "All right, Hal. Don't freak on me. Did she act normal?"

"Normal?" I said, as though it was a foreign word that I didn't quite understand.

"Sure. I mean, Cleo would have turned around and smiled at you when you walked out of the store, right? Did she?"

I shook my head. "Why does that matter?"

"Well, if you were just making her up, she would have acted normal, right?"

"How do I know? Cleo's dead and that probably changes a person."

Roberto blinked at me. "Okay, what happened next?"

I clenched my fists at my sides and saw it all again in my mind. "She walked away. When she got to the intersection, she broke into a run. After she disappeared around the corner, I heard three rifle shots and screams."

Roberto nodded like a psychiatrist humoring a mental patient. "Just like that day."

"Yes, just like that day!"

"Yeah, okay. Chill. I get it." Roberto got to his feet and exhaled a long breath, before announcing, "I'm having a glass of your mom's fancy wine. Want one?"

"No."

Roberto pulled open the door to the wine cellar and trotted down the stairs to the basement. A few seconds later, he called up. "The really filthy bottles are the good stuff, right?"

"They're the ones my parents save for special occasions. I guess so."

Roberto trotted back up the stairs with a dust-covered bottle and blew the filth off onto the kitchen floor. "Here's a 1992 cabernet with a cool name: Screaming Eagle. At least it's American. I hate that French shit."

Roberto opened and closed drawers until he found the corkscrew. After he'd pulled the cork, he smelled it like a professional, set it on the counter, and opened the cabinet door to pull out two fancy wineglasses.

"I said I didn't want one."

"Yeah, I'm not deaf."

After he'd filled both glasses, he walked back and set them on the table. "Let's dissect this, okay?"

I sank down onto one of the chairs, "You're not going to tell me I need to check myself into an asylum, are you?"

"'Course not." Roberto lifted a glass and took a dainty sip of wine, which he swished around his mouth before swallowing. "Where's the sugar?"

"What?"

"The sugar."

I pointed to the flowered sugar bowl on the counter. Roberto went to get it, then dumped a bunch into his glass and stirred it with his finger. After he'd sucked his finger clean, he nodded approvingly and sat down again. "How many girls with black hair do you think live in Colorado?"

"I would know Cleo anywhere. It was her."

"Hey, I believe in ghosts, so I'm not saying it wasn't her—but I just want you to think about other possibilities."

"Like what? Either I'm seeing a ghost, or I'm delusional. There are no other possibilities."

"Sure there are. For example, maybe somebody's pulling a fast one. Maybe you're being conned."

"That's ridiculous. Why would anyone do that?"

"Money, for one."

"Money? I'm sixteen. I don't even own a car. What could I possibly have—"

"Not from you, bright boy. Your parents. Your mom is a trust-fund baby. She's worth, what? A couple of million?"

"My mom?"

"Christ, you are such a babe-in-the-woods when it comes to the real world. Your parents own a Lexus. At every Christmas party your mom wears rubies the size of meteorites. On the phone, you said Dr. Who offered to take you to Egypt with him. Who's paying for your trip? Surely not him."

I inhaled a breath and held it while I considered the implications. Nobody had talked about that, at least not with me. But somebody must be paying for the trip. "My parents, I guess. Why?"

"How much are they paying? Just for your room, board, travel, and being babysat by Moriarity for a few weeks? Or are they paying for their genius son to be trained by a professional archaeologist? Hell, Moriarity may even be giving you college credits for your work. So figure your parents are also covering college tuition, fees, and books, and the total has got to be pretty high. And just maybe he hinted that it would be nice if your parents donated a chunk of cash to help fund his excavation. You know, as a thank you. Because without him they'd have to put Hallucination-Hal in a straitjacket, and that would certainly cost more."

Tucking my hands into my jeans pockets, I balled them into fists. "Yeah, maybe. So what?"

"Well, Hal, what if your parents backed out? Moriarity could lose a lot of cash. Sooo . . . what's the best way to make sure they don't back out?" He pointed a finger at me, then lifted it and made circles in the air around his right ear.

"Make them think Moriarity is my last hope?"

Roberto gave me a decisive nod. "And he has to be coaching them.

'Poor DID Hal. He's never going to get well without a once-in-a-lifetime trip to the Land of the Pharaohs. You don't want to take that chance, do you, Mr. and Mrs. Stevens?' Crap like that always works on parents. That's how Hornsby got his Porsche. I swear to God his therapist was in on it. Six months later Dwight sold the Porsche to the guy for a song."

"I didn't know that."

"Oh, yeah, the story was all over school. You were just so wrapped up in Cleo that you missed it."

That was probably true. Cleo had been my whole life. The love of my life. Cleo and the ancient world were all I had ever really cared about. "What did Dwight do with the money?"

"Bought himself a two-week trip to the whorehouses in Thailand. Came home bow-legged and dripping. Took massive doses of antibiotics to clear it up, I guess."

I grimaced. "Could we get back to my delusions? The visual images are way more pleasant."

"Oh, yeah, sure." Roberto's forehead knotted in deep thought. "Anyway, you get it now, right? You may not be crazy, and you may not be seeing a ghost."

My thoughts started to churn. Though I felt better about what had happened at Starbucks, the new direction of my thoughts did not ease my nerves. "But if that's true, then Moriarity, or someone else, staged the whole thing."

"Totally. Hired a girl that looked like Cleo from the back. Fired some rifle shots, got her to scream. Pretty simple stuff when you think about it."

"Jesus." I flopped back in my chair. "Do you really think so?"

"Makes the most sense." He shoved one of the wineglasses across the table to me. "Now, sit and let's talk about this rationally. If the chick isn't Cleo, you need to stop going catatonic every time you see her. You're playing right into Moriarity's hands."

I took a long drink of cabernet and shivered, which had nothing to do with the wine, but Roberto said, "Try some sugar. Makes it drinkable."

Just as he shoved the flowered bowl across the table to me, I heard my parents' Lexus pull into the driveway outside, followed by another car.

We both upended and drained our glasses.

"You wash the glasses, Hal. I'll stash the bottle."

I jumped up to obey, while Roberto carried the half-full bottle over and hid it in the garbage can under a bunch of greasy paper towels. As though he didn't have a care in the world, he wiped his hands on his hair and ambled over to look out the window.

"Bad news, Hal," he said. "The second car is a sheriff's cruiser."

CHAPTER THIRTEEN

By the time my parents opened the front door and walked inside with the officer, Roberto and I were slouched on the living room sofa with our hiking boots braced on the coffee table.

Mom gave Roberto an evil look, pointed to the front door, and said, "Go home, Robert."

"Oh, okay." Roberto exchanged a glance with me and walked for the door. "Call me later, Hal."

"Yeah."

I eyed the sheriff's deputy. I didn't know him. He'd never interviewed me before. Young, maybe mid-twenties, he had black hair, brown eyes, and a scowl. His silver badge reflected the light streaming through the windows. I had grown sick to death of these interviews. Couldn't they leave me alone? I'd told them everything I knew on the first day.

"Let's go into the kitchen to talk," Mom said. As she walked across the room, she pulled off her black sweater and tossed it onto a chair. "Deputy McDougal, may I get you a something to drink? A cup of coffee?"

"No, thank you, Dr. Stevens."

Mom and Dad walked toward the kitchen.

Just before Roberto stepped outside, he drew a couple of pentagrams in the air, plus some other squiggles, and seemed to cast them at me. He mouthed the word *protection spell*.

I gave him a thumbs-up.

When Roberto was gone, Dad called, "Can you please come into the kitchen, Hal."

I rose and went to my chair at the table, where I sank down and waited for the bad news, which is what it had to be. The deputy pulled out a chair beside me.

"How are you today, son?"

"I'm not your son, sir."

Mom made a threatening sound deep in her throat, but I tried not to notice.

The deputy started over. "Sorry. How are you today, Hal? Do you prefer Hal or Halloran?"

"Hal is fine."

While Dad busied himself making a pot of coffee, Mom eased down onto the chair at the end of the table, and said, "Deputy McDougal was a participant in a meeting we had today at the police department, as was Dr. Moriarity. We have granted the deputy a few minutes to speak with you."

"I want an attorney."

"We have waived your right to an attorney in this instance, Hal," Mom said.

"I'm not saying a word without an attorney present." I clenched my jaw.

Mom started to say something really unpleasant, but Dad cut her off: "That's okay, Hal. You don't have to say anything if you don't want to. You can just listen."

Deputy McDougal seemed to be trying to decide how to proceed. Clearly, he'd planned on talking with me, maybe even *needed* to talk with me. But after a few seconds, he turned away and looked at the end of the table where Mom sat and Dad stood with his hands on the back of her chair.

"At today's meeting, Dr. Moriarity laid out the details of the trip he has planned to Egypt. While we are hesitant to allow your son to leave the country—"

I blurted, "You can't stop me! You have no evidence that I have committed a crime."

"What I'm trying to tell you, Hal, is that the final results of the autopsy just came in this morning," the deputy said. "And our office agrees that it may be safer for you to be away for a while."

"The autopsy?" I said in a quavering voice. No one had told me there had been an autopsy. But, of course, there had been an autopsy. It was a murder case. The idea of Cleo being cut apart . . .

Without realizing it, I squeezed my eyes closed and sagged forward to prop my elbows on the table. Grieving, I whispered, "What did you find?"

Deputy McDougal waited a short while, giving me time, I guess, before he answered, "Ms. Mallawi tried to fight off her attacker. And she got a piece of her. The blood beneath Ms. Mallawi's fingernails belongs to a woman."

I sat there like a speechless lump.

Mom said, "So you think she was killed by a woman?"

"Obviously, at this point, we can only say she fought with a woman, but it seems likely that her attacker was also her killer. We have no evidence that anyone else was involved. However, this is an ongoing investigation."

I looked up at him with tears in my eyes. When had that happened? "Sir, did you find any other evidence left by the woman? Tracks, murder weapon?"

The deputy shook his head. "No. But the rainstorm washed away a wealth of evidence. By the time we got there, the only tracks we could find belonged to you and Mr. Dally."

"What about the claw marks? Did you find out how they were made? Did the woman have a knife? Or was she——"

"Our forensic experts are still analyzing that information, so I'm not at liberty to answer that question."

I must have looked terrible. Everyone was staring at me like my face had turned green.

God bless Dad. He cleared his throat and Mom and Deputy McDougal turned away from me to look at him. "Why do you think it's safer if Hal goes away for a while?"

McDougal studied me for five awful seconds, before he said, "In Hal's initial discussion with Officer Sackett, he told him he thought an Egyptian demon named Ammut, wearing an Egyptian Army uniform, killed Ms. Mallawi."

I swallowed hard. "Yes."

"Is Ammut male or female?"

"I . . . female, I think, but I'm pretty sure the demon can appear as either. Why?"

He shrugged, as though it didn't really matter. "Just curious. There is a cult in Denver that worships Ammut, among other demons. Their high priest is a pretty scary guy. Has multiple felonies on his record."

From a locked door somewhere inside me, Cleo's voice whispered: *She and her priests have successfully kept me from reaching the Island of the Two Flames for over two thousand years.*

Dad said, "Then you think members of the cult killed Cleo?"

"I have no evidence to suggest that, but we are checking into all possible leads."

Placing my hands on either side of my skull, I pressed hard, trying to force out the lingering images I had conjured of the autopsy. "Thank you. Really."

Mom had never been known for being subtle. She stood up and gestured to the front door. "My son is finished speaking with you, Deputy. Have a nice trip back to your office."

McDougal looked a little startled at being told to leave. "Oh, well, thank you. I appreciate the opportunity to speak with your son."

"Of course, you do. Goodbye," Mom said.

While Dad led the cop to the door, Mom sat down again and silently glowered at the tabletop. We both jumped when the front door closed. Dad walked back into the kitchen and dropped onto a chair beside Mom.

His voice was ominous. "Well, what do you think, Jenna?"

Mom lightly ran a hand through her short blonde hair. When she looked up at me, her professional look was gone. She was really worried. "I want you to answer me, Hal. Do you have the medallion that Dr. Moriarity is looking for?"

"N-no," I stammered. Why had Moriarity told them about the medallion? Had he wanted them to turn my room upside down searching for it? "I don't know what he's talking about."

"Why didn't you tell us that he'd asked you about an ancient medallion?"

"Because I didn't have it, so it didn't seem important."

"It is important. *Very* important," Mom said. "Dr. Moriarity suspects that Cleo was attacked by someone trying to find that medallion. Which means, if you have it, they may come for you next."

Time seemed to stop between two heartbeats. Nothing moved. If Ammut's priests would kill a sixteen-year-old girl for the medallion, they would certainly kill me. They must want it badly. Why? Was one of the Denver whackos a Sem priest? *Oh, God . . .*

Dad leaned toward me. "Hal? Are you all right? You just went pale."

My parents were watching me like vultures, just waiting for me to keel over so they could pick my mental bones clean.

I took a deep breath. "Is that why you agreed to let me go to Egypt?"

Dad held my gaze. "You've always wanted to go to Egypt, son. We think it will be emotionally healing for you to do that."

Mom added, "But we also think you'll be safer out of the country until they can catch the murderer. Dr. Moriarity agrees."

"What about Roberto? He's a target, too."

"We know," Dad said. "Dr. Moriarity has spoken with Robert's parents, and they've agreed to allow him to accompany you to Egypt. You're leaving at the end of the month."

I sat up straighter. "That's only three weeks. That's not much time to prepare."

"No, it's not, but we'll help you."

"How?"

Mom rose from her chair and went to the sink to wash her hands, which I found a little curious. Did she feel soiled after talking with the deputy? She dried her hands on a paper towel and opened the cabinet door to toss it in the garbage. Something seemed to have caught her eye, but she said, "Your father is going to buy supplies and archaeological equipment for you, while I take care of making appointments for the infectious disease shots you'll need. Dr. Moriarity will get the necessary visas for you to enter the country. You'll be listed as members of his field crew. Egypt will only allow you to stay for one month."

I closed my eyes and nodded as though exhausted, which I was. "Okay. Good. Thanks. I'm going to my room."

As I rose from my chair, I saw Mom's eyes widen suddenly, and I trotted up the stairs. When I reached the landing at the top, I turned back. Mom stood curiously examining the garbage. It took a few seconds for her to decide to stick her hand in the mess and shove aside the greasy paper towels. The curious look on her face changed to one of horror.

"Dear God!" she yelled loud enough for it to echo through the house. "There's a $7,000 bottle of wine in the garbage!"

I tiptoed into my bedroom and closed the door.

Nobody came up to yell at me, so I spent most of the day curled on my bed, sleeping, climbing to the top of the ancient lighthouse with Cleo.

It would have been okay with me if I'd never woken up.

CHAPTER FOURTEEN

The day we left, we insisted our parents not accompany us to the airport. Instead, we said goodbye in Georgetown, and rode to the airport with Dr. Moriarity, who kept glancing suspiciously at my carry-on shoulder bag. Maybe because the tan canvas bag had belonged to Cleo or maybe because he knew what it contained.

As we proceeded through the serpentine line toward the security checkpoint, I fell as far back as I could. I didn't want Moriarity to be watching the X-ray monitor when my shoulder bag went through.

"Roberto? Keep him busy for me, will you?"

"Sure thing."

Roberto went through the line ahead of me, picked up his carry-on—his worn-out gym bag—and proceeded to join Moriarity on the other side of security, where he engaged Moriarity in a lively conversation.

By the time I'd stepped out of the body scanner, a redheaded TSA agent already had my bag in his hands. "Is this your bag? You don't mind if I open it, do you?"

"No, sir."

The man carried my bag to the rear, unzipped it, and pulled out small metal box where I kept the medallion safe. He examined it, apparently decided it was just a piece of jewelry and put it back in the box. After he shoved the box into my shoulder bag, he handed me the bag and said, "Have a nice day."

"Thank you."

I slipped the strap over my shoulder and walked out to meet Roberto and Moriarity.

So far so good.

In the fluorescent light, Moriarity's graying brown hair and beard looked more silver, almost white. He had a knowing expression on his face, as though no one had to tell him why it had taken me so long to get through security. Like a laser, his gaze focused on my bag.

"Everything okay?" he asked.

"Yeah. My laptop is in the bag. They had to turn it on and stare at the screen for a while."

"Uh-huh," Moriarity said as though he didn't believe a word of it. He checked his watch. "All right, boys, we have two hours before our flight. Let's go find some lunch. I didn't have breakfast. I'm starving."

Moriarity turned right and walked toward the Elway's restaurant in Concourse B.

We followed.

Keeping him in sight wasn't difficult. The professor wore light green chinos and a tan shirt with hiking boots. His fedora was classic Indiana Jones, including the ingrained dust and soot, presumably from sitting around a thousand campfires at exotic archaeological sites. The man had been twitchy all morning, irritable, clearly eager to get out of America.

Denver International Airport was bustling. Dodging the numerous baby strollers, shrieking children, rolling bags, and rushing people took real concentration, which wasn't easy given that the overhead loudspeakers kept calling out names and announcing departing flights. I felt a little overwhelmed by it all.

When we reached the door of the Elway's, the front of my red T-shirt was damp. I shook sweat-soaked blond hair out of my eyes and surveyed the crowded restaurant.

Over the din of conversations, I said, "Do you see him, Roberto?"

"No. Oh, wait. There he is." Roberto pointed. "Way in the back."

Moriarity waved to us from where he sat with a menu open in front of him. We worked our way around the tables. I was proud of myself. I only stumbled over the luggage in the middle of the floor twice. After I'd almost tumbled into the laps of the idiots who'd left them there, it was a little curious to me that they made no attempt to move them. I must not understand airport etiquette. Probably because it's an oxymoron. When we slid into the booth on the opposite side from Moriarity, he tossed us the menu.

"The Smash Burger is good," he said and began scanning the crowd like a cop, squinting at people before his gaze moved on. What was he looking for? A person?

"I don't like Smash Burgers," Roberto countered, and sank back against the booth. Since I had the menu, Roberto folded his arms across his chest, and examined Moriarity. A curious expression came over his face. He asked, "So. Once we get to Egypt, what then?"

Moriarity waited until the waitress had set his beer in front of him, took a long drink, and used his tan sleeve to wipe the foam from his beard. "Then, Robert, you're mine."

Roberto stared at Moriarity. The staring match lasted so long I felt like there was some sort of struggle of wills going on, and I suspected it presaged the month ahead.

"I'm having the chicken-fried steak burrito," I announced and handed Roberto the menu.

Moriarity took another drink of beer. "To answer your question, as soon as we get off the plane, we're going to pick up the Jeep my student has left for us in the parking lot, then head out into the depths of the Egyptian desert. We will be completely out of contact. Keep that in mind. And it's going to be a long hard hike. The sand is too deep to drive the Jeep to my friend's cave."

My heart rate quickened. "Samael Saqqara? The man who helped excavate the mysterious medallion you keep talking about?"

Moriarity pinned me with bottomless black eyes. "That's right, Hal. For a few hours, or maybe days, it's just going to be you two and me, hiking alone through sand dunes that seem to go on forever. The entire region is swarming with insurgents, not just Daesh, but tribal groups and local militias. They are well-armed and brutal, and they hate Americans. We cannot allow ourselves to be captured. I'm not trying to scare you, but I don't know if you two flabby boys are up to it. Don't either of you engage in sports? Football? Basketball? Maybe a little baseball?"

Still absorbed by the menu, Roberto didn't look up when he said,

"Gangster Cyclops from Centaurus: Death Mission Edition. Become Death, bro. Way more interesting than a couple of dudes tossing their balls around."

Moriarity looked distressed by being called bro. He took another long drink of beer. "You're really are obsessed with death, aren't you?"

Roberto started to answer, but I interrupted. "Don't worry about us, Dr. Moriarity. We'll be fine on the hike. We've been running and lifting weights. We're in better shape than you think."

"I just want to prepare you boys for the worst," Moriarity continued. "It's an ugly world out there in the backcountry regions of Egypt. This could well be life or death. Understand?"

Roberto closed the menu, set it aside, and looked up at Moriarity through the stringy hair hanging over his wide eyes. An apocalyptic tone entered Roberto's voice. "I'm having the Ding Dong with two scoops. You?"

CHAPTER FIFTEEN

As we descended toward Port Said, fog cloaked the plane like a shimmering blanket, and beads of water began to stream across the wings outside the window. I heaved a sigh. After twenty-one hours in the air, including changing planes twice, I felt like I'd been beaten with a stick. Roberto was still asleep in the seat beside me, so I watched the shreds of coastline below appear and disappear as we descended through the silver haze.

When the turbulence increased and the plane began to bounce around, I leaned back in my seat and found Moriarity staring at me. The professor sat across the aisle reading the latest issue of *Antiquity*. Originally, he'd sat in the aisle seat beside Roberto, but changed seats when it became clear that airplane food caused Roberto some fragrant gastrointestinal distress.

Moriarity smiled at me. I smiled back.

"Almost there," he called.

"I see that."

Moriarity's hair stuck out at odd angles, as though he'd had an uncomfortable night of shifting positions, trying to sleep. Who hadn't? I suspected my blond hair looked pretty much the same.

At the sound of our voices, Roberto roused and straightened up in his seat to blink around the plane. "Where are we?"

"Descending toward Port Said."

"Awesome." He leaned across me to gaze out the window at the glimpses of city and blue ocean flashing by below. "The countryside is so green. I thought it was all desert. Sand dunes that went on forever, you know?"

I shook my head. "No, this is an agricultural area. Historically, it was famous for growing flax." I pointed to the east. "Do you see that broad marshy plain?"

"Yeah."

My gaze clung to it. "The ruins of Per Amun are out there. I don't know where exactly. It used to sit two and half miles from the sea, between two branches of the Nile River, but even by the third century it was four miles from the sea. Per Amun was the most important port in ancient Egypt, after Alexandria. In 55 BC, Marcus Antonius saved the people of Per Amun from the wrath of Ptolemy Auletes, who wanted to put them to the death after—"

"Why is it so far from the sea today?" Roberto interrupted. He could always tell when a history lesson was coming, and tried at all costs to avoid it.

"The branches of the Nile started silting in during the first century BC. Eventually, the Nile changed course, and the shoreline was pushed farther and farther away."

"Oh. Cool."

I looked back at Egypt. This was the first time I'd felt truly alive since Cleo's death. The small round window became my entire universe for a few minutes. As the plane headed down, the pilot began to circle, and more of the country appeared. To the south, for as far as I could see, the Nile River cut a vast blue swath through the landscape. Green fields lined the Nile's floodplain, but the desert that stretched beyond them to the west was mesmerizing. In the morning light, the sand resembled a vast ocean, rising and falling in tan waves, cut here and there by cliffs and canyons, and speckled with green oases.

This was my Cleo's homeland, the place she had spoken of with such love and despair in her voice. I closed my eyes and tried to imagine her here with me, leaning across me to look out the window. What would we be doing? We'd be discussing the past. She would be pointing things out to me, laughing, quoting Plutarch.

When I opened my eyes and gazed out across the land that Julius Caesar, Ptolemy, Marcus Antonius, and Cleopatra had walked, this world vanished. Time melted away. . . .

Far back in my mind, I could hear vast armies on the move, horse tack jangling, whinnying mixed with human voices, and the roar as thousands of men marched out of Per Amun on their way to Alexandria in 30 BC.

Cleopatra's scouts had told her Gaius Julius was coming. She was frantic. She knew what he would do when he won. Egypt would be no more. He would steal her treasury, pillage her country, and turn Egypt into just another Roman province. Then he would kill her children and lock her in chains to be paraded through the streets of Rome as the glorious proof of his triumph, before condemning her to a Roman dungeon for the rest of her life. Many captured rulers had killed themselves, or gone mad, in the dungeons of Rome.

Willing to do anything to save her children and her country, Cleopatra made one last desperate gamble. She deceived Antonius into thinking she was dead in the hope that the man she loved, the father of three of her children, would in turn commit suicide. In utter despair over her death, Antonius tried. But when he thrust the sword into his chest, he missed his heart. Gushing blood and faint, he begged his servants to finish the job. To a man, his loyal officers and friends deserted him and fled, most in tears.

When Cleopatra heard Antonius' anguished cries echoing through the palace, she ran to the unfinished roof of the mausoleum where she'd taken refuge and called out to her servants below. Her secretary answered that Antonius was not dead, but lying half-dead on the floor. Stunned, Cleopatra lowered ropes and ordered that Antonius' limp body be tied so she could lift him. She drew him up herself, aided by her two servants Iras and Charmion. Bleeding to death and in agony, Antonius watched her the whole time. Plutarch said, "Never was there a more piteous sight. Smeared with blood and struggling with death he was drawn up, stretching out his hands to her even as he dangled in the air."

When Antonius had at last been pulled into the room and placed on the couch, a distraught Cleopatra began weeping and tearing at her clothing. Antonius silenced her. He asked for a sip of wine. He told her that she must now concentrate on her own safety, and make the best arrangement with Gaius that her honor would allow. As he lay dying in Cleopatra's arms, Antonius told her he loved her. He forgave her. . . .

Slowly, as though my soul didn't want to return to the present, the plane's window crystallized before my eyes, and my lungs filled with air. Outside, a magnificent vista stretched into infinity. The Nile flashed by through clouds of fog.

The idea that this land was haunted by demons and ghosts did not seem strange. In fact, the reverse would have been stranger. Egypt was an ancient and magical place. Some of the most important events in history had occurred here. Events that had changed the entire world. "In Egypt," Cleo had once said, "the dead are not dead. They stare you in the face every day." I wasn't sure what that meant, but I wanted to find out.

I felt Roberto shift in his seat. He leaned close to ask, "Any suspicious activities from Dr. Who while I slept?"

"No. He spent the night dozing and reading. Got up a couple times to go the bathroom in the rear. Had two glasses of wine. Some coffee."

"He never tried to reach under your seat for Cleo's shoulder bag?"

I shook my head. Throughout the trip, Roberto and I had taken turns staying awake to monitor Moriarity's movements. He'd never so much as accidentally reached for my bag.

When he saw us looking at him, Moriarity unfastened his seatbelt and returned to sit beside Roberto. He gestured to the window. "Want me to tell you what you're seeing out there?"

"If you have to," Roberto said.

Moriarity gave Roberto an askance look, then leaned toward the window and pointed eastward. "Right about there, where the marshes look so green? That's where Pompey Magnus was killed."

I lurched forward so fast my nose hit the window. "Where?" I didn't realize I'd shouted until the redheaded woman in front of us turned around to give me a dirty look.

Through a yawn, Roberto said, "What's a pompous Magnus?"

Excited, I answered before Moriarity could: "In 60 BC, Gnaeus Pompeius Magnus joined with his rivals Julius Caesar and Marcus Licinius Crassus to form the First Triumvirate of Rome. They ruled together for seven years, but the alliance collapsed in 53 BC, when Pompeius talked the Roman Senate into demanding that Caesar give up his army, which he refused to do. Instead, in 49 BC, Caesar led his legions across the Rubicon River into Italy and declared war against Pompeius and his forces."

"Huh." Roberto grunted. "Is that where the phrase, 'to cross the Rubicon' comes from?"

Nodding, a huge grin came to my face. "Yes."

"So did Julius Caesar win?"

"Oh, yeah. In August of 48 BC, Pompeius' army chased Caesar to Pharsalus in Thessaly. Caesar was outnumbered two-to-one, but he had a good strategic position. And Marcus Antonius was in command of the eleventh and ninth legions. Nobody was better at fighting a land battle than Marcus Antonius. Caesar's smaller forces completely defeated Pompeius."

"And," Moriarity added, gazing at me with a smile, as though proud of my knowledge, "Pompey fled to Egypt, hoping that King Ptolemy XIII, Cleopatra's younger brother, would give him sanctuary. Unfortunately for Pompey Magnus, Ptolemy was afraid of the wrath of Julius Caesar, so he invited Pompey Magnus to come ashore at Per Amun, and when Pompey arrived, Ptolemy ordered that his head be chopped off."

A glow filled Roberto's blue eyes. "Where's his head? Can we go see it?"

Moriarity paused. "You're a curious kid, you know that?"

"Well . . . Yeah."

As the plane banked and swerved over the ocean, Moriarity looked out the window. Two cruise ships left gigantic Vs in the water as they coasted up the shoreline. Alexandria was visible in the distance, sitting like a shining jewel on the blue sea. My heart actually caught in my throat. All of my life, I'd wanted to see this sight.

Moriarity said to Roberto, "So, as to Pompey's head. To try and gain favor, Ptolemy sent Pompey's head to Caesar, which enraged Caesar, who'd been looking forward to magnanimously pardoning his most ardent enemy. The historian, Appian, says that Caesar had Pompey's severed head buried in Alexandria. Which is—" he pointed— "right there."

Roberto didn't look. He kept his eyes on Moriarity. "Yeah, but is the head in a museum now? How about the other body parts? Where are they?"

"Has anyone ever told you that you're a little disgusting?"

"Sure. I asked Molly Henson for a date three days before we left."

Moriarity continued, "On the other hand, you, Mr. Dally, are the stuff that legendary archaeologists are made from. They've all had an unhealthy interest in the dead. Of course, so do mass murderers." He gave Roberto a pointed look, but Roberto didn't seem to notice.

"Whatever. I'm probably going to be a video game designer anyway."

"Video games are utterly inane. Hopefully, you'll grow out of it."

Roberto scratched his chin and tilted his head to study Moriarity's bearded face with a careful eye. "You know, next time you should try passing yourself off as a chimpanzee. It would be more convincing than an intellectual."

Moriarity stared at him. "Did I mention that your parents said I could ship you home any time I wanted to?"

"Yeah? Can you make sure I have a twenty-four-hour layover in Thailand?" Roberto turned to me and said, "*Lay*over."

I started laughing and couldn't stop.

People all across the plane turned around to give me ugly glares. Smothering my mouth in my sleeve only made it worse, because then my shrieks sounded like a dying turkey buzzard's flopping toward doom. Finally, two little boys in the seats behind us started shooting spit wads at me between the seats.

When one of the misaimed projectiles stuck to Roberto's face, he whirled around to say, "Hey! Don't make me crawl over this seat!"

The barrage ceased.

As a flight attendant hurried down the aisle toward us, Moriarity seemed to be trying to sink into his seat.

"I'm sorry," the dark-haired woman said to him, "but your sons are causing a commotion."

"I apologize. I'll take care of it," Moriarity assured her. As she walked away, he gave us a threatening look.

A few seconds later, her voice crackled over the loud speaker: "*May I have your attention, please? We will soon be landing in Port*

Said. Please put up your tray tables and return your seat backs to their original positions. Thank you for flying with us. The local time is 8:13 AM. The temperature in Port Said is 37 degrees centigrade, or approximately 99 degrees Fahrenheit. We hope you have an enjoyable stay here, or wherever your final destination takes you."

The plane bucked and jumped as we neared the landing strip. Along the shoreline I saw weathered fishing boats, the casino I'd noted on maps, and a beautiful beach filled with people, who, at this height, appeared as tiny colorful dots.

I leaned back in my seat to ride out the turbulence until the wheels touched down.

Once the plane eased up to the jetway, the unclicking of seatbelts started. Finally, we rose, gathered our things, and slowly shuffled down the aisle toward the forward door.

We marched through the airport and out to the baggage carousel without incident, though I almost broke my neck whipping my head around to stare at people. The array of colorful clothing, hats, and languages was fascinating!

It didn't take long for our backpacks to show up. Shrugging into the shoulder straps, we pushed forward in a herd, not a line, toward passport control and customs.

Once we'd made it through, Moriarity said, "The restroom is just ahead. You might want to change clothes while we're in there. We have a long hot drive ahead of us today."

Ten minutes later, I exited the restroom wearing a clean blue T-shirt and jeans. The medallion was back in its usual place, duct-taped to my ankle. I waited for Roberto, who emerged wearing a clean white T-shirt, but the same pair of worn jeans.

Moriarity met us just outside the restroom door. "You can call your parents now. Tell 'em you made it okay, and this is the last contact you'll have with them for a while. There's no cell service where we're going."

I pulled out my phone, checked the text message from Mom, saying, *Are you there yet? Worried about you,* and then started punching in numbers. The phone rang a dozen times. No one answered, so I left a message: "Mom and Dad, we just landed in Egypt. It's beautiful here. This is the last call I'll be able to make. Dr. Moriarity says we're not going to have cell service. I love you. Don't worry about me. I'm okay."

Off to my left, Roberto had his phone to his ear, talking to his parents.

When Roberto shoved his phone back in his pocket, Moriarity said, "All right, let's go. It's only a short walk to the parking lot."

Just as I stepped outside the terminal, a blast of hot humid air hit me, along with the din of honking horns, and the smell of exhaust fumes. It was real sensory overload. People rushed in all directions around me, dragging rolling bags toward taxi stands, onto buses, or across the busy road toward the parking lot in the distance. I counted at least a dozen languages in the first five minutes.

Moriarity pointed. "See that beat-up white Jeep in the first line of the lot? That's ours. Follow me."

We crossed the road as part of a multilingual bumping and crashing crowd.

CHAPTER SIXTEEN

N ine hours later, Moriarity pulled to a stop on the side of a dirt road and shut off the engine. While the dust boiled up around the Jeep, I checked my watch. Ten minutes to six and it was still hot. The Jeep had no air-conditioning, so we'd been riding the entire way with the windows down and dust gushing in around us every time Moriarity slowed down. Roberto and I both looked like filthy drowned rats. Our dusty, sweat-soaked shirts could have come straight out of a mud bath.

Moriarity pulled his water bottle from his pack, which took up the entire front passenger seat, and took a long drink. Then he put on his fedora and turned around to look at us where we sat in the back. His graying brown hair and beard glittered with beads of sweat. "Grab your packs, hats, long-sleeved shirts, your water bottles, boys. From here, we walk."

"Why can't we drive?" Roberto said.

"Sand is too deep. Jeep would be bogged down in five minutes."

Roberto and I reached into the rear to pull the necessary items from our packs, and climbed out.

As I put on my white shirt, I scanned the desert. No people, no houses, no roads. It was beautiful and stark, unlike any place I had ever been. At any moment, I expected to see a camel caravan crossing before me, or a band of armed insurgents exploding from the dunes. Nonetheless, I felt strangely free. For most of my life, I'd lived inside my head, dreaming ancient dreams, but right now, at this moment, I was just here. I mean really *here*, feeling the heat and the light breeze that swept the desert. There were no thoughts in my head. The constant grief that plagued me eased.

I took a drink from my water bottle and hooked it to my belt.

Roberto walked up beside me. "This is the middle of fucking nowhere. I don't even see a goat trail, do you?"

"No."

"Where do you think we're going?"

I shrugged. "I assume he'll tell us. But the only real topography out here is that ridge in the distance."

To the west, the sun shone bright red as it sank through a dust haze toward the horizon. Beneath it, a ridge wound its way through the dunes like the twisted and broken backbone of some long-dead monster. I couldn't tell how tall the ridge was, but it appeared to be at least one hundred feet, maybe two hundred feet tall in places.

Roberto narrowed his eyes at the ridge. "I hope that's where we're going. Look at that shadow. That's the perfect place to make camp. I've never been this hot in my entire life."

"Me either."

Keep in mind we'd grown up in the forested Colorado high country. We weren't used to this kind of heat. If it got to eighty-five degrees in Georgetown in the summer, it was probably the hottest day of the year.

I put on my hat and studied the ridge. The shadow of the cliff did look inviting.

Roberto's brown hair hung around his face in sweat-matted locks. He shoved it off his forehead, and asked, "How hot do you think it is now?"

The Jeep door slammed behind us. I heard the locks click.

"I don't know. Still over 100, I'd say."

Moriarity came around the Jeep adjusting his fedora and stood beside me. He wore a long-sleeved tan shirt. "Actually, I suspect it's around 38 Centigrade."

"How hot is that?" Roberto asked.

"You, Robert, are going have to learn how to calculate in centigrade, which is easy to do. Just multiply the centigrade temperature by 1.8 and add 32. So, 38 x 1.8 plus 32 equals 100.4 degrees Fahrenheit."

"Wow, thanks. That was really helpful," Roberto lifted his watch and tapped the glow-in-the-dark dial. "But I think I'll just check my watch."

Using his sleeve to mop his forehead, Moriarity said, "Oh. Does your watch have a thermometer?"

Roberto replied, "No. Get it?"

I hated to interrupt their budding friendship, but I had to ask, "We don't have much time to hike, Dr. Moriarity. How far is Samael's house?"

While the professor scowled at Roberto, he answered, "He lives in a cave in that cliff you see to the west, but it's farther than it looks. We have a good two-hour hike ahead of us."

Roberto headed out across the sand.

"Hold on," Moriarity called. "Before we go, I need to warn you. Watch out for snakes. Especially cobras. The bite of a cobra works through neurotoxins and anticoagulants. First, the venom paralyzes you, and then it liquefies your insides. By the time the tremendous swelling sets in, you feel like your body had been dipped in acid and set on fire. Many victims use knives to slice open their own skin so the bulging flesh can spill out. Understand?"

Roberto chewed a hangnail and spat it out. "No snake handling? Shit. I was looking forward to that."

CHAPTER SEVENTEEN

As the smoky veils of twilight settled over the desert, the crests of the dunes shaded a dark purple, and I thought I smelled trees and water. Maybe even the fragrance of flowers. Was it real? Was there an oasis ahead? Or was it just my cottony mind playing tricks?

I stopped to look around and to rest for a few seconds. Moriarity and Roberto continued walking ahead of me. I had to admit, I was tired. The worst part of the hike was the sand. It dragged at my hiking boots, making each step a chore. But we had to be close now. Just ahead, the ridge rose out of the sand like a dark fortress, its steep cliffs clearly visible in the dusk glow.

"You okay back there?" Moriarity called. When he turned around to look at me, wind fluttered his hair beneath the brim of his fedora.

"Sorry. Just looking at the desert. Pretty out here."

I rarely took my gaze off Moriarity. The medallion taped inside my right sock wouldn't let me. Each time I forgot and started to lose myself in blissfully looking around, the artifact felt heavier, as though in warning. Or . . . I thought it did. But for a couple of hours, my imagination had been running wild. I was just beginning to understand the first Christian ascetics. As early as the late first century, Christian monks had retreated to the wasteland of Egypt's desert for the solitude they believed necessary to seek God.

And I could feel it, too. A supernatural presence, as though the divine permeated the very air I breathed. Often, I heard invisible footsteps in the sand behind me, but when I turned to look, I saw nothing.

"Just keeping walking, guys," Moriarity said. "We're almost

there, and I guarantee you that tonight will be the most fascinating night of your lives."

It was a measure of Roberto's exhaustion that he didn't have a comeback for that. He just plodded along behind Moriarity.

As we got closer, the vertical cliff loomed two hundred feet above us. Cracked and broken from millennia of weathering, giant fissures rent the stone. They resembled black veins worming their ways across the cliff face.

For another hour, I panted along behind Roberto, struggling just to put one boot in front of the other.

When darkness fell in earnest, it finally started to cool down, and stars flickered to life. My God, it was amazing. In Colorado, the mountain peaks obscured most of the sky, so I could only see a small slice of stars. Here, in the flat desert, the stars stretched from horizon to horizon. The only thing blocking the view was the cliff to my left, and it felt small and insignificant in this vast bowl of glittering galaxies.

I stumbled and winced. I'd finished off my water bottle an hour ago, and I'd been feeling queasy ever since. Probably dehydration. Out here, a person could not drink enough to stay hydrated. The searing heat sucked every ounce of moisture from the human body. If only I could just rest for a while, I was sure I'd . . .

"*Hal*," Cleo softly called.

I came to a dead stop. The words had been as clear as a bell. As adrenaline surged through my veins, my gaze searched the darkness. In the bright starlight, every dune cast a shadow. The interplay of light and dark, along with the grains of sand that sparkled as they blew across the ground, was almost mystical. Was I so desperate to see her, to talk with her, that my unconscious was manufacturing auditory hallucinations? Suddenly, I missed her so much I could barely stand it. For most of the day, I'd forgotten my grief.

Moriarity called, "Did you say something, Hal?"

"Did I? I . . . I thought I heard . . . Something." I hadn't called her name, had I? I didn't remember doing that.

"Why did you stop, Hal? We have to keep going."

Roberto said, "Leave him alone. He just needs to catch his breath."

They stood twenty paces ahead of me, little more than two black silhouettes against the backdrop of dark cliff. I couldn't make out either one's face, but Moriarity's glasses flashed with starlight when he started shifting position, as though impatient.

"Come on, Hal!" Moriarity called. "We have to go. It's not safe out here."

I forced my feet to march forward, leaving her behind. It would hurt her feelings, but I couldn't help it. I was pretty sure that if Moriarity thought I was completely crazy, he'd strip me naked to find the medallion, and put me on a plane home. As a matter of fact, I couldn't figure out why he hadn't already done that, but he probably hadn't had the opportunity.

The professor did not wait for me to catch up. He took off at a quick walk, making up time. Roberto followed him.

I started falling behind almost immediately. I just didn't have the energy left to push . . .

"*Hal, don't go.*"

I froze.

Off to the right, something moved, trudging through the deep sand. Little more than a faint black shape, it looked human. And the sky . . . the sky was bleeding . . . red streamers ran from the stars like rain . . .

I jerked when rifle shots echoed across the night . . . like physical blows . . . and I longed to shout, to run . . . I couldn't breathe. The pungent scent of pine filled my nostrils.

Roberto shouted, "*Hey! You okay?*" He ran back to me. "What's wrong? You yelled."

She was still out there, maybe thirty feet away. I could see her black hair blowing in the wind. I was scared now, because there was no longer any doubt about my sanity. No one else had heard the shots or her voice. Only me.

"Yeah. I—I'm okay."

Roberto turned around to follow my gaze. "Do you see something?"

"I'm just . . . Really worn out, Roberto. Dehydration, I think."

"Yeah, Christ. I've been pissing orange for an hour."

That's all this is. Dehydration can bring on delusions. I haven't lost my mind. I'm not crazy.

Roberto looked back at Moriarity who'd crossed his arms and was giving us an unpleasant look, like we were both wimps.

"Hal, if we don't stop soon, I'm going to pitch a fit. You don't look so good. Are you sure you're okay?"

Nodding, I whispered, "Yeah, let's keep going. I need to get to a place where I can rest."

"All right, but don't push yourself. I'm afraid you're going to have a heart attack or pass out on me."

I nodded. "Okay."

Roberto started walking along the cliff face again, but he kept turning around to make sure I was following him.

When I searched for her again, the black shape was gone. All I saw was wind blowing across starlit dunes.

I put my head down and concentrated on placing one hiking boot in front of the other.

CHAPTER EIGHTEEN

As the trail curved westward, I could see dozens of caves dotting the cliff wall. They resembled unblinking black eyes. Ahead, palm trees swayed in the starlight, and I definitely smelled water and flowers. "Is that where we're going to camp? That oasis?"

"Yes," Moriarity called over his shoulder. "Keep walking."

To the north, I saw the flicker of lights, maybe lamps. They were pinpricks in the darkness, but definitely there. A small village? Or an insurgent's camp?

When we got to within a hundred paces of the caves, a pond, fringed by palms and other trees, glowed in the starlight.

Moriarity stopped and lifted his hat so he could wipe his drenched forehead with his sleeve. "I want you two to sit down for a minute. I need to talk to you."

Roberto gestured to the cliff. "Let's get to the caves and then sit down. They'll be cooler."

"No. Sit down. Right here." Moriarity stabbed a finger at the ground. "Get comfortable."

Roberto and I exchanged a glance and dropped to the sand, and I do mean dropped. I hit so hard I grunted when I landed. Moriarity knelt in front of us and removed his water bottle from his belt. As he slowly unscrewed the lid, his gaze fixed on the watery reflections cast upon the cliff by the starlit pond. Finally, he tipped up the bottle up and gulped it dry. I wanted to kill him. He had that much water left? And he hadn't offered to share when he knew I was on my last legs?

Lowering his empty bottle, Moriarity propped it on his knee. "There are some things I need to tell you about Samael before you meet him. He's a bit odd."

"Odd?"

"First, he's a famous digger. Never forget that. The man is a legend in the archaeological world. I think he's worked on every important archaeological excavation in Egypt over the past forty years. He was at Karnak when they opened up the tomb of—"

"Odd in what way?" Roberto interrupted.

Moriarity gave him a disapproving look. "Well, for one thing, his memory has started to go. He forgets things, asks the same questions over and over, and mixes up words. When he can't remember something, like where he put an object, he often makes up a story about monsters or fallen angels to explain the disappearance. There's no telling what he'll say to you."

I asked, "How old is he? Is this Alzheimer's?"

Moriarity tilted his head as though uncertain. "Sometimes, I think so. Other times, I suspect he's schizophrenic." Without a trace of humor, he added, "Which you, Hal, should understand better than most."

My spine stiffened. "Are you saying I'm schizophrenic?"

"No, I'm saying you have a well-developed imagination. Don't you agree?"

"Oh. Yeah," I conceded, and Roberto frowned at me like I should never let Dr. Who think he was right.

"Have either of you ever been around a seriously mentally ill person before?"

Roberto said, "Oh, hell, yeah. My Aunt Louise collects the shriveled body parts of saints and puts them on her mantel. Every holiday she makes us pray before them, as though a chunk of tongue can hear us."

Moriarity stabbed a finger at Roberto. "That's exactly the irreverent tone I want you to banish from your voice right now. As an archaeologist, it is not your job to disbelieve. It's your job to listen and learn. Get it?"

"Yeah. Sure."

"Good. If we can get him to talk about it, I suspect he has information that you will find extremely important. Especially you, Hal."

I pulled off my hat and batted the dust out on my pant leg. "What information?"

Moriarity's lips curled into a knowing smile. "Samael claims to have visited the Island of the Two Flames."

"He's been to the land of the dead?" Suddenly there wasn't enough air in the world. My lungs were starving. "I didn't know the living could get to the Island of the Two Flames."

"It's not easy, believe me." Moriarity bowed his head and grimaced at the sand.

Forcing a swallow down my throat, I said, "You sound like you've tried, Professor."

"I did once." Moriarity's eyes narrowed as though in pain at the memory. "Samael told me he could take me there. Unfortunately, he got lost. Or said he did. We came back here after three days of walking along the Nile, searching for it."

"So he really believes it exists?"

"It does exist." Moriarity tilted his head to the right and gave me a strange look. "Isn't that why you came here? To find it? You asked me about it at the funeral."

"I came here to study archaeology with you. But I'd definitely go if Samael offered to take me."

"You might never come back. You understand?"

"Yeah. Okay."

Moriarity's mouth pressed into a hard white line as he gazed down at the oasis where the palms shimmered. The cliff that cradled the oasis looked taller, more ominous. The caves were pits of darkness. He pointed to one of the holes on the far end of the cliff. "All right. You see that cave on the far end? That's where we're going. But you must promise me that no matter what Samael says or does, you will listen respectfully. He's very frail. Don't hurt his feelings. Just play along with whatever he says."

Slightly offended, I said, "I understand the tenets of anthropological field work. I won't act like a stupid American tourist."

"Great, but it wasn't really you I was worried about." His bushy eyebrows drew together as he squinted at Roberto.

Roberto squinted back. "I will be the soul of discretion."

"You'd better be," Moriarity warned, shoving himself to his feet.

By the time we neared the caves, the moon had risen and moonlight blazed from the cliff. Off to my right, the pond resembled an oblate silver coin, the surface so calm I could see the perfect reflections of palm fronds sprinkled with stars.

As we paused to replenish our water, Roberto said, "I smell a campfire."

"I do, too."

The scent grew stronger as we walked. Actually, I sort of staggered my way toward the caves, with my legs on the verge of buckling. Thirty paces away, firelight flickered over the interior of one of the caves in the middle of the cliff. Given the heat, it seemed unbelievable that anyone would have a fire going out here, but I guess if you had no electricity, you had to light your cave and cook your food somehow.

"Is that it? Is that where Samael lives?"

I tried to walk around Moriarity to get there faster, but as I passed, he caught my sleeve and dragged me back. He was studying the yellow circle of light, apparently searching for anything amiss. "For forty years, Samael has lived in that cave down on the far end of the cliff. Not in the middle."

As the moonlight brightened, I could see better. "The cave that's boarded up? He used to live there?"

Planks had been nailed across the front, as though sealing something inside.

"Yes." Moriarity released my sleeve. Peering into the firelit cave, he whispered, "Curious."

"Maybe he moved," Roberto said. "People do that."

Rubbing his chin with the back of his hand, Moriarity replied, "Maybe." Then his eyes widened, and he stared hard at the darkness ahead. "What's that?"

"What?"

"I don't know . . . I thought I saw . . ." He shook his head, and there was a long pause. "Probably nothing. Just reflections off the pond."

But Moriarity shoved his hand inside his shirt, pulled a small pistol from a shoulder holster, and gripped it tightly.

"Nothing?" Roberto said. "You just pulled a pistol."

"I thought it was illegal for foreigners to carry pistols in Egypt," I said.

"It is. But insurgents and extremists can be anywhere, and they're naturally drawn to remote oases. I wouldn't be caught dead out here without a pistol." He cocked his head. "Do you . . . Do you hear that? Sounds like howling."

I listened. The sound was low-pitched, barely audible. "I think it's a voice. A male voice. Deep."

"If so, it is not Samael's voice." Gripping his pistol, Moriarity cautiously headed for the cave.

Roberto followed less than two paces behind him.

I just kept standing there with my shaking knees locked. *Don't go.* Is this what she'd meant? Don't go to Samael's cave? Everything inside me was telling me to turn around and run. But this man might be able to help me get Cleo to the Island of the Two Flames.

I hurried forward and stood awkwardly behind Moriarity and Roberto, both of whom had stopped just outside the cave entry.

It didn't take me long to figure out why. The warmth coming out of the cave was drenched with the scents of gunpowder and machine oil. Not only that, someone was moving around inside. Feet tapped the floor of the cave. Back and forth, scurrying, as though the person knew we were standing just outside, and he was waiting for us.

Moriarity said, "I want both of you to stay here. Let me check this out first. I'll return shortly."

Roberto jerked a quick nod. "You bet."

The professor vanished inside the cave, and we watched his shadow move across the firelit walls like a dark ghost calmly searching for something it had lost centuries ago.

"Dr. Who is starting to weird me out," Roberto whispered. "Did you have any idea he was carrying a gun? It must have been stashed in the Jeep."

I shook my head. "I didn't know, but I suspect he's met a lot of extremists, robbers, and looters during his time in the Egyptian desert, so maybe it isn't so weird. Maybe it's practical."

"Yeah, maybe, but it's still illegal. He could end up being beheaded. Then what will we do?"

Roberto's nose was dripping sweat from the hike, and he was still breathing hard. I'd never considered what we'd do if something happened to Moriarity, but it might be wise to start. "Head for Per Amun by ourselves, I guess."

"You think it's going to be easy to catch a camel ride out here, Hal?"

"He's probably not going to be executed tomorrow, Roberto," I pointed out. "At least, I hope—"

Moriarity suddenly laughed out loud, and said, *"What were you doing? Hiding from me?"*

A soft indistinct voice answered.

Then Moriarity called, "Hal and Robert? Come in and meet Samael."

CHAPTER NINETEEN

When we stepped into the cave, we found Moriarity standing beside the fire with a hunchbacked elder who was at least in his late sixties, and maybe early seventies. A toothless and short man, Samael had stringy gray hair dangling over his shoulders. As though frightened, he kept shifting his weight from one foot to the other and giving Moriarity worried glances.

"Come over here, boys."

I staggered forward, utterly exhausted, but stopped when my gaze was drawn upward. The firelit roof soared thirty feet over my head and was covered entirely with ancient Egyptian hieroglyphics, as well as several inscriptions, most in ancient Greek or Latin, but a few were in modern Arabic. Even the walls were covered with writing. Though the main chamber was about fifty feet wide, several smaller chambers jutted off in different directions. Ancient Egyptian and Roman artifacts, probably looted from local archaeological sites, hung from pegs that had been driven into the rock walls: carnelian-encrusted swords, golden theatrical masks, bracelets, collars, and magical amulets. The wealth of two-thousand-year-old mosaics alone would have kept a smuggler living nicely for the rest of his life. Why hadn't someone stolen these priceless artifacts from this frail old man? Antiquities' looting was big business in Egypt. Half the Egyptian military was supposedly involved in selling off their country's priceless heritage.

As I crossed the floor on shaking legs, I said, "This place is a museum."

"Yes. Samael has been collecting artifacts his entire life," Moriarity extended a hand to me. "Samael Saqqara, this is my friend, Hal

Stevens. The boy still standing near the entry like a bad statue is Robert Dally."

"Come and let me look at you?" Samael waved me forward with a parchment-like brown hand.

The old man was a walking skeleton. The sharp bones of his face stuck out as though flesh barely covered them. But it was his cataract-covered eyes that left me uneasy. They sank so far back into Samael's skull, they resembled holes filled with ice.

As I slowly continued toward him, I passed a wealth almost beyond belief. An Egyptian chalkstone relief—carved by a master stoneworker—leaned against the wall to my right. It depicted Cleopatra wearing the headdress of the Mother-goddess Mut, surmounted by the horns of the Cow-goddess Hathor and the disk of the Moon. *Magnificent.* I'd seen something similar in a book about the Hathor Temple at Denderah. Hathor was a curious deity who dwelt in a thick sycamore grove that overshadowed tombs. She fed the souls of the dead with water, wine, figs, and meats. Next to the chalkstone relief, a sandstone panel around ten feet tall and fifteen wide leaned against the wall. It showed Cleopatra with Caesarian, her son by Julius Caesar. She was depicted as Isis, while Caesarian was Pharaoh bringing incense to the gods.

The panels must weigh several tons each. The frail old man standing in front of me could not possibly have dragged the reliefs in here, so how long had they been in this cave? Had someone two thousand years ago brought them here to hide them? To protect them? Or maybe as offerings? To what? Reliefs like this often held secret messages if you knew how to read the hieroglyphs. Cleo had taught me basic hieroglyphics, but I was no expert. Still, I'd give anything for a few days to try and decipher the secrets.

When I got close enough, Samael reached toward me with a claw-like hand and groped for my shoulder. His ragged linen shirt and pants fluttered around him like a burial shroud. "You're tall, aren't you?"

"Not really, sir. I'm five-nine. That's pretty average in America." I spread my feet to brace my weak knees. I really needed to sit down and rest my legs.

"Well, you're much taller than me." Samael's toothless mouth opened in what must have been a smile, but it looked a little scary. "How old are you?"

"Sixteen, sir."

Samael's white-filmed eyes never focused on anything. Clearly, the old man was blind, or mostly blind. How could a blind man be one of the best diggers in Egypt?

"There is an ancient veil of grief that hangs about you, Hal Stevens." He gently patted my shoulder. "Please, sit down. I can see you are tired."

"Actually, the grief is recent," Moriarity said. "A close friend of his, my niece, Cleo, died a few weeks ago. You remember Cleo?"

"Yes, of course." Grief tightened Samael's wrinkled brown face.

While I sat down, Moriarity walked around the cave with his pistol in his hand, exploring the smaller caves. At a dark chamber in the rear, he stopped. "You have enough ammunition and guns in here to supply an army, Samael. And it smells like you keep them well oiled."

The old man grunted as he lowered himself to sit on the opposite side of the fire from me. "Well, as you know, you can't be too careful out here in the desert."

"Yes, I do know." Moriarity returned his pistol to his shoulder holster and walked over to the fire to sit down cross-legged beside Samael. "Robert? Come over and sit down before you fall down."

Roberto seemed fascinated by the dozen or so Roman lances, called *pili*, which leaned beside the entry. He was running his hand down the shaft of the longest one. "How old are these?"

"Couple of thousand years," Moriarity answered, then he gave Samael a pained look. "How long have you been blind, my friend?"

"About one month. It is not so bad. I can now see things I could never see before. The threads of the past have finally all come together."

Moriarity bowed his head as though in sympathy for the old hermit. How did Samael do it? He lived out here in the middle of nowhere. Was he just dedicated to being alone?

Roberto took his time crossing the floor. He seemed to be as riveted by the collection of ancient weapons as I was.

Swords, stilettos, and knives lay end-to-end around the circumference of the cave, like some curious magical circle of protection. As well, a wealth of amulets and ostrich feathers stuffed the small natural hollows of the cave walls.

"What's with the feathers?" Roberto asked.

"Hmm?" Moriarity had been staring hard at Samael, as though in surprise or shock. When he looked up, he said, "Oh. The feather was the emblem of lightness. Ancient Egyptians believed that sins weighed down the heart, so its lightness had to be proven against the weight of an ostrich feather. At death, the heart was placed on one side of the scale, the feather on the other. If the heart was as light as the feather, the person was found worthy, and Osiris, the god of the underworld, opened the door to the afterlife."

"What happened if your heart was too heavy?"

"Then the demon Ammut, who guards the Lake of Fire in the underworld, devours your heart, which assures that your soul must wander restlessly for eternity. Which is undoubtedly your fate, Robert. Now. Sit. Down." He stabbed a finger at the floor.

Roberto crouched beside me and gave me an askance look. Clearly, this whole place, the ancient inscriptions and weapons, the cave filled with guns and ammo, was not sitting well with him. To make matters worse, Samael was staring blindly at him from across the fire with a beatific expression on his ancient face.

"Ah, Robert," Samael said with affection, "I'm so glad to see you again."

"I've never been to Egypt before."

"Oh, yes, you have. You've been here for over two thousand years, dear boy. You are a loyal and faithful *shabti*."

Roberto glanced at me, and I shrugged. We both turned to Dr. Moriarity for illumination.

Moriarity ran a hand through his dusty hair. With an uneasy smile he answered, "I forgot to tell you that Samael can see into the Kingdom of Osiris. His whole family has special gifts—"

"What's a shabti?" Roberto frowned at Moriarity as though pretty certain he wasn't going to like the answer.

Moriarity tossed his fedora aside and spread his hands as if trying to decide whether to give an answer or a lecture. "Shabtis are mummiform figurines. You'll see some before we leave Egypt. Shabtis are substitutes. Let's say the dead have a task to perform, but, for whatever reason, can't. The dead assign a shabti to substitute for them to make sure the task is accomplish—"

Roberto turned to me. "What's a mummiform figurine?"

I said, "A painted figurine made in the shape of a person. Don't you remember Ms. Lawrence talking about them in her class about the reign of Amenhotep III? She mentioned mummiform figurines, though she didn't call them shabtis. Remember?"

Roberto gave me a blank look. He was usually zoned out in history class, secretly playing computer games on his phone under his desk. "So, were these shabtis slaves in the afterlife?"

"*Are*, Robert," Moriarity said. "Shabtis serve forever."

Roberto gave me a disgusted glance as he slumped into a cross-legged position beside me. "Yeah, well, if I'm a shabti, why I am sitting here in this world?"

"Ah . . ." Samael lifted a finger as though about to share some great secret. His toothless mouth hung open, revealing the pink tongue. "That is an important question. The dead person must wish to accomplish some task in this world, and the responsibility falls to you, as his or her substitute."

"Oh, okay, got it." Roberto replied with exaggerated politeness as though it all made perfect sense now. "So will the dead person talk to me or something when the time comes? You know, to give me a clue as to what I'm supposed to do?"

For several long moments, Samael just stared blindly in Roberto's direction. In response, Roberto's eyes narrowed more and more, until he was gazing at the old man through slits.

As Samael reached down to pull the tripod closer and arrange the legs so that the pot dangling in the middle hung directly over the flames, his bony arms seemed to glide through the air. For all his skeletal gawkiness, the old man had a light birdlike manner, as though he had hollow bones. He said, "You will know when the time comes."

Roberto rolled his eyes.

Samael couldn't have seen it, but he smiled and gestured to the pot. "I just brewed olive blossom tea. Please drink. I know it was a long hot walk getting here. There are cups right there beside the hearth."

"Thanks. We're all dehydrated."

In truth, I was so dog-tired and thirsty all I wanted to do was curl up and sleep for a week.

Moriarity reached for one of the chipped cups resting beside the hearthstones and dipped it into the pot. He handed the first cup to me. The next went to Roberto. I found it strange that the good doctor did not dip a cup for himself. Was he afraid to drink it?

As I drank the delicious brew, I noted the poorly patched holes in the bottoms of Samael's woven-reed sandals. Hot sand must constantly torment the old man's feet. Strips of reed protruded from a basket in the rear. Did his blindness prevent him from repairing the holes? Was there no one who came to check on him? To bring him supplies like new sandals? How did Samael survive out here alone?

"This is good tea," I said. "Thank you. Would you mind if I have another cup?"

"Of course. I'm delighted it pleases you."

I gave the cup back to Moriarity, who refilled it and handed it back. He kept watching me, then his gaze would shift to Roberto. What was he waiting for? To see if we dropped dead? It would be just my luck if the old man was the reincarnation of Livia, the wife and poisoner of Emperor Augustus Caesar.

Moriarity turned to Samael. "Before I tell you why we came, how are you, Samael? With your new blindness, how can you survive out here? I'm worried about you."

A gust of wind moved through the cave, fluttering the old man's gray hair and bringing the pleasant scents of flowers and water.

"It was a difficult year, James. Too many monsters to fight. They seem to be everywhere."

Moriarity said, "I'm sure that's true. All the wars raging across Africa and the Middle East have turned human beings into savages. My informants tell me that Abu Katan is overflowing with insurgents."

The elder reached down and felt around the hearthstones until he found an ancient bronze stiletto that lay half-hidden near his drinking cup. He clutched it tightly. "I sincerely wish my tormentors were human. They'd be easier to kill."

Moriarity's gaze slid sideways. In a totally serious voice, he asked, "Are the demons still tormenting you? I thought you'd lost them?"

Samael nodded. "I did, for many summers, but Ammut is very persistent. She knows how committed I am. I was Charmion in a former life, you know? Ammut came to me again about a month ago. I have to be very careful now, lest I make a mistake and she gets into my cave. If that happens, my holy quest is over."

At the name "Charmion" my eyes widened. If it was the same historical figure, this old man believed he was the reincarnation of Cleopatra's most loyal servant, the woman who was with her when Cleopatra ended her own life. Plutarch had written that when Octavian's forces burst into the room, Cleopatra was already dead and Charmion was dying. Stumbling and almost unable to stand, Charmion was clumsily trying to arrange the diadem on Cleopatra's head, before she, too, collapsed.

"Ah, now I understand why you moved to this cave." Moriarity gestured vaguely to the walls and ceiling. "I can't believe you've never shown me this place before. The magical protection spells carved into the walls and ceiling here are fascinating. Do they keep demons out?"

"They have for thousands of years, but I must continue to be vigilant."

I watched the strange elder over the rim of my cup. Moriarity was listening hard, his bushy brows knitted in concern. I drank more tea and tried not to be judgmental. After all, I had no right to judge anyone else's delusions. Given that I was hearing voices *and* seeing things, my mother would say my DID was in full swing tonight.

"The monsters are demons?" I asked.

"Some of them are," Moriarity answered, reaching for a cup, then dipping it full of tea.

I guess since neither Roberto nor I had fallen over clutching our throats, he figured it was safe.

While Moriarity gulped tea, Samael said, "There are several varieties, but the red ones with frozen eyes are my greatest enemies." Samael lifted a crooked finger and tapped his temple. "That's how I was blinded. One of Ammut's helpers touched me. You must never let them touch you."

My teacup stopped halfway to my mouth. "I'm not familiar with an ancient Egyptian demon that meets that description."

"Oh, there have been many varieties over the ages. These are very, very old. They have roamed this world since the beginning of time when Set murdered his brother Osiris."

Mesmerized by his voice, I whispered, "I see."

Samael's blind gaze went back and forth between Moriarity and me. "Didn't you hear it howling when you arrived? It was very loud."

Slowly, I lowered my cup. "I thought I heard a voice, but Dr. Moriarity heard howling."

Samael gestured to Roberto. "Did you hear its cries?"

"I didn't hear anything."

Samael nodded. "That makes sense. They wouldn't hunt you, since you're already dead."

Roberto turned to give me a dirty look, as though it was my fault.

I shook my head wildly, to say, *How could I know you were a dead shabti?*

Roberto didn't look convinced. After all, I was the Greco-Roman-Egyptian-history whiz kid of Georgetown High. I'd won the Colorado Classics Award three times. He figured I knew everything else, why not that little tidbit?

Samael added, "I really hate the ones that sound like animals. I'll think I'm being followed by an ordinary jackal, or one of the village dogs, until I see them hulking along after me. That's when I know I'm in trouble." He bowed his arms at his sides and rocked his shoulders back and forth to demonstrate how they "hulked." "If you hear its howls, it intends you harm. Beware, my friends."

The lines at the corners of Moriarity's black eyes deepened. "Why are they chasing you?"

"They recognize me. They don't wish me to keep my promises to the dead."

Samael peered at the flickering fire for a few seconds, then his gaze shot to the cave entrance as though he'd glimpsed something moving out in the darkness. He seemed to be holding his breath.

My heart stuttered. I jerked around to look. Wavering silver reflections danced through the palms, cast by moonlight on the pond, but I saw nothing else.

Roberto said, "Why don't you move into a village? Wouldn't it be safer there?"

"The village is not safe at all. It's an insurgent hive filled with madmen. Here, at least, I have magic to protect me." His skeletal hand panned the room.

"Well, can't you find an exorcist to destroy the demons or drive them away?"

The elder groped for the woodpile, lifted a branch, and tossed it onto the flames. Then he extended his hands to the warmth, as though he were cold. "You can kill monsters, but demons cannot be destroyed. They are as old as the world, and maybe older. I don't know for certain. I entrap them with spells or lock them in caves as best I can, but . . ."

As the fire ate into the fresh tinder, flame shadows fluttered over the cave like gigantic amber butterflies. Despite the fact that the temperature in the cave was around eighty degrees, Samael was shivering.

Moriarity said, "Is that why your old cave is boarded up?"

"Yes." The elder's gray head dipped in a nod. "I trapped one in there. It tries to kill me every time I walk by the boards. The demon is always waiting, always testing the boards, trying to escape. You must be very careful if you walk past it."

With great tenderness, Moriarity said, "I'm prepared at all times now. Ever since my niece was murdered, I take no chances."

"She was murdered? You only told me she'd died."

"Yes, it was murder. There's no doubt."

My despair, which had been at bay for most of the long hike, returned with a vengeance. Just behind my eyes, I could see Cleo smiling. I suddenly didn't have the strength to lift my cup to my mouth to drink.

Samael turned to peer blindly in my direction. "How did you two survive the attack that killed her?"

"It's a long story," Moriarity answered for us. "I wasn't there when it happened. Hal and Roberto found her."

Samael seemed to be thinking about that. He rolled the stiletto between his palms. His next question was so soft, I almost didn't hear it: "Did it follow you home, Halloran?"

Roberto stiffened and whirled to stare at me.

I forced a swallow down my throat. *Did I tell him my full name?* "It?"

Samael turned toward the cave entry again and frowned. He *did* see something out there. "You don't have to answer. I know you've seen it. A memory clothed in human flesh, tiptoeing up beside you wearing a smile that died weeks ago, speaking in a voice that goes straight to your heart. She's been sending you dreams, hasn't she? Dreams of the past?"

Roberto was breathing like he'd run a hundred miles.

I couldn't move.

For a time, the old man blinked at the fire. "It is such a hazard, you know? The lonely dead seem to think that archaeologists can do something to help them reach the Island of the Two Flames. It's probably because we are the first people to touch them in thousands of years. It makes them cling to us. They think we are their last hope." He paused to gaze outside again, before asking, "Is that why you came here? To take her to the island?"

I was going into some kind of shock, I could feel it. My body was numb, my hands ice-cold. *I have to give this man the medallion.*

Roberto leaned close to my ear to whisper, "Don't you dare wig on me, Hal, or I'm out of here."

I closed my eyes for a few moments. Managed a nod.

"Actually." Moriarity leaned toward Samael. "We came for another reason. Before her death, my niece gave Hal the medallion her father claimed to have found with the bagsu along the Great Horus Road."

"What's a bagsu?" Roberto asked.

"It's a ceremonial dagger," Samael said.

Roberto grunted as though that fact meant nothing to him.

"A bagsu?" The bronze stiletto flashed with firelight as he rolled it faster between his palms, spinning it. "Oh, yes, the one with the blue lotus. I helped him pull it from the skeleton's fingers."

Moriarity had gone so still, his eyeglasses caught the flickering light and held it like a mirror. "I need that dagger, my friend, and I need to know exactly where you found it. Where was the grave?"

Samael hesitated. "I don't know what happened to the bagsu. But I do remember the grave."

And it occurred to me for the first time that Cleo's father must have been searching for Queen Cleopatra's grave when he'd stumbled upon the grave of her Sem priest. Had Cleo told her father she wanted to be released from this world? Was he trying to help her? As I was?

Moriarity said, "Your mind is wandering, Samael. I asked where you found the grave."

"Yes, forgive me. I was thinking . . . Well, sometimes I get lost in the past. Let me try to recall for a moment. It's been a long time, after all." His white eyes fixed upon me, as though he was trying to communicate something critical to me. Something I did not understand.

"I *know* you remember, Samael."

The old man clutched the bronze stiletto more tightly. The weapon had been held so often it had a polished sheen in the firelight. The other stilettos near the hearthstones were similarly shiny. Was the elder so worried about monsters that he never let the weapons out of his reach?

Finally, Samael took a deep breath and, following a long exhalation, said, "The grave is a good distance from the eastern end of the fortress wall in Pelusium. I can't tell you precisely where, but I think I could take you there."

Moriarity's black eyes glowed with sudden triumph. "Great. Did you hire the crew chiefs I requested? Are they already at the site and excavating?"

"Oh, yes. They arrived a week ago."

"Thank you. Then we need to leave early tomorr—"

"Don't thank me, James." Samael aimed the bronze stiletto at Moriarity's heart. "Old and powerful forces live there. It is a dangerous place. You know it as well as I do. They'll try to kill us before we're done."

"Kill us?" Roberto's voice had squeaky nasal quality. "Who will? You're not serious, right?"

The old man turned toward the cave entry to look outside again, and despair twisted his face. After a few deep breaths, he answered, "You have nothing to worry about, my young friend. Only the living must fear the scales of justice."

CHAPTER TWENTY

As Moriarity and Samael lay down to sleep by the fire, Roberto and I walked over to throw out our space blankets close to the *pili* at the mouth of the cave—just in case we needed to run for our lives. Before I stretched out on top of the silver material, I pulled a lance down and placed it on the blanket beside me. The shaft was covered with Greek writing. Though Roman soldiers came from all over the empire, and spoke dozens of different languages, Greek was the language of science and magic. Which were pretty much the same thing, at the time. The script was beautiful and flowing. It was a Roman prayer, asking the gods to keep the bearer safe. *Ginest-hoi.*

Roberto grabbed a pili, as well, and lay down with it, facing me. He had an annoyed look on his face. We both waited until we thought the other two men had gone to sleep, which wasn't easy. I was flat worn out.

Finally, I whispered, "You okay?"

"Oh, yeah, I'm fine. For being dead."

"You should get some rest."

"The dead don't need sleep."

"Okay. Valid point."

"What was that silent teat-a-teat between you and Samael over the location of the grave?"

"I think you mean, tête-à-tête, like a private conversation."

"Really?"

"Yeah."

"Well, that's not nearly as interesting." He seemed to be contemplating it. A branch broke in the fire, and sparks flitted around the cave like fireflies. Roberto blinked at them. "Did you get the feeling that the old guy didn't want to tell Dr. Who where he found the grave?"

"I did. And did you catch that odd statement when we were still standing outside? When Moriarity asked if Samael had been hiding from him?"

"Yep. Do you think he was cowering somewhere in one of the small caves, hoping Moriarity wouldn't see him?"

"Sounds like it."

Neither of us spoke for a minute, and I absently started reading the hieroglyphics and other ancient inscriptions on the ceiling. The cave was wreathed in cloaking spells that winked in the firelight.

"That doesn't make any sense," Roberto hissed. "If he'd really been afraid, he would have been cowering in the guns and ammo cave with one of the pistols in his hands, and the good doctor would currently be splattered all over the walls."

"Samael doesn't strike me as the violent type. Despite his weapons cache."

Roberto rolled over onto his back and frowned up at the deeply carved inscriptions on the ceiling. In the flickering firelight, the ancient letters seemed to dance upon the stone as though alive. He pointed. "What do those say?"

"Most are cloaking spells to hide the cave from passersby. Others are magical protection spells for specific people. A few are prayers to ancient gods and goddesses."

Roberto drew a couple of pentagrams and squiggles in the air, probably counteracting their magic, or some such.

I yawned and glanced out the cave entry to the wavering moonlight on the palms. Is that what Samael had kept looking at? Could he see the flickers with his cataracts? Or had he seen her out there? *Did she tell him my name?*

"Roberto?"

"What?"

"Tell me if you see eyes growing in the back of my head, okay?"

"Vice versa, dude."

CHAPTER TWENTY-ONE

I'm in a deep, dreamless sleep when I hear faint sounds. I'm not sure where I am. Someone is talking to me, but I can't really understand the words. Finally, the sounds congeal . . .

And I become aware of waves dashing upon a nearby shore, the squeal of shore birds, and hot wind against my face.

In the distance, a woman stands on a low, grassy promontory with her white robes flowing about her in the sea breezes. Her copious jewels gleam in the sunlight, which seems to accent her magnificently braided and arranged black hair. Despite the sweltering mosquito-infested coast, she looks like the queen she is.

My steps are heavy today, for I am truly exhausted. Armor jangling, I trudge up the slope to stand beside her to gaze out at the vast armies spread over the Greek lowlands. The splendid chaos creates a glorious spectacle. Men in gold-spangled purple-red robes weave through Thracians in black tunics overlain with brightly polished armor, and Macedonians wearing brilliant scarlet cloaks laugh with Medians in richly hued vests. The entire vista is an ocean of glints and shimmers. Gleaming helmets, gilded breastplates, jeweled bridles, dyed plumes, and decorated pili rise and fall as men move through the huge camp. I have Armenian cavalry, Ethiopian infantry, Median detachments, and far too much gaudily attired royalty for my tastes. In total, I command 230 ships, 50,000 sailors, and 115,000 troops. Unfortunately, my former brother-in-law, Gaius Julius, commands 120,000 soldiers and 300 Roman war galleys.

In an amused voice, I call, "My officers tell me you are abusing them. They are upset, my queen."

She turns her stunning kohl-darkened eyes upon me. Truly, she has the face of a goddess—a fierce goddess. Tucked into the belt around her slender waist, she carries a small golden dagger, for we both fear there may come a time when we will need to end our lives with dignity. "What upsets them is my status as your equal partner, my love. I should have them all flayed alive."

I sigh. Over and over I have heard what an "infuriating and exhausting presence" she is in this camp. "They are worried about the battle to come. Perhaps if you would relent—"

"Perhaps you have forgotten that I command Egypt's military forces. War preparations and operations are my duties. If your officers object, let them swim across the strait and throw themselves upon Little Gaius' mercy. See if he welcomes them with open arms. As I have."

Squawking birds wheel over my head, their wings flashing in the sunlight. She has backed herself into a corner, which I have told her on numerous unpleasant occasions. The stormy arguments that resulted have achieved a legendary status among my men.

I slip my arm around her shoulders and hug her against me. "Please, listen to me. The men are hungry, their moods sour. We have, of necessity, curtailed rations. And, as you well know, female commanders are not popular, not even in Egypt. Perhaps, just this once, you could step aside and allow me to take charge—"

"I was shunted aside by military commanders once before, you know? I wound up in the Sinai desert, homeless and abandoned. I will not trust my fate or the fate of my country, to a man again. Not even you, my dearest love, and you are the greatest and bravest general in the world."

Despite her kind words, I pull my arm from her shoulders and rest my hand upon the hilt of my belted sword. The familiar feel comforts me. "Just give me a little more freedom to wield my tools as the need arises. I am not blind to the fact that the fate of the Ptolemaic dynasty hangs in the balance. I—"

"Gaius Julius has declared war on me. Not you. After all, you are his brother-in-law. This is my fight. Not yours." Tears of anger glitter on her lashes. Her lovely face has gone red, her breathing shallow. Worse, a slight tremor has entered her voice. She is afraid, desperate even.

I tenderly say, "I will never abandon you. You must know that by now. Never. You are the mother of my children, and I love you with all my heart."

She abruptly turns, wraps her arms around my waist, and buries her face against my chest. "Do you give me your oath?"

"Do I have to say it? Of course, I do."

As I kiss her scented hair, my gaze seeks the distances. This is my fault. I had planned to trap little Gaius in the Ambracian Gulf, but instead have found myself and my troops bottled up and unable to move. A good general or admiral always attacks when he has the upper hand, not when his enemies do. Caesar's blockade, the unbearable weather and malaria, and the utter boredom have affected my troops in predictable ways: Slaves, soldiers, and kings alike are deserting me, abandoning the cause. It has unnerved me, I admit it. To make matters worse, I have been ill so often of late that I've even imagined Cleopatra might be trying to poison me, to be done with me, so she can come to some arrangement with Caesar that will make this battle unnecessary. Gods, I pray not. She does not know him as I do. He can't be trusted. Ever. And I know—really, I do—that she would not betray me. She needs me. She loves me.

I bow my head and close my eyes for a few moments. Strange haunting images flash . . . a magnificent lamp-lit tomb filled with marble statues of the gods, their disembodied arms reaching for me through the veil that separates life from death . . . Loneliness that strips a man to his bare bones. . . .

I jump when her soft fingers trace lines down my cheek. "Forgive me for adding to your troubles. I'm just so worried."

Smiling, I grasp her hand and kiss her palm. She is a mere thirty-eight and still so lovely. "All will be well. You'll see. Just trust me . . ."

The shrill scream brought me bolt upright, gasping for breath. Roberto and I almost knocked each other over as we lurched to our feet and looked around the cave. The fire's coals had burned down to flickering red eyes that cast scant light. I couldn't seem to shed the dream, the visions of the ships in the bay, Cleopatra's magnificent eyes, the paralyzing dread in Antonius' heart.

Samael was stumbling across the cave with his hands extended before him, as though feeling for obstacles.

"What's wrong?" I shouted. "What happened?"

"Where are they? Where are my weapons? Do you see them? Who took my sandals? I can't find them!"

Turning, I noticed that the lances that had been by the door had vanished, as had the lances Roberto and I had placed on our blankets beside us. Worse, all the knives, swords, and stilettos that had formed the magical circle around the circumference of the cave were gone. *Someone came in here. . . .*

"Do you see them?" Samael cried and flung an arm toward the cave entrance. "Are they standing there?"

"No," I answered. "The lances are gone."

"Not the lances! *Them.*"

Through the entry, I could see the first gleam of dawn watering the darkness, turning the air faintly blue. "I—I don't see anything."

"Please, look for my weapons?" Samael yelled. "I need them!"

Moriarity finally threw off his blanket and ran for the old man. "Samael, calm down. Everything is fine. Don't worry. I'm sure they're still here. Everything is all right."

"No, it's not! One of them was in here. Can't you smell it? That bitter tang to the air?"

Moriarity smelled the air, then shoved graying brown tangles out of his eyes. He wasn't wearing his glasses, and was squinting. "I don't smell anything except wood smoke, my friend."

Samael cried, "Please, please, find my weapons. The monsters are out there right now waiting for me!"

Moriarity turned to us. "Hal? Roberto? Did you take Samael's weapons?"

Simultaneously, we answered, "No way," and "Of course, not!"

Samael backed away from Moriarity with a wild look in his blind eyes. "Blessed Osiris, how was it possible for the creature to enter this cave? How did it get past the spells? Why aren't we all dead?"

Roberto leaned sideways to whisper to me, *"Don't tell them I cast a spell last night, okay?"*

I gave him a disbelieving look and whispered back, "I'm pretty sure you're not powerful enough to counteract the spells of ancient Egyptian magicians."

"Really?"

"Really."

"That's depressing."

While I fought to slow my heart rate, I wondered if this wasn't an example of Samael's dementia. He was alone out here. As his brain continued to lose itself in myths and magic, he had no one to straighten reality for him. That explanation was a lot more comforting than the possibility that an ancient demon had reached down and pulled a Roman lance from my hand while I slept. Was "it" the same demon that had killed Cleo? The thing that had leaned out from behind the tree to stare at me?

Roberto said, "Did you hear anything last night?" His eyes looked like wide blue moons.

"No."

Moriarity put his arm around Samael's hunched shoulders and guided him back toward the fire. "Samael, please, come and sit down by the fire. Let me make you a cup of tea. It will help calm your nerves. While I take care of Samael, why don't you boys search for tracks?"

"Sure, we can do that," Roberto said, and looked at me. "You go left. I'll go right."

"Got it."

We began carefully walking in opposite directions around the circumference of the cave, searching for tracks in the main chamber, but also checking the adjacent chambers. Roberto stopped for an unusually long time in the guns and ammo cave before moving on.

It was hard for me to focus. I couldn't quite get away from the scenery and scents of the Greek lowlands. I could still hear seabirds squawking in my ears and smell the salt in the air. The worst part was the certain knowledge that tens of thousands were depending upon me, and I didn't know if I could save them. Strangely, it had never occurred to me that the legendary Marcus Antonius, the hero of Philippi, the man known as the new Dionysius, might have been frightened that day as he looked out across the Gulf of Ambracia at Marcus Agrippa's fleet.

"Find anything?" Moriarity called.

"All the tracks in the cave belong to the four of us," Roberto said.

I nodded in agreement, though I wasn't sure I'd know a demon footprint if I saw it. Besides, Roberto was a much better tracker than I was. Every autumn he hunted deer and elk with his father.

Samael covered his elderly face with his hands and wept as though his heart were breaking. "It was in here! It was here!"

Moriarity crouched beside him. "My friend, are you sure you didn't rise early and move your weapons? Perhaps you've forgotten."

"How could I forget such a thing? It's impossible. Someone or something took them. If it wasn't you three, it must have been one of the monsters. Now I'm defenseless! They're going to kill me. They'll follow me until the moment is right and then—"

"You still have plenty of guns and ammunition in that rear chamber."

"Those are for the extremists and thieves. Bullets won't kill monsters, you fool. I need those ancient magical weapons!"

Moriarity dipped the old man a cup of last night's tea from the pot and placed it in his hands. "Drink this. You'll feel better, and don't worry. Right after breakfast we'll start searching for your weapons. I'll bet we've found them within the hour."

Samael clutched his cup hard and tried to take a sip, but his arms were shaking too badly. He lowered the cup to his lap. "Be careful. It's waiting for one of us to step outside." He shivered.

"Are you cold?" Pulling several branches from the woodpile, Moriarity placed them on top of the coals in the firepit. He blew gently upon them until flames fluttered to life, and firelight flickered over the walls and roof of the main chamber. "Give me just a few moments, Samael, and I'll have breakfast made. That'll warm you up."

Samael sobbed. "James, you and the boys are not safe here. You must leave immediately."

"Sure, that's fine. Right after we find your weapons, we'll pack up our things, and yours, and leave for Pelusium."

Samael lifted his head and blinked up at Moriarity with tear-filled eyes. "Do you think the boys could search the boarded-up cave before breakfast?"

"Of course, they can. Can't you, boys?"

Roberto and I stood like proverbial pillars of stone, glancing at each other. Clearly, neither of us wanted to search a cave that contained a captive demon.

"No, I'm sorry I asked. It's too dangerous. Just leave me and go! Make me a wooden spear from an olive limb outside, and I'll be all right. I've killed plenty of monsters before. I'll break off their fangs and stab them in the livers. That's how you do it. I've killed hundreds of them."

"I will personally make you a spear, but I'm not leaving you here alone," Moriarity replied in a soft voice. "You're coming with us. We need you."

"Yes, I'm sure I can find the grave again. Despite my blindness. I'll find it."

"While I'm making cereal for breakfast, the boys will search the boarded-up cave, *won't you, boys?*" he repeated.

"Oh, yeah, sure," I said. "We'll do it."

Roberto gave me a look like I'd lost my mind.

Samael stared blindly at the cave entry as though terrified of what might step through next. "Just you, Halloran. Leave Robert outside to stand guard. The instant you smell them, scream. Do you understand? You must not wait, or it will be too late to save you."

"Oh, yeah. I will."

Samael extended a crooked finger. "That small cave over there has a big stash of torches. I keep them for guests to use when they go out at night."

"We have flashlights in our pockets," Roberto said and drew out his motorcycle key with the pen light on the ring. "We'll be okay."

Moriarity rose to his feet. "While you boys get started, I'll go fetch some water from the pond for cereal. If you're not back in thirty minutes, I'm coming to look for you."

He reached for the teapot on the tripod, unhooked it, and carried it outside.

When he was gone, I said, "Roberto, can you wait for me outside. I'll be right there."

"Yeah, sure." He glanced suspiciously at Samael, then followed Moriarity out into the brightening dawn.

Samael was biting his lip, rocking back and forth, and whispering to himself in a language I thought might be ancient Egyptian.

I went over, crouched beside him, and said, "Sir, Cleopatra Mallawi asked me to give this to you." I pulled the medallion from my pocket and placed it in the old man's clawlike hand.

Samael sucked in a breath, then ran his fingers over the jewels and the Greek letters around the rim of the pendant. When he slowly lifted his blind eyes to me, I felt like I was caught in the frozen gaze of a long-dead magi.

Softly, for my ears alone, he said, "She's been waiting for you for so long. It's on the altar behind the pyramid. Hurry. Go. Before they understand why you are here."

"What pyr—"

"*Go.*" He thrust a bony arm toward the cave entrance. "But the shabti must remain outside. If he tries to enter before you have completed her task, he will be lost forever. The demons will be watching you very closely now. Never forget that."

CHAPTER TWENTY-TWO

I stepped out into the faint lavender gleam of morning feeling completely confused.

The air was intensely fragrant, filled with the scent of olive blossoms and damp soil. Birds chirped. In every direction, the dunes glittered into infinity. I saw Moriarity bending down and filling the pot from the pond; Roberto stood about five paces away, hands on his hips, watching him.

When I started for Roberto, I saw sandal prints. The woven pattern, with gaps showing the holes in the bottoms, was pressed into the dirt. Samael's missing sandals. The man's trail led to the left, running along the cliff face toward the demon cave.

"Roberto?" I knelt to get a better look at the sandal prints. "Did you see these tracks?"

He trotted back. "Yeah. Samael's tracks."

"He must have gone out during the night."

"He's old. He probably went out fifteen times to pee."

As I rose to my feet, I said, "Why didn't either of us hear him? He's blind. He shuffles and makes noise. We should have heard him gathering up his weapons."

"We were tired, Hal. Really tired. Especially you. For a while, I thought you were going to drop dead."

"You weren't the only one. I was having a really hard time at the end."

A sudden thought struck me. *Had* I heard Samael gathering his weapons?

"Wait a minute. Last night, I had a really vivid dream. I dreamed of a battle, and I could hear clanking armor, jingling horse tack, crashing swords. Maybe I interpreted Samael's noise as part of my dream."

"Yeah, probably. Let's follow these tracks, find the weapons, and get back for breakfast. I'm hungry."

"Me, too."

As we started walking along the base of the towering cliff, Roberto said, "I suspect the old geezer gathered up all the weapons and carried them outside to hide them. Poor old guy."

"But why would he do that? He made such a big deal out of the fact that he needed them to fend off demons."

Roberto studied the tracks that dimpled the sand ahead of us. "My grandpa used to do strange things, too. Toward the end, he was afraid my dad would take his guns away from him, so he'd hide them. I think he wanted his pistol as a last resort for when the pain got too bad. When he couldn't find it, he'd call me up crying and begging me to come over to help him. I once found his Colt .45 stuffed in the toilet tank. Been there awhile. It had rusted up pretty bad."

"That's sad."

"Yeah, well, he didn't have much longer to worry about it. He'd be dead in a couple of months."

"When was that?"

"Last year."

I gave him a sideways glance. "You never told me about that."

Roberto shrugged. "Don't talk about it much. I still miss him. He was more my dad than my dad has ever been."

I'd never heard that tone of voice from Roberto. He must have really loved the man. This was a side of my friend that I'd never seen, and I wondered why. Maybe he just didn't want anyone to see him vulnerable. At school, he was always on the fringe, the kid who never fit in. It wasn't just because he was a Biker Witch, Roberto seemed to go out of his way to keep his distance from other people. Of course, so did I. After all, our classmates had the skills of Torquemada, the infamous torturer of the Inquisition.

"Roberto, don't these tracks look way larger than Samael's feet?"

"Yeah, but even the slightest wind can blow out tracks, and when they refill with sand, they look bigger."

"Oh, okay."

The sun edged above the eastern horizon, and a wave of golden light rolled across the desert. The shadows cast by the dunes resembled long fingers, all pointing westward toward the village of Abu Katan. Already, I could hear faint voices on the wind. On occasion, they sounded really loud, and I realized that was probably the source of the man's voice I'd heard last night when we first arrived. Voices carried unbelievably long distances out here.

My hiking boots sank into the sand as I swerved around a boulder that had cracked off the cliff and fallen across the old trail. The chunk of stone stood taller than I did and had to weigh at least a ton.

The braying of camels carried from Abu Katan. The village was too far away to make out anything except a white shimmer of buildings dotted with palms.

"You think it was somebody from Abu Katan?"

Roberto shrugged noncommittally. "Could be. They must know Samael lives here, right? He has to go into town every now and then for supplies. Over the years, somebody must have gotten curious and tracked him back here. I would have. Wouldn't you?"

"You bet."

"So they know he's here. Do you think he trades artifacts for food and clothing?"

"Probably. A lot of people in Africa do."

"That would give anybody a reason to follow him." Roberto stood up and heaved a breath. "Why is he alive? By now, some unscrupulous character should have cracked his skull and cleaned out his cave."

A gigantic whirlwind careened over the dunes in the distance, rising high into the morning sky. My gaze absently fixed on it. "Locals are probably scared to enter these caves. They're sealed with magical spells, and people out here believe in magic. Whole villages have been slaughtered in Africa because some ignoramus thought the inhabitants were witches casting spells to make people sick."

"Seriously?"

"Yeah, so you might want to watch the pentagrams in the air bit. If somebody sees, you could wind up with an ax in your forehead."

"Noted."

For good reason, the image took me back to Actium, to the feel of the armor weighing down my shoulders, the tug of the heavy sword at my hip. I found myself marching along the shore past thousands of dead bodies and ship timbers that kept washing in . . .

"Did you hear me, Hal?"

"What? Oh, sorry." I shook my head. "No, I didn't. What did you say?"

Roberto sighed, "Nothing important. Where were you this time? Listening to some moldy Babylonian?"

"A Roman. Can't shake a dream I had last night. It was so real."

Roberto took great pains not to disturb any of the tracks as he carefully led the way along the cliff face toward the boarded-up cave. "What did you dream?"

"I was at Actium in 31 BC."

Roberto's gaze lifted, and he scanned the ledges on the cliff above, as though afraid something might be up there and preparing to leap down upon us. "What's Actium?"

Worried, my gaze shot upward, but I saw only birds perched in the crevices. "It was a great sea battle that Marcus Antonius and Cleopatra lost to Gaius Julius, who would shortly thereafter become known as Augustus Caesar, Emperor of Rome."

Roberto rubbed his fingers over the stone, as though feeling the cool morning temperature, before he slowly started tracking again. "Marcus Antonius lost? I thought you told me he was some great general?"

"Oh, he was, but at about three o'clock, Rome's left wing moved to outflank Antonius. In response, Antonius veered northward. As the center of the line opened, sixty ships under Cleopatra's command hoisted sail and broke through the middle of the battle, creating confusion on all sides. Antonius had no idea what she was doing. I think he panicked. Moments later, Antonius climbed into a small galley and rowed after her."

"Wait a second? Are you telling me he abandoned his fleet in the middle of the grind?"

I nodded, feeling the same wrenching despair Antonius must have felt.

"What happened to his fleet?"

"It was destroyed."

Roberto peered at me from the corner of his eye. "Some hero."

I inhaled a breath and held it for a time, before I added, "Well, he never forgave himself. When Antonius boarded Cleopatra's flagship, he walked to the prow and spent three days sitting with his head in his hands, refusing to speak with anyone, including Cleopatra. He loved her desperately, but he must have known in that instant that his love had cost him everything."

Somewhere down in the village, dogs barked, then children laughed, as though playing with the dogs. They sounded so close.

Roberto said, "You really dreamed all that stuff about Actium?"

"And it was vivid. Like I was really standing there in 31 BC. I could smell the sweat of the army and Cleopatra's perfume."

Roberto scratched his chin. A fuzz of brown beard had grown. At home, his parents refused to allow him to grow one, so he was obviously taking advantage of his newfound freedom. "You have to stop reading all those history books. They're ruining your mind, bro. Try romances, instead. They give you much better dreams."

"Yeah? What did you dream?"

"Oh, Jeez, it was awful." Roberto knelt down to examine a scuffed place on the ground. Seemed satisfied it was nothing. But as he rose, a frown lined his forehead. "I dreamed I was locked in a museum with a bunch of Greek statues and I couldn't figure out why all their penises were so small. I kept going from statue to statue, staring at them, over and over. It was exhausting. Like being in some kind of horror movie loop."

It took a minute to reorient my thoughts, then I headed for the boarded-up cave twenty paces ahead. Roberto came along behind more slowly, which gave me time to study the old weathered lumber. Many of the outer boards had been nailed over others, crisscrossing in places, sometimes three deep. It was a poor job, done fast and furious, as though the builder had been eager to get the boards up and get away as quickly as possible. A moldering scent seeped through the cracks, like moss that had been growing in darkness for a thousand years.

Roberto walked up beside me and started scanning the haphazard carpentry.

I took the opportunity to say, "Aristophanes said small penises were a sign of intelligence."

Roberto tugged his gaze from the boarded-up cave to give me a deadpan look. "Because he had a pinworm, right?"

"Historians didn't record that, but—"

"You remember that football player, Barney O'Donnell? That guy had a pinworm and an IQ of twelve. After gym, I used to stare at it in the shower."

"His IQ?"

"Oh, yeah, that's what I meant."

CHAPTER TWENTY-THREE

Roberto stepped back from the boarded-up entry with a frown on his face. "Whoever did this was serious about keeping people out."

"Or keeping the demon in."

"Do you really think there's a demon in there?"

I wiped my forehead with my sleeve. It was already starting to get hot. "Samael believes it. He's terrified."

"Yeah, but the old guy is not right in the head, Hal, you have to admit."

He was giving me that look that said, *Come on, don't get weird on me.* So I said, "Yeah, he's strange all right. But we're not exactly normal, you know."

"That's what makes us interesting."

While I moved closer to the cave to sniff the air penetrating between the boards, Roberto crouched and brushed at the dirt beneath the lowest board. A metallic tang seeped from the cave. I could taste it in the back of my throat, like sucking on a copper penny.

"Look at this, Hal."

"What did you find?"

With his finger hovering above it, he drew the outline of knee prints. "Somebody knelt here." He hesitated, then added, "And the sand here is a different color. Do you see this?"

I did. It was darker. "It looks like someone scooped fresh sand over the bottom of the board to block a gap."

Roberto continued brushing at the dirt until he'd revealed the hole beneath the board. The bedrock had been perfectly smoothed, as though someone routinely lay on his belly to slide beneath the board to get into and out of the cave.

Roberto stood up and we both stared at the hole while we listened to the sound of birds singing in the olive trees by the pond.

"Yeah," Roberto nodded. "Given that the sand is still a different color, it looks like somebody crawled under the bottom board recently. Maybe an hour ago. Do you think that's where he hid the weapons?"

I took a deep breath to fortify my courage. "I guess I'll go look."

"All right, but . . ." Roberto reached down the front of his pants. "Take this with you." He pulled a pistol out and handed it to me. "I picked this up when I was searching the guns and ammo chamber."

I didn't know much about firearms, but I knew that was a semi-automatic. "I thought that was a codpiece."

"If it was, it'd be bigger."

Which I knew from personal experience was true. Roberto had tried wearing one for the first time at last year's Valentine's Day dance. It hadn't worked out so well. I think the glue was old on the tape he used to strap his mom's sanitary napkin to his leg, because it kept working its way down all night until it fell out on the floor when he was dancing with Molly Henson. Most people would have been humiliated, but with fifty people watching, Roberto had calmly bent down, picked it up, and said, "Christ, Molly, can't you strap these things in better?" before he'd handed it to her and walked off the dance floor.

Glancing at the gun, I said, "Bullets don't work against demons. Didn't you hear Samael?"

"Yeah, I heard. What if it's not a demon?"

I backed away from the weapon. "I'm not good with guns, Roberto."

He shoved it into my hand. "This is the safety. Switch it down when you're ready to pull the trigger. It's not complicated. And if I'm eaten by a demon while you're in there, I expect you to take whatever is left home to my parents."

The pistol was heavy. I stuffed it into the back of my pants, and dug in my pocket for my flashlight. "Even if all that's left is demon shit?"

"Gift wrap it and give it to my Aunt Louise. She's a religious fanatic. She'll have people praying over it in no time."

Stretching out on my stomach, I shone the flashlight inside the cave. Nothing happened, so I slid forward and stuck my head beneath the board to look around. As my flashlight beam illuminated the walls, my excitement grew. "My God, this is amazing. This whole cave is covered with Egyptian hieroglyphics, Roberto."

"Any sign of demons?"

"No."

"Then save the wallpaper for later. Look for weapons."

I slid under the board, thankful for the weight I'd lost, and rose to my feet inside the cave. The main hieroglyphic panel was gigantic, covering the entire northern wall from floor to ceiling. The magnificent colors were still brilliant. A woman I thought might be Cleopatra was carrying a platter of food and a cup of wine to the kneeling figure of a man. One of the souls of the dead? Ammut sat on her hippopotamus hindquarters a short distance away with her crocodile jaws gaping to show sharp teeth. All around the figures were images of war, of huge ships with people inside, and countless rows of soldiers standing with lances in their hands.

"Dear God," I whispered in awe, "this is stunning. And really atypical for Egyptian hieroglyphics. At least, I think so. I'm no expert—"

"Weapons?" Roberto interrupted.

My heart in my throat, I answered, "No weapons. Yet."

"Keep moving, Hal. We only have another fifteen or twenty minutes before Moriarity gets worried."

Panning my flashlight around, I didn't see anything threatening, no snakes, no mice, not even an insect scrambling across the floor. Which, when I thought about it, was curious. This was a perfect place for snakes and mice, not to mention spiders and scorpions. Even more interesting, there was a slight breeze in here.

Before I realized what I was doing, I was walking toward the rear of the cave with my flashlight beam flipping around. The hieroglyphics seemed to go on forever. The colors were so vibrant they looked like they'd been painted yesterday. I'd been studying color symbolism, so I knew the brilliant red in the paintings symbolized the protective power of the blood of Isis, whereas Osiris had green skin, and . . .

I stopped.

About fifty paces into the cave, my flashlight beam blazed from a pyramid of gold, silver, and bronze. Astonished, I couldn't take my eyes from it. Thousands of lances, spears, swords, daggers and other weapons had been arranged into a pyramid in the middle of the floor. A ring of ancient oil lamps, cold and dark, encircled the pyramid.

"Unbelievable," I whispered. "Samael must have spent his whole life collecting Roman weapons."

As I walked closer, I thought I heard Roberto calling me, but the voice was so faint, I dismissed it. If he were really calling me, he'd be shouting, and the breeze moving inside this cave led me to believe there was a vent hole somewhere, maybe a crack in the cliff that allowed air to pass through the cave. The whispering was probably the wind meandering along the rock walls.

Reaching the ring of lamps, I halted and let my gaze drift upward. Jewels glittered everywhere. The moment was almost bizarre. The stack of weapons stood twice my height, and everything had been beautifully, even lovingly, organized. The square frame of the pyramid was formed by lances that had been arranged according to length, the longest at the bottom, the shortest toward the top of the pyramid. The peak was composed of daggers. There was even a pattern to the placement of the jewels. All the rubies seemed to be on the north side, the emeralds on the south. My flashlight didn't do it justice. I could only imagine what this structure looked like when the ring of oil lamps glowed and sent random flickers dancing through the skeletal depths of the pyramid. It must literally blaze to life.

Awe expanded my chest. This was clearly a shrine, a monument to the deaths of a thousand heroes. How many more wonders like this existed in the maze of caves that honeycombed this desert ridge?

As I listened, I understood the whispers. The breeze played the lances like a musician. It was symphonic and ethereal, but soft. Just a caress of melody against my ears.

Slowly, I curved around the ring of lamps, and shone my flashlight into the depths of the cave. The hieroglyphics continued for as far as I could see. Beyond the halo of light, tongues of darkness licked at the walls, as though marking the boundary where this world stopped and the dark underworld of Osiris began.

My flashlight beam blazed on a golden chair—a throne? It stood on a raised platform. I was momentarily stunned. The chair's armrests were sculpted lion heads and the feet were lion paws. The chair back was painted with an image of a woman seated on a throne, maybe Cleopatra, and a man kneeling before her with his head resting in her lap. The purple, red, and white colors of their clothing were as brilliant today as they must have been thousands of years ago when first painted.

And lying in the seat of the chair was a single dagger . . .

As though being drawn by a hand tugging on my shirt, I walked closer. The dagger, also made of pure gold, glittered wildly in my beam. I picked it up. *I've seen this before . . .*

As my throat constricted with emotion, I was once again standing on the hilltop overlooking the Gulf of Ambracia filled with hundreds of ships, my arms around the mother of my children, fearing the death of everything I loved.

Tears blurred my eyes. I thought about the men who'd died fighting after I ran away and the thousands of bodies that had washed up on shore. For weeks after the battle, distraught soldiers had remained to search for friends and loved ones. All across the vista, the scrubby Greek lowlands flashed with weapons dropped by men who simply could not go on.

My head was pounding. I closed my eyes and sobbed.

What was the matter with me? I felt foolish weeping over the deaths of people I had never known in a battle that had been lost more than two thousand years ago, but I couldn't help it. The tragedy lived inside me as though it had been passed to me in my very genes.

When I finally caught my breath and opened my eyes, I heard footsteps.

Light as a cat's.

"Hello?"

Something old and powerful stood in the cave before me. Though I could not see it, I felt it there, watching me.

My heart in my throat, I stuffed the dagger in my shirt pocket and pulled the pistol from the back of my pants. While I aimed it at nothing, I retreated one step at a time. My flashlight beam whipped around the cave, grazing the colorful hieroglyphics and flashing across the ceiling. I saw nothing. I wasn't sure how much time had passed, but surely if I'd been in here for longer than twenty minutes, Roberto would have come looking for me.

When I'd finally edged around the magnificent pyramid of weapons, I did the only thing I could. I pivoted and charged back for the boarded-up entrance, where I hit the ground on my belly and slithered through the hole into the sunlight.

Roberto jumped when I emerged. "What took you so long? I was starting to panic out here! Didn't you hear me calling you?"

"Sorry." I got to my feet, and shoved the pistol into his hand so I could dust off my pants. "I found the weapons, thousands of them."

"You did? Why didn't you bring a few with you? The old man would—"

"They form some kind of shrine, Roberto. I'm not touching that thing."

When I turned back to stare at the boarded-up entry, I could sense it standing just on the other side, its ear pressed against the wood, listening to our voices.

My throat suddenly went dry. Falling to my knees, I scooped dirt back over my exit hole, and waited. A moment later, I felt the presence fade, as though it had turned around and started walking away into the dark tomb. In my mind's eye, I could see it standing beside the pyramid, the circle of oil lamps alight, and casting flickering reflections through the ancient weapons. "It" was strong and commanding. But not alive. Not human.

A well-developed imagination Moriarity had called it. My mom would have diagnosed this as another *dissociative episode* from her *unhinged* son.

But I couldn't help wondering why it hadn't followed me out beneath the boards and freed itself?

Unless, of course, it was already free.

Roberto gasped. "What's that thing in your pocket?"

CHAPTER TWENTY-FOUR

Y ou can't tell anyone about this, Roberto." I pulled it from my
pocket and handed it to him. "I'm pretty sure this is what Cleo
sent me here to find. This is the sacred dagger, called a bagsu, that
belonged to her in 30 BC."

While he smoothed his fingers over the gold, he said, "It's so
small. The blade is barely three inches long."

"Long enough to stab yourself in the heart, I guess."

"Definitely. What makes you think it belonged to Cleo in 30 BC?"

I knelt, unstrapped the duct tape where I'd kept the medallion,
and retaped it around the dagger, making sure the blade was covered.
As I pulled my sock up over it, I said, "Samael told me the dagger was
waiting for me, and this was lying there all by itself. This has got to
be it."

"Okay, whatever. Tell me about the shrine."

As we walked back along the trail, the fragrance of water and
olive blossoms blew up from the oasis, and we heard what sounded
like wood being chopped. I debated on whether or not to tell Roberto
about the presence I'd felt in the cave, but I just couldn't convince
myself to do it. I was having enough problems. If my only friend
abandoned me because he thought I'd lost my mind . . . Well, I wasn't
sure I could face life without even a single friend.

"Fifty paces into the cave, there's a pyramid made from ancient
Roman lances, spears, swords, and daggers. About twice my height,
so maybe twelve feet tall."

Roberto slowed down to veer around the chunk of rock in the
middle of the trail. "Why would someone build a pyramid of old
weapons?"

"It had a ring of oil lamps around it. I swear it looked like a monument to fallen heroes."

"Or dead enemies, Hal. Which means it isn't a shrine, just a victory monument. It's like saying, 'My enemies can bite me.'"

I considered that possibility. It had felt sacred to me, but ancient things always did. Cleo had once told me I was clairvoyant and could hear the voices of the dead. But I think I'm just a historian. Historians spend most of their lives mourning the deaths of people who've been moldering in the ground for centuries. It's a curious kind of penance for having been born too late to know them when they were alive.

I said, "Yeah, you're probably right."

As we cleared the boulder, we saw Moriarity down in the olive trees sharpening a length of wood with his knife.

Roberto stuffed the pistol into the back of his pants and pulled his T-shirt over it to hide it. "Looks like Dr. Who is about finished with the spear he promised to make Samael. Are you going to tell him about the weapons pyramid?"

"Do you think I shouldn't?"

"Depends. Do you want to get to the site so we can start helping Cleo, or stay here for two months while Moriarity dismantles the thing and studies every nick and rust spot in the swords?"

"He has a field crew waiting for him, Roberto, I don't think he'd . . ." I stopped talking because Roberto was giving me that look that said, *do you really want to take that chance?*

"Okay. Maybe you're right."

Moriarity didn't see us yet. He stood up with the weapon in his hand, and seemed to be testing its weight and balance. In the distance behind him, the wind had whipped up a minor sandstorm.

It was just after seven AM, and my blue shirt and jeans already stuck wetly to my body. The temperature had to be in the high eighties. I was not looking forward to hiking across the desert to get back to the Jeep. Relief filled me when we walked into the shade of the palms to wait for Moriarity. This was such a beautiful place. The wind-blown shadows of the trees wavered over the water bubbling from the spring.

"Thirsty?" I asked as I knelt down and dipped up a handful of cool water. The pond tasted slightly salty, as though composed of the tears of thousands of caravan pilgrims that had stopped here over the centuries. I was sure crossing this brutal desert had never been easy.

A soft voice came from Samael's cave. Probably the old man talking to himself. Tilting my head, I listened, but didn't hear it again and rose to my feet.

"What's it taste like?" Roberto asked.

"A little salty, but good."

Roberto crouched and started dipping up water with both hands, drinking.

"I have the feeling we'd better drink a few gallons before we start for the Jeep. It might be a real scorcher today."

Moriarity moved around the edge of the pond, using the newly made spear as a walking stick, and a shocked expression lit his bearded face when he saw us. He wore his fedora, a long-sleeved white shirt, and tan chinos. The black rims of his glasses perfectly framed his bottomless black eyes.

From the corner of his mouth, Roberto said, "He looks surprised to see us. Why?"

"Don't know."

When he got close enough, Moriarity called, "Find the weapons?"

I shook my head. "No. Any chance they could be in some of the other caves? This whole ridge is honeycombed with them."

Moriarity stopped in front of us and pushed his fedora back on his head. Examining me with one suspicious eye, he said, "You didn't actually go inside the boarded-up cave, did you?"

"Sure, I did."

"And you found nothing?"

"No, why?" Heat flushed my face when it occurred to me that perhaps he knew what was in there.

Moriarity's dark gaze slid to Roberto, and he stared at him unblinking. "Did you go into the cave with Hal?"

Roberto shook his head. "No. I stayed outside. I figured that way I could run for help if Hal screamed that he was being eaten by a demon."

Moriarity nodded. "That sounds exactly like something you'd do, Robert."

"Yeah, so. No weapons."

As though the wood had grown slick beneath his palm, Moriarity took a new hold on the spear. "Samael will be happy to see you alive. He was certain you'd be killed by the demon the instant you entered its prison."

"But he asked Hal to do it anyway? That is *really* cold, bro. Why didn't you say no?"

"You survived, right?"

Smiling, Moriarity hiked past us with the spear propped over his left shoulder and headed for Samael's cave.

As we followed five steps behind, Roberto lifted both hands and made strange symbols in the air, clearly casting a spell on the good doctor. When he'd finished, he whispered to me, "Curse."

"Great," I said with my brows lifted.

Moriarity entered the cave ahead of us, and shouted, "What the . . . *Put that down!*"

Roberto and I broke into a run. When we slid to a stop inside the cave, we found Samael cowering in the guns and ammo cave with a revolver in his old, trembling hands, aimed at Moriarity's belly.

Roberto whispered, "That revolver is loaded, Hal. Don't push him."

What would have ever given Roberto the idea that I might push someone holding a gun on me, or rather, on Moriarity? Of course, given that Samael was blind, if he fired there was no telling who the bullet might hit.

Moriarity dropped the spear and edged forward with his hands up. "Samael, it's just us. There's nothing to be afraid of. Do you understand? It's me, Hal, and Robert. That's all."

"It c-came in here," Samael stuttered, "while you were gone. I was napping, but I smelled it. Look what it did?" He thrust a gnarled finger at the place where Roberto and I had stowed our backpacks and rolled space blankets.

When I turned, the sight left me speechless. Our belongings were scattered everywhere, and I was heartily glad I hadn't brought any underwear, because Roberto's camo jockey shorts were laying out for everyone to see. As well as the large box of strawberry-flavored condoms he'd brought.

"Well, it's gone now, so you can put down the gun."

"Are you sure?"

"Yes, my friend. It's gone."

Slowly, the old man lowered the revolver and sagged against the boxes of ammunition behind him. "I couldn't stop it. It's so big and powerful. *Monstrous.*"

"It's all right. None of us expected you to battle a demon over a few pairs of jockey shorts." Turning to Roberto he said, "Jungle camo?"

"Yeah, need a pair?"

"What was it looking for?" Moriarity walked over to kick through the contents of our packs. After five or six seconds, he stopped and reached down to pick up a mangled chunk of metal. "Hal?"

My heart lurched. The locked box where I'd kept the medallion was almost unrecognizable. It was a twisted hunk of junk. All I could think of was that Moriarity must have taken it outside and smashed it with a rock while Samael was napping.

Moriarity held it up to show the empty interior. "Tell me you have the medallion?"

Don't . . . don't let . . . My aunt and uncle can't get their hands on it.

I heard her dying voice so clearly, she might have been in the room with me.

"It was in that box."

"You're lying!" The professor lifted the mangled metal box as though he planned to bludgeon me with it, and strode across the room with an enraged expression.

Seeing Roberto's fingers go tight around the gun tucked into the back of his pants, I quietly said, "Don't."

Moriarity stopped a pace in front of me. For several seconds, he looked confused, as though he didn't know what to do now. Finally, he hurled the box into the cave wall, sank to the floor, and lowered his head into his hands.

"Dear God. There's no reason to go to Pelusium now. How am I going to tell her I've lost—"

"*Her?*"

Moriarity stopped as though realizing what he'd said, but he did not look up. Moving his hands to cover his face, he went still and quiet.

I looked at Samael. The pistol still dangled limply from his right hand. Despite our presences, he had not put it down. He was clearly terrified. His blind eyes moved constantly, as though searching the cave with his faint vision.

If I made the wrong decision, it could cost me everything.

Turning to Moriarity, I said, "Who is the woman you're afraid to tell that you lost the medallion?"

Moriarity used his fingers to massage his forehead. As though deciding what to tell me, it took several moments before he answered, "My wife. Sophia arrived at the site a week ago. She's already searching for the old excavation unit where the medallion and bagsu were found. But the Sem priest's burial is meaningless without them."

"What Sem priest burial?" Samael asked.

Spreading my feet as though bracing for a fight, I said, "I have the bagsu, Dr. Moriarity."

Samael made a small sound of dismay.

The professor lifted his head. A strange glow entered his eyes, as though he'd known it all along. He rose to his feet and loomed over me. "Where's the bagsu? Show it to me."

"Let's pack up and head for Pelusium before it gets too hot. I'll show it to you later."

"Where's the medallion?"

"I have no idea. That's the truth."

I walked wide around Moriarity and went over to start picking up my belongings and stuffing them in the right pockets of my backpack. A few seconds later, Roberto joined me.

The first thing he reached for were his condoms. As he jammed them in his pack, he glanced at Moriarity, and softly said, "You should have let me shoot him. Now we're going to have to sleep with one eye open."

CHAPTER TWENTY-FIVE

The Jeep trip to the site was silent, brooding. We stopped once for a bathroom break and to buy lamb kebabs for dinner, then we piled back into the vehicle and took off in a cloud of dust.

Staring out the window, I watched the sunny dunes pass until they changed to a constant stream of villages and green fields, and hours later turned into reeded marshes soft with starlight. The Nile Delta was stunningly flat and crowded, but birdsong filled the warm night air, and it was cooler here near the seacoast. I couldn't shake the premonition that I'd made the wrong choice telling Moriarity I had the dagger. The sense of foreboding had settled into my blood like the wet snowflakes that fell in Colorado in April.

I kept second-guessing myself. It must have been Moriarity who destroyed the medallion's metal box, then tore through our packs looking for it. Now he knew I carried the dagger with me at all times.

On the other hand what if Samael had told the truth? A monstrous demon had entered the cave while he was alone and thrashed through our belongings searching for the medallion . . . or the dagger? Memories of turquoise skin, red hair, and an Egyptian Army uniform flashed behind my eyes. Had it followed me to Egypt? Was it the thing that looked and sounded like Cleo?

Though I kept thinking about that possibility, I just didn't believe it. The person I kept hearing and seeing was Cleo. *It was her.* Or rather, her soul. There was no doubt in my mind. It was Cleo, and she needed me.

And, yes, I know that sounds like the talk of a madman in the grips of DID. Believe me, the possibility that I am not sane is never far from my mind.

To the north, the dark ocean spread for as far as I could see, but westward, the lights of Port Said shone, and in the distance, Alexandria's glow lit the sky. I kept seeing planes descending toward an airport in the east, but I had no idea which one. Probably Tel Aviv in Israel. Maybe Jerusalem.

Roberto shifted in the seat beside me and sand trickled down his pants to patter on his hiking boots. We were all covered with it. Every time my teeth came together, sand grated. In front of me, Moriarity drove with his fedora canted at an angle on his head, and Samael slept. I'd given Samael the pair of sandals I'd brought with me and, holding tight to Moriarity's arm, while using his makeshift spear as a walking stick, he'd made it across the desert in much better shape than I had in my hiking boots. As soon as we'd stowed our packs in the rear of the Jeep, however, Samael had fallen asleep as though completely exhausted.

The dirt road swerved around the marshes, and the scents of water and damp earth filled the night air.

The most spectacular part of the trip was driving over the long suspension bridge that crossed the Suez Canal. About a half hour later, Roberto suddenly sat up in his seat.

"What's that?" He extended his arm in front of my face to point at something.

Awe swelled my heart. Starlight gleamed whitely on the standing marble columns that ringed the stunning ruins of a massive D-shaped amphitheater. "My God," I said, "We're here."

"This is Pelusium?"

"It must be."

A short distance away, I saw at least one hundred tents and twenty or thirty ramadas. Tables had been set up beneath the ramadas and the tops were heaped with boxes of what looked like bagged and tagged artifacts. Lanterns glowed inside many of the tents.

"This excavation is huge, Roberto," I softly said. "I had no idea there would be so many people here."

Roberto leaned close to reply, "Dr. Who is serious, bro. He wants that grave."

Moriarity stopped the Jeep on the far western side of the field camp, and called over his shoulder. "Grab your packs, boys. Those tents on the west are reserved for us. Yours is the small one."

Roberto rolled his eyes, like, *of course it is.*

When I stepped out of the Jeep, and my foot first touched the soil of Pelusium, a light-headed sensation possessed me. In my mind, there were no ruins, no automobiles in the parking area, no one speaking English. The city stood before me exactly as it had in 48 BC, when Cleopatra's younger brother Ptolemy XIII became sole ruler of Egypt. Thirteen at the time, Ptolemy had watched Gnaeus Pompeius Magnus wade ashore, then ordered his beheading. Cleopatra had tried to raise a rebellion against her brother right here.

Right here.

I bowed my head to stare at the ground. I could be standing in the footsteps of Cleopatra, or Ptolemy, or Marcus Antonius, even Julius Caesar himself. Those towering historical figures had influenced all of Western civilization. The person I was today was because of who they had been more than two thousand years ago. Reverence filled me. Closing my eyes, I could feel them all around me. Ancient Egyptians believed that dreams were portals to the afterlife, planes upon which the gods and the dead spoke to the living. Deep inside me, I knew if I just listened hard enough, they would tell me what to do.

Roberto's boots came up beside me. "You ought to try being here in this world. It's way more interesting than whatever's happening in your head."

"I doubt that."

"Oh, sorry, I didn't know you were thinking about sex."

"Surprisingly, I wasn't. I was remembering that, in the Battle of Pelusium in 525 BC, the oncoming Persian Army carried cats as living shields against the Egyptians."

"Cats?" Roberto sounded mystified. "I'll bet they got the holy shit scratched out of them."

"Maybe, but cats were sacred to Egyptians. The Persians knew their foes would be hesitant to spear a cat."

"Did the Persians win?"

"Absolutely."

Roberto took a deep breath of the marsh-scented air and let it out in a rush. "It's been a long, scary-as-hell day, Hal. Let's go stuff, and I do mean *stuff,* our packs in that tiny tent. I'll take first watch."

"No. Let me do it. I won't be able to sleep for a while anyway. I'm too excited."

"Affirmative."

We walked to opposite sides of the Jeep and reached into the rear to pull out our packs. As we shrugged into the shoulder straps, we watched Moriarity helping Samael slide out of the passenger door. It was a slow process.

"Hold onto my arm, my friend," Moriarity instructed.

"Where's my walking stick?"

"Right here."

Moriarity supported the old man while he gingerly edged from his seat, then he placed the stick in Samael's hand. "I'm going to take you to your tent, and I'll return for our things."

"All right," Samael said in a frail voice.

When he drew even with me, Samael stopped and looked up with those eerie demon-touched eyes shining like pearls. "You feel her coming, don't you? The *Weret-Kekau.* She's almost here."

My gaze riveted on the amulet he wore on a leather cord around his neck. I'd never seen it before. As though he could see my gaze, Samael walked closer. Reaching down, he lovingly cradled the amulet in his gnarled fingers to show it to me. It was a stone carving of the demon Ammut, the handmaiden of The Judgment. Her crocodile head was discernible even in the faint light.

"A prayer for justice," he explained in that kindly old voice. "There are many such charms found here at the site. Tomorrow, I will find one for you to wear. It will protect you against destruction. Evil against evil. You see?"

The air was redolent with a bitter tang, like copper on the tongue. The same scent that had pervaded the boarded-up cave. And I could *feel* something moving in the darkness not more than a few paces away.

"Thank you," I said. "For finding me a charm tomorrow."

Roberto walked around the Jeep and said, "Can I have one, too? This is kind of a creepy place."

Samael tilted his head and peered blindly at Roberto for several seconds. "They only protect the living."

"Oooh. I forgot I was dead."

After a moment, Samael slipped his arm through Moriarity's, and they walked away toward the tents.

When they were far enough away, Roberto said, "What was that mumbo jumbo about something *coming?*"

"The *Weret-Kekau* means The Great Magic. It was one of the many names for the goddess Isis. Cleopatra was supposedly the reincarnation of Isis."

"So, what does that mean? Cleopatra is coming?"

A vague prickling taunted the back of my neck. The feeling I'd had that something was out there in the darkness evaporated, but the air still carried the coppery bitterness. "I don't know, Roberto. I'm pretty sure the old guy is insane."

Roberto shrugged his pack into a more comfortable position. "*Pretty sure?* Bro, come on."

"Let's go check out our palatial tent. That's got to be a whopping five square feet of space." Roberto hiked off for the tent with his pack swaying back and forth.

My feet sank deeply into the sand of the ancient Nile Delta as I trotted to catch up.

The square tent was actually six by six feet, which meant we had a whopping thirty-six square feet. It was going to be close quarters, but I didn't mind.

After we'd stashed our packs on either side of the tent near the entry flap, we pulled out our space blankets and arranged them. Roberto immediately stretched out and went to sleep.

To allow the evening breeze to flow through, I tied the tent flap back, then crouched inside the doorway to keep watch. The crescent moon had just risen, flooding the site with a silver glow. Dozens, maybe hundreds, of square holes and massive back dirt piles cast shadows across the site. It seemed impossible that the crew had only been excavating for a week, but I didn't know much about archaeological field techniques. Maybe a crew of two hundred could move that much dirt in seven days?

At around midnight, I stood up and yawned. The lanterns had all been shut off. The camp slept for the most part. Snores and coughs and quiet voices carried.

Really tired, I'd start to doze off and then jerk awake. I needed to get my blood flowing to stay alert. I decided I'd walk to the closest excavation unit. It was less than thirty paces away, which meant I could still keep an eye on our tent.

The night was so perfect I felt like I had stepped into one of those historical photographs of Egypt that fill the Internet. The ruins of Pelusium were cast in gray tones, the monumental amphitheater like a gigantic half-open mouth; its standing columns reminded me of broken teeth. The dust of ancient civilizations blew through the silvered light. But beneath all that, beneath the ruins and marshes and tents, I could see the ancient city rising from the flood plain, embraced by two meandering arms of the Nile. I *knew* this place as surely as if I myself had walked here two thousand years ago. Right over there to my left, Caesar's cavalry horses stood, tack jangling as they stamped their feet to dispel flies. The helmets of centurions glinted as they walked the line, checking on the guards who stood watch between the dark forms of horses. The ancient voices that filled the darkness spoke mostly Greek and Latin. I could understand some of what they were saying, discussing the treachery of Cleopatra and Marcus Antonius, talking about how hungry their families were back in Roma. More than anything, I heard the downright hatred in their voices. These were the soldiers who ravaged my dreams. The people I knew in my heart were going to kill me and everything I loved.

I trudged forward to look down into the excavation unit. Small, it covered only about ten by twelve feet. Darkness prevented me from seeing anything clearly, though moonlight gleamed from potsherds embedded in the western wall.

A dark form loomed to my right.

I spun around with my heart in my throat just as the man unslung his rifle and ran toward me. A click sounded as the safety on his weapon was shifted into firing position, but then he abruptly stopped.

"Ah! You are one of the young men from Colorado, yes?" the soldier called.

"Yes, sir." My voice sounded a little terrified, because I was. "Is it okay if I'm out here?"

The soldier slung his rifle over his shoulder and strode closer. He was about my height, with short black hair, wearing a camo uniform I'd seen a thousand times in my repeating nightmares. Egyptian Army. How strange that it hadn't occurred to me that the military would be guarding the excavation. Of course, it was. Looting was at an all-time high in Egypt. All across Africa and the Middle East, archaeologists were being killed for trying to protect antiquities. Dead archaeologists and destroyed sites were bad publicity. Images of the ravaged city of Palmyra in Syria flitted behind my eyes.

The man's teeth glinted with moonlight as he came to stand beside me. "Which are you?" he asked in heavily accented English.

"Hal Stevens, sir."

"From mountains, yes?"

"Yes, my home, Georgetown, Colorado, sits in the Rocky Mountains."

He smiled. "Dr. Sophia tells us you are coming. Someday I wish to go see buffalo in Colorado. They are majestic animals, yes?"

I smiled back. "Yes, they are. We have a park close to us with buffalo and elk, as well as other animals."

"You wish to see a little of site tonight?" he asked in a friendly voice.

Turning around, I looked at the tent. I was supposed to be standing guard, making sure neither of us was murdered in our sleep, not out wandering around the site. "Thank you, but I should probably go back and get some sleep. It's been a long day."

"Please? Let me to show one thing? Just found today. Right there," he pointed to the next excavation unit about ten paces in the distance.

"Okay. Thank you," I said, not wanting to offend the first person I'd met at Pelusium.

He led the way to the dark rectangle rimmed with moonlight.

When he pulled his flashlight from his belt and shone the beam down into the pit, my muscles contracted all at once.

"She is magnificent, yes?"

"Oh, y-yeah."

I stared at the huge, partly uncovered stone statue hulking in the bottom: massive clawed feet, long jutting face, jaws gaping to show sharp rows of teeth arranged in a monstrous crocodile grin: the demon, Ammut.

"See? Look also there." He aimed the beam at the northern part of the excavation.

My gaze traced the long red brick wall which extended the length of the unit. At the far end, shadows coalesced into one gigantic arm and the fingers of a human hand. Faint barking echoed, maybe from camp dogs, or maybe from packs of feral dogs that roamed the land of the dead. Wind buffeted the soldier's sleeves. Cold wind. Odd for this time of year. I crossed my arms for warmth.

The solider thrust out his hand in a traditional American greeting. "I am Corporal Bektash. Please to call me Tashir. I work as guard for Dr. Corbelle."

I gave his hand a firm shake. "Nice to meet you, Tashir. Please call me Hal."

Looking back at the face of the demon, I thought I saw Ammut's stone eyes slowly turn to meet my gaze. It had to be a trick of the moonlight, but my heart froze in my chest. Her carved pupils glittered.

She knew me.

I could feel it.

She'd been waiting for me to get here.

A terrible premonition swelled to certainty inside me. In the not too distant future, maybe even tonight, I would be locked in the battle of my life with an ancient demon over the condemned soul of the woman I loved, and I had no idea how to fight a demon.

"Much more to see. Come?"

"No, thanks, Tashir," I said and hooked my thumb over my shoulder to indicate my tent. "I'm going back now and try to sleep."

"Yes. See you at morning, Hal."

He waved as I walked away with my skin crawling, hurrying toward our tent. Through the open flap, I could see Roberto sprawled on his stomach sound asleep.

Crouching down just inside the tent, I fought to keep from shivering. An icy terror had started to pulse through my veins. What was that cloying taste in the back of my mouth? The metallic tang of old blood, dried for millennia, just mixed with my saliva? Something . . .

Roberto seemed to sense my dread. He roused and sleepily said, "I saw you out there with that guy. What were you doing?"

"Staring into the deepest darkest pit of hell. I'll show it to you tomorrow."

He yawned the word, "Okay," flopped to his side, and went back to sleep.

CHAPTER TWENTY-SIX

Dim sounds penetrated my sleep, metal clanging, quiet voices, the rattling of boxes of artifacts being moved. I didn't want to wake up. Roberto had taken over watch at two am, and I was pretty sure I'd only been asleep for a few hours. But the smell of campfires and coffee drifted on the air. Rolling to my back, I opened my eyes and blinked up at the canvas roof over my head. Wind buffeted the tent. When I looked for Roberto, I found him sitting cross-legged just outside the door, his body darkly silhouetted against the lavender gleam of dawn.

I pulled my hiking boots from the corner of the tent, where I'd stashed them last night, and slipped them on. I'd slept in my jeans and blue T-shirt, but I figured they'd be good for another day or two.

Roberto looked in at me. Brown hair blew around his face. He was wearing a tan long-sleeved shirt, but when the wind gusted, I could see the pistol tucked into the back of his pants. "Go back to sleep, Hal. People are just starting to get up out here. You could get another hour or two of shut-eye."

"No, I'm up." Reaching for my green long-sleeved shirt, I put it on and crawled out of the tent to sit on the sand beside Roberto.

The cool morning breeze buffeted the tents that stretched for a good two hundred yards to my left. A few people stood talking near the largest tent in the middle of the camp. Obviously, that was the cook tent. I could see big coffeepots on grates over open fires. A few more people were already at work beneath the ramadas, shifting boxes around. But my gaze clung to the ruins.

Naturally, I'd read everything I could find on Pelusium, including the works of Herodotus and Strabo and even a rare Greek papyrus from Egypt, but the reality was stunning. Standing walls or fragments of walls crisscrossed the vista, littered with massive chunks of broken columns. The impressive D-shaped amphitheater seemed to be the heart of the archaeological site, but the most impressive ruins were of the late-sixth-century Roman fortress, which I'd researched before I'd left. With seven-foot-thick walls and thirty-six towers, the fortress dominated the site. I'd studied both ancient and modern maps online, but this . . . This was amazing. As the sky continued to brighten, and I could see more of Pelusium, a profound sense of wonder filled me.

Roberto said, "I thought Egyptians built in gigantic blocks of stone, like the pyramids."

"My God, you were listening in class."

"Don't get excited. I got that from you and Cleo." He looked out at the theater. "This place looks like it's made of bricks."

"The ruins are mostly red bricks and mud bricks." I lifted a hand and pointed to the green strip to the north. "You see that?"

"The reeds? It's a marsh, right?"

I drew up my knees and propped my arms on them. "Now it is, but twenty-five hundred years ago, it was a branch of the Nile River." I turned around to the south and drew a line with my hand. "All that green out there is the other branch. The two branches embraced Pelusium like two arms." I extended my arms to show him.

"Yeah?" He pointed to the northern marsh. "So, when you look out there with your historian's brain, what do you see? I've been trying to imagine what this fallen-down wreck looked like in its prime."

I smiled. In my mind's eye, I could see everything perfectly. "There are big barges moving along the Nile, filled with pots—amphorae—of honey, wine, and oil. Some are moored and offloading supplies. This is a bustling port city with quays and customs offices. It's also an industrial city. There are salt vats for distilling salt for sale, very fine workshops for textiles and glass, pottery kilns, and jewelry and statuary artists plying their wares along the docks. On the outskirts of the city, farmers grow flax and grains for breads. Cattle and other livestock graze in the distance. Everyone is busy working or worshipping. There are temples to a variety of gods and goddesses here. Isis is the local favorite."

"And what's that?" he pointed to the fortress. "It looks burned in places."

"That's the Roman fortress, built in the late 500s. It was burned, probably during the Persian Invasion of AD 619."

"The guys with the cat shields?"

"That was in 525 BC. Persians burned this fortress over a thousand years later."

A gust of wind peppered us with sand. When it was over, Roberto pushed tangled brown hair away from his blue eyes. His face shone with a dusting of silt. "So. I'm starving. Why don't you show me the deepest darkest pit of hell, then we'll go look for a cup of coffee and some flapjacks?"

I took an uneasy breath, said, "Sure," and rose to my feet.

As we walked out toward the excavation unit, the sun cleared the eastern horizon, and the ground glittered wildly. Far out over the distant ocean, dark clouds were gathering, and I wondered if it might rain later on in the day.

Roberto kicked at some artifacts, which made me cringe. "What's this green stuff?"

"Slag from glassmaking, I think. There was probably a glass workshop here. I didn't see this last night in the dark."

We passed the closest excavation unit with the potsherds sticking out of the walls, and continued on. As my feet took me closer, my heart started to race, and sweat beaded my hooked nose.

When we stopped at the edge of the pit, Roberto waved a hand at the excavation and said, "Hey, look at the big dog."

"That's not a dog. That's Ammut."

"Oh, *holy shit!*" He leaped backward. "The demon? That's what she looks like? A mutant collie?"

"Actually, if you look closer, you'll see that her long muzzle is a crocodile snout, and she has the paws of a lion. Her hippopotamus hindquarters are still buried."

Roberto edged closer to peer down at Ammut. "Hal, I hate to tell you, but this doesn't look anything like the turquoise-skinned creature you described—"

"Yeah, Moriarity said I may have seen Set, the brother of Isis."

Roberto bared his teeth at the demon. "Look at all those needle teeth! Reminds me of Stef Brown." His gaze slid to the gigantic arm and hand at the opposite end of the unit. "Who does the arm belong to? Dog catcher?"

"Don't know. They have to excavate more of it."

With the dawn, I could see things I could not last night. A small pool of water had gathered around the fingertips of the hand, and the arm wore a spiral serpent bracelet. They were common in ancient Egypt, but it reminded me . . .

Behind us, I heard Moriarity call, "You're up early, boys."

Turning, I saw him step from his tent and pull his fedora down against the breeze. As he rolled the sleeves of his white shirt down and buttoned them, his glasses flashed with sunlight.

"Wanted to see the site," I called back.

Moriarity walked to the edge of the excavation unit and looked down to see what we were staring at. His brows plunged down over his nose. "She's new, and well preserved," he noted. "If you were to conjecture, *Dr. Stevens*, what would you guess this might represent?"

I shifted uncomfortably. I hated it when teachers pinned me in class. My mind always went utterly blank. But I said, "Well, all I have is the front of Ammut and an arm with a humanlike hand, but I wonder if these statues might recreate 'The Judgment' scene. Which would mean the Devourer is sitting at the base of the Scales of Justice and the arm belongs to a statue of Osiris. Maybe."

Moriarity nodded admiringly. "That is exactly what I wonder. Good work. Obviously, we won't be able to answer that question for a few days."

Roberto asked, "Why is there water down there?"

"You're walking on top of ruins right now. They are everywhere just below the ground, but the deeper we sink our excavation units the closer we get to the water table. It's very close to the surface here."

He looked around the huge excavation, studying the people who were up and about, then he said, "Come on, let's get a cup of coffee, and I'll show you the other main attractions."

"Thanks."

As we walked, the ground became wetter until mud stuck to my boots. Roberto's head kept whipping around, trying to take every-thing in, just as I was. The whole site seemed to be enveloped by salt-crusted mud and wetlands, the legacy of the two extinct branches of the Nile that had once embraced the city.

"Is it always this wet?" I asked.

He laughed softly. "Though it looks like we might get a shower later this afternoon, this is the dry season. If we're lucky, we can work from March through October, because when the winter rains start, it's impossible."

Roberto kicked a chunk of green glass, and Moriarity shouted, "Stop that! You do not EVER kick at artifacts, Robert!"

"Well, what was that?"

"A fragment of a molded glass bowl that dates to the around 200 BC. Now, listen up. You do not collect artifacts, or move them, unless you are under the direct supervision of one of my crew chiefs. You may pick them up, look at them, and put them down in exactly the same place. That's all. Understand?"

We both nodded.

When we arrived at the big cook tent, which stretched about twenty by thirty feet, my stomach started growling from the rich scents. I noticed there was a dinner bell suspended from a post, which I assumed notified the archaeologists when food was ready. Ten long tables, each surrounded by wooden benches, stood on the eastern side of the tent. This early in the morning they rested in full sun, but by afternoon, they would be shaded.

"Dr. James!" the gray-haired man stirring one of the big pots sit-uated on the grates over the fire called, smiling broadly. He had a mouthful of broken yellow teeth. "It's good to see you."

Moriarity walked around the fire and embraced the cook like an old friend. "And you, Shihab. You look well, my friend."

"Yes, very well. Where is Dr. Sophia?"

"I let her sleep. She'll be here soon. What do we have for breakfast this morning?"

Shihab lifted the wooden spoon from the big pot. It was covered with a sticky brown substance. "I heard you would be here today, so I made your favorite cereal of teff and flax."

"Is it ready?"

"Yes, please." He gestured to the bowls and spoons nested on the table just inside the tent.

"Follow me, boys."

Moriarity led the way into the tent and stopped to point. "Do you see that black box on the shelf over there? That's a satellite phone to be used only in case of emergency. Got it?"

"Sure."

Moriarity picked up a bowl and spoon. "Grab a cup, too. And if you want tea, it's in the big box on that shelf." He pointed to the opposite side of the tent.

The canvas walls were lined with wire shelves filled with cardboard boxes, and bags, fresh vegetables, and pomegranates, along with a healthy supply of bottled water stacked in the very rear.

When we walked back outside and held out our bowls, Shihab filled them with gelatinous brown goo.

Roberto smelled it and wrinkled his nose before he took a bite. Around a mouthful, he said, "Hey, Egyptian Malt-O-Meal. Tastes like mud. So it has honey in it to disguise the flavor, right?"

"Milk and honey," Moriarity said. "But it is most certainly not Malt-O-Meal. Teff is an ancient grain that originated around 6,000 years ago. The tiny seeds were so revered by ancient Egyptians they were placed with pharaohs in the pyramids as their last meal for traveling to the land of the dead."

I took my first bite and smiled as the rich earthy flavor filled my mouth. "This is really good."

"Glad you like it. Let's find a seat and come back for coffee."

We followed him to the tables, set our bowls down, and took our cups back to the fire.

"The usual?" Shihab asked.

"Yes, thank you," Moriarity replied, "and you can give the boys the same as me."

Roberto said, "I may not want it. What is it?"

"It's my favorite blend of Egyptian coffee. You'll like it. I think."

As the Arab lifted the big coffeepot and began to pour Moriarity's cup full, I smelled spices, but I couldn't identify them. Once we had steaming cups, Moriarity led us back to the table, and we slid onto the bench opposite him, facing the tent.

I sipped my cup, and said, "This is delicious coffee. What are the spices?"

"Cardamom, anise, and red pepper." Moriarity took a healthy sip, smiled at the flavor, and said, "What do you think, Robert?"

"Nasty. Give me Starbucks any day." He set his cup aside, made a face, and dug into his cereal.

More of the crew began to emerge from the tents, yawning, stretching their arms over their heads. As I ate, I noticed that an attractive blonde woman, tall and athletic, was coming our way. She wore her hair in a braid that fell down the back of her long-sleeved ivory shirt. I guessed her age as mid-thirties. She had one of those authoritative strides that told me she was in charge of something. After grabbing a cup of coffee, she walked toward us.

Roberto leaned close to whisper, "Dear God, please let her sit by me."

Instead, she slid onto the bench beside Moriarity, which made him grimace and shove his bowl away. "LaSalle. How are you?"

As she sipped her coffee, her arm muscles bulged through her shirt. "Are you going to make me sue you, Jim?" she said in a deep gravelly voice.

"I had complications in Colorado. I'm sure Sophia told you about my niece's death."

"I'm not talking about you getting here two weeks late. Where's the excavation report from the 2010 field season? How many years do I have to wait before I have the information necessary to publish my article in *Antiquity*?"

Moriarity ignored the question, and instead said, "Boys, this is Dr. LaSalle Corbelle from the Royal Ontario Museum in Canada. LaSalle, let me introduce you to my newest crewmembers." He held a hand to me. "This is Hal Stevens, and the boy with drool at the corners of his mouth is Robert Dally."

Roberto wiped his mouth on his arm, and said, "Hi."

I nodded to her. "Hello. I didn't realize different countries worked here at the same time."

Dr. Corbelle gave Moriarity one last disgusted look, then turned to face me. "Currently, five countries are excavating here. Canada, the US, Switzerland, Poland, and, of course, Egypt. We all use the same tent camp to minimize the impacts to the site, but our excavations are in different areas. How do you like Egypt so far? Have either of you been here before?"

Roberto said, "Egypt's hot, but pretty."

She gave him an approving nod and looked at me. "What about you, Hal?"

"This is my first trip to Egypt, but I'm looking forward to learning much more about the site and country. Have you found any indications of where Queen Cleopatra might be buried?"

Dr. Corbelle sat back, as though surprised by my question. "I have not. Personally, I think that's just another of Jim's wild theories. I don't think she's buried anywhere near here. I have my money on the ruins of the ancient temple to Osiris at Abusir, which is about thirty miles from Alexandria."

I drank coffee for a few seconds before I worked up the courage to say, "Would a woman who was believed to be the reincarnation of Isis be buried in a temple to Osiris? Isn't it far more likely that she would be buried in a temple to Isis?"

Moriarity suppressed a smile.

Dr. Corbelle said, "Yes, it is possible. But many suggestive artifacts have been found in the Temple of Taposiris Magna, that's the name of the temple to Osiris. For example, temple carvings showing two lovers in an embrace, coins bearing a likeness that may be Cleopatra, and even a ceramic fragment that shows a man with a cleft chin, as Marcus Antonius is supposed to have had."

"So you think both of them might be buried there?"

"I think it's possible. Do you disagree?"

I tried to organize my argument. This woman obviously knew way more than I did. Nervous, I stammered, "Well, no, I—I don't think so. Gaius Julius wanted to conquer them in every way possible. He hated them. Cleopatra had specifically asked him to bury her with Antonius, so burying them far apart would have been his final triumph over her." I swallowed hard. "Don't you think that's possible?"

Her blonde brows lifted as she nodded. "You're a thinker, Hal Stevens. Yes, I do think it's possible. Probably not likely, but certainly possible. Why don't you ditch Jim and come to work for me? My excavation is right over there in front of—"

"I'm not letting you steal more of my crewmembers, LaSalle. Forget it. You already took Tashir and Ronald. Hal is working with me. However, I'll gladly give you Robert the Drooler." He flicked a hand at Roberto.

Roberto's mouth quirked.

Dr. Corbelle tipped her cup, finished her coffee, and stood up. She was tall for a woman, as tall as I was, so around five-nine. "Hal? Robert? Come over to my excavation anytime, and I'll show you around. And if you decide you want to defect to the Canadian part of the site, I'll put you to work."

"Thank you, Doctor," I said. "We'd like to see your excavation."

"Good." When she swung back around to Moriarity, her smile vanished. "Get me that overdue report, Jim. Or I'll have the museum sue you for breach of contract."

She walked away like a tigress on a hunt, all rippling muscles and power.

Roberto reached up to grip a fistful of the white T-shirt over his heart. "Good Lord, my heart actually hurts. Falling hard here."

Moriarity shoved his fedora back on his head. "Then you'd better have two PhDs, a curriculum vitae a thousand pages long, and a boat-load of money. She's embarrassingly rich and acts like it. We worked on a joint US-Canadian project in 2010, and it was the worst field season of my life."

Roberto said, "What's a curriculum vitae?"

"It means," Moriarity answered, "that somebody like you, who can't even spell archaeology, is doomed. Now finish up your breakfast, and I'll take you to an interesting part of the site."

CHAPTER TWENTY-SEVEN

J ust as the other field crews started to fall into line for breakfast, and a variety of languages filled the air, we rose from the table and Moriarity led us out toward the ruins of the Roman fortress. The cool air blowing in off the ocean smelled of salt and sea.

I brought up the rear. Walking along the massive seven-foot-thick wall was sobering. It stretched high over my head, and in the yellow morning light the red bricks had an unearthly orange glow.

We followed Moriarity along a path that wound around puddles and between jumbled piles of ancient bricks, which I assumed had toppled from the fortress wall over the millennia.

Cleo had described this site a hundred times, but in her stories the Roman fortress was always a dark brooding wall that hulked over the earlier Egyptian ruins, like Rome still exerting influence over the conquered Egyptian people even after fifteen hundred years. To me, this morning, it was a bright exciting monument to an ancient culture I'd spent my whole life studying. Rome. A happy place. For me. As the path veered closer to the wall, I knew I was walking in the footsteps of ancient Roman legionnaires.

And right before my eyes, it all came into focus . . .

I heard the clip-clopping of horse hooves, bits jangling, Roman cavalrymen calling up to the soldiers guarding the walls as they rode by. It was night in the vision, but moonlight showed me the gleam of helmets and swords hanging from belts.

"This way, boys." Moriarity veered off from the fortress wall and headed westward. We walked in silence for a time, just absorbing the scents and sounds of the archaeological site. As the breeze shifted, I smelled coffee and cardamom. The cardamom was especially intense here.

"Incidentally," Moriarity said. "We've had a number of artifacts disappear from inventory on this site and later wind up for sale on the open market. So, if you see anyone pocketing an artifact, I want you to report it to me immediately."

The path took us out into the flats where there was nothing—no ruins, no people, no artifacts. In another thirty paces, however, I saw the excavation on top of a low rise. Maybe one hundred feet in diameter, its circular shape was outlined by rows of carefully placed red bricks.

"Now watch your step up here," Moriarity called. "The stairs down will be very slick this morning."

When we arrived at the rim, I could see down into a bowl-like depression; it was filled with fog. Mist snaked around inside, obscuring most of the interior, but I caught glimpses of walls and numerous smaller chambers arranged around the exterior of the circle. On the far side, a life-size marble statue of Isis lay on its back, its stone eyes apparently fixed upon the shimmering clouds hovering above it.

Moriarity guided us to the mud-brick staircase. "Be careful."

Moriarity trotted down into the bottom of the depression and stood looking up at us. His bearded face was little more than a dark splotch covered with a hat.

Roberto and I took the steps more carefully. Coated with mist, they were slick beneath our boots.

"Look around you, boys. See the different sizes of bricks distinguishing the layers through which you are traveling?"

Turning to my right, I saw what he meant. There were seven distinctive layers of bricks. The uppermost bricks were the largest, but they grew smaller in size as the stairs descended, as though they were funneling us down into the misty depths.

"You're watching the journey of the soul as described in Re theology. The rim of the temple is the realm of light. The dim realm of the cemetery god Seker occupies the fourth and fifth hours of night, which is where you're currently standing." He extended a hand to indicate the fourth and fifth layers of bricks. "The sixth hour is an approach to the land of Osiris, which is where I'm standing on the floor of the temple, and the seventh hour, which can only be reached through the tunnels in the temple, is the Kingdom of Osiris."

Looking around, I thought I saw one of the tunnels wavering through the mist; it was a partially excavated hole in the wall to my right. When I stared, trying to see it better, I had the feeling I was being watched by old and unearthly eyes.

"The Kingdom of Osiris is the netherworld realm of Duat, isn't it?"

Far back in my head, I could hear Cleo's soft voice telling me the dagger . . . *will allow my soul to climb out of the netherworld of Duat and travel to the Island of the Two Flames.*

"Yes. Each hour is guarded by demons controlled by priestly magical formulae. So be careful. Each step you take is a symbolic journey down into the land of the dead."

Awed, I softly said, "I've never read about anything like this."

"'Course not. This site is absolutely unique. Wish I was in charge here, but LaSalle Corbelle has exclusive rights to excavate this structure. As a matter of fact, we shouldn't even be here. Only she and her students are allowed."

Roberto leaped off the bottom step and vanished into the densest part of the white cloud. I could barely see him moving around down there.

Slowly, I took the stones one at a time, trying to imagine how it might have felt to be an ancient priest descending these stairs into the misty underworld—the guardian demons held at bay only through the strength of my magic. Above me, the risen sun went from being a yellow ball to a hazy white blur. It sounded like a thunderstorm down here. Every ledge was wet and dripping, and the sounds seemed to be magnified. Was the temple designed to be an echo chamber? Even Roberto's breathing reverberated around the walls.

Moriarity opened his arms to the temple. "You should ask LaSalle if you can work here for a day. I'd ask for you, but if I did, she'd say no."

As I stepped down into the sixth hour, the approach to the Kingdom of Osiris, I saw the three subterranean passageways arranged at regular intervals around the floor. The tunnels. Each had a set of stairs that led down. I aimed a hand at the passageway to my left. "What's down there? What does Duat look like?"

"I don't know. Like you, I just got here. I have no idea how far back that tunnel has been excavated. Now, I have to run. I need to get my teams organized in their excavation units. When you're ready, come find me at the far end of the fortress wall."

Trotting back up the stairs, he left Roberto and me alone in the misty temple. Roberto had his head tilted back, gazing upward at the carved heads that thrust from each layer of stone. "Are those the demons that guard the hours?"

"I guess so," I said. "I can't see them very well. When sunlight finally floods the temple and the mist evaporates, we'll be able to see more clearly."

While I was gawking, Roberto scrambled over a giant chunk of fallen wall and looked down the other side. "Oh, buddy, you're going to want to see this."

"What is it?"

He gave me an irritated look. "How would I know? I'm waiting for you to come tell me."

I climbed up the wet bricks and stood next to him. The fog in the bottom shredded like an old gauze curtain, and suddenly there it was, cloaked in mist, looming from a dark pool of water. A sarcophagus. Mostly buried, all I could make out from above was the beautiful face painted on the stone. A woman. I understood instantly why Corbelle restricted access to this temple. Most of the pyramids had at one time or another been looted for the treasures they contained. Finding an intact sarcophagus was remarkable.

"So, what is it?"

"It's a sarcophagus, a stone container that holds at least one coffin with a mummy. Some sarcophagi had three coffins inside, like King Tut's."

"There's a mummy in there?"

"Probably."

"Let's go look at it." Roberto leaped down and splashed into the pool of water beside the sarcophagus. As he studied the painted image, he said, "There's a weird bird with a human face painted on her chest. What's that about?"

Wedging my feet on the slick stones, I stepped down next to him. The water came up over the toes of my boots, but it was going to be a hot day. They'd be dry soon. "Ancient Egyptians believed that human beings had two souls, the Ka and the Ba. The Ka remained with the body. Priests opened the mouths of the dead so the Ka could eat and drink the offerings brought to the grave by loved ones. The Ba soul was portrayed as a human-headed bird, but it had the ability to take on different forms. It's the Ba that travels to the afterlife. The shadow, the Khaybet, was alive, too, though."

Roberto looked a little unnerved by that idea. "The shadow was alive?"

"Yeah, later on, it was like witchcraft. If you could capture and control someone's shadow, his Khaybet, you could control him."

"How would somebody catch a shadow?"

I shrugged. "Magical net? You'd know better than I would."

"So, after you caught it, did the person walk off with no shadow?"

"I have no idea."

Roberto shoved brown hair away from his blue eyes and squinted at the bird. "Bro, I have got to find a spell for that. Wouldn't it be radical to be the only kid in school without a shadow?"

"You'd try to capture and control your own shadow?"

"Sure. Why not?"

"Well," I said with a shrug. "I guess I don't know enough about it to comment, but the Khaybet was powerful. What if your own shadow tried to get you?"

"Would it do that?" Roberto asked with wide eyes. "Like, grab me around the throat and beat my brains out on a concrete floor?"

"Maybe. I don't know."

Roberto glanced uneasily around the temple for a few seconds, before he said, "Okay, quality advice. Got it."

I started methodically working my way around the sarcophagus, studying the painting more closely. The woman had elaborately braided black hair and green eyes. A transparent clinging dress sculpted her body. The purple color was still stunning. Murex shells? Pearls hung around her neck and studded her hair. Part of the painting was missing at the top of her head, but I thought she might be wearing a cobra headdress. Cobras had been the symbols of Egypt. It was hard to imagine that this could be anyone but Cleopatra, but surely Moriarity or Corbelle would have mentioned the fact that Cleopatra's sarcophagus had been discovered in this temple. Since neither had, it must not be her. Maybe another Ptolemaic queen?

"Woah," Roberto commented. "I didn't know ancient Egyptian women wore see-through dresses."

"Cleopatra is sometimes portrayed as wearing transparent dresses. I've never seen anyone else, though. But I'm not a specialist in Egyptian dress. I'm better with Roman and Greek fash—"

"Hello," a frail old voice called from above us.

We both twisted around to look up. Standing on the rim of the temple, propped on his walking stick, was Samael. The hunchbacked elder wore a toothless smile. "Come. Both of you." He waved a gnarled hand at us. "I wish to show you a grave."

"What grave? The grave of the Sem priest?" I asked, but I was already hurrying toward the staircase that led out of the temple with Roberto less than three steps behind me.

Samael cocked his head curiously. "What Sem priest grave?"

"The Sem priest grave where you and Hassan Mallawi found the bagsu."

"Who told you we found it in the grave of a Sem priest?"

Stunned, I said, "But I thought you found it in a grave."

"Yes, we did."

CHAPTER TWENTY-EIGHT

Walking with Samael was agonizingly slow work. Every step he took had to be calculated. He looked around, propped his walking stick, gingerly stepped forward, then repeated the process. Look, prop, step.

"Samael, would it help if you held my arm?" I said and extended my elbow toward him.

He groped around until he found it, then slipped a skeletal arm through mine. "Thank you. The grave is over there." He gestured with his stick.

The area ahead was a flat expanse of nothingness. Just bare ground scattered with a few chunks of what looked like the brownish slag of brickmaking.

While we slowly made our way, I asked, "Have you seen the sarcophagus in the temple excavation? Or . . . Heard about it?" I revised, realizing that he couldn't see it.

"No, but it's not important." He continued plodding forward out across the empty expanse of sand.

"How can you say that? The sarcophagus has a painting of a woman wearing purple with a cobra crown. I thought it might be——"

"Listen," he hissed and cocked his ear. "Let him tell you."

"Who?"

I concentrated on the wind, trying to hear something unusual. Laughter and ordinary conversation came from the archaeologists eating breakfast around the cook tent. Roberto and I exchanged a glance, and Roberto shrugged to tell me he heard nothing interesting.

In the distance, at the far end of the Roman fortress wall, Moriarity stood with ten students. He was pointing at something and talking, but he kept glancing our way. I could see his mouth moving.

We walked until we were at least a quarter mile from the site before I saw the excavation and my steps slowed. The dirt that had been removed created a small mound. "Is that it, Samael?"

"Yes. He's calling and calling."

As we got closer, I could see the partially excavated skeleton in the bottom of the pit. The left side of the man's skull had been crushed, probably with a club. There were no grave goods, no fabrics, no jewelry, no pots of food . . . no evidence that he had been prepared for his journey to the afterlife. Instead, it looked like he'd been stripped naked and carefully, even lovingly, placed in the grave with his hands folded across his chest.

Roberto crouched and stared down. "Somebody did not like this dude. They bashed his skull in. You really hear him talking?"

Samael released my arm and grunted as he lowered himself to sit on the ground. "Come. Sit with me. Let us wait. You will hear, too."

Roberto sat down cross-legged to the old man's left. I continued standing for a time, surveying the people. Students had started dispersing from around the cook tent, heading out across the site. Several marched to the artifact boxes stacked on the tables beneath the ramadas and began shifting them around. The rest streamed away in different directions, presumably heading to their excavation units to start digging.

Samael cocked his head again, and his toothless mouth hung half-open while he listened. "In my dreams, they are alive. You know? They come to me weeping, pleading for help. This one . . ." He aimed a hand at the skeleton. "He says his name is Philopator Philometor Caesar. He—"

"*What?*" I instantly fell to my knees beside Samael to stare down at the skeleton. "It can't be."

Roberto said, "Who is he?"

"Well . . ." I sucked in a stunned breath. "Could be the son of Julius Caesar and Cleopatra, better known as Caesarian. Born in June of 47 BC, he was murdered on August twelfth, 30 BC, right after his mother committed suicide. She'd ordered him to run away and hide, but messages reached him from Gaius Julius, telling Caesarian that he need not be afraid. Gaius Julius told him to come back to Alexandria, that Egypt needed a ruler. Of course, when Caesarian returned, Octavian had him murdered."

"Was he buried here? In Pelusium?"

I shook my head. "No one knows where he was buried. Gaius Julius wanted him to disappear from history, just as he wanted to obliterate all traces of Marcus Antonius and Cleopatra."

I tried to convince myself that Caesarian had been carried here and placed in an ignominious grave, but it didn't seem likely. Gaius Julius could have dumped him in an ignominious grave in Alexandria just as easily. On the other hand, hauling him out of the city and far away would have lessened the chances that someone loyal to Caesarian might have been watching. And, after all, there had been an enormous Roman camp here. As the only blood heir to both Julius Caesar and Cleopatra, Caesarian was the legitimate ruler of both Rome and Egypt. And he was the greatest threat to Gaius Julius, who was only an adopted son of Julius Caesar. A known grave would have provided a rallying point for a rebellion. Of course, the graves of Cleopatra and Marcus Antonius might have done so, as well. Which was probably why they, too, had been dumped in ignominious graves. Gaius Julius was nothing if not thorough.

Roberto looked up from the grave with his blue eyes squinted. "Don't get too excited, Hal. He's probably going to turn out to be some poor shabti schmuck who survived on an ancient version of teff ramen and canned cat food."

"Why would you think that?"

"Don't you remember that naked ninety-year-old in The Springs that the Meals on Wheels lady found moldering in front of his TV surrounded by empty cans of dog food?" He held out a hand to the skeleton. "Same thing. Ptolemaic variety."

It amazed me that Roberto had absorbed who the Ptolemies were. That was true progress on his part. "Poor old guy. That was a tragedy."

"People get lost in the shuffle, bro."

We both turned to Samael, and I knew Roberto was thinking the same thing I was: *Just like Samael, living isolated and alone, forgotten by everyone.*

"Has the Ka said anything else?" I asked.

Samael used his walking stick to brace himself while he wobbled to stand up. "He says I must pay the shabti for the services he renders the dead."

Samael reached into his pocket and handed Roberto the extraordinary ancient medallion that Cleo's father had given her. Quietly, he said, "Do not forget the task you've been given. And tell no one you have her medallion. Both people and demons will kill you for it."

Roberto looked dumbstruck. His mouth was hanging open. "Wow. Sure. Whatever."

Samael turned to me. "You understand now."

"What? No, I don't. I don't understand anything," I protested. "Ask Caesarian if he knows where his mother is buried?"

Samael gazed at me with those strange milky eyes. "Please? Before you go, cover him?"

He turned and meandered off, sort of heading toward where Moriarity was working at the end of the fortress wall. The old man kept walking in small circles, then listening, as though for the sound of voices, then walking again. Or maybe his dementia had set in with a vengeance, and he had no idea where he was or where he was going. I'd take care of him in a few minutes.

When he was far enough away that he couldn't hear me, I quietly said, "He's blind. How could he find this grave? It's out here in the middle of the flats, far away from the ruins."

Roberto stuffed the fabulous medallion in his pocket and stood up. "Did you know he was going to give me the medallion?"

"'Course not. How could I? I'm not a shabti."

"Yeah? How do you know?"

"Oh." That was a disturbing possibility. "Right. Point taken."

He shook his head and the four pentagrams dangling from his left ear flashed with sunlight. "Look at the dirt pile, Hal. It's fresh."

"You mean someone dug up the body this morning?"

"Or last night." Roberto reached down and grabbed a handful of the dirt to rub it between his fingers. "See how the dirt is a darker color? It was just turned over not long ago."

My gaze was drawn back to the skeleton that lay in the grave. Ancient Egyptians buried their dead with great care. This young man had been buried with nothing. Even if it were Caesarian, there was no way to identify him. Just as his enemy had intended.

Grief tightened my chest. Cleo had always spoken of her first son with such love in her voice. "Help me cover him up, then we'll go help Samael get to Moriarity."

"Why does he want the skeleton covered again? Isn't the whole point out here to dig stuff up?"

"I don't think he wants anyone to know he dug this up. If he's the person who dug it. The excavation wasn't done scientifically. See how the hole is kind of oval? Archaeologists dig square holes. This was a haphazard act done by somebody who just wanted to get the dirt out fast."

"Maybe the old guy already knew it was here? Maybe he found it years ago?"

"And came back to look at it?"

Roberto rubbed his jaw. His sparse brown beard was improving. "If this burial was his personal secret, why would he tell us? We're nobodies. Less than nobodies. We're not even archaeologists."

"Maybe that's why."

As I started scooping dirt back into the hole, I looked down at the man below me. Caesarian had been seventeen when he'd died. His parents were dead. His younger half brothers and half sisters were about to be hauled off as prizes of war and given to Octavia, the sister of Gaius Julius, who was also Marcus Antonius' former wife. She would raise them as the royalty they were, but Rome would never let them forget that their parents were traitors.

I had often tried to imagine what it must have been like for them. Almost a year after their parents' deaths, the ten-year-old twins and six-year-old Ptolemy Philadephus were forced to march down the streets of Rome in chains as part of Gaius Julius' glorious anniversary celebration of his victory over their mother. A painted figure of their mother lying on her deathbed with an asp was followed by Gaius Julius in a magnificent purple cloak. Oddly absent at the anniversary gala was any reference to Antonius. It was already as though he had not existed at all. Over and over again for the rest of their lives, the three children would be bombarded with Roman propaganda, forced to see plays portraying their parents as despicable deviants, plays re-enacting their parents' suicides. By the time they were twenty or thirty, did they actually believe their parents had been evil people?

When we'd finished covering up the skeleton, I bent down and lightly rested my hand atop the dirt pile. In my mind, I told Caesarian the other side of the story, told him that *I* mourned him, and thousands before me had mourned him. Maybe, after all, that was a historian's prime directive? Learn the truth and tell the dead, so they could rest easier.

Roberto watched me with a curious expression. He'd gotten sunburned on our hike to and from Samael's remote cave, and his freckles seemed larger and darker. "Is that, like, a Vulcan mind-meld?"

A smile came to my face. "Yeah. Pretty much. Come on, I'm sure Moriarity is waiting. And Samael is never going to get there without our help."

We dusted our hands off on our jeans and headed for the blind old man wandering aimlessly across the desert.

CHAPTER TWENTY-NINE

With Samael holding onto my arm, I led him at a slow walk toward where Moriarity stood looking down at two students kneeling in the bottom of the shallow excavation. The other eight students had gone to a nearby pit to start digging. Both of the men with Moriarity appeared to be in their mid-twenties. One had short sandy-colored hair. The other was a dyed platinum blond with black roots.

Moriarity didn't even glance at us until we stopped two paces away, then he turned and asked, "Did you find something out there?"

"Just murex shells," I lied.

Samael's fingers dug into my arm, as though to thank me for lying.

Moriarity scanned my face with shining black eyes, looked out in the direction of the covered-up grave, then back at me. "Are you sure?"

"Yeah, why?"

After studying Roberto and Samael, Moriarity gestured to the students in the pit. "Jonathan Jones and Mike Bates, this is Hal Stevens and Robert Dally. These are the kids I told you about from Colorado. Jonathan and Mike are graduate students. Their job today is to teach you boys the fundamentals of excavation."

"Sure," Mike said, but looked a little annoyed at being saddled with that task when there were far more interesting things to do. "Why don't you both climb down here, grab a trowel, and we'll get started."

Moriarity nodded. "Samael and I need to find an old excavation unit. Let me know if you have any problems. Otherwise, I'll see you at the cook tent for lunch, and you can update me on the boys' progress."

"Will do, boss man," Bates replied.

Moriarity grabbed Samael's arm and dragged the elder away, speaking to him in a hushed voice.

"What was that about?" I asked.

Mike Bates shook his head. He was tall and wiry. Sandy hair flew around his oversize ears. "I don't know, but he was not happy that Samael took you two out there. Was that really all you found? Murex shells?"

"Yeah," Roberto said. "They're everywhere. You must have been out there a hundred times. Didn't you see them?"

Bates had been working hard this morning, because sweat drenched his bulbous nose. "No, that part of the site is absolutely off-limits to everyone. Moriarity is saving it to be excavated years from now, when archaeological tools and techniques are better. He wants it left undisturbed."

Jones climbed out of the pit and stared me down with hard brown eyes. He had a physique like Arnold Schwarzenegger, made more impressive by the stretched-to-the-max synthetic blue shorts and muscle shirt he wore. I actually flinched and took a step backward. "And yet you two were out there, and with Samael, no less."

"What do you mean, 'with Samael no less'?"

In an almost theatrical manner, Jones shook dyed platinum hair out of his eyes, before answering, "That old man is as famous as you can get in this part of the world. In archaeological circles he's called the Oracle of Egypt. He has a supernatural ability to find sites. He's a legend."

"More like a prophet," Bates corrected. "I'd give anything if he'd take me by the arm and lead me out across a site. Like he did *you two*."

Mystified by their hostility, I threw up my hands in surrender. "Hey, it wasn't our fault. We didn't know it was off-limits, and Samael asked us to follow him out there. What were we supposed to do, say no? Would you have?"

Bates' fierce expression tightened. "I—"

"So," Roberto interrupted. "Do you have a PhD?"

"I'm a graduate student working on my PhD, brainless. Right now I just have a master's degree."

"Oh. Okay. So I guess that means we can't call you Doctor Bates. We just have to call Master Bates, right?"

"You little . . ."

When Bates took a threatening step toward Roberto, Jones grabbed his shoulder and pulled him back. "Listen, kids. Mike is trying to save you a lot of grief. If Moriarity finds you out there by yourselves, he'll throw you off the excavation."

"No joke?" Roberto asked. "He'd actually kick us off the excavation for going out there by ourselves?"

"No doubt about it. Two years ago a woman from the University of Chicago sneaked out there in the middle of the night. It was more of a prank than anything, but she ran straight into Dr. Moriarity who was excavating by himself in the moonlight. The next morning, he put her in a Jeep and drove straight to Port Said, where he dumped her at the airport without so much as a word of goodbye. Carla still hates his guts."

"Well, that's not surprising," Roberto commented. "Dr. Who is kind of a psycho."

"Hey!" Jones half shouted. "The guy chairs my dissertation committee, okay? I don't want to hear your trash talk, *fairy boy.*" He flicked his left ear to demonstrate that he was referring to Roberto's earring.

"Yeah, whatever."

As usual, I was seeing their story play out in my mind, watching Moriarity bent over in the darkness, pulling dirt back with his trowel when something gleamed silver. "Can you excavate in moonlight? It seems like you'd miss a lot."

Bates and Jones exchanged a knowing look—as though the answer was obvious—but neither wanted to be quoted later.

After a few seconds of silence, I asked, "So, I've been wondering about the location of the Great Horus Road. Is it close to here?"

Jones rolled his eyes. "Christ, you are buffoons, just like Moriarity said. Look down. You're standing right in the middle of it. It ran in

front of the fortress wall. That's why there's a gatehouse over there."
He flung an arm to point at the massive brick structure we'd seen
earlier. "That's how military forces entered Pelusium. They came up
the road and turned in at the gate. Get it?"

"Thanks. I should have thought of that."

Jones shook his head as though really upset with my stupidity.
"Now come here, *boys*." He reached down, picked up two trowels and
shoved them at us. "Climb in here. Let's get started. Once Mike and
I have taught you the basics, we can return to our own excavation
unit where there is actually something important going on."

Roberto jumped down first and looked around. The unit stretched
about ten feet across and ten wide. "What are we excavating? I don't
see any artifacts."

"That's right, bright *boy*," Jones said. "This three-by-three-meter
unit is a sterile pit. There's nothing in it. You don't think Moriarity
would actually let you two dunces excavate archaeology on your first
day, do you?"

Bristling over the way he kept stressing the word *boy*, I clenched
my jaw to keep from saying something I'd regret. These guys really
resented having to spend the morning with us. Had Moriarity actually told them we were buffoons?

Of course, when it came to archaeology, we were. But I still didn't
like being described that way.

Roberto seemed oblivious to the general hostility. He was preoc-
cupied examining Jones' shorts, which were made of the kind of
shiny material that would survive a thousand years of sun and dust
storms and still reveal that he had no dick.

In a genuinely concerned voice, Roberto said, "*Dang*, bro, if I were
you, I'd seriously think about strapping on a tampo—"

"*Not now*," I interrupted.

Roberto reluctantly closed his mouth and pretended to be squinting out at the field crews scattered across the ancient site. Metallic
clangs sounded as tools were laid out for the day's work.

"What was he going to say?" Jones asked in a hostile voice. His
face had gone bright red, which contrasted sharply with his dyed
hair. He was clenching and unclenching his fists, as though he had a

pretty good idea what Roberto was about to say. Probably because Roberto was not the first person to notice his "shortcomings."

"Nothing," I replied. "We didn't have a chance to grab our own dig kit this morning. Do you have brushes and dental picks we can borrow?"

"The only thing you'll need today is trowels." Jones flung an arm out to point to the three-by-three-meter unit. *"Now get in the pit."*

CHAPTER THIRTY

By the time the lunch bell clanged, Roberto and I had excavated a ten-centimeter-deep level in the designated three-by-three-meter unit, which means we'd carefully used our trowels to scrape out a roughly ten-foot-square hole, four inches deep, with absolutely nothing in it. But we'd kept the pit walls straight and square, and learned to use our trowels like an artist rather than a bricklayer. Just before Jones and Bates left us alone to move to their own unit, they had not so politely explained that we were no longer to use terms like inches and feet to describe measurements, because it meant we were "stupid pricks."

Wiping my forehead on my sleeve, I gazed out across the site. As a couple hundred people started moving slowly toward the cook tent, dust puffed beneath their feet and drifted across the majestic ruins of the ancient city. We'd been hearing snippets of conversation all day, but now it picked up, punctuated by laughter.

"I'm hungry. This is hard work," Roberto said.

Standing up, he stretched his tired back muscles. As his thin brown beard grew out to meet his chin-length hair, it covered his biggest freckles, leaving his blue eyes as the centerpiece of his triangular face. Though it was wispy, the beard made him look older, maybe eighteen or nineteen. His sweat-soaked white T-shirt, like my blue T-shirt, was covered with windblown dust and stuck to his chest.

Roberto climbed out of the pit and extended a hand to help pull me up. I took it gratefully. "I'm hungry, too. Let's go eat so we can come back here and excavate more nothing."

"Yeah, I have to admit, archaeology isn't nearly as interesting as I thought it would be. I got over my sandbox fetish when I was six."

Every time I swallowed, my teeth grated on sand. "Well, I'm sure it would disturb someone if we accidentally screwed up the find of the century."

"You think?"

Our back dirt pile—all the sand we'd dug from the pit—had been steadily growing until now it was a meter tall. Jones and Bates had informed us that if we were bright we'd dump the sand on the west side of the pit so that the pile would cast a shadow over us in the afternoon. Shade, after all, was a valuable commodity out here. We veered around it and headed for lunch.

Roberto led the way along the face of the fortress wall, which had just started to cast a narrow shadow. As we trudged through the sand, I noticed that the thick wall radiated cool air, and wondered if the eroding bricks sucked moisture up from the water table, absorbed it and, through evaporation, kept the wall cooler than the surrounding air temperature? It made me think of the old evaporation coolers people in Colorado had shoved into their windows before the advent of modern air-conditioning.

By the time we'd grabbed plates and bottles of water from the cook tent, and stepped into the food line, all the tables were stuffed with crewmembers from across the huge site. People who couldn't find a chair wandered off to slump down with their plates in any shade they could find, usually beside a tent. I saw Jones and Bates sitting at the far end of the table—the same table where Moriarity and Corbelle sat across from each other, wearing unpleasant expressions. Moriarity was shaking a finger in Corbelle's face.

Roberto, who was ahead me in line, turned to say, "Where are we going to go sit?"

"As far away from Jones and Bates as possible."

As the line pushed forward, the spicy fragrance of the food filled the afternoon.

I turned to the redhead, about twenty or twenty-one, who stood behind me. She wore a canvas hat pulled down tight against the breeze. "Excuse me, can you tell me what we're having for lunch?"

She had a turned-up nose and green eyes. "That's taamiyya. It's deep fried patties made of fava bean paste and green herbs. You're new here, aren't you?"

"Yeah, we just arrived from Colorado where it was still snowing. It's an adjustment. The heat, I mean."

She smiled, "I'm Sarah Wadsworth. From Arizona originally, though I'm at McGill University in Canada. Pelusium temps are pretty much like Phoenix, though it's more humid here, because we're so close to the ocean. So, I sort of came pre-adjusted." She pointed. "Do you see the salad at the end of the table? There's a dish right beside it filled with tahini, a sauce made from sesame paste. Try it. It's really good. Has a cooling effect."

"Okay, thanks. I'm Hal Stevens. From Colorado."

I started to turn back around, but she said, "I've heard we're having tagine for dinner. You'll like that dish."

"Really? What is it?"

"Pigeons stuffed with rice and spices, then cooked in a stew with onions and tomatoes. It's good. Trust me." When I started to turn around, she stopped me again, asking, "So if you're from Colorado, you must be working with James Moriarity." She sounded excited by that prospect.

"Yeah."

"You're lucky. What's he like? I almost went to CSU just so I could study with him."

The last thing I needed was for word to get around the site that I thought Moriarity was a murdering maniac and maybe even the high priest of a demonic cult in Denver, so I said, "I don't know him very well yet. This is our first day onsite with him. He seems okay."

"Yeah, it's his wife who's the scary one."

"Really?"

"Oh, wow, yeah. You'll see. Haven't you ever met Dr. Mallawi?"

"Sure, a few times, but we've never really talked."

"If you're smart, you'll try not to. She's loves embarrassing students in front of the entire field crew. Don't get in her sights, Hal Stevens. You'll regret it. She's been sick a lot, though. So maybe you won't have to worry."

"Sick?"

"Yeah, really sick. One of LaSalle's interns joked that she was being poisoned by a graduate student who really hates her guts. But somebody else said she's having a bad pregnancy."

"She's pregnant?"

Sarah shrugged. "Guess so."

A haunted sensation crept through me. How many months pregnant was she? I kept thinking about Cleo saying she didn't want to be reborn . . . that wasn't Cleopatra in her womb, was it?

When we finally reached the table where the food was spread out, Roberto started filling his plate. Taking a piece of pocket bread, he loaded it with taamiyya patties, then moved on to the salad.

I did the same while I thought about Sophia's unborn child.

We stepped out of the line and stood looking around for a place to sit down.

Roberto said, "Where to?"

"I was thinking—"

"I'm sorry," Sarah quietly interrupted. "Would you mind if I join you?"

"Not at all," I said. "Sarah, this is Robert Dally. Roberto this is Sarah Wadsworth from Arizona."

"Hey, Sarah."

"Hi, Robert."

Roberto led the way, weaving around groups of people who stood talking, or sitting together on the ground, to get to our tent at the far western side of the field camp. A few curious looks were cast our way, but nothing unusual.

In front of our tent, a narrow strip of shade about twenty centimeters wide had formed, so we slumped down in it and started eating.

I took a big bite out of my taamiyya and concentrated on tasting the different flavors. "Umm, good."

Around a mouthful, Roberto said, "Falafel, but spicier. Not bad. Don't these people believe in eating meat?"

Sarah said, "Give it time, Robert. Egyptian food grows on you."

"Yeah, well, I'm a buffalo steak kind of guy. Birdseed isn't exactly my cup of tea," Roberto noted.

"You should have tried the tahini," I pointed to the sauce on my salad. "Sarah recommended it, and it's great."

Roberto leaned over to get a closer look at the sauce. "What's it taste like?"

"Ground sesame seeds."

"When you find a sauce that tastes like hamburger, I'm in."

Sarah tucked a lock of shoulder-length red hair behind her ear and unscrewed her water bottle to take a drink. "Don't you guys have hats? The afternoons out here can be brutal, and you're already beet red, Robert. That's exactly how I looked after two days in the sun here. Be smarter than me."

"Yeah, I'll take it this afternoon. Moriarity dragged us away before dawn this morning. We didn't have time to get anything we needed."

"He's probably in a rush. We work ten-fours out here. Ten days on and four days off. Our ten-day ends tomorrow."

"So everybody will be leaving tomorrow night?"

She nodded as she bit into her lunch. Around a half-chewed mouthful, she said, "Everybody except LaSalle. She never leaves the site. She spends the entire time excavating by herself until we get back."

Sarah was staring up at Roberto with appreciative eyes, smiling, which made Roberto squirm slightly. He wasn't accustomed to female attention. At least not positive attention.

"So you're in Fort Collins, Colorado, right?" she asked, making conversation.

"Georgetown," Roberto said. "Up in the mountains to the west."

Sarah frowned as though puzzled. "How far is that from Fort Collins? Do you have to drive back and forth every day?"

"Forty-five minutes, maybe an hour," Roberto answered. "I wouldn't drive it every day for all the money on earth. I-25 traffic is the stuff of nightmares."

"But don't you study with Dr. Moriarity at CSU?"

"God, no, I'm at Georgetown High. I'll be a senior next year."

"Ooooh." She drew out the word as though Roberto's status had just plummeted in her eyes. "I see. What about you, Hal?"

"The same." I used my sleeve to wipe tahini off my mouth.

"Really? You guys look older. I thought you were freshman in college, maybe even sophomores, like me. I've never seen high school students out here. At least, not students from America. Sometimes they bus Egyptian high school students out here to take a look at the site, but not often. How did you get on Moriarity's crew? He only brings graduate students here, and very few of those."

Roberto used his chin to gesture to Jones and Bates, who had finished lunch and were headed back out toward their excavation unit on the far end of the fortress wall. Jones threw his massive shoulders around like the Hulk. "Like Master Bates and the penile-ly deprived Jones?"

Sarah squelched a smile. "Yeah, well, Mike and Jonathan are at the bottom of Moriarity's totem pole out here. More like the professor's slaves than graduate students. For the past two summers they've gotten stuck with all the crap work. If somebody has to drive into town for toilet paper, they get the job."

Roberto chewed and swallowed. I suspected he was mulling over that new information, probably thinking it explained a lot. I, on the other hand was contemplating the fact that they were both at CSU, both his students, and both trying hard to work their way up in his hierarchy so they stopped being saddled with all the crap work. How far, I wondered, would they go for him?

I'm sure it was just my overactive imagination, but I couldn't help wondering if they weren't temple lackeys in an ancient Egyptian cult in Denver, duty-bound to carry out the orders of the high priest. Which was a crazy thought, but until I knew who or what had killed Cleo, paranoia was going to be my best friend. Better safe than sorry.

"So, are you part of Dr. Corbelle's crew?" I asked.

"I am. We've been here for about two weeks."

"You like her?"

"Oh, yeah, LaSalle is great. She worked at Tanis, you know? I mean, she's a taskmaster. If she tells you to do something, she means now, not in two minutes. But if you watch and listen to her, you learn a lot."

"What are you excavating?"

She lifted a hand and pointed to the east. "A spectacular Roman bath with polychrome mosaic floors. This is only the second bath found at Pelusium."

"Really? And this was a big city, right?" Roberto said. "There must have been a lot of really filthy people."

Sarah squinted, not quite sure if he was serious or joking. "So, are you, like, archaeologically challenged?"

"More like completely clueless."

She stared at him. "Wow. Historical morons are rare in this circle. You're more interesting than I thought."

"Yeah, I don't know how you missed that earlier."

"When you get off work today, why don't you come over? I'll show you around the bath."

"Thanks. We'll try to do that."

"Well, I should go find out what's happening with the rest of the crew. See you two later, I hope."

When we were alone, I said, "Sarah was definitely giving you the eye, bro."

Roberto stuffed the last chunk of food into his mouth and chewed. "Yeah, well, I'm not interested in any woman who wants to spend all of her time in an old bathroom. Besides, she has to be nineteen. Why would she be interested in me"?

"Pedophilia?"

Roberto grinned as he dusted the crumbs off his hands and reached for his water bottle. After taking a long drink, he wiped his mouth on the arm, and his gaze drifted over the desert and the ruins, before settling on the fortress wall. The shadow on the eastern side was getting longer, looking more and more inviting. "Hal, you ever going to tell me what really happened in that cave?"

The sudden change of topics made me blink. My cheeks went hot. "Not unless I have to."

"You saw something, didn't you? The demon?"

"No, and I didn't actually *see* anything. But there was . . ." How did I describe it without sounding totally crazy? "A presence. Something old and powerful. But not evil. I think it was just curious about me."

"It scared you, though. When you crawled out and starting shoving dirt over the hole, I knew you thought something might crawl out after you."

Taking another drink of water, I swallowed slowly, deciding what I should tell him. "The pyramid of weapons really set off my imagination. It felt alive, as though each spear, sword, and dagger held the soul of a soldier just waiting for the command to rise and fight again."

"A command from the thing in the cave?"

A tingle went up my spine. "You just scared the holy hell out of me. I hadn't thought of that."

Roberto suddenly sat up straighter. When I turned to see what he was looking at, I saw Cleo's Aunt Sophia standing talking with Sarah Wadsworth. A tall black-haired woman with a narrow waist and long legs, she wore a long-sleeved white shirt and chinos. Dr. Mallawi kept nodding at whatever Sarah was saying, but her gaze was fixed squarely on me and Roberto.

"Are they talking about us?"

"Looks like it."

When she walked away from Sarah, Dr. Mallawi headed straight for us.

"Here she comes," Roberto said. "What do you think she wants?"

"To engage us in charming conversation?"

Dr. Mallawi tramped across the sand with her head down. She looked so much like Cleo that it was heartbreaking for me. I inhaled a deep breath and held it in my lungs for a few seconds, hoping the emptiness filling me up would go away.

Dr. Mallawi stopped a couple of paces away, and said, "How are you two doing? I understand you're learning to excavate?" She had just a slight accent.

"Yeah, it's fun. Good to see you again, Dr. Mallawi."

"And you, Robert. Are you having fun?"

Roberto replied, "Oh, yeah, hot sandboxes are very interesting to me. Ever since I was three, I've had this thing——"

"Hal," she interrupted in a clipped voice. "I need to ask you for the bagsu."

My smile vanished in a heartbeat. "It's in our tent. Buried in my pack."

"Go find it, please?"

She pointed to the tent, as though expecting me to instantly rise and obey her orders.

The canvas tent flaps were tied closed. Had we done that before we'd left this morning? I thought about trying to delay this, but I didn't know how to get away with it. I'd told Moriarity I had the dagger, and he'd told Sophia. This moment has been inevitable. The question was what was I going to do after I produced the dagger? There was no way I was just handing it over to her or anyone else.

Rising, I went to kneel in front of the door and begin untying the flaps. As soon as I threw them back, my heart leaped in my chest. "Oh, my God! Not again."

"What?" Roberto jumped up and ran to look inside the tent. All of our belongings had been ripped from our packs and strewn across our sleeping bags. "Someone broke into our tent and rifled through our packs!" he cried. "Who would do that?"

I ducked into the tent and started sorting through the mess. While I did, my thoughts were churning.

"Get out of my way!" Dr. Mallawi shoved Roberto aside, and forced her way into our tent.

"I don't see it anywhere!" I said. "It's gone!"

She started throwing our belongings around. In self-defense, I grabbed my dig kit and our hats and crawled outside.

Roberto stood casually in front of me, chewing on a hangnail. After he'd ripped it off and spat it out, he gave me a sly smile, and said a little too loudly, "Goddamn it, this is the third time someone has fingered my condoms trying to find that stupid dagger. It's just a freaking old knife."

I handed him his Colorado Rockies baseball cap, which he flipped onto his head. I'd brought a roll-up canvas hat with a six-inch brim. As I unrolled it, Dr. Mallawi crawled out of the tent and stood up with her green eyes blazing. The wind buffeted her white sleeves.

"Jim told me you were probably carrying the dagger with you at all times. I don't know why I fell for this little charade of yours. I want it right now." She held out her hand.

"What charade?"

"Give it to me!"

I pointed a finger in her face. "You'd better search the field crews out here to find that dagger, or your little cult in Denver is going to be really upset that you didn't put it back in the grave."

"What cult in Denver?"

"I'm tired of people jerking us around! Come on, Hal," Roberto said indignantly. "Let's grab another bottle of water from the cook tent and go back to our sandbox."

He stalked away so fast I had to trot to catch up.

When we were twenty paces away, he said, "Good thinking, but that only bought you a few hours, Hal."

I shook my head. "I didn't do it, Roberto."

"You didn't empty our packs onto the floor?"

"No."

"No shit? You were the last person in the tent this morning. I just assumed . . . A delaying tactic, you know?"

"Yeah, it would have been a smart thing to do. Wish I'd thought of it."

"Well, if you didn't do it, who did?"

My thoughts returned, once again, to Samael. I didn't see him anywhere in camp. I looked over my shoulder at his tent just a few paces away. The mesh front was zipped closed to keep insects out, but the flaps were tied open. I thought I saw a body stretched out on a blanket inside. Had he decided to take a nap during the heat of the day?

Roberto followed my gaze. "You think he did it?"

"Maybe."

Roberto scratched his wispy beard as though it itched. "My money is on Dr. Mallawi. I think she ransacked our tent while we were excavating."

I considered the possibility. "I'm not ruling it out, but when she crawled into the tent with me, her expression was genuinely surprised. I don't think she's responsible."

Roberto waved a hand at the field crews walking across the site. "Well, there are around two hundred other possibilities. Plus one."

I glanced at him. Sweat-soaked brown hair dangled around his sunburned face. "What do you mean? Plus one?"

Quietly, he said. "If it was a demon that emptied our packs in Samael's cave, who's to say it didn't follow us here and do it again?"

I frowned at the chunk of ancient green glass sparkling in the sunlight in front of me. "Right."

CHAPTER THIRTY-ONE

Around seven, the dinner bell clanged, and the field crews began to climb out of pits and wipe their sweaty faces on their sleeves. Conversation and laughter erupted as people stopped work for the day and moved toward the tents, their faces shining in the deep amber gleam cast by the setting sun. As the day cooled off, the scent of the marshes became stronger, filling the air with the fragrances of water and greenery.

My gaze was on Moriarity and Mallawi who stood about fifty paces away with Samael and three Egyptian laborers. The hunchbacked elder was standing in the bottom of a meter-deep unit, smiling beatifically, but no one was paying him the slightest attention. Moriarity and Mallawi were engaged in a heated conversation. Mallawi kept waving her arms at her husband, as though to drive home some point.

Roberto, who sat cross-legged on the far end of our excavation unit, said, "Dear God, tell me it's quitting time?"

"Yeah, looks like our first day as archaeologists is over. Let's pack our tools in the dig kit and head for our tent."

"Great. I've had enough fun excavating hot sand to last me a lifetime." He handed me his trowel, and jumped out of our pit. As he dusted off his pants, he said, "Don't these people know that a work day is 8 to 5?"

I tucked his trowel into my kit, along with mine, and reached for the other tools. "They only have one month here, Roberto. I guess they work as long as they have light."

"Yeah, well, this qualifies as an Asian sweatshop."

While I finished packing my brushes and dental tools, I watched

Moriarity and Mallawi walk purposefully for one of the ramadas where the artifacts were bagged for transport. They'd left Samael and the three laborers by the pit to clean up. Tools clattered as they put them away.

Samael climbed out of the pit and slowly turned around as though getting his bearings, maybe from the constant sea breeze blowing in off the ocean, then he cocked his ear to listen for voices. The laborers seemed afraid of him. They'd moved a few paces away and stood whispering to each other, while they cast uneasy glances at Samael. *The Oracle of Egypt.*

Alone, Samael started making his way across the site, using his walking stick to steady his steps.

Roberto said, "Where's he going? There's nothing out there."

"I think he needs help finding his way."

"Okay, why don't you give me the dig kit, and I'll take it back to our tent and stow it. Then I'll meet you at the cook tent."

"Sounds good. See you there."

I handed Roberto the pack and climbed out of our unit. After I dusted off my pants, I trotted toward Samael.

When the elder heard my approaching footsteps, he stopped and stared at me with those eerie white eyes. "There you are."

"Yes, sir, I thought you might need help getting to dinner."

He gave me a toothless smile. "Not yet. Come look, please?"

"Did you find something?"

"Yes. At the unit dug by James and Sophia."

I noticed that the three other laborers had sat down on the rim of the excavation pit and started smoking cigarettes.

When we arrived, one of the men smiled at me with rotted teeth and extended a hand to the excavation. "See? Look. Samael found."

I knelt and frowned down at the entwined skeletons. Their lower bodies were covered by a limestone stela: a large inscribed tablet. About one meter wide and two meters long, it must weigh two hundred pounds. It was a beautiful thing, but what struck me was the Greek word on the stela: *Kleopatra.*

I suddenly seemed to be looking down at myself from a great height, and the magnificent city of Per Amun was alive below me, bustling, both branches of the impossibly blue Nile filled with barges and fishing boats. The scents of lime-laden dust and lemons rode the breeze as the two bodies were placed in the grave.

"Can I jump down to get a better look?"

Samael said, "Carefully, yes."

I lowered myself into the rectangular pit and studied the stela. The Queen of Egypt, dressed in male garb, stood on the right side of the stone, offering a baby to the goddess Isis. Though this stela was much larger, I'd seen photos in a book that showed a similar stela in the Cairo Museum. The museum's stela had been inscribed during the first few months of Cleopatra's reign, and was the oldest evidence of her rulership. At the time she had shared the throne with her brother, though his name was absent on both this stela and the one in the Cairo Museum.

My heartbeat sped up when I shifted my gaze to the entwined skeletons. The large skeleton on the right had his arms around the small skeleton, which I assumed was a woman.

"What did Dr. Moriarity and Dr. Mallawi think about this?"

The laborers watched me with half-squinted eyes. They'd risen and begun collecting their tools.

Rotted teeth said, "They argue. She thinks it is two women. He don't."

"Does this part of the site date to the first century BC?"

"Yes."

Samael stared down at the skeletons with such an expression of love, his wrinkles twisted into odd cavernous lines. "Per Amun is where it began for the Ptolemies, you know? Her most magnificent relative was Alexander the Great. After his death in 323 BC, Alexander's general, Ptolemy I, seized Egypt. In 321, Ptolemy kidnapped Alexander's body and brought it here to Pelusium. In 102, Cleopatra III defeated her brother and won Egypt here. And in 48, Cleopatra VII launched the rebellion here that would lead her to become the Queen of all Egypt. So many moments in her family history were tied to this city. It was very dear to her."

"Then you think more of her children may be buried in Pelusium?"

Samael gave me a toothless smile. "She would not have buried her loved ones in Alexandria out of fear that those graves would be obliterated by her enemies. Or worse, the bodies exhumed to be paraded through the streets of Rome as symbols of Octavian's victory."

"Which is exactly what would have happened. Octavian hated her."

Samael gestured to the skeletons. "Do you see that hand? The larger skeleton's left hand? That's where we found it."

The dagger. He doesn't want to mention it in front of others.

I tried to imagine how the dagger would have lain in the skeletal fist. The fist had been wrenched into a strange unnatural angle, which meant the hand had been deliberately twisted to hold the dagger in a certain way.

"So he was a Sem priest?"

Samael's old head tottered on the frail stem of his neck. He looked like he was about to faint from heat prostration. "No. Come, now. Let us leave the Ka souls in peace and find water. Been a hot day."

He waved for me to come out of the pit, which I did not want to do. If this wasn't the burial of the Sem priest, as Moriarity believed, then the small skeleton in front of me might be Cleopatra. If it was . . . Could the larger skeleton be Marcus Antonius? Had they been buried together after all, as she'd requested? *If so, I need to place the dagger in the grave beside the woman.*

Swallowing hard, I climbed out of the pit and gripped Samael's elbow. As I guided him toward the cook tent, I said, "Samael, have you heard their voices? Is it possible that the bodies are Cleopatra and Antonius?"

He shook his head. "It's two women."

Though I had the urge to rush, I couldn't. Samael needed me to walk slowly. He was swaying on his feet, as though completely exhausted by the day's labors. "Why did Dr. Moriarity think it was a man and a woman?"

Releasing my arm, he touched his forehead. "James said the larger skeleton had a male brow ridge. Sophia disagreed. She wished to ask Dr. Corbelle to look at skeletons. He didn't want to."

"Why would they ask Dr. Corbelle?"

"They are archaeologists. Corbelle is a biological anthropologist. She knows more about skeletal remains than they do."

As the mystery deepened, my historical imagination started running wild. After Antonius' death Cleopatra had asked for and obtained permission from Gaius Julius to prepare Antonius' body for burial. She spent two days purifying his body with oils of cedar and cinnamon. Then, on August 3rd, 30 BC, she begged that she be allowed to bury Antonius herself, a request Gaius Julius granted.

"Plutarch wrote that Cleopatra buried Antonius with her own hands, feverishly, lavishly."

"Yes, that's right. Iras and I helped her. I have forgotten many things from that time, but not that terrible day. Afterward, she tried to starve herself to death. It was heartbreaking. When Gaius Julius discovered she was ill and refusing to eat, he sent soldiers to watch over her every move, and threatened her children if she tried to kill herself."

"And she pleaded for an audience with Gaius Julius, didn't she?" This discussion was so fascinating I couldn't take my eyes from the old man.

"Yes. He came. On August 8th, Cleopatra found herself face-to-face, for the first time in her life, with her mortal enemy. Six years younger than she, Gaius Julius was about five-foot-seven with blond hair. He was so uneasy in her presence, he spent the entire time squirming and shifting. She asked only one thing: 'Grudge me not burial with him.' She wanted only to rest with Antonius."

The old man had tears in his voice, as though seeing it all again in his memory.

"Plutarch wrote that he made her no promises."

"True. Just before she died, she'd begged the soldier, Epaphroditus, to carry one final letter to him, asking again to be buried with Antonius."

I watched his wrinkles deepen as he closed his eyes against emotion.

"Was she buried with Antonius?"

A pained smile came to his face. "By that time, I was dead. I do remember that before Antonius' death, she had consulted with a handful of merchants about transporting the bodies of her loved ones to safe places. She fully expected they would all be murdered and paraded through the streets of Rome. She would have done anything to avoid that humiliation."

That was an interesting detail, if true. According to Plutarch, Gaius Julius honored her request and buried her with royal splendor beside Antonius in the center of Alexandria adjacent to a temple of Isis. Which would have been strange, indeed. Why would Gaius Julius go to such lengths to create a monument to Cleopatra and Marcus Antonius that would last for centuries, and then go to even more extraordinary lengths to erase them both from every historical record? Plutarch recorded that Alexandrian priests came to Gaius Julius to offer him 2,000 talents, an extraordinary sum, to preserve the many statues of Cleopatra that adorned the city. The only reason they would have made that request was if those statues were being systematically destroyed by Gaius Julius or his soldiers. The soon-to-be emperor began rewriting history even before her death, but afterward he was in a hurry to get rid of the evidence. He dedicated himself to making certain her name and beautiful face were forgotten. So a monument seemed extremely unlikely.

As we walked, Samael's shuffling feet created an erratic rhythm in the sand. He was holding tightly to my arm, his fingers digging into my flesh. This must be hard for him. He'd been on his feet for most of the day. At the cook tent, people had already started to line up. The benches at the tables were filling fast. By the time we got through the dinner line with our plates, there would be no places to sit, just like lunch. The spicy scent of the tagine wafted on the breeze, making my empty stomach growl.

I looked around for Dr. Corbelle. I didn't see her, or most of her crew. They'd probably gone through the line first and were already gone. Except for Sarah, who sat at the far table with Moriarity, Bates, and Jones.

To the west, the sun perched like a brilliant red ball just above the horizon. Full darkness was an hour away, but that didn't give us much time to eat and go see the other excavations. Plus, I was really tired. I was eager to eat and go to bed. It was my turn to sleep first, for which I was really grateful. Though I'd be up at two am for my watch, I'd get a solid six hours of sleep.

As we neared the food line, I said, "Samael, could I ask you a question in confidence?"

The elder looked up at me. "Of course."

"You've been to the Island of the Two Flames. How did you get there?"

The wrinkles around his eyes deepened. He propped his walking stick and took another careful step forward. "There is a passageway."

"Where? Why couldn't you find it when you tried to take Dr. Moriarity?"

We had reached the food line. As I walked Samael past the people to get to the far end of the line, the scent of stale sweat rose. It had been a very hot day. I wondered how someone took a shower out here.

Samael exhaled a deep breath. "I could have."

"But I thought—"

"He wasn't ready."

The old man frowned blindly at the sand. He kept putting one foot in front of the other. It had been so long since I'd asked the question that I thought he wasn't going to answer, but then he softly said, "Why do you wish to go to the island of the dead?"

"I promised a friend—a dead friend who I loved very much—that I would help her get there."

Samael gently squeezed my arm. "I knew her, too, you know."

My head jerked around. "You knew Cleo?"

"Oh, yes. She was a sweet child. I played with her on this very site when she was young. She was very special and very dear to me."

"It never occurred to me . . . But of course, you must have known her. You worked with her father for years."

"Yes."

I licked my chapped lips, before I asked, "Did you believe she was the reborn Queen Cleopatra?"

"There was not a doubt in my heart. The instant I looked into her eyes, I recognized her. And she knew things about me and ancient Egypt that no child her age could possibly have known."

Before her death, I had always sort of believed Cleo. Then, afterward, I definitely believed her; but it was sobering to hear that the Oracle of Egypt believed her, as well.

As we neared the rear of the line, Roberto emerged from our tent and trotted toward us. He still wore his Colorado Rockies baseball cap. Brown hair stuck out at odd angles beneath the brim. I waited for him to arrive, then we stepped into the line and started slowly moving forward.

When we reached the table, I picked up a plate for Samael. "Can I fill your plate for you, Samael?"

"Thank you, yes. It's hard to hold a plate and keep my balance."

Roberto said, "Want me to fill your plate, Hal?"

"Sure, thanks, Roberto."

As I used tongs to place a pigeon on Samael's plate, the elder bowed his head. He seemed to be gazing at my hand while I spooned vegetables and sauce onto his plate. At the end of the table, a bread basket waited. The warm sweet fragrance told me it was teff bread. I put a roll on Samael's plate, and over my shoulder told Roberto, "Two rolls for me, please?"

"*No problemo,* bro."

Roberto had both plates balanced on his left arm while he scooped up food with his right hand. He'd given me two pigeons which I really appreciated. I was losing weight out here. Fast. But that meant I was always hungry.

I exited the line with Samael still holding tightly to my arm and looked around for a place to sit. From the far table, Dr. Moriarity stood up and waved at me.

"Over here, Hal. Jones and Bates are finished."

I could tell that Jones and Bates were not finished. Their plates were still half-full, but both rose and yielded their places. As they walked away, they gave me unpleasant glances.

I set Samael's plate down, then held his hand while he slid onto the bench and moved down to sit next to Sarah Wadsworth. She looked positively starstruck to be sitting next to the legendary old digger. When I slid in beside Samael, I moved down as far as I could. There was enough space, just barely, for Roberto's narrow butt. Setting both of our plates down, he crammed himself next to me and smiled across the table at Moriarity.

"I want you to know that we found absolutely nothing today."

Moriarity's brows lowered. "Of course not. That's why you're there. To practice digging up nothing."

"Well, tomorrow, could you throw in a few crappy artifacts and cover them up just so I can discover them?"

"No," Moriarity said with a grimace. "That's called 'salting' a site. It's unethical."

"Even in Arab culture?"

Moriarity forked a bite of pigeon into his mouth and chewed while he stared at Roberto. "In any culture. It's basic professional ethics."

Ripping open his roll, Roberto stuffed it with strips of pigeon, then strained the onions from the tagine sauce and mounded them on top the pigeon strips. Before he ate it, he dipped his sandwich into the tomato sauce, soaked it up and finally took a big bite. Red dripped down his chin, which he wiped off on his tan sleeve. "Hey, by the way, can I buy one of those potsherds with the wolves on them for my girlfriend Molly?"

"You have a girlfriend?" Moriarity sounded astonished. "Does she know that?"

"I'm going to give her the potsherd as an engagement present."

"I see. Which potsherd?"

"The one with the wolf bearing its fangs. I passed it on my way back to our tent."

Moriarity looked at the ramada in question and seemed to be trying to place which sherd Roberto meant. "That's not a wolf, it's a jackal."

"Whatever. The fangs are cool. Just like the hookers on Colfax Avenue in Denver. They have these fake fangs they wear. You know? If a guy thinks she's a vampire, he—"

"How do you know what hookers do on Colfax?" Moriarity scowled at him. "You're sixteen."

"Yeah, but thankfully I have degenerate friends."

The entire table had turned in our direction. Sarah, especially, seemed completely absorbed by Roberto's story. Her eyes were glowing. I was starting to like her. I figured it was to her credit that she could appreciate the debauched way Roberto's mind worked.

When Roberto looked at me, the four pentagrams dangling from his ear caught the sunset and blazed with a reddish fire. "What was in the pit Samael took you to see?"

Samael tried to answer, but he had a mouthful of teff bread, so I said, "The grave of Cleopatra and Marcus Antonius."

"What!" Roberto cried in shock. "Are you sure?"

"It's two skeletons with their arms wrapped around each other and a big plaque, a stela, over them that says Cleopatra in Greek. So, I think—"

"That is pure speculation." Moriarity's brows lowered thunderously. "At this point, all we know is we have two skeletons and an interesting stela."

"Any sign that they killed themselves?" Roberto had gone back to eating in earnest, shoveling food into his mouth, which he talked around with no apparent difficulty. "I mean, Antonius should have a sword cut on his ribs, right? He stabbed himself in the heart, didn't he?"

"'Course not. It's far more likely that he aimed too low and punctured his abdomen or guts. If so, he suffered greatly before the end."

"Really?"

"Of course. No one wants to die from peritonitis. As the gut juices leak out into the body cavity, it's horrifyingly painful."

"Good tip, thanks."

"That's why Roman generals didn't really like to kill themselves. They assigned the duty to one of their servants or trusted officers. In Antony's case, the man was named Eros."

"Then why didn't Eros kill him?"

"Honor. He committed suicide instead."

Roberto nodded. "Probably self-preservation. If he'd refused, Antony would have been really pissed."

Roberto chewed pigeon while staring blankly at Moriarity, his mind far away. I figured he was still dreaming of Colfax Avenue. It was the only possible explanation.

A quirky smile had come to Sarah's lips. I swear it looked like true love. Although, I had to admit, what I was interpreting as appreciation could just as easily be morbid fascination. That would be more typical of female responses to Roberto.

"Hey, Robert," Sarah said. "When you're finished eating, let me show you our excavation, okay? The Roman bath is beautiful. It'll only take a half hour. Unless you want to stay longer, and then my schedule is open."

Hope tinged that last sentence. Roberto noticed it, too. He gave her a slightly mystified squint, but said, "Yeah, sure. Hal and I have got the time."

Her face fell. She sighed and went back to eating tagine.

"I think I'll pass. I'm really tired. See you at the tent when you get back, Roberto."

"You sure?"

From the corner of my vision, I saw three Egyptian Army soldiers walking together along the fortress wall. I wondered if they took their dinner in a different place.

"Yeah, I'm sure. I'll see you back at the tent."

Since we'd left Colorado, we'd never been more than a few paces apart, and always within yelling distance in case one of us was in trouble. But Sarah's Roman bath couldn't be that far away, could it?

Roberto said, "I'll only be gone thirty minutes, Hal."

I tipped my water bottle and finished it to the last drop, then crushed the plastic in one hand and said, "Have fun."

CHAPTER THIRTY-TWO

After Sarah and Roberto left the table, Samael looked at me with shining white eyes.

His soft old voice was shaky. "This is one of those rare nights where you can feel Duat bleeding into this world."

"Can you?"

His head tottered in a nod. "Oh, yes. Ghosts and demons have slipped through the breach and walk all around us right now."

Accidentally swallowing a bite of pigeon whole, I had to force it down my throat, before saying, "Do you see them?"

"They are everywhere, Halloran." For a few seconds he closed his tired old eyes and rubbed them. "You must promise me something."

"Sure. What?"

He reached out, took my hand, and pressed something into it, then closed my fingers around it. Very quietly, he said, "When I was Charmion, she made a final request of me. She knew she would probably be resurrected, and if she was, she would need an army to take back her country. Please, now and then, add a weapon, for her army to come—"

Moriarity said, "I can't hear you, Samael. Could you speak louder, please?" He leaned across the table to get as close as possible to hear better.

Samael sucked his lips in over his toothless gums and sat that way for a time, before he replied, "Just telling Halloran that I must go to my tent. It has been a long day for me. Will you help me, Hal?"

"Happy to."

Rising, I waited for him to slide down the bench, then extended a hand to help him up. The old man held tight to my fingers, grunting as he rose to his feet.

"Wait." Moriarity stood up. "I'll take him, Hal. I need to speak with Samael."

For an instant, the old man went rigid, as though afraid. "Don't forget, Halloran. I won't always be here to remind you."

"I won't forget."

Moriarity walked over and pulled Samael's hand from my arm, then took him by the elbow. "Let's go to your tent where we can talk in private."

"I just thought Hal would like to see the grave," Samael defended. "I saw no harm in—"

"What did you tell him?"

"Nothing! I just . . ."

They walked off, leaving me standing alone, my mind already spinning hypotheses about their conspiracy of silence. What were they hiding? Opening my hand, I stared down at the gift Samael had given me. It was a stone amulet of the demon Ammut, the handmaiden of The Judgment. Her crocodile head was tilted up to stare at me.

"A prayer for justice. There are many such charms found here at the site. Tomorrow, I will find one for you to wear. It will protect you against destruction. Evil against evil. You see?"

But the amulet in my palm was not just some charm he'd found at the site. It was his personal magical protection. No doubt about it. The same leather cord. The same symbol. Why would he give me his amulet?

Slipping the cord around my neck, I tucked the amulet inside my shirt. Which, frankly, was a little terrifying. The entire table full of graduate students stared at me. They did not look happy to have me around. Probably because Jones and Bates had been telling unflattering stories about me and Roberto. Unfortunately, I suspected most of the stories were true. We were ignoramuses when it came to archaeology. To make matters worse, the legendary Samael seemed to gravitate toward us whenever he needed help, which apparently created a lot of envy among the crews.

After I'd walked a short distance away, I heard heated conversations break out. My name was passed around, as well as Roberto's, and the tones of the speakers' voices were none too pleasant.

I didn't care.

Twilight was settling over the delta, bringing with it the scent of the sea and the lush green fragrance of the marshes. Though I was really tired, I felt better after dinner, so I headed out into the forbidden part of the site. No one tried to stop me, which I found mildly interesting. Either no one saw me, or they wanted me to get into trouble. I'm sure it would have pleased quite a few of the graduate students if Moriarity threw me into a Jeep and drove straight to Port Said to dump me at the airport.

As I picked my way across the sand, trying to remember the route Samael had used to find the Caesarian grave, I worried about how fast darkness fell out here. In Colorado, twilight hung over the peaks for ninety minutes to a couple of hours, depending upon the time of year. Here it seemed to fall like a hurled rock. The tents already blazed as lanterns were switched on, which gave the field camp a soft glow. After about fifteen minutes of wandering aimlessly, I saw the temple ahead of me. At this time of night, it looked like a big black circle floating in a gray ocean of sand.

Trudging onward, the stone steps materialized in the twilight.

When I arrived, I discovered that the interior of the temple was not nearly as dark as it had looked from a distance. I didn't even need my flashlight yet. If I waited until I was in the bottom, the approach to the Kingdom of Osiris, before I pulled my flashlight from my pocket and switched it on, there was a good chance no one in camp would be able to see the gleam.

I took the stairs down one at a time. Unlike mornings, the steps were not slick with dew, but dry and warm from the heat of the day. When my hiking boot hit the floor of the temple, I heaved a sigh of relief. Empty and unbelievably quiet, I felt as though I'd stepped into another world, a magical place where the ghosts of ancient Egyptians reverently moved around me, going about their sacred duties to the gods. Whispers—almost not there—wafted through the temple air, along with the faint scent of something sweet and exotic. Sandalwood? Myrrh? Samael's words about Duat bleeding into this world rang in my ears. I couldn't get his words about Charmion out of my mind. It finally occurred to me that Samael had wanted me, and me alone, to go into the demon cave. Why? What could I. . . ?

A crack sounded to my left, and my heart almost stopped.

When I whirled around, breathing hard, all I saw were collapsed walls and tumbled stones. The first stars had been born above me, and their pale silver light flickered over the flaking hieroglyphics. I thought the painted figures moved, turning to face me, as though they only came alive at night.

Tugging my flashlight from my jeans' pocket, I turned it on and shone the beam around the temple. The whispering ghosts died. Even the exotic fragrances vanished beneath the unnatural onslaught of modern technology.

I wandered around, studying everything that cast a shadow, and eventually worked my way over to the sarcophagus. It remained barely excavated, just as I'd seen it at dawn, but the woman's beautiful eyes shimmered in the starlight, which made me wonder if ancient artists added crushed emeralds to their paint? It was spectacularly unearthly. Her lips were so red they seemed to be melting, like red crayon held over a flame.

Shining my flashlight around, the tunnel to the north swallowed the beam.

My feet seemed to move of their own volition, taking me to the tunnel whether I wanted to go or not. An eternal two minutes later, I found myself squatting in the mouth of the tunnel, aiming my light down the throat at a descending rock-cut stairway that extended thirty or forty feet into the earth.

It must have been excavated just today.

I stepped onto the first stair, and my boot grated on what seemed to be large pebbles. Strange moldering scents encircled me as I continued down. When I hit the bottom step, I discovered a stunning corridor to my right. Maybe five feet across, the white plastered walls gleamed. My flashlight illuminated dozens of cartouches stamped into the plaster. I'd seen the cartouche of Tutankhamen, so I knew what a cartouche was—an oval ring encircling the hieroglyphic name of a person. As I leaned closer, I realized this cartouche was the face of the god Dionysus: the god of wine and revelry.

Did this corridor connect the temple with a subterranean burial chamber of the gods? Fabulous images of King Tut's tomb paraded through my memory.

Slowly, I edged forward, trying to take everything in at once.

By the age of twelve, I'd studied pictures of every artifact found in Tut's tomb and read every historical report about its discovery and excavation. When the museum exhibition came to Denver, my parents took me to see it. They almost couldn't get me out of the museum. I spent all day staring at the wealth of gold and jewels. Mesmerized by the painted face of the boy king, they'd had to drag me away from that exhibit because the museum was closing its doors. The last person to step outside, I'd felt completely hollow and stunned, as though leaving ancient Egypt had torn my soul from my body.

And here I was, staring down a corridor just like Howard Carter had in 1922. On November 26th, he'd made a small hole in a blocking wall and inserted a candle. Looking into what would become known as the Antechamber, Carter felt hot air blowing around him, escaping from the chamber. He later wrote, ". . . presently, as my eyes grew accustomed to the light, details of the room within emerged slowly from the mist, strange animals, statues, and gold—everywhere the glint of gold."

Trying to control my excitement, I walked faster. Cartouches flickered beneath my bouncing flashlight beam. Twenty paces later, the corridor dead-ended. As I studied the wall in front of me, I wondered what lay on the other side. A tomb? Dirt? This might be an ancient ruse, a blind corridor designed to mislead tomb robbers, but faint images of gold flitted through my . . .

Scratching.

I tilted my head to listen.

What is that?

Clothing catching on eroded stones in the tunnel above? Or an animal? Mice? Snakes slithering along the floor?

A sudden sweltering rush of air filled the corridor. Jewelry clinked, and the scent of sunbaked stones slaked with water blew around me.

I distinctly heard footsteps.

Barely audible, a voice whispered. I concentrated, trying to understand the words, but I couldn't. I was afraid to move, afraid the person would hear me. Perfectly aware that the abject terror pulsing through my veins was unwarranted—because, of course, the voice came from someone in the camp—my adrenaline level was so high I was shaking like a leaf in a gale. It occurred to me that it was probably Roberto. He'd returned to our tent, found me gone, and come looking for me. I wanted to call out to him, but some instinct told me to stay quiet.

I listened, straining to hear more. The corridor had suddenly gone as silent as the old abandoned goldmine shafts that sank into the mountains in Colorado.

My right hand started to ache from being clamped around the flashlight. I forced myself to move it from my right hand to my left, and let my right arm fall to my side, hoping to restore circulation. In no time, a fiery tingle stung my fingertips. Forcing myself to think, it finally occurred to me that as soon as the person in the tunnel stepped down into the corridor, they'd see my flashlight. If they hadn't already. I turned it off.

Absolute darkness, warm and heavy with camphor, enveloped me.

My panicked breathing was loud. I fought to control it.

In the back of my mind was the knowledge that by now anyone in camp who knew me would have called my name. No one had.

A foot thumped as the person stepped off the last stair and entered the dark corridor ahead. I could *feel* them looking down the corridor. More footsteps. Whoever was coming toward me was ghostly quiet.

Gulping air, I held my breath.

"Halloran? Are you here?"

Hearing her call my name was so shocking my knees went weak. I sagged against the wall. *Cleo? Or is that the demon calling me?*

Fumbling for the switch, I turned on my flashlight.

Cleo stood in front of me wearing a white T-shirt and jeans. Black hair hung to her shoulders, framing her pretty face. She smiled. "Don't be afraid, Halloran. It's just me."

"You're not here," I whispered. "You can't be. You're dead. I held you in my arms when you died." Grief struck like an avalanche inside me. I sobbed, watching her through a blur of tears.

Her smile faded to an expression of love. "I miss you so much. I came to warn you. You must listen to me . . ."

She walked forward with her arms out as though to embrace me, and sheer terror exploded in my body.

Like a chased animal, I wildly ran straight at her, tripping and stumbling down the corridor, trying to get out.

As I shoved past her, knocking her back into the wall, she cried, "Please, don't go back. They're waiting for you!"

I lurched into the tunnel and scrambled up the stone stairway like a madman. When I emerged in the starlit temple, I sprinted around the ancient stone walls, and leaped up the stairs two at a time to get out, then ran headlong for camp.

"*Hal?*"

Spinning around, I saw movement, a blurred face, coming fast.

I crashed into the tables by the cook tent, and fell hard on my left shoulder. Splintered wood cartwheeled around me, followed by startled voices as the field camp came abruptly awake and people began to stagger outside.

Before I could get to my feet, something heavy hit me from behind, flattening me, then pinning me to the ground. I cried, "Let me go! What do you want?"

"You're too clever for your own good, Hal Stevens." The man patted me down with the expertise of a police officer, paying special attention to my legs. "Where is it?"

"What?" I screamed, trying to get the attention of someone in camp.

People started running my way, their flashlight beams jerking around wildly in the darkness.

My assailant slammed my head into a broken table leg, which knocked me half-senseless, then he pressed his mouth against my ear to whisper, "If it's not in your tent, and it's not on you, you hid it somewhere. Is that what the old man was trying to dig up?"

"Who are you?"

As people streamed toward the cook tent, the man shoved me hard one last time, then he jumped to his feet and ran away.

By the time I'd managed to twist around to search for him, I was surrounded by archaeologists asking me what had happened, questions I almost didn't hear.

My gaze had fixed on the only movement out there in the starlight. A dark slender form slowly walked back toward the temple. I put my hands over my ears to block the harsh voices bombarding me, and shouted, "Shut up! Be quiet!"

I needed to watch her, to listen for her voice. She had her head down, as though unbearably sad and alone.

"Move!" I heard Roberto order. *"Get out of my way!"*

As he shouldered through the crowd to get to me, a din of uneasy conversation broke out among the archaeologists. They kept casting uncertain glances my way and hissing to one another.

Roberto finally reached me and dropped to one knee to my left. Brown hair framed his frightened blue eyes. "What happened, Hal? Are you all right?"

"I'm okay."

"No, you're not. You're bleeding."

He helped me to sit up, which was the first time I actually felt my head wound, probably from having my head slammed into the table leg. Or from my crash into the tables? Warm blood ran down my left temple.

LaSalle Corbelle and Sophia Mallawi appeared at the rear of the group of students and instantly a pathway opened in the crowd as people moved back to allow them to get to me.

Corbelle made it first. She crouched beside me and studied me with concerned eyes. "Hal, you're hurt. What happened?"

"I—I was attacked. A man hit me from behind. Knocked me to the ground."

Roberto rose to his feet and glared out at the gathering of students. Fists balled at his sides, he looked ready for a fight. "What cowardly piece of shit did this? *Jones*, where are you?"

From the pale halo of light in the rear, Jones called, "I didn't do it! It's midnight. I was sound asleep in my tent, like he should have been."

Midnight?

My gaze shot up to the sky, trying to see the stars to verify that he was right, but there were too many flashlight beams blinding me. How could it be midnight? I'd only been wandering around for thirty minutes or so. Not *four hours?*

Sophia Mallawi worked her way around the legs of an overturned table and knelt to my right. The gray in her dark hair winked in the roving flashlight beams. "Come on, Hal. Let's get you to my tent. I have a medical kit there. We need to take care of that head wound right away. You'll probably need to stay with us for the night, so we can monitor you."

As Sophia and Roberto took my arms to help me to my feet, Corbelle grabbed a handful of my shirt. "I have a nurse on my crew. Let me take Hal to see her."

"No, he's our student, and we promised to take care—"

"I want to go with Dr. Corbelle," I said as I staggered sideways into Roberto.

Roberto grabbed me to hold me up. "We're going with Dr. Corbelle," he announced.

"That's not a good idea," Sophia said angrily. "You should come with me!"

"Not a chance." Roberto stared down Sophia Mallawi long enough to walk me out of the murmuring crowd.

When we reached the other side, Dr. Corbelle led the way in front of the line of tents. Every person in Pelusium must be awake. Tents glowed all across the field camp, and I saw yawning students making their ways back to their beds.

Roberto hissed, "I've been looking for you for hours! I was worried sick. Where were you?"

In a voice too low for Dr. Corbelle to hear, I answered, "With Cleo."

CHAPTER THIRTY-THREE

When we reached Corbelle's tent, the first thing that struck me was the size. It was as small as our tent. I'd just assumed she had a huge tent, like Moriarity's.

When she threw back the front flap, the white glow of the solar lamp hooked to the roof pole flooded out. "Go in, Hal. Sit down. I'll go find our nurse, Lacey."

"Okay."

I ducked inside, followed by Roberto. A rumpled white sheet covered her sleeping bag, which must be what she slept under on hot nights like this. She'd stowed her backpack near the flap. I noticed that all the zippers were closed, which was probably a reflection of her fastidiousness. Nothing was out of place. Stacks of books and manuscripts were neatly arranged in the northern corner.

I slumped down on her sheet. Really shaken. The combination of supernatural terror mixed with the rage and helplessness of being attacked had left me feeling shattered. I couldn't seem to catch my breath.

Roberto knelt in front of me, his face a mask of confusion and fear. "You saw Cleo?"

"She—she came to warn me. She told me not to come back to camp because they were waiting for me."

Quietly, Roberto said, "Let's keep that tidbit to ourselves, okay?"

God, I felt miserable. Letting my head fall forward, I forced myself to breathe in and out. "I'm not totally stupid, Roberto."

He sank down cross-legged in front of me. "I just meant that it might give people the wrong idea—"

"Really?" I asked in exasperation. "You think?"

Hiking boots pounded the sand outside, hurried steps. Dr. Corbelle and a black-haired woman in her mid-twenties ducked into the tent carrying a small bag, which made it downright crowded. The canvas walls shook as they tried to find a place to sit beside me.

Roberto headed for the door. "I'll wait outside."

I watched him duck through the flap and took a deep breath to steady my nerves.

"Hi, Hal. I'm Lacey Borden," the woman said as she scanned my head wound. She had a flat nose and a dimple in her chin. "How'd you get this?"

"I'm not sure. It either happened when I crashed into the tables, or when my attacker slammed my head into a broken table leg."

"How old are you, Hal?"

"Sixteen."

"When's your birthday?"

"May 22nd, why?"

She held up a hand with three fingers out. "How many fingers do you see?"

"Three. Look, I don't have a concussion. I'm just bleeding." Warm streamers continued to pour down my face and splat on my Levis.

"Is your vision blurry? Are you sick to your stomach?" She took her flashlight and shone it in my eyes, no doubt checking the size of my pupils. If one was larger, it meant I had a concussion.

"No. No blurriness and no nausea. Really, I'm okay."

Lacey frowned at me, but hesitantly said, "For the moment, I believe you. I think this is just a laceration. Head injuries bleed like crazy. Let me treat that wound."

Dr. Corbelle was sitting in the background to my left, watching me, but she said nothing while Lacey opened her bag and drew out a package of wet wipes to cleanse my wound. The ointment she applied as a final touch burned.

As Lacey closed her bag, she said, "I want to see you first thing in the morning. And if you have any dizziness, nausea, or double vision tonight, I want to see you immediately. My tent is the last in line to the north. You understand? Send Robert to come get me."

"I understand, and I will. Thank you for your help. I really appreciate it."

Lacey pulled aside the tent flap and said, "Did you hear that, Robert?"

"Yeah, got it. I'll beat feet for your tent if he pukes or thinks I've been cloned."

"Good."

Dr. Corbelle said, "Thanks, Lacey. I'll bring Hal to your tent in the morning."

"Good night, all."

Lacey crawled out of the tent, leaving me alone with Dr. Corbelle.

Narrowing her eyes, Corbelle said, "Look at me, Hal. I want to know the whole story. What happened tonight?"

"Could I . . . Would you mind if I tell you tomorrow? I'm pretty shaken."

When I crawled toward the doorway, her question stopped me. "One of my students said she saw you climb out of the temple. Is that true? And don't lie to me."

I turned back, and my gaze locked with hers. No matter what, I wasn't going to tell her the whole story. I had no idea who my friends were.

I sat down again. "Yeah, it's true."

"What were you doing there? It's dangerous at night."

I gestured helplessly with one hand. "Exploring the tunnel that leads to the corridor covered with cartouches. Didn't mean any harm, I was just curi—"

"Stop." Her expression had turned deadly serious. "None of the tunnels in the temple have been excavated more than a few feet deep. There is no corridor covered with cartouches."

A hollow floating feeling came over me. I stared at her with my mouth half-open. "But I saw . . ." I never finished that sentence.

I bowed my head and massaged the back of my neck. The muscles felt like knotted ropes. That made it simple. It was perfectly obvious now. There was no corridor. No Cleo. I had imagined it all, conjured both from the depths of my historical imagination. What a wretched excuse for humanity I was. My grief and pain were manifesting themselves in ever worsening hallucinations.

But it was so real. . . .

"Which tunnel, Hal?"

"The one closest to the sarcophagus."

Corbelle sat back, and her gaze thoughtfully drifted over the tent for a few seconds. "Are you sure it was *that* tunnel?"

"Yes, why?"

"Probably nothing, but that's a strange tunnel. I found it five years ago. When everyone else was afraid to come to Egypt, I came just to excavate the temple." She leaned toward me. "That tunnel was the only one that had been bricked up. When we got behind the meter-thick wall, the floor was scattered with a peculiar artifact."

"What artifact?"

"Rare ceramic cartouches of Dionysus. They are absolutely unique. I've never seen anything like them. It was as though someone had tossed them down the stairs before the final brick was shoved into place to seal the tunnel."

I swallowed hard. "Do you have something I can draw on?"

She looked around, pulled a notebook from the stack of papers behind her, and handed it to me. She had the most intense blue eyes I've ever seen. Dr. Corbelle examined my every move as I sketched.

When I thought I'd gotten it right, I handed her the notebook. "That's the cartouche that was stamped into the plastered walls of the corridor."

She glanced up at me, then back at the sketch. "I understand that you're quite a historical scholar. Have you ever seen this symbol before?"

"No. I mean, I know it's Dionysus, but—"

"You sure you've never seen this before. Maybe in a book?"

"Never."

When she tossed the notebook to rest on the stack of papers and focused on my face, I knew she was trying to make up her mind about something. "I noticed you were talking to Sarah Wadsworth today. Did she tell you about the tunnel?"

I shook my head. "Did she help excavate it?"

"No, but she's a member of my crew. People in camp talk. I can't figure out how else you would know about this cartouche. You've been here barely a day and you——"

"Then it is the same cartouche?"

"It is. Yes."

An unpleasant tingle ran up my spine. I covered my face with my hands and tried to figure out what was happening to me. Either I was in the middle of a temporal rift the likes of which would have stunned Captain Kirk, or . . .

"Hal, don't worry about this." She gently placed a hand on my shoulder. Her fingers were warm. "Though you're not showing signs, I suspect you're suffering from a mild concussion. Someone mentioned the tunnel and the cartouche, and after you were attacked, you mixed up the memories. Adrenaline has a way of reshuffling the brain. Do you see what I'm saying?"

"Yeah. Thanks. I'm sure you're right."

She gave my shoulder a friendly squeeze and removed her hand. "If you don't mind, I'd like to pick you up around six in the morning and take you to Lacey's tent for another evaluation."

"Fine." My hands started to shake. I clenched my fists to stop it, but not before Dr. Corbelle noticed.

"Let's change the subject, okay? I need to know about your attacker. You said it was a man. Did you see his face?"

"He was muscular and had a deep voice. That's all I can tell you. He kept me pinned facedown the whole time."

Wind buffeted the tent. The solar lamp above us started swinging, casting odd shadows over the glowing walls.

"Why did he attack you? What did he want?"

I hesitated only a moment, but it was long enough to make the lines at the corners of her eyes tighten.

"He thought I was carrying an artifact."

"An artifact? One you'd stolen from the site?"

"An artifact I brought with me from Colorado. It was found here several years ago by Hassan Mallawi, supposedly in the grave of Cleopatra's Sem priest."

She gave me an indulgent smile. The white glow of the lantern turned her deeply tanned face into burnished bronze. "That's amusing. I knew Hassan. He was a very good archaeologist, but I doubt that even he could have identified the specific priest assigned to carry out the Opening of the Mouth ritual for Queen Cleopatra. It's not like they wore signs around their necks."

"Roman slaves wore collars bearing the names of their masters."

"Yes, but . . ." Dr. Corbelle stopped. A somber tone entered her voice: "Why would your attacker have suspected that you had that particular artifact?"

"His daughter was my friend. Before she was murdered, she gave it to me."

She paused. "Is this . . . Wait a second. Is this part of Hassan's crazy theory that his daughter was the reborn Queen Cleopatra? Dear God, that's what got him and Maggie killed."

"What do you mean?"

Dr. Corbelle tilted her head back to stare up at the tent roof, while she apparently contemplated what to tell me. "Okay, look, I don't know the whole story, so I probably shouldn't say anything—"

"I need you to tell me, please."

Instead, she asked, "First, you tell me something. Did your attacker say why he wanted the artifact?"

Words rushed out of my mouth before I considered the ramifications: "No. But Dr. Moriarity brought Samael here to help him find the Sem priest's grave, so he can put the bagsu back in the skeleton's hand—which is where he thinks it came from."

"Why?"

"Apparently, when you see the dagger in the Sem priest's hand, it gives you a clue to the location of Cleopatra's grave. Moriarity told me he wants to become a legend, like Howard Carter and Lord Carnarvon. Both he and his wife have demanded that I give them the dagger."

Dr. Corbelle shifted her intense gaze away from me—which was a relief—and focused instead on the starlit darkness visible through the tent flap. "Good God, I hope this isn't part of that bizarre cultish crap Sophia was involved in."

"What bizarre cultish crap? How did it get Hassan and Maggie killed?"

She ran a hand through her hair, as though stalling. "Hal, I shouldn't be the one to tell you this—"

"Please. I need your help."

It took another ten seconds before she said, "There's a legend that if Cleopatra can be reborn in the perfect vessel, the perfect body, she will rally the people of Egypt and launch an apocalyptic rebellion that will lead to Egyptian world domination."

"But Hassan didn't believe that. Cleo told me her father wanted her to reach the Island of the Two Flames."

"That may be true, but his sister Sophia did believe it. She talked openly about it, and she was gaining a following. People had started to flock around Hassan's daughter every time he took her outside. That really upset people in the government. I think they were waiting for Hassan and Maggie that night."

"I think Moriarity believes it, too."

"He's never struck me as the cult type. How do you know?"

"He told me he wants Cleo to be reborn."

I wondered why Cleo had never told me about any of this. Maybe she didn't remember? Or maybe it was too painful.

"Did you give Jim or Sophia the bagsu?"

"Wait . . ." I was really shaking now. "Is that why Cleo was killed? I thought it was because someone wanted the dagger. Was it really because someone thought my Cleo wasn't the 'perfect vessel'?"

She took a deep breath and exhaled the words: "Tell me the truth. Tonight, did you think your attacker was Jim Moriarity?"

I flexed my fingers. I'd been clenching them for so long that they'd started to ache. "I thought . . . It might be."

"Did you give him the bagsu?" Dread filled her voice.

"No."

She exhaled the word, "Okay. Where is it? Is it safe?"

"I really need to rest. Good night, Dr. Corbelle. Thank you for your help."

When I turned for the doorway, she said, "One last thing, okay?

The Royal Ontario Museum has its own private security. I think you need a bodyguard. Let me assign one of my people—"

"I haven't seen any private security guards."

"Glad to hear it. They're supposed to be invisible. Most of my crew doesn't even know they're there. But they're *good*. Promise me you'll think about it?"

"I will. Thanks. Again."

CHAPTER THIRTY-FOUR

I crawled to the doorway where I ducked out into the warm night air and stared at my best friend. Roberto didn't say a word, but I could see his worried expression. He didn't like it that I'd told Corbelle about the dagger.

I headed for our tent.

Roberto walked along beside me. "Are you sure that was a good idea?"

"I've never been this scared in my life, Roberto." The breeze had picked up. Across the camp tents jostled and creaked. "I figured someone else needed to know just in case something unfortunate should happen to me. Or you. Or both of us."

I stumbled.

Roberto grabbed my arm to keep me from falling. "You're still shaky, Hal. Hold on to me while we walk. I should never have left you alone tonight. God, I'm sorry."

I placed my hand on his shoulder to steady my steps as we walked. "I wanted you to. How did it go with Sarah?"

"Pretty boring, actually. She got orgasmic over a bunch of broken rocks glued together to form pictures on the floor of a bathroom."

"I suspect that was a priceless Roman mosaic."

"Yeah. Well." He tilted his head back to stare up at the night sky and seemed to be appreciating the brilliant patterns of the constellations. "Did the creep that attacked you steal the dagger?"

I thought about lying. If I said yes, the dagger would be safer. And my friend would be safer. Not only that, I was pretty sure the only person I could absolutely trust was me.

"No, I hid it, Roberto. I was afraid——"

"Do *not* tell me where. I don't want to know. That way, if I'm captured, they can't torture it out of me."

"But what if something happens to me. . . ?"

Footsteps padded across the sand in the darkness to my right. I whirled around with my heart in my throat, searching every possible place where she might be standing.

Roberto looked out into the starlight, then gave me a concerned glance. His largest freckles resembled painted splotches. As he reached around to pull the pistol from where he kept it tucked into the back of his pants, he said, "What's wrong?"

"Nothing. I thought I heard . . . Nothing."

Frowning, Roberto whispered, "Are you sure you're all right? You're starting to worry me."

I didn't need to ask why. Demons. Ghosts. Nonexistent corridors. Footsteps of invisible people. Had I not been injured in the attack, I suspect Roberto would have thought I'd imag—

I kept walking, but the shifting sand beneath my boots no longer felt solid or even real.

My whole body had gone numb.

Egypt was an emotionally charged place for me, and this had been a traumatic day in more ways than one. When had I first started feeling that perplexing sense of disconnection? Like my own body was unfamiliar? I knew exactly when. It had started the instant Samael showed me the grave of the entwined skeletons. Perhaps that, and the marker that bore Cleopatra's name, had triggered a dissociative flight of fantasy?

That's ridiculous. I have bruises everywhere. I smelled the man's breath, for God's sake.

"Roberto? Can I ask you . . ."

"What?"

Feeling stupid, I made an airy gesture with my hand. "Did we actually board a plane to Egypt? Are we really here? Or did my parents institutionalize me, and I'm huddled in the corner of a padded room dreaming all this?"

Roberto came to a dead stop. With a passion I'd never heard before, he said, "You think this is all a delusion?"

"Well, think about it." My voice sounded pathetic even to me. "It could be. What if I am just some crazy kid that can't get over the murder of the love of his life?"

Roberto shoved his hands in his jeans pockets and balled them into fists. "First off, asking me to tell you what's real and what isn't is kind of a waste of time. I don't know myself. And if I'm a figment of your imagination, I'm going to tell you what you want to hear, right?"

That was sobering. "I wish you hadn't pointed that out. You're the only thing that's been keeping me sane. If you're not real, I'm lost."

I started to walk off, but he grabbed my shoulder to stop me.

"Second, we need to stay frosty, bro. I don't understand why they're in such a hurry to get their hands on the dagger. They haven't found the grave of the Sem priest yet, have they?"

"I don't think there ever was a Sem priest burial, Roberto. When we were standing over the entwined skeletons, Samael told me the dagger had come from the hand of the larger skeleton, and it wasn't a Sem priest."

"But it still might be, right?"

"Yeah, I guess."

"We have to figure this out, Hal. By attacking you tonight, they've taken this thing to the next level. They must be in a hurry."

The wind whispered through the ruins like a sad human voice calling out for someone to listen. "I think it has something to do with the bizarre cultish crap Dr. Corbelle mentioned tonight."

"I didn't understand any of that. I mean, did Cleo ever tell you she was supposed to grow up and lead Egypt to world domination?"

"No."

We started walking again.

After ten paces, Roberto quietly said, "Hal, listen, we have round-trip tickets. Do you want to go home? For fifty bucks I'll bet we can hire some student here to take us to the Port Said airport."

My gaze traveled along the length of the dark Roman fortress and moved out into the ruins until it came to rest on the amphitheater. When the wind gusted, sand blew around the circular walls in a glittering starlit haze. Too beautiful to be real. This was the kind of visual effect Steven Spielberg would create in a science fiction epic.

An alien landscape that took the breath away with its sheer other-worldly magnificence.

Maybe that's exactly what I needed. A nice trip to the local Colorado sanitarium where they could dope me up and check my feces every day.

Night birds chirped out in the marshes, and the sounds carried across the site.

"Roberto, do you want to go home? It's okay if you do."

He was silent for way too long before he said, "I was there when she died, Hal. She'd want me to help you, which means I'm staying."

As we trudged through the sand, my fear started to ebb and my brain worked a little better. "I suspect they've taken this to the next level because they're afraid we're going to find Cleopatra's grave before they find the Sem priest."

"What happens if we do?"

"No idea."

"Let's say we put the dagger in Cleopatra's grave, can't they just pull it and go stuff it into the Sem priest's hand?"

"Sure. If there is a Sem priest."

When we got close to Moriarity's tent, the sound of hushed voices rose, but stopped instantly. They must have heard us coming.

We passed in silence.

Continuing on, I halted in front of Samael's tent. The old man was absolutely silent. Was he actually in there sleeping? Maybe he was awake and staring blindly at the roof pole in his tent, thinking about Cleopatra's rebellion to come. I considered calling out to him, asking him if we could talk with him for a few minutes.

"Do you think we should knock on his tent?" Roberto asked.

"No. He looked exhausted at dinner. Let's leave him alone."

"But he has to be awake. How could anyone sleep through the hullabaloo that's rocked the camp over the last thirty minutes?"

Jerking a nod, I softly called, "Samael? Are you awake?"

No response.

I motioned to Roberto. "We'll talk to him tomorrow. Besides, I'm tired, and I hurt. I need to sleep."

Just ahead, the front flap of our tent whipped back and forth in the wind. I longed to get inside where I could collapse onto my sleeping bag and hopefully fall into a dreamless sleep. As the adrenaline evaporated from my body, I felt completely drained.

And scared.

Really scared.

Ducking beneath the flap, I got on my hands and knees and crawled onto my sleeping bag where I stretched out, fully dressed, and closed my eyes. It was too dark to see anything inside, but the walls seemed to be breathing; shifting with life, whispering. And somewhere in the distance faint laughter echoed through the ruins. It must be my imagination, but the things I was hearing . . . It sounded like there was more going on outside than night wind and human voices could account for. Things moved, tiptoed toward the tent. I considered ancient Roman ghosts, with spears and shields up, and had the urge to flee for my life. But I was less afraid of them than of the thing that had shaped itself into my Cleo, right down to the subtle nuances of her accent.

Unless, of course, it had been Cleo.

Dear God, a person could go crazy thinking about this.

Outside, Roberto sat down on the sand. The magazine of his pistol clacked as he released the catch to let it fall out so he could check the ammunition. Finally, he slapped the magazine back into the gun, and there was another click. Switching the safety on?

Or off?

My bodyguard. The only person on earth I could trust.

CHAPTER THIRTY-FIVE

*H*al?" a soft voice called. "Hal?"

Rousing from deep slumber, I answered without opening my eyes. "Roberto?"

"It's about a quarter to six. I thought you might want to get up and comb your hair before Dr. Corbelle gets here."

My body felt like lead. It took real effort to move my arms and legs into a sitting position. When I managed to sit up, I discovered that I ached all over and had a monstrous headache. Wincing, I rubbed the sleep from my eyes and yawned. Cool morning wind blew over me, bringing me the scent of coffee.

By the time I'd crawled forward and unzipped the mesh screen. I saw the two cups half-buried in the sand beside Roberto.

"Where did you get coffee?"

"Sarah is an early riser. She came by a little while ago to say hi. I asked her to bring me two cups from the cook tent." He lifted one of the cups and held it out to me. "How are you feeling this morning? There's only one of me sitting here. You see that, right?"

Smiling, I took the cup. "Yeah, I see that. Thanks for asking." As I slumped down on the sand beside him, I said, "My guard duty started at two. Why didn't you wake me?"

"Figured you needed the rest more than I did."

I sipped the coffee. It was still warm and tasted wonderful. "I appreciate it, but you're going to be falling asleep on your feet by noon."

"I'll survive. No nausea or blurred vision?"

I shook my head. "No. Except for some impressive bruises and a few nasty cuts, I'm okay. Just a headache."

Most of the camp stood around outside the tents, talking and laughing, but a few students wandered the ruins. One dark-haired woman was sitting in a lotus position on top of the fortress wall with her eyes closed. Meditating in the gleam of sunrise, I supposed.

"So Sarah came by, huh?"

"Yeah, she can't stay away from me. I had no idea I was so good at casting love spells."

I took a drink of coffee. "Thank God you brought all those condoms."

"Yeah, and to think that I was worried I'd have to use them as water wings to swim home."

"No chance of that now. Just don't forget to *wear* one."

"What are you, my mom?"

"I'm serious. You don't know what kind of diseases they have in Arizona. I read somewhere that the prairie dogs around Phoenix have bubonic plague."

"Sarah doesn't look like the type to hook up with prairie dogs, but I've been wrong before."

Dr. Moriarity's tent shuddered as he unzipped the mesh screen and threw back the flaps to duck outside carrying his fedora. He hadn't buttoned his white shirt, so I could see the gray T-shirt he wore underneath. Looking out across the ruins, he didn't seem to see us at first. Instead, his gaze fixed on LaSalle Corbelle and Lacey Borden who were walking toward him. While he waited for them to arrive, he buttoned up his shirt, then put on his fedora and arranged it at a jaunty angle on his head.

"LaSalle," Moriarity greeted her with a cold smile. "Good morning."

Dr. Corbelle slowed down long enough to say, "Morning, Jim," and continued walking toward me and Roberto.

To my chagrin, Moriarity followed Corbelle. While Moriarity smiled at me in a sympathetic manner, I sized him up, trying to decide if that was the body that had knocked me flat last night. Could be, but I wasn't sure, and my attacker had been Egyptian. He'd had a slight accent. Of course, he could have deliberately disguised his voice. By the time the man hit me, I was so terrified that little details were the least of my concerns.

"Decided I'd come to you this morning, Hal. How are you?" Lacey called. She carried her medical bag over her shoulder.

"Fine. I really appreciate you helping me last night."

Roberto and I stood up.

Lacey stopped in front of me and studied my face, paying special attention to the purple goose egg above my left temple. "That's going to hurt for a while. Any additional bleeding last night?"

"There was a little on my space blanket this morning, but nothing to get excited about."

"How did you sleep?"

"Straight through. I don't even recall dreaming."

She looked at me speculatively, as though not certain that was a good thing. "Do you have a headache this morning?"

"Yes, but it's bearable."

"On a scale of one to ten, how bad is it?"

"I don't know, a five, maybe." Actually it was an eight.

"Do you have aspirin? Ibuprofen?"

"Aspirin. I'll take a couple before we go to work today."

She pointed a finger at me. "Do it. No macho bullshit. Real men *do* need to keep brain inflammation down. If you have a mild concussion, working today is going to make it much worse. Understand?"

"I'll take it slow."

"Okay, but if your headache gets worse, stop work and come see me. In fact, I recommend you do not work today. You should stay in your tent and sleep. LaSalle, do you agree with me about that?" As the morning breeze picked up, black hair blew around Lacey's face.

"That's good advice, Hal. We can always—"

Moriarity interrupted, "In fact, since you are *my* student, Hal, I insist you stay in your tent today. Besides, I need to talk to you. Sophia told me about last night's attack. I need more details if I'm going to find the culprit."

Without realizing it, my shoulders hunched forward in self-defense. The last thing I wanted to do was spend time with Moriarity. I lied, "Later, okay? I promised Dr. Corbelle I'd help her today, and I'd like to try and do that. If you don't mind?"

Corbelle straightened up. In an authoritative voice, she said, "That's right. I asked Hal to help me at the temple. If he's able to. Do you have any objections?" Her deep gravelly voice had an edge, as though daring him to get into a fight with her.

Behind his heavy black-rimmed glasses, Moriarity's eyes appeared bug-like. His gaze went back and forth between me and Corbelle. Obviously, he suspected collusion, but he warily replied, "No problem. However, Hal, you should always get such things approved with me before you agree to them. You're on my crew." To Corbelle, he said, "By the way . . ." His expression contorted as though he hated to say it, "I was hoping you could come take a look at some skeletal remains for me."

Corbelle's head jerked toward him. "Skeletal remains? You found a burial? Where?"

Moriarity vaguely waved his arm to the north. "Samael found a grave yesterday and Sophia suggested—and I agreed—that we need a biological anthropologist to take a look at it. If you don't mind?"

She hesitated for a couple of seconds. "Of course not. I'll be there right after breakfast. Where is it?"

"I'll show you," I said.

"You've seen it, Hal?"

I nodded. "Samael showed it to me. It's interesting. Two entwined skeletons covered with a stela that says Cleopatra in Greek."

"Really? I can't wait. Male and female?" She'd directed the question to Moriarity.

"That's why I need a biological anthropologist. Sophia and I disagree about that."

Corbelle tucked a wind-blown lock of blonde hair behind her ear. "Okay. See you after breakfast."

"Hal? Roberto?" Moriarity said. "Why don't you join me for breakfast? We can talk for a little while before you show Dr. Corbelle the burial."

Roberto and I exchanged a glance, but since I didn't see any way out of it, I said, "Sure. Meet you at the cook tent."

"I'll save you places at the table. Don't be late." Moriarity turned and strode for the breakfast line that was already forming up.

The four of us watched him go.

Corbelle said, "Take your aspirin, Hal, then we'll walk you to breakfast."

"It'll just take me a second."

I ducked back into the tent and dug around in my pack until I found the bottle my father had forced me to pack. Silently, I thanked him and his obsessive need to over-prepare for every eventuality. Popping three aspirin, I grabbed my dig kit and our hats, and ducked outside again.

As I handed Roberto his Rockies' hat, I said, "I didn't want you to forget that."

"Thanks, buddy." Roberto flipped it on his head and pulled the bill down to shield his eyes.

Lacey and Roberto led the way to breakfast, while Corbelle and I followed a couple of paces behind them.

Pointedly, Corbelle said, "I'm glad you used me as an excuse, Hal. Being away from Jim will give you a while to think things through. But I really believe you need protection. Have you thought more about my offer last night?"

"I have. Thanks, but I don't want a bodyguard. I'll be fine."

She started rolling up the sleeves of her ivory-colored shirt. "All right. The offer remains open, so let me know if you change your mind." With an edge in her voice, she asked, "Do you have a gun?"

"No. Why would you think that?"

She shrugged. "They're available on every street corner, and you're from the American West. It occurred to me that you might have purchased one."

"No."

"Okay. Just wanted to make sure."

Roberto didn't show the slightest interest in this conversation. He kept his eyes forward, just walking to breakfast.

As we neared the cook tent, the sweet earthy scent of teff filled the air. We collected bottles of water, bowls, and spoons, then got into line. As we slowly moved forward, I said, "Sounds like you know something about Colorado?"

"A little. The Royal Ontario Museum occasionally works with the Denver Museum of Natural History, so I've been there a few times. Lovely city. The mountains are beautiful."

As I scooped cereal into my bowl, I searched through the crowd for Samael. I didn't see him. He was probably still sleeping. I didn't see Sophia Mallawi either, but Moriarity sat at the closest table. True to his word, he'd saved us two places.

Corbelle said, "I'm going to sit with my crew, Hal. Why don't you find me when you're finished with breakfast, and we'll head out to the grave."

"Sounds good."

Corbelle and Lacey split off and went to sit at the last table, while Roberto and I slid onto the bench beside Moriarity. Unfortunately, Jones sat across from us. I tried not to notice him as I spooned warm cereal into my mouth. I also tried to avoid looking at the evidence of my mad flight last night. The broken pieces of the table I'd demolished lay stacked like firewood down near where Corbelle and her crew sat. Losing one table meant there were even fewer places to sit for meals. People kept giving me dirty looks, and I knew that was probably why. Not to mention the fact that my shrieking had dragged them from their tents in the middle of the night.

Moriarity finished his cereal and picked up his coffee cup. After a drink, he said, "Tell me what happened last night, Hal."

Swallowing a lump of cereal, I said, "Somebody hit me from behind, knocked me flat, and slammed my head into a table leg."

"I know that much. Sophia told me. Did he say anything to you? Why did he attack you?"

If Moriarity was the man who attacked me, he knew the reason. If not, I didn't want to discuss the dagger in front of a table filled with strangers.

Lifting my gaze, I found Jones watching me with curious un-blinking eyes.

"Where's Dr. Mallawi this morning?" I asked, trying to change the subject.

"In bed. She hasn't been feeling well since she arrived in Egypt. She's been throwing up all morning. I think it's a touch of malaria. She's battled the illness off and on for her entire life. You didn't an-swer my question, Hal. Why were you attacked last night?"

I wondered if that was true, or if he just didn't want anyone to know his wife was pregnant.

"All the guy said was 'Hal Stevens,' then he beat me up and ran off."

Jones' mouth quirked in disbelief.

Moriarity loudly scraped his bowl with his spoon, ate the last bite, and shoved his bowl aside. "That doesn't make any sense. Did you get into a fight with someone on the site? Was this a payback?"

Moriarity's bearded face was stern, foreboding, as though he blamed me for the attack. I forced myself to maintain eye contact with him.

"No fights."

"Why were you at the cook tent at midnight? You should have been in bed. If you had been, none of this—"

"He was out wandering the off-limits part of the city," Jones said. "One of the women on Corbelle's crew saw him step out of the temple and run for camp."

Moriarity raised his voice. "What? My God, Hal, that was foolish and dangerous! We only have six guards at this site. What if a terror-ist had sneaked in and secreted himself in the temple? It's the perfect place to hide. You would have walked right into his rifle."

Roberto shifted to my right. "Yeah, well, he didn't, did he? He was attacked in camp, right where we're sitting, by someone who knew his name. Get it?"

Moriarity's mouth pinched into a white line. "Yeah. I do. But I don't understand why. What possible reason—"

"He wanted the same thing you did," I answered in a low voice and chewed another bite of my cereal. Across the table, Jones perked up, and his gaze slid to Moriarity.

Moriarity's face slackened. "Did he get it?"

"Someone stole it from our tent earlier in the day. I didn't have it," I answered and shoveled another bite into my mouth.

The air seemed to go out of Moriarity's body. Sagging forward, he set his coffee cup down and used his fingers to massage his forehead. Jones watched him with a curious expression, as though he thought he ought to say something, but didn't know what.

Finally, Jones asked, "What was stolen? I could start asking around. You know, see if anyone has seen it."

Roberto elbowed me and tipped his chin. "Corbelle is finished with breakfast. We should hurry."

At the far end of the table, Corbelle had just stood up. I quickly gobbled the rest of my cereal. She said a few last words to her students, then walked toward us. I noticed that all of her crew had started rising and were filing out toward the temple.

Moriarity called, "LaSalle, I need to line out today's work with my crew chiefs. Why don't you and the boys go ahead without me, and I'll meet you at the burial in a few minutes."

Corbelle nodded. "That's fine."

We slid across the bench, and I smiled at her as she approached.

Extending a hand, she said, "Lead forth."

Roberto walked out front as we headed for the mysterious entwined skeletons. I walked beside Dr. Corbelle.

"You look a little better, Hal. Is your headache easing after the aspirin?"

"Yeah, thanks."

Which was sort of true, though I kept seeing things from the corner of my eye—floating shapes, starlike, flashing off and on. They seemed to swoop in from the marshes, then hover right in front of me before winking out. Some had a reddish tint; others shone a pale yellowish-white. One reddish-brown light kept flying straight at me. Which I found interesting. In ancient Egyptian artwork, males were usually depicted with reddish-brown skin, while females were painted lighter, their skin a mixture of yellow-and-white paints. Maybe the lights were the souls of long-dead men and women who had once lived here? If so, what did they want? I wasn't sure I liked my newly acquired skill of talking to the dead. As a matter of fact, I knew I didn't. More likely, however, the flashing lights were evidence of a mild concussion. Or maybe I had a migraine coming on and this was part of the aura? God, I hoped not.

"Going to be a hot one today." Corbelle lifted her ivory sleeve to wipe her face.

Already sweating to beat hell, my heart was pounding as well. "I have to admit I'm not looking forward to that. In Georgetown, Colorado, it's probably going be seventy-five to eighty degrees today."

She smiled, and the world seemed to brighten. The colors of the site actually glowed. The distant green of the marshes turned luminous. "You're not adapted to Egypt yet, Hal. And today, of all days, you might want to sleep during the heat of the day."

"If I start feeling badly, I will."

It was always stunning how fast the temperature rose out here. Despite the constant sea breezes, by seven in the morning, you could feel the night's coolness evaporating and the air warming up.

"Dr. Corbelle? I notice that your students call you LaSalle, and I was wondering—"

"I'd be delighted if you called me LaSalle. What took you so long? Most of my students just do it automatically."

"I can understand that. You're a lot more open and approachable than Dr. Moriarity."

"Well, Jim is . . . Jim."

That had been one of the first things I'd noticed, Moriarity's students called him *Dr. Moriarity*, and LaSalle's students immediately felt comfortable calling her by her first name. That simple little thing bridged the gap between professor and student and made it easier to ask questions and, therefore, to learn more. At least, for me it did.

"Maybe sometime you could tell me more about biological anthropology? I don't understand why Dr. Moriarity and Dr. Mallawi disagreed about the sex of the skeletons."

Her blonde brows drew together. "I don't either, honestly. It's usually a slam-dunk if you have a skull or pelvis. Are they missing from this burial?"

"The skeletons looked whole to me, but I don't know anything."

She smiled again. "I suspect you know more than you let on, Hal. Have you ever noticed that when you speak, people listen? That's because they're learning something. You're a natural teacher."

The praise made me sheepishly stare out at the Roman fortress wall. It cast a long shadow this time of morning. "Thanks, I appreciate you saying that, but I know how much I don't know. I'm looking forward to getting to college where I can study what I want to."

"Is high school getting boring?"

I lifted a shoulder. "I'm kind of a misfit, so it's not much fun."

"Well, of course, you are," she said, and gave me a strange look. "I was, too. You don't know it yet, but you're going to be brilliant at whatever you choose to do. I, frankly, hope it will be anthropology, but I know right now you're more interested in focusing on history."

"Are they incompatible?"

"Not at all. In fact, I insist that my students study both. It's the only way you can actually understand a culture. Why don't you come study with me in Canada?"

"Do you teach? I thought you just worked at the museum?"

"I work full-time at the museum, but on the side I teach a couple of courses in biological anthropology, as well as consulting with police departments across North America. Besides, I'll give you a part-time job at the museum which should cover your tuition. You'll enjoy it."

"Thanks. I've always wanted to visit Cana—"

"What the . . ." Roberto came to a dead stop in front of us, then broke into a dead run. "*Hal?*"

It didn't matter that I had no idea what had set him off, I charged after him at full speed, trying to catch up, shouting, "Roberto? What's going on?"

LaSalle's feet pounded after me. She was tall and athletic, but my legs were longer. I outdistanced her pretty fast. All across the site, people straightened from their work, and looked in our direction. A wave of students began walking toward us.

By the time Roberto reached the excavation pit, I was still ten paces behind, but I saw what had caught his eye. The pit walls had caved in, half-filling the excavation.

Roberto leaped down into the pit and started scooping out dirt with his hands. I ran as hard as I could. When I got close enough, the sight that met my eyes made me stumble.

"Oh, my God!"

I jumped down beside Roberto and helped him throw out the dirt. He worked at the bottom of the excavation, while I cleaned out the top portion. When I finally got down to the skulls, I sucked in a breath. The stela sat at an angle, covering most of the skulls. "They . . . They've been crushed."

LaSalle arrived and climbed down into the pit with us. Gently, she said, "Please move aside, Roberto. I need to take a look." But the expression on her face told me she already knew the answer to the question of "why?"

Roberto climbed out of the pit and knelt on the edge looking down. "It looks like somebody used the stela to bludgeon the skulls to bits."

"Maybe. We can't be sure yet."

LaSalle pulled her trowel from the sheath on her hip, and started carefully scraping away the fresh dirt. As the skeletons slowly emerged, it became clear that fragments of the skulls scattered the dirt.

LaSalle stood up and studied the positions of the skeletons in the grave. Most of the bones remained exactly as they'd been yesterday, placed as though each had been gently lowered into the grave, then their arms arranged around each other. But it was no longer easy to tell, because there was still a lot of dirt over them.

"Looks like somebody out here is superstitious," she whispered to herself, then carefully scooped away some of the dirt from the hip bones of the skeletons, whereupon she frowned. Her gaze darted back and forth between the crushed skull of the larger skeleton and the hip bones.

Rage filled me. I had no idea why I was so upset over this desecration, but the crushed skulls really stunned me. "Why would someone shatter the skulls of ancient skeletons?"

People began shouting and running toward us.

Exhaling hard, LaSalle leaned back against the crumbling pit wall. "There are many possibilities. Someone may have wanted to make sure the Ka souls could not escape and wander around the site. Or the person who did this was trying to prevent us from identifying the remains. And there are about a million other possibilities. I know this is a shock, but vandalism like this occurs all the time at archaeological sites. This might even have been an accident."

"An accident?" Roberto said. "How do you accidentally smash skulls?"

"Think about it, guys. If someone were trying to move the heavy stela by himself, he might have stumbled or lost his hold and accidentally dropped it on the skulls. This is not necessarily a malicious act."

"But what was he doing trying to move a stela in the middle of the night? That implies he didn't want to be seen." Roberto propped his hands on his hips and grimaced as the first of the students began to arrive and encircle the pit.

LaSalle's blonde brows pulled together, which deepened the crow's-feet at the corners of her blue eyes. "Most of the students here knew nothing about this burial, but some of them probably heard rumors. If one came out to take a look in the moonlight, he may have gotten excited, tried get a better look, and accidentally dropped the heavy stone."

"And then tried to cover it up by caving the pit walls over the top of it?"

"Possibly. What I'm saying is let's not jump to conclusions."

When people started crowding around us, I backed up, then wandered a short distance away. Roberto trotted over to stand beside me.

LaSalle called, "Everything is all right, folks. Just some vandalism."

"Let me through, please! Coming through. Move!" As though he'd been occupied elsewhere and only just heard the news, Moriarity pushed forward to stare down at the shattered skulls. "Who did this? Somebody knows! Tell me right now?"

In the back, murmurs started: "Bates must have been drunk as a skunk when he . . ."

"Can't say that, he . . ."

"I was with him last night after dinner and he was talking about . . ."

Moriarity gingerly lowered himself into the pit and knelt beside the crushed skulls. "Jones! Get over here."

Jones' dyed platinum hair shone whitely as he passed through the students and crouched near Moriarity.

"Where's Bates? Send someone to find him this instant. Then I need to re-excavate this burial so we can determine the extent of the damage."

"Got it."

Jones tapped someone on the shoulder, issued instructions, and the young man took off at a run.

"LaSalle, did you find any evidence of who did this? Tracks? Anything left behind?" Moriarity stared at her through enraged eyes. "You must have come to some conclusions. You routinely work with the police—"

"All I have are guesses. The soil shoved over the burial is pretty dry, so this is hours old, but—"

"Give me a time."

"If you pressed me, I'd guess the vandalism probably occurred between ten last night and around two."

Jones straightened up and clenched his fists at his sides. As though he was calculating in his head, his eyes darted around, then they came back to me with the force of a blow to my belly. "That's the time Stevens claims he was attacked last night."

"So?" I said.

"So, you're a liar. I checked for footprints this morning. All I found were your tracks running from the temple to the cook tent. There was no one behind you and no signs of a fight by the tent." He flexed his fists at his sides. "Setting up an alibi, *boy?*"

Roberto shouted, "There were a hundred people around the tent for breakfast! Any tracks left from last night were long gone. There's no way you could have determined there hadn't been a fight."

All eyes turned to me.

I felt like I'd been body-slammed. I couldn't breathe.

"That's enough." LaSalle ordered. "There is no evidence that this is anything but an accident."

"Yeah. Sure." Jones clenched his jaw. "The only people out here who might have been ignorant enough to pick up a heavy stela are these two."

Moriarity aimed his trowel at Jones. "Jonathan shut your mouth. I'm tired of your bullshit."

CHAPTER THIRTY-SIX

Moriarity ordered, "All right, go back to work. This is over. Return to your excavation units." When the gathering did not immediately disperse, Moriarity clapped his hands. "Right now! Go on."

Students wandered away, but their dark voices rode the wind. Many turned around to stare curiously at me, then whispered to each other.

As though searching for anything reassuring to cling to, my gaze fastened on LaSalle, where she stared down at the entwined skeletons. Wisps of blonde hair had come loose from her braid and blew around her somber face.

When there were only five of us remaining, Moriarity said, "This is my fault. I should have posted guards over this."

"Jim," LaSalle said in a kind voice. "Don't blame yourself. These things happen at sites. You know they do."

"It never occurred to me that anyone would deliberately harm this burial."

"What makes you think this was deliberate?" LaSalle glanced at me, then her blonde brows slanted down over her blue eyes. "I see no evidence of that. Do you?"

"No. I just . . . I wonder. Bates was inordinately interested in this burial yesterday——"

"Oh, yeah, burials have started to freak him out. He's been intensively studying ancient Egyptian demons," Jones said, "and drinking a lot, and ranting. I swear to God it's like he's somebody else. Somebody I don't know."

LaSalle narrowed her eyes at Jones. "You're not suggesting that Mike Bates vandalized this burial because he was afraid of demons, are you?"

My brain was playing tricks on me. The reddish-brown light flashed right in front of my eyes. As soon as I reached for it, it disappeared, only to reappear a few feet away and start working its way closer to my face again in a slow, bobbing manner. The ancient ghost of a man trying to tell me something?

Jones lifted his face to look up at her. There was something frightened behind his eyes. "No, no. Of course not. Just saying is all."

LaSalle walked around the excavation pit to stand with her back to the sun. "All right. I know this is a bad time, but while we wait for Bates, can we talk about the entwined skeletons? I see why you had problems identifying the sex of the remains."

Moriarity walked over to stand beside her, looking down into the pit. "Go on."

Roberto and I edged closer to listen.

LaSalle knelt on the rim of the excavation and pointed to the larger skeleton. "The heavily built skull, along with the large brow ridge, would instantly make you think this was a male. However—" she shifted positions to point at the hips, " —the pelvis is definitely female. This is a woman. The other skeleton is also female. Therefore, you have two women lying here with their arms around each other, covered by a stela that tells me they may have been associated with Cleopatra."

"So. They were Cleopatra's slaves? Servants?" He took a deep breath and let it out slowly.

"Possibly. Do you see the thick bones of their right arms? They were heavily muscled, which means these women did a lot of hard physical labor. However, they were well-fed because I see no signs of malnutrition. If they were slaves, they were elite slaves."

Moriarity's eyes narrowed behind his glasses.

The strange scent of myrrh blew across the site. Where could that be coming from? Was it real?

LaSalle said, "Iras and Charmion?"

Moriarity gave her a small smile. "That's called 'wild conjecture.'"

"Maybe, but the only two women unquestionably associated with Cleopatra—"

"Without more information, there is no way to guess the identity of these two women."

"Not definitively, but the stela is suggestive."

Moriarity's brows drew together. "Agreed. Suggestive. And it would be interesting, wouldn't it? We know from historical documents that Cleopatra's two personal servants committed suicide at the same time she did."

"With poison," I said. I'd started feeling a little nauseous. Flashing lights, strange scents, and now I was sick to my stomach. How long did I have before I'd have to go lie down in our tent? Maybe thirty minutes, if I was really lucky.

LaSalle nodded. "Yes, Plutarch tells us that by the time Octavian arrived, Cleopatra was dead and Iras and Charmion were nearly dead."

As understanding dawned, I gasped a deep breath into my lungs. Charmion must have been tasked with placing the bagsu in Cleopatra's grave. Suddenly, it all made sense. Before Cleopatra ended her life, she must have asked Charmion to place the dagger in her grave so she could open the channel of light and find her way to the Island of the Two Flames, but Octavian had the palace surrounded. He would never have allowed her servants to carry out any Egyptian burial rituals. When Charmion knew she could not complete the task Cleopatra had given her, she chose to die with her queen. The dagger had probably been found on Charmion's body by one of the house slaves assigned to clean up the room, so it was buried with her.

But why would Charmion and Iras have been buried in Pelusium? Seemed a strange choice, unless maybe they'd been born here? There were virtually no historical records about Cleopatra's slaves.

I had to find Samael to ask him for more details about what had happened that terrible August day in 30 BC.

Myrrh again . . . The fragrance strong and exotic.

I searched the site, trying to see who might be burning the sacred incense, but saw no one, and no clouds of smoke.

Moriarity swallowed hard, glanced around as though he smelled it, too, then his gaze returned to the entwined skeletons. "If Iras and Charmion are here, LaSalle, Cleopatra may be here as well."

"Yes, but there is absolutely no reason to believe that these entwined women—"

"If I'd been the budding young emperor, I would have scooped up all three bodies and gotten them out of sight before anyone knew what had happened," Moriarity said.

"You would have hauled the three bodies away together?"

"At least those three bodies. He was in a hurry," Moriarity said. "Nine days had already passed since Antonius' death. As soon as the common people heard that Cleopatra was dead, they'd start spinning their own stories of what had happened. Octavian would have wanted to stop that before it began."

"Yes, he would have. To stop a rebellion. If the Egyptian people thought he'd murdered her . . . Well, I see what you're saying." She folded her arms across her chest. "If he got rid of the evidence fast, he could broadcast his version of the truth, but I really don't think—"

"I'm going to personally expand this unit today. We excavated here yesterday because Samael was certain this was the same place where, several years ago, he and Hassan Mallawi had found a burial." Moriarity bowed his head and exhaled hard while he massaged his forehead. "But I never expected to uncover two women—"

"Jim, if Octavian was trying to hide the evidence, he would not have buried her with her servants. He would have buried Cleopatra far away from anyone or anything. And he'd have made certain no one could ever identify her."

"Or just weighted her down and dumped her body in the ocean. That would have taken care of it."

As though in a dream, I found myself in the body of Gaius Julius gazing down at Cleopatra where she lay dead upon her golden couch, her flowing purple robes draped artistically around her, as befitted the daughter of kings. "Her son, Caesarian, was murdered two days after she died. Would his body have been hauled away at the same time?"

If Caesarian, Iras, and Charmion were all here, it made it far more likely that she was here, as well.

Moriarity rubbed his bearded jaw. "I'd say that's a good guess. If we knew where Caesarian was buried, we could at least hypothesize—"

"We do know. At least, I think we know," I blurted out the words without thinking.

"Yeah," Roberto pointed to the west. "He's right over there."

Both professors turned to give us incredulous looks.

LaSalle said, "No one has ever definitely identified his grave, guys, so anything you've read is speculative at best. He probably—"

"Samael showed us the grave. He had partially excavated the skeleton."

LaSalle appeared stunned. "When? How did he know it was—"

Roberto said, "The burial is out in the forbidden part of the site. After he showed it to us, he told us to cover it back up."

"Is that what you were doing with him yesterday morning?" Jones asked. "Looking at a burial?"

"Yes."

Moriarity's heavy shoulder muscles contracted and bulged through his white shirt. "Why didn't you tell me about that?"

"Samael asked us to cover it back up. So, at the time, I thought he didn't want anyone to know about it."

Moriarity straightened to his full height and scanned the dig. Students had finally made it back to their excavations and were hard at work, but low disgruntled voices carried on the wind. "Where is Samael?" he asked. "Has anyone seen him this morning?"

When everyone shook his or her head, Moriarity's gaze returned to glare angrily at me. He'd clamped his jaw hard.

LaSalle asked, "Can you find the burial again?"

"Sure."

"Take me there, please."

LaSalle motioned for us to lead. When Moriarity stood up to follow, she said, "I thought you were going to wait for Bates, and then excavate the rest of the burial so we'd know the extent of the damage? Would you rather have me do it? I'll be happy to."

Moriarity aimed a hand at the burial. "I am the only one who gets to excavate this."

He stepped down into the pit and lightly brushed the dirt from the smaller skeleton's chest. "Are you ready, Jones? Where's your trowel?"

"Right here, Dr. Moriarity." Jones pulled his trowel from his back pocket and climbed into the excavation.

The reddish-brown light flashed in my face again, and I felt something touch my cheek. "Let's g-go," I stammered. "It's due west."

LaSalle wiped her sweating face with her hand, and turned westward. "Curious that you would say that."

"Why?"

"The Egyptian Book of the Dead speaks of many 'secret portals of the West' that lead to otherworldly spheres. One of those spheres, the Lake of Fire, is guarded by a demon known as the 'Devourer,' responsible for swallowing shadows, and pulling out hearts."

"Ammut," I said.

She nodded. "Yes."

In unison, Roberto and I turned around to look at the partially excavated statue of the demon near our tent.

Dust blew around the two students who crouched on the rim looking down at her.

CHAPTER THIRTY-SEVEN

A s we walked across the sand, getting farther and farther from the entwined skeletons, my nausea diminished a little, but I was still shaky and sweating profusely. The damp warmth of the morning wasn't nearly hot enough to explain my excessive perspiration. This had to be a concussion. My blond hair was plastered to my aching head as though I'd just stepped out of a shower.

In the slanting sunlight, the ruins cast blocky shadows that stretched westward, toward the land of the dead: The Beautiful West, it was called. It also happened to be the direction of the temple and the grave of Caesarian. Looking across the vista, I noted that many of the excavations where students had been working yesterday stood abandoned, their tools left neatly arranged on the ground waiting for them to return. However, the screens and shovels seemed to be missing. Had they hauled them elsewhere?

None of us said a word until we passed the temple, whereupon I came to a stop.

There had to be twenty men and women lined out in different rooms of the temple, digging, but eight students were excavating the tunnel. *My tunnel.* Two students dug with shovels, while four others screened the dirt that came out, and two more scooped the dirt into buckets and hauled it up and out of the temple. The back dirt pile on the south side was growing fast. What really surprised me was that I could see the men working in the tunnel about fifteen feet back. Only fifteen feet. Dirt filled the rest of the tunnel, and probably had for centuries.

A delusion. That's all it was.

LaSalle halted beside me. "You didn't think I was just going to ignore what you told me last night, did you?"

Tears burned my eyes. "Then, you believe me?"

"Not yet. But I've spent twenty years excavating with Samael—" she said his name in a reverent tone, "—and I learned that if he told me to dig somewhere, I dug."

"But why would you believe me?"

"Because, for some unknown reason, he trusts you. I think he sees something in you that few people ever have." She held up a finger as though making a point in a classroom, but then aimed it at my head. "I'm wondering if you don't have a touch of the same clairvoyance that he has."

"You believe in clairvoyance?"

The students in the temple had just noticed her presence on the rim above, and they started whispering to each other.

"I can't explain how he does it, but Samael has a gift for finding burials. He says the dead call to him." She fixed me with intense blue eyes. "And now I wonder if they speak to you, as well, Hal Stevens."

You have no idea.

"Thank you. I don't know if that's true or not, but . . . thank you."

Turning away from the temple, I tried to get my bearings, searching the flats for the place where Samael had taken us to see the grave. "Roberto? What do you think?"

"It's this way," he said, extending a hand.

As we walked, chunks of black and brownish slag, as well as green glass slag crusted with salt, dotted the sand.

LaSalle said, "It's interesting that Samael told you he'd found Caesarian's grave out here. This was a bustling manufacturing district. It is unlikely that Octavian would have buried him here. Somebody would have noticed. Somebody would have asked what the soldiers were doing. But if you were a common laborer, burying a family member, no one would have asked questions."

"Then he may have been buried in secret by potters or brickmakers or glassmakers. Common people?"

"Exactly right."

Roberto said, "Are you saying that some servant made off with the body of Cleopatra's son and brought him here to bury him? That was ballsy."

"Why would a servant risk his life to do that?"

Wind buffeted her ivory sleeves around her muscular arms. "Out of love, maybe. Or patriotism. Loyalty. Or simply because he hated Rome. Who can say?"

The more I learned about Gaius Julius, the more I could see myself risking death to defy him. In my mind, he had become far more than a pivotal historic figure; he was evil incarnate.

LaSalle's pace slowed, and her eyes slitted. "Is that it?"

Roberto squinted at her. "Are you telling me that you can see it from here?"

"It's that slight soil discoloration, I assume."

Roberto nodded. "Yeah, come on."

By the time we stood around the discoloration, LaSalle had her trowel gripped in her left hand. "Let's see what we've got. This is going to take time, so you may as well sit down. Or you could go back to your tent and catch a nap, Hal."

Shaking my head, I sat down to watch. "I'm not leaving."

Roberto continued to stand, but he wasn't watching LaSalle. His eyes moved constantly across the site, noting where people walked, what they were doing.

With the expertise of a surgeon, LaSalle removed the discolored soil, leaving the irregular borders of the undisturbed grave intact. She continued slowly and methodically working her way down, until her trowel clicked on bone. Pulling her brush from her belt, she gingerly feathered away the soil until she was staring into the empty eye sockets of Philopator Philometor Caesar. She grunted softly, and kept brushing at the loose dirt.

"Well . . . hello there," she said to the dead man when she'd finished uncovering the skull. "Hal? Roberto? Come closer. I did not expect to find this so soon."

Roberto came to crouch beside me, and we both focused on the man with the crushed skull.

LaSalle said, "Obviously, he was clubbed to death, but do you see the 'cracks' in the skull here and here? These cracks are called sutures. They are not related to his crushed skull. These are natural growth lines that fuse, grow together, as you become an adult. Your sutures, for example, are still open. But mine are fused. So, how old do you think this person is?"

"Our age?" Roberto said. "Sixteen?"

"Correct. I'd guess the age of this person at somewhere between fifteen and eighteen. What's the sex of the remains?"

I leaned forward. "From the heavy skull and large brow ridge, I'd guess it's male."

"Good. You're learning. Here's another interesting thing." She used her brush to push more dirt away from the neck bones. "What do you see here?"

Roberto leaned over to point to the vertebrae. "These two neck bones are broken. What does that mean?"

"It means," she said with a sigh, "that after he was dead, he was beheaded. Whoever carried him here brought both his body and his severed head. During burial, that same person took the time to carefully arrange his head in its anatomically correct position." She turned to me. "Do you think Octavian or his soldiers would have treated their enemy with such consideration?"

That familiar hollow expanded my chest. "No."

"I don't either."

"Then, you think this is Caesarian?"

She shook her head. "I find nothing so far to suggest that. In fact, it could just as easily be a glassblower's son who committed a crime and was beheaded for it. Or even Marcus Antonius Antyllus. Antonius' son by Fulvia. Antyllus was sixteen when he was beheaded just a few days before Caesarian was killed. And those possibilities are pure speculation. All we have here is a young male, between the ages of fifteen and eighteen, with cranial trauma, who was beheaded."

"But if he is either Caesarian or Antyllus, it means they were not mummified, and they were buried with nothing."

"Correct. But that's a very big 'if.' There's no evidence to support your hypothesis."

"Not yet, but if true, it may mean Cleopatra and Antonius' bodies might have been treated the same way."

LaSalle shook her head. "Not Antonius. We know from historical records that she cleansed his body, prepared him for the afterlife, and buried him with her own hands."

I said, "That's the version Gaius Julius allowed to survive. So we know it's the version he wanted us to believe. But we don't know if it's true or not."

"Correct."

Clouds of dust rose as two cars drove up the road and pulled into the parking lot with the other vehicles. Men in uniforms stepped out. The soldiers who guarded the site trotted over to meet them, then they all walked together toward the cook tent.

"Changing of the guard?" I asked.

"Yes. Six in, six out."

Though my brain was foggy, something interesting had occurred to me. Had my attack last night been merely a distraction? When I'd yelled, the entire camp had awakened and rushed toward me, which would have given the criminal time to vandalize the entwined skeletons. But that would mean two people had been working together: my attacker and the vandal.

LaSalle rose to her feet. "Thank you for showing me this. I'll need to get approval from the Egyptian authorities to finish excavating here, so I'm going to tell you exactly the same thing Samael did: Please, cover it back up for now."

"Okay."

Scooping up the dirt, we filled in the small hole she'd excavated, and rose to our feet. The instant I straightened, I felt nauseous again, and shaky. I was starting to feel really awful. "If you don't mind, I might go lie down in our tent for a while."

"Feeling sick, Hal?" Roberto asked.

"Just a little. Nothing to worry about."

LaSalle nodded. "Good idea. Get some rest. When you feel better, come and see me in the temple. While Hal sleeps, do you want to help me excavate the temple, Robert?"

"Nope. I'm staying with Hal. Thanks. See you later."

LaSalle waved and turned to walk toward the temple.

As we headed back to our tent, I saw Mike Bates trotting toward the entwined skeletons. When he arrived, a shouting match broke out. Above all the other voices, I could hear him yelling, *"I didn't do it!"*

CHAPTER THIRTY-EIGHT

Each step I took heading back across the site felt like a hammer swung into my skull. My heart was thundering in my chest as the pain level increased.

Roberto seemed to sense it. He slowed down to walk at my side. "You okay?"

"Sick," I whispered. "I'll be all right."

"Lacey was right this morning. You should have stayed in bed."

"You're the one who stayed awake all night. You should sleep, too."

"When you're better, it'll be my turn."

"I think you should do it now. It's broad daylight. No one would dare attack us in our own tent in broad daylight. And you look terrible. Your eyes are puffy."

"I'll think about it."

As we continued forward, I frowned at the wind. Icy air blew in my face, but it wasn't constant. Sometimes it shoved me so hard I had to brace myself so I wouldn't stagger. Other times, it turned hot, unbearably hot. Then it suddenly stopped altogether, as though holding its breath, waiting for me to understand. It was frighteningly animate. When it stopped, I felt certain something or someone had blocked it, and that something was towering above me, evaluating me with sparkling inhuman eyes.

"Weird cold wind," I said.

"Cold?" Roberto asked. "It feels like a blow torch."

"Oh. Thanks for telling me."

When we reached our tent, I practically fell to my knees and crawled inside. I managed to lie down before I collapsed in a heap.

Roberto ducked under the flap. "I'm going to lie down, too, but I'm not sleeping, just resting my eyes with my pistol in my hand."

"I think it's safe for you to sleep for a while, too."

"No chance. I don't trust anybody, 'cept you."

Roberto dragged over his pack, unzipped one of the compartments, and I heard pills rattle as he shook them out. "Where's your water bottle?"

Basking in the darkness behind my closed eyes, I said, "There's one stuffed into the middle compartment of my pack."

Roberto rummaged around for a few seconds, then he came to kneel beside me. "Take these, Hal."

I opened one eye to see three white tablets and a water bottle. Swallowing the aspirin all at once, I washed them down with water, and handed the bottle back to Roberto. "Thanks."

The sound of the mesh screen being zipped closed filled the tent, then I felt Roberto stretch out on his sleeping bag beside me. Metal clinked against metal, as he tucked the pistol down the front of his pants. When I briefly opened my eyes, I saw his fingers go tight around the pistol grips.

Softly, he said, "Hal, do you think it was Bates who attacked you last night?"

"Could have been. Didn't sound like his voice, though."

Shifting around for a comfortable position, his jeans made a scratchy sound against his nylon bag. "What about Jones? He's the one I'd peg for the job."

"Could have been."

"I know you didn't see his face, but can you guess how tall he was? How much he weighed?"

Pulling my pillow over my eyes, I covered it with both arms, pressing down to block out as much light as I could. My headache felt a little better, though sparks flitted and soared through the blackness. "He was shorter than me. When he had his mouth against my ear, I could feel his toes digging for purchase above my hiking boots. So . . . I don't know, maybe he was five foot six. As to weight, I'd say around one-sixty."

"There are probably fifty guys here that meet that description. But very few of them know your name. Did he have an accent?"

"Yeah. Egyptian, but he could have been disguising his voice."

There was silence for a time, while Roberto thought about that.

In the interval, I observed the dark gray behind my eyes, and the fluttering light gray around the edges, and made special note of the dove-gray sparks flying around. A guy could suffer sensory deprivation from covering his face with a pillow. Which is exactly what I wanted. I'd had enough of strange scents and lights today.

"When you said you saw Cleo—" Roberto started slow, "—I was wondering . . . Did you think it was really her?"

"Or a shape-shifting demon, you mean?"

"Right."

"She looked and sounded like Cleo."

"But demons must be really good at disguise. I mean, they live forever, right? They've had a lot of practice screwing with mortals."

Yawning, I said, "I guess so."

"If they're immortal, how do you kill one?"

I could feel myself falling to sleep, my breathing getting deeper and slower. "Kryptonite?"

"See, that's what makes me nervous. I don't like danger I can't pull a gun on."

Metal clinked against metal again. And again. And again. It sounded like he was rubbing something with his pistol.

"Tell me you're not doing what it sounds like you're doing?"

The clinking stopped. "What does it sound like?"

"You're being careful with that pistol, right?"

"Are you really asking me if I'm using the gun to scratch my balls?"

"I know the answer to that. Where's your finger?"

"What?" He sounded worried.

I hugged the pillow tighter over my face. "Is it on the trigger?"

"Of course not. I took a gun safety class. Rule number one is: know where your finger is."

I had to ease up on the pillow over my face because I was smothering myself. When I did, the dark gray behind my eyes shimmered into soft gray and I felt myself drifting off. . . .

In the dream, I'm not afraid.

I open my eyes and see Cleo at my bedside, holding my hand, smiling. "My God, Halloran, are you awake?"

"Yeah . . ." I inhale and let it out slowly as I look around the room. I'm in a hospital with white, white walls. There's an IV in my arm, and a bag filled with clear liquid dripping into it. "Where am I?"

"You're in Denver. You've been in a coma for a month." Crying softly, she squeezes my hand. "How do you feel?"

"I'm okay, Cleo."

A coma? I should have known. My injured brain has been concocting bizarre stories while I slept. Don't know why, or what happened . . .

"I love you, Halloran. I've been here every day, begging you to wake up."

She loves me. We're going to go to Egypt together some day to find Cleopatra's grave.

But for now she's smiling at me, holding my hand. Tears of happiness glisten in her eyes. She's so pretty. Her fingers are warm where they twine with mine. Dear God, let me stay here in the hospital. I just want to hold her hand for a while. Let me do that . . . And I'll be good.

CHAPTER THIRTY-NINE

*D*ally? Stevens?"

Moriarity's voice barely penetrated my dream. I rolled over to go back to sleep.

Then I heard Roberto say, "Yeah. What?"

"I need you to come out here." Moriarity's voice sounded higher than normal, as though straining against emotion.

Roberto's hand lightly shook my shoulder. "Hal? Gotta get up. Sorry."

"I'm awake."

I dragged myself to a sitting position and rubbed my eyes. Through the mesh screen, I could see several pairs of legs shifting uneasily outside, as well as students walking across the site, heading toward the cook tent for dinner. The pale glow of dusk had fallen over Pelusium.

"Did I sleep for so long?" I turned to Roberto.

"You needed to. How do you feel?" He was combing his hair with a blue comb, which he handed to me.

"Better. Almost no headache now." As I combed my sweaty hair, I watched him crawl forward and unzip the mesh screen.

The people gathered outside murmured softly. I could only identify two voices: Moriarity and Corbelle. I didn't think I'd ever heard the other two men before.

Roberto ducked outside first, but I wasn't far behind. My gaze touched on Moriarity, then LaSalle, noting her worried expression. Moriarity looked like a damned soul awaiting judgment. The other two men might have been stone-cold Egyptian killers. They wore no expressions. Both carried notebooks in their hands.

Moriarity extended his hand to us. "This is Hal Stevens and Robert Dally. My students from Colorado. Boys, this is Officer Fatimid and Officer Sattin. Robert, I think you met Detective Sattin in Colorado."

"Yeah."

The tall lanky man, Officer Fatimid, didn't speak. He just looked at the older man next to him, waiting for Officer Sattin to take the lead.

"Who found the body?" Sattin asked in a calm voice.

"What body?" I said.

"I did," Moriarity replied. "I was out checking my students' excavations—"

"*What body?*" I interrupted.

"But I was less than ten seconds behind Jim," LaSalle added, ignoring me. "So, basically, the two of us arrived at the same time."

"I see." Sattin jotted down a couple of notes, then lifted his pen from his notebook and aimed it at Moriarity. "Who moved the body from the excavation pit?"

Moriarity licked his lips nervously. "I did."

I glanced between them. *"Will somebody tell me what's going on?"*

"Hal," LaSalle said gently, "there's been a death. Just relax and answer the officers' questions as best you can."

"Who died?"

Sattin watched me like a hawk, studying every detail, my shock, my rapid breathing, then he turned back to Moriarity. "I'll answer that in a moment," he said, and turned back to Moriarity. "Why did you move the body?"

"He was covered with dirt. I wanted to get a better look at him, to search for wounds."

Sattin's bushy black brows knitted as he wrote more notes. "Did you find any?"

"No."

"And where were you last night, Dr. Moriarity?"

"Asleep with my wife in my tent. She'll verify my story."

"I'm certain she will." Sattin smiled politely. "And you three, where were you?"

LaSalle said, "Asleep in my tent. Alone. No one can verify my story."

Roberto and I exchanged glances. I'd learned my lesson about telling the police the whole truth, but I wasn't sure how to formulate a believable lie. I hadn't had much practice, and worse, I had no idea who was dead. Fear was burning through my veins. "I was out looking at the site in the starlight until around midnight."

"And I was wandering through the camp trying to find him," Roberto said.

Sattin fixed Roberto with dark unblinking eyes. "Can anyone verify your story, Mr. Dally?"

"I talked to lots of people, asking them if they'd seen Hal, so I guess so. Am I a suspect?"

Sattin swiveled to face me. "Can anyone verify your whereabouts, Mr. Stevens?"

Back in Colorado, before I got smart, I would have said, *Sure, just ask the ghost.* Fortunately, I knew better. "I don't think so, sir. I was by myself."

He stared unblinking into my eyes for several seconds, before writing in his book, and I was pretty sure that over the years he'd developed a sixth sense for when someone was lying. "When did you two find each other?"

"Around midnight. I was over by the cook tent when I was attacked."

"Attacked?" Sattin asked in surprise. "Why has no one told me about this assault?"

Moriarity made an airy gesture. "It didn't seem important, not with everything else going on."

Sattin looked annoyed. To me, he said, "Who attacked you?"

"I don't know, sir. He hit me from behind, knocked me to the ground. I screamed and woke the whole camp. People started running toward me, including Roberto. That's what scared him away."

"Can you describe this man who attacked you?"

"No, never saw his face."

Sattin aimed his pen at my face. "Is that how you got that purple bump on your head?"

"Yeah. The guy slammed my head into a broken table leg."

"Did anyone else see him? Perhaps as he ran away?" Sattin looked around. When everyone shook their heads, he frowned down at his notebook and wrote something. "Later, I'd like to see the place you were attacked, and I'll need to speak with rest of the camp."

"Of course," Moriarity said.

Sattin closed his notebook. "Let us return to the corpse with Mr. Stevens and Mr. Dally."

The officer led the way past the tents and out toward the Roman fortress wall, the students in the dinner line watched us with dire expressions. A few were crying. That set my heart to pumping.

I almost stumbled when I saw the police van parked near the sterile pit we'd dug yesterday. Beside it, a man knelt over a sheet-covered body.

A dead body was found covered with dirt near our pit?

Sattin walked around the excavation to stand over the kneeling man. Around forty, he had rich brown skin and sunken eyes. They spoke in Egyptian for a few minutes. Though they were speaking quickly, I could pick up a few words. Sattin kept asking, *"Emta, Hussein?"* which meant 'when, Hussein,' so I assumed he was asking about time of death, and then Sattin said, *"Ana mish fahem,"* "I don't understand." In response, the man on the ground shook his head and rose to his feet. They talked for a while longer before Officer Sattin turned his attention to the sheet-covered body.

"Dr. Corbelle," he said, "please describe how the body was lying in the excavation?"

LaSalle walked over to stand beside Dr. Hussein. "On his back, his arms and legs sprawled." She demonstrated and continued talking. Occasionally, Sattin nodded or frowned.

Roberto leaned close to whisper, "You're weaving on your feet, Hal. You okay?"

"Yeah." I was weaving? I spread my feet and forced myself to take deep breaths. There was a trowel lying in the northeast corner of the pit. Had we left a trowel?

Though twilight was settling across the delta, waves of heat rose from the sand, spawning a mirage that made it look like a thin layer of shimmering water covered the ground. The Roman fortress wall seemed to be floating in the air just above the water.

Without waiting for authorization, I walked over to the sheet-covered body and threw it back to see who lay beneath.

Samael's mouth had frozen into a final silent scream, and his dead eyes stared blindly up me, as though begging me to do something.

I staggered backward, breathing hard. He gave me his protection amulet, the stone amulet of Ammut. It was hanging around my neck. Without it, he was completely vulnerable. He . . .

Robert cried, "Wh—what happened? Oh, my God!"

Dr. Hussein quietly walked over. "That's what we are trying to discover."

I choked out the words: "He can't be dead! He was just an old man. Why would anyone kill him?" I wiped my face on my sleeve, and took a deep breath.

"How did he die? Was he murdered?" Roberto asked.

Officer Sattin frowned at him. "Why would you think that, Mr. Dally?"

"Moriarity said he was covered with dirt. Samael couldn't have done that by himself, right?"

LaSalle extended both hands in a calming gesture. "There are no signs of violence, Robert. He was old. He may have just suffered a heart attack or a stroke. When he fell into the pit, he probably struck the back dirt pile, and it cascaded over the top of him. We won't really know until Dr. Hussein has a chance to examine him in his lab."

"But I was attacked last night, too!" I half shouted. "Maybe we were attacked by the same person?"

The color drained from Roberto's face. Subtly, he reached around to check for the pistol tucked into his pants beneath his shirt, then he scanned the crowd running toward us. His breathing had gone shallow. I could see his chest rising and falling with swift breaths.

And it occurred to me that carrying a firearm without the approval of the Egyptian authorities was a crime punishable by imprisonment.

"Hal, try to calm down. We don't know Samael was attacked. There's no sign of a struggle. No sign that he tried to run. Maybe—"

"How can you say that? Why would his body be lying sprawled in this pit? That doesn't make any sense. Someone killed him and dumped him in there! They're sending me a signal."

LaSalle said, "He may have just come out to look at the excavation, suffered a heart attack, and fallen backward into the pit. That's what it looks like."

Officer Sattin leisurely walked around to stand between Dr. Hussein and me. He stared at me with narrowed eyes and a half-smile on his dark face. Scary. "Both you and Mr. Dally think a murder was committed. Why? What kind of a signal do you think someone was sending you?"

Turn over the dagger, or you're next....

The same hollow ache I'd felt at Cleo's death was back and beginning to fill me up inside. "I don't know. I'm sorry, I'm not thinking straight."

"That's true," LaSalle said. "Hal is suffering from a mild concussion he received during his attack last night. He's been in bed most of the day, Officer Sattin."

"That may be, Doctor," Sattin said in a friendly voice, "but Mr. Stevens thinks Samael Saqqara was murdered to send him a message. So I must ask Mr. Stevens to explain himself."

I hated talking to the police. It always got me in hot water. "I just meant . . . He was my friend. And my friends keep dying, and I don't know why." Tears blurred my eyes.

Moriarity's expression changed, going from shock to grief to downright fear, as though he'd just made a connection that I had not. "Officer, my niece, Hal's girlfriend, was murdered about a month ago in Colorado. That's what he means. I brought him to Egypt in the hope of easing that trauma. He's been having problems coping with his grief."

"I see."

Sattin gestured to Fatimid who scribbled in his notebook. I had the feeling Fatimid was extremely competent, the ideal second-in-command who followed orders without fail, whether it be cleaning the departmental urinal or herding people into cattle cars. No muss. No fuss. He'd get the job done.

As though utterly devastated, Moriarity crouched beside Samael and gripped the old man's stiff hand. He choked back sobs.

LaSalle walked around the pit and knelt in front of him. "Jim, don't. He wouldn't want you to—"

"I should have never asked him to come here. He didn't want to. And I knew he was blind, and there was a very small chance he might be able to relocate the old excavation."

"He loved being here, Jim. He told me so. He was an archaeologist. This is where he spent the happiest days of his life."

Jerking up his chin, he stared at Hussein through blurry eyes. "What's your estimate of time of death, Dr. Hussein?"

"Sometime between eight last night and midnight."

I felt the blood drain from my head. About the same time the entwined skeletons had been vandalized. And the same time I was attacked.

Those were also the four hours that I could not account for. The four hours when I was in the ancient corridor covered with cartouches. Where Cleo came to me. Was it possible that I'd suffered some kind of a blackout? That I'd vandalized the entwined skeletons and then . . .

I couldn't even think the words.

Officer Sattin tucked his notebook in his chest pocket and looked up at the darkening sky. "It's getting late. We'll return tomorrow. For now, we are assuming this is not a murder. Do you have plans to leave the site?"

Moriarity nodded. "Everyone is leaving tonight, including me. My wife is ill. She has a doctor's appointment in Alexandria tomorrow afternoon, but we'll be staying at the Hilton, if you need us. I'll be taking Hal and Robert with me. I want to make sure they're sa—"

"We're not going," I said.

"I'm not leaving you here alone, boys. You have no idea what's—"

"We'll be with LaSalle. Sarah said she never leaves on the four-days."

"True." LaSalle propped her hands on her hips. "I'll watch out for them, Jim. Take as long as you need in Alexandria."

"All right. I guess." Moriarity turned to Sattin. "Or would you rather that I cancel the four-day and my wife's appointment?"

Sattin mildly shook his head. "Not necessary. But if anyone does not return to work after the four-day, I need to know about it."

"Of course."

Dr. Hussein turned to Fatimid and asked something in Egyptian, then they gently wrapped Samael in the sheet and carried the body to the police van where they stowed it in the rear and closed the doors.

As Fatimid got in behind the wheel, he said, "*Masa' el khayr*," which meant "good evening."

"*Inshallah*," LaSalle called back. "God willing."

Sattin got into the passenger side of the van without a word and slammed the door.

Weak-kneed, I balled my fists and watched them drive away, but my eyes kept straying to the sterile pit where I'd buried the dagger. Was that Samael's trowel? Had he been hunting for the dagger? Was it still there? I had to find it, to move to it, before the police returned to do a closer examination of the murder scene—and I was sure it was a murder scene.

"Come on," Moriarity said. "Let's get dinner. It's been a rough day."

CHAPTER FORTY

The sounds of plates and forks clattering carried on the light breeze blowing across the site. When I turned to study the students eating dinner, I found almost every eye glued to us. The few that weren't on us were watching the van disappearing in a cloud of dust.

LaSalle stood in silence with us for what seemed an eternity before she said, "If you're feeling well enough, I'd like to show you both something before we head to dinner. It won't take long."

Though I felt like my insides had been hollowed out, I said, "Sure. I don't think I could stomach any food right now anyway."

Roberto said, "Where are we going?"

"The temple." LaSalle started walked westward.

"Did you find something today?"

"We did. Something very interesting."

"What is it?"

LaSalle's voice turned a little dark. "You need to see it with your own eyes."

My legs felt heavy as we marched toward the purple glow on the horizon. The sun had just sunk into the underworld, and the night birds had started calling across the waving stems of papyrus. For some reason, the air smelled more salty and fragrant at nightfall. I drew it into my lungs, holding it like a healing tonic, before slowly exhaling.

To my left, Roberto trudged through the sand with his head down. I could see his teeth grinding beneath his sparse beard, thinking hard, no doubt. As I was.

When he caught me staring at him, he whispered, *"We're in trouble."*

I nodded.

I just didn't know what to do about it. Run? We could run. We could also hide, maybe return to Samael's cave in the desert. Or we could stay and face the danger. But I knew the safe choice. If we were smart, we'd grab the dagger and head for the Port Said airport.

Far back in my mind, I could see Cleo staring at me with forgiveness in her eyes.

When we reached the temple, LaSalle said, "Be careful. The water table was up today. The steps are weeping."

She took the stairs down one cautious step at a time.

Roberto followed next, and I finally stepped onto the top stair. The different sizes of bricks that funneled me downward into the darkness shimmered with moisture. I could feel it tonight. My body turned light as a feather, as though my flesh was gone, and only my soul journeyed downward toward the land of the dead. At the fourth and fifth hours, the dim realm of the cemetery god Seker seemed to come alive. I heard faint inhuman laughter echo around the walls. My gaze shot upward, but I was having trouble locating the source of the voices. They seemed to come from the gaping mouths of the carved heads that thrust from each layer of stone. The demons that guarded the hours.

Stop this. You're terrifying yourself.

Taking my imagination in firm hands, I realized the cackling must originate from drops of water falling onto ledges below. Actually, when I thought about it, the sound was more like a rattle than a cackle.

By the time I reached the approach to the Kingdom of Osiris, the walls breathed. Though I knew it was the reverberations of Roberto's and LaSalle's breathing, it still unnerved me, just as it must have the ancient priests who'd entered this temple two thousand years ago.

High above, the sky shaded to slate blue as night deepened, turning the pools of water scattered across the floor into leaden eyes.

Was she here? Was Cleo waiting for me? I glanced around, but saw nothing.

LaSalle must have seen me reach into my pocket for my flashlight because she called, "No flashlight, please, Hal. I want you to see it in natural light first."

"Okay." However, I clutched my flashlight in my hand, my finger on the button, ready to turn it on in an instant.

Roberto called, "Wow. This is amazing, Hal."

As I got closer, I could see Roberto inside the tunnel. LaSalle remained outside, standing straight and tall, as though she were an ancient priestess guarding the gate to the Kingdom of Osiris. Her blonde hair and ivory-colored shirt glowed in the faint light of evening.

Roberto scuttled backward, out of the tunnel, and stared at me with wide eyes. "Your turn, buddy. Be careful, the stairs are slick in there."

Gripping my flashlight as though it were a magical sword that could slay demons, I hesitated at the mouth of the tunnel to glance at LaSalle. "What's down there?"

Her face shone like polished marble when she turned to look into my eyes. "Go see for yourself. But no flashlight. You'll ruin it."

I suddenly realized that I was not a courageous person. My cowardly streak was growing wider by the instant. Girding myself, I stepped into the tunnel and began climbing down the wet stairs. The deeper I went, the more familiar it became. Except now, in the twilight gleam, the plastered walls glowed as though backlit. Reaching out, I touched them and felt crushed shells beneath my fingertips.

"My God." My whisper rang through the tunnel as though I'd shouted. "The entire passageway was painted with crushed pearls."

"Correct," LaSalle called down. "This is no ordinary tunnel to the Kingdom of Osiris. This is a royal gateway to the afterlife."

"Can I turn on my flashlight now?"

"Yes, and I want you to walk all the way to the bottom of the tunnel."

Switching on my flashlight, the beam seemed to set the walls aflame. The pearlescent shimmer almost blinded me. With one hand braced against the wall, I continued climbing downward until I hit the bottom stair. There, to my right, was the corridor I had walked last night. It had been excavated all the way back to the dead end. The cartouches stamped into the walls cast shadows in my flashlight beam.

"It's here," I whispered in awe. "I didn't dream it. It's really here!"

At that revelation, fear charged my muscles. If the corridor was here, did that mean I had not imagined Cleo? Had she truly come to warn me? If I'd stayed and spoken with her, would she have told me they planned to kill Samael? Would she have revealed the identities of my enemies? Of *her* enemies? Why hadn't I trusted her?

Shining my beam around, I searched for her, hoping to see her, but I saw only the empty corridor and shimmering tunnel.

"Come out now, Hal. Let's talk," LaSalle called.

Her voice boomed around me, magnified by the tunnel and corridor. Turning, I switched off my flashlight and climbed the luminescent passageway lit only by the first stars born in the sky.

Euphoria filled me. My feet did not seem to be touching the steps, but striking the air just above them.

When I emerged and stood between LaSalle and Roberto, my best friend said, "Is that what you saw in your dream?"

All I could do was nod.

"I knew it."

LaSalle nodded, too, but I wasn't sure she was aware of it. It was one of those faint nods a person gives when they are deep in thought, not really here in this world. "Did you glimpse anything beyond the dead end? What lies on the other side, Hal?"

"I didn't see anything."

"Even in your imagination? When you first saw the dead end, did your mind flicker with images? Samael's used to."

The whole experience had possessed a surreal quality, so I wasn't sure I should tell her, but I said, "Gold. The glitter of gold in lamplight. But I thought I was just being influenced by Howard Carter's first glimpse of Tut's tomb."

"Could be. We won't know until we get behind that wall."

Roberto propped his hands on his hips. "If everyone is leaving for four days off, you won't have this excavated for a while."

"I'm not leaving. I plan to break through that wall tomorrow morning. Want to help?"

"Yes," Roberto and I said at the same time.

After a short hesitation, I asked, "LaSalle, the cartouches stamped into the walls, do you have any idea whose name they represent? There are hundreds of them down there."

"No. But the name must have been very important to whoever built that corridor."

Dusty starlight filled the temple, reflecting from the standing walls and shining upon the pools of water on the floor. The laughter started again, barely there, just a distant cackling, and I noticed the tiny trickles of water that ran down the walls like silver threads.

LaSalle followed my gaze. "Yes, that's a curious feature of this temple. Though it sits at the highest point of the site, about seven feet above sea level, the temple walls soak up water from the shallow water table and sometimes, always at night, streams penetrate through the cracks and flow down the walls. It's a beautiful sight, especially at moonrise."

Aching loneliness swelled my chest, but I had the feeling it did not belong to me. It belonged to someone else, someone old and tired, someone who had lost all hope.

As though reading my thoughts, LaSalle frowned. In a low voice, she said, "I've been wondering . . . Do you feel Samael's soul out there tonight? Does he call to you?"

Roberto shook his head. "Not to me."

Stars reflected in the largest pool of water three paces in front of me. Like jewels, they twinkled and flashed.

"No," I replied.

She jerked a nod as though it had been a silly question and she knew it. "I was just wondering. I thought, if he was going to speak to anyone, it would be you. I wish I knew what happened to him last night."

I stood there like a lump on a log, mute.

"Well," she said at last. "You two must be starving. You missed lunch today."

As she led the way around the puddles, she passed the flaking hieroglyphics on the northern wall.

I said, "LaSalle, what's this panel talking about? So much of the plaster has flaked off I can't get the gist of the story."

Smiling, she said, "Yes, it is hard to figure out. On the far left, do you see the image of Set? He's the blue guy. Then on the opposite side, see the cow's horns embracing the solar disk? It seems to be floating, attached to nothing."

"Yes."

"Two thousand years ago, you would have seen a beautiful woman in a sheath dress, probably carrying her son Horus in her arms. The disk and horns would have been perched upon her head."

"Then the story is of Isis, Set, and the murder of Osiris?"

"Actually, I think that's Cleopatra in the guise of Isis. Can you see the faint images of the cobras next to her?"

I shook my head. "Not in this light."

"Tomorrow, you'll see them. This particular Isis Temple—"

"This is a Temple to Isis?"

"Yes, I assumed that Jim had explained that."

"No, he didn't."

. . . adjacent to a temple to Isis.

LaSalle gave a nod to the crumbling wall that blocked the view of the sarcophagus. "Have you seen the partial painting of the woman on the sarcophagus?"

"Yes, but we weren't sure what it meant."

LaSalle waved an arm for us to follow her. "Come on, let me show you."

She carefully scaled the giant chunk of fallen wall and climbed down the other side. I heard her feet splash in water when she landed. Placing my boots with care, I climbed next, followed by Roberto.

When we stood beside her, looking at the beautiful face painted on the stone, LaSalle said, "I can't wait to get this fully excavated and see what's inside. Given her purple dress and elaborately braided hair, I am fairly sure she is a member of the Ptolemaic dynasty." She reached out to hold her finger over the fangs of the cobra on the woman's headdress. "If the painting were intact and showed three cobras, we'd know this is Cleopatra. Two cobras would tell us this is her half sister, Arsinoe IV."

Dust suddenly gusted across the top of the temple as the wind picked up. All around me, the standing walls sighed and whimpered.

"Are you saying this sarcophagus might belong to Cleopatra's sister?"

LaSalle gestured at the painting glowing in the starlight. "I think it's possible that her body was brought home from Turkey, where Antonius killed her, to be buried in Egypt. But, regardless, this particular Temple to Isis seems to be dedicated to Ptolemaic women."

Robert's gaze drifted over the clouds moving through the darkening sky. Lightning flashed, and the temple blazed like the white throat of some primeval serpent. "Let's get out of here. This is a creepy place to start with, but if there's a storm coming, I really don't want to be here."

"I'm with you."

Our boots splashed in puddles as we climbed back up and stood atop the wall.

Strangely, LaSalle stayed beside the sarcophagus. "I'll be just a little longer. Go on without me. I'll meet you at the tables."

Roberto said, "Okay, see you there."

"No," I said. "We're not leaving you alone out here. There's a murderer on the loose."

"Hal," she said in a soft voice. "I'm pretty good at determining cause of death. I work with homicide investigators all the time. I was in Denver working with the FBI just a month ago. I'm sure Samael died from natural causes. I'll be fine, and I'll be right behind you."

"Okay, but if you're not there in fifteen minutes, I'm coming back."

"I appreciate your concern. Thanks."

Hesitantly, I walked after Roberto.

When we'd trotted up the stairs and reached the rim of the temple, I turned around. I couldn't see her from up here, but I had a bad feeling about leaving her alone.

"Want us to save you a seat at the table?" I called.

"Sure. Thanks."

Water gurgled near the sarcophagus, as though she were wading through the pool examining the painting in the flashes of lightning.

Switching on my flashlight, I led the way to dinner. The beam bounced in time with my steps.

Roberto said, "She's braver than I am."

"Me, too. By a long shot."

I took the most direct route back, moving in silence through the lifeless, wind-lashed ruins.

CHAPTER FORTY-ONE

B y the time we arrived at the dinner line, most of the students had finished eating. There was no laughter tonight. No playful horsing around. As I watched the last of the archaeologists meandering out toward the parking lot to leave for four days, I noticed that my headache had vanished. My brain was working better, thank God, because I had a lot of thinking to do.

Roberto picked up two plates and forks in the cook tent. He handed me one set.

"We should fix a plate for LaSalle, too." I picked up another plate.

Three Egyptian laborers were still in the tent. They looked eager to have us finish so they could start cleaning up. They'd already begun washing dishes. Soft clattering filled the air.

We filled all three plates with spicy goat kebabs on skewers, rice, and salad. At the end of the line, sat a clay pot of tahini, but by the time I got there, it was almost gone. I tilted the pot and scraped the dregs over my rice. Roberto grabbed three bottles of water and we headed for the abandoned tables.

It was the first time I'd seen the tables empty. Sitting in front of the only lantern, our faces had a pallid gleam.

Roberto glanced at the tent where laborers spoke in soft voices, and whispered, "We could be murdered in our sleep tonight. You get that, right?"

"I get it. But I don't think they'd dare kill again so soon after Samael."

"Maybe not, but I have to admit it freaked me a bit when I saw Moriarity pull out of the parking lot."

"Did he?" I asked, alarmed. "You sure?"

"Oh, yeah. He's gone. It's just you, me, and my Ruger pistol." He patted the gun stuffed into his pants beneath his shirt.

"And LaSalle."

"Yeah. Do you really think Samael was murdered?" He took a long drink of his water and exhaled hard. Sweat-soaked brown hair stuck to his cheeks and forehead.

Leaning across the table, I replied, "The guy who tackled me last night asked me . . ."

Two dishwashers came out and started wiping off the empty tables with wet cloths. Before they disappeared, they gave us curious glances. Dishes clanged and clinked again as they apparently returned to washing.

"Asked you what?" Roberto took a bite and chewed.

"He asked me about the dagger, then said, 'Is that what the old man was trying to dig up?' Now I'm wondering—"

"Tell me that is *not* where you hid it?"

I just looked at him.

"Oh, my God." Roberto squeezed his eyes closed for a second. "Okay, let's be calm about this. The first thing we have to do is go see if it's still there."

"Agreed." I chewed a kebab and swallowed. "Roberto, do you think he killed Samael before he attacked me or after?"

"He used the past tense, didn't he? '. . . *was* trying to dig up?' Must have been after. Do you think Samael told him you had the dagger?"

Using my fork, I cut a chunk of goat in half and ate it while I thought about that. "Maybe."

Inside the cook tent, the Arab dishwashers must have put away the last of the plates and forks. The metallic clashings died down. One of the men walked out and gave us a questioning look.

"About done?" he called.

Roberto called back, "You can go home. We'll wash our own dishes."

"Okay." The man lifted a hand.

A short time later, the men walked out of the tent and headed for the parking lot.

We ate in silence for a while, watching the lightning flash in the distance. It occurred to me that after my assailant had run away last night, he might have gone back to the pit to dig for the dagger. When he'd finished, he'd shoved Samael's body into the pit and left. With the dagger? Or was it still where I'd buried it?

On the eastern horizon, the first sliver of the moon edged above the delta. If the clouds didn't completely obscure the sky, in a few hours I'd be able to go search the pit for the dagger without having to use my flashlight.

While I waited, my body vibrated with adrenaline. I tried not to swallow my food whole, but it was a challenge. The only thing I wanted to do was get to that pit and determine if the dagger was still there.

Roberto finished his food, and set his fork aside. "Hal, listen, I want you to play an imagination game with me. You're really good at that."

"Sure."

"Okay, I'm Samael, you're the murderer. I—Samael—have been worried about the dagger. After all, I found it in Charmion's hand, and I was Charmion in a former life. Maybe I considered it mine, but it was taken away from me by Hassan Mallawi. After searching your tent, I've been trying to figure out where you'd hide the dagger, and I've concluded you must have hidden it in the sterile pit. So I'm going to go search—"

"Why didn't you conclude I had it strapped to my body?"

"Because I've gotten to know you a little. I'm pretty sure you're smarter than that."

"Okay. Next?"

"I grab my trowel and leave my tent at around eleven last night. I'm blind, but I don't want to be seen, so . . . what do I do?"

Pausing, I considered. "The moon is heading toward the western horizon. You walk in the shadow cast by the fortress wall. That gives you the cover of darkness, but you can also keep one hand against the bricks to steady yourself."

"And I know the pit is right at the end of the wall. All I have to do is follow the wall, and I'll be there. But I have to walk carefully. I don't want to fall, so it takes me about thirty minutes, right?"

I thought about it. "Right."

"When I get past the end of the wall, I stop and listen to make sure I'm alone, then I feel my way forward with my feet until I find the pit. What are you doing?"

Shifting points of view, I tried to get into the murderer's mind. It took a few seconds before I could feel the coolness of night around me, smell the bricks radiating the heat of the day. The predator inside me suddenly woke. "I see you. And I'm close, maybe just on the other side of the fortress wall."

"Why are you out there at midnight? Were you restless? You couldn't sleep? Why couldn't you sleep?"

"I've been watching the pit, waiting . . ."

From out of the moonlight, I saw a figure walking toward me, coming from the temple. Like a mountain lion, her muscular body flowed with each step. Elegant. Silent. I stiffened involuntarily when it occurred to me that she was walking exactly the same path Cleo had last night.

Roberto whirled around. "It's LaSalle."

"Sorry. I—I'm just jumpy."

"I certainly hope so."

Digging into my dinner, I shoveled a mixture of deliciously tender goat meat and rice into my mouth. The tahini gave each bite a light sesame flavor that I found comforting.

As she passed, LaSalle waved. "Good night. Get some rest, you two."

"Aren't you having dinner?" I called. "We fixed a plate for you."

"Thanks, but not hungry. I'll see you in the morning."

"Okay . . ." My voice trailed away. I'd been hoping to question her more about what had happened today while Roberto and I slept, but I guess that would have to wait.

When she was out of earshot, Roberto said, "Back to the imagination game. You were watching the pit, waiting for us? Why would you assume we'd be out there at midnight? That doesn't make any sense."

I blinked. Picking up my bottle, I took a long drink of water. It was just barely cool. "I've changed my mind."

"About what?"

"About why I'm out there. I'm out there at midnight because it's my job."

Leaning back on the bench, Roberto stared at me. He must be thinking about my description of the demon I'd seen the day Cleo died. The Egyptian Army uniform.

Bracing both elbows, Roberto glanced around the darkness, then leaned across the table to whisper, "Listen, Hal, if that's true, we've got to—"

"What do you do when you see me?" I had to continue the game to the end. It was imperative now.

Roberto swallowed hard. "I don't see you. But I hear you coming. I hear your feet on the sand."

"Why don't you run?"

Roberto lifted his gaze to my face. His breathing has gone shallow. "I know you."

"Did you recognize the sound of my steps?"

"No, you spoke to me. I recognized your voice."

"Okay. You have less than five minutes to live. What do you hear?"

With a light shake of his head, Roberto said, "You ask me if I found the dagger."

"Why do I think you're looking for the dagger?"

In the dim gleam of the solar lantern, I saw Roberto's shoulder muscles contract beneath his shirt. "Because I told you I'd get it. I guaranteed it. Why else would I out be out here at midnight?"

"Is that why you've been making such good friends with the kids from Colorado?" It hurt to say the words, but they sounded true.

"Oh, fuck. Of course."

Our gazes locked. "So you and I are in this together. Why do I kill my partner?"

"Maybe we're not that good of pals. Maybe the only reason we're in this together is that we both want to find the grave of Cleopatra. What do I say to piss you off enough that you'll kill me?"

Trying to think like the murderer, I said, "You tell me you found the dagger, but you're not giving it to me."

"Yeah, but you're bigger and younger than me. Just take it from me. You don't have to kill me."

"True. But now that I have it, I don't want anyone to know I've got it. No one. Which means you have to go."

Thoughts danced behind Roberto's eyes. He took another swig of water. "Doesn't work. In five minutes you're going attack Hal Stevens, and ask him where the dagger is. Which means I didn't give you the dagger."

"Oh. Right." My imagination was floating through possibilities. "Maybe when you heard me coming, you were scared. You hid it."

"Or maybe I left my tent at ten o'clock, an hour earlier."

"Which means you found the dagger long before you saw me just before midnight. What were you doing with the dagger for an hour?"

"You tell me, bro."

In my mind, I could feel Samael's shaky old body, and feel him turn around, start to walk away in the direction of the entwined skeletons.

A surge of fear went through me. "You walked over to place the dagger in the hand of the large skeleton."

"Why?"

Rubbing my stinging face, I replied, "God, I wish I knew. Samael said— "

"Let's go find out." Tipping his bottle up, Roberto drained it dry and set it on the table with a clunk. "Even if we don't find the dagger, we can improvise, use something else."

Chugging my last swallow of water, I stood up, leaving the dirty dishes, and LaSalle's full plate, behind.

Roberto led the way toward the sterile pit where I was sure an old man had been murdered.

CHAPTER FORTY-TWO

As we crossed the field camp, the full moon wavered through dark clouds—there one instant, gone the next. On the few occasions when it broke through, the watery gleam of moonlight painted the ruins, then it vanished, and rain sprinkled around us.

The fragrances of damp bricks and earth rose.

When we arrived at the fortress wall, I said, "Let's walk on the side Samael would have walked."

Roberto looked up at the sky. "Right. By midnight, the moon would have been on the other side of the wall."

I took the lead, trying to imagine how the blind old man would have made his way along the wall, feeling with his left hand while he used his walking stick to steady his steps.

"Roberto? Did you see his walking stick at the pit?"

"No, but the police probably collected a lot of evidence before we got there."

"Then why didn't they pick up his trowel?"

Behind me, I heard Roberto stop walking. He hesitated. "I don't know. That doesn't make any sense. Maybe in Egypt, if they have no evidence that a crime was committed, they don't touch stuff. Or maybe the police used it to dig up something and left it there."

Continuing along the fortress, I veered wide around fallen stones and toppled sections of walls. Each time lightning flashed in the distance, the ancient city came to life in front of my eyes. I could see outlines, actinic afterimages, of the soldiers who had once stood here. Helmeted and cloaked in armor, lances held at the ready. If I strained hard enough, I could hear horses whinnying and pawing in the nearby stables, and smell the scent of date beer in the air. Somewhere, bronze mugs clanked together, and men laughed.

At the end of the fortress wall, I halted and waited for the next lightning flash. The sterile three-by-three-meter unit appeared and disappeared. Stepping forward, I peered down the opposite side of the wall. In the next flare of brilliance, I searched for anyone or anything that might want to kill us. Nothing human moved. Just misty rain falling. We were apparently the only people out walking the site in the storm. Where were the guards? Huddling in one of the ruins until the rain stopped?

I trotted forward and crouched by the pit. Roberto came forward slowly. He had one hand behind him, on the pistol tucked into the back of his pants. When he knelt beside me, he didn't look at me. He was scanning the lightning-strobed world. His face blazed an instant before the bang of thunder crashed above us.

"That was close."

Roberto nodded. "Yeah, let's hurry. Grab the trowel and start digging."

Jumping down into the pit, I grasped the well-worn trowel, clearly an artifact of hundreds of digs, and felt its weight in my hand. Then I moved to the northwest corner and started digging. The sand was wet and heavy. I dug with my heart in my throat. *It has to be here.*

After two minutes, I tossed the trowel aside and slumped down in the pit on the verge of tears. The back dirt pile loomed beside me, a full meter high. It definitely looked like a body had toppled into it. A big swath of dirt had been knocked out. "It's not here."

"Figured that." Roberto rose to his feet. "Okay, let's head to the skeletons."

He extended a hand to me. I clasped it, letting him pull me to my feet. As I climbed out of the unit, I felt like a fool. Why hadn't I chosen a better place to hide it? I could have secreted it in a gap in the temple bricks, or buried it beneath a toppled wall. But I was afraid of being seen. Burying it in a pit that everyone knew contained nothing made sense at the time.

Roberto headed toward the entwined skeletons. Marching forward like a resolute infantryman, he had his head down, driving against the rain, planting each step in anticipation of the next.

Soaked to the bone, it occurred to me that we had been young once, just over a month ago. Before Cleo's murder. But I didn't think that was true anymore. My soul felt as hollow and as old as these dark ruins. Though, in truth, the ruins were not so much dark as the sky above was so ruptured with brilliance. For the moment, I tried not to think about how heartbroken Cleo would be that I'd lost the dagger. Besides, if she were out here, walking unseen beside me, she already knew. And I prayed she was out here.

Two paces ahead of me, Roberto sidestepped something, and pointed to the ground. "Big puddle, Hal."

"Thanks."

Making a wide detour around it, we continued to the site of the entwined skeletons, and stood looking down at the black tarp the archaeologists had pulled over the grave to protect it while they were gone.

"Let's get this off," Roberto said.

As we pulled the tarp back, rain fell upon the dead. The rain-drenched stela flashed when the sky exploded with light, and I swear the figure of Cleopatra seemed to turn her stone face and look directly at me . . . asking me to do something.

Dripping water, Roberto got down into the pit, and carefully positioned himself over the larger skeleton. "Hal, loan me your flashlight. It's about the right size to fit in the skeleton's closed fist."

Digging in my soggy pocket, I pulled it out and handed it to him.

Roberto slipped the flashlight into the ancient fingers and we waited for the next flash. Instead, the full moon crawled from behind a cloud and silver washed the world.

We stood there with our heads cocked, trying to fathom what it meant.

"I don't get it," Roberto said. "With the skeleton's fist twisted at that weird angle, the flashlight looks like a long pointing finger."

"What's it pointing at?" I stretched out on the lip of the excavation and tried to sight down the length of the "finger" to see what might be in the distance. "It aims at the fortress wall."

Roberto scratched the back of his neck, as though unhappy. "But the fortress dates to the sixth century, right? So it wasn't here when they were buried."

"Right, but . . . Could the blade have been pointing to the temple? Or to Caesarian's grave?"

He frowned at the fortress wall. "I'd give anything to be standing on top of the fortress wall right now. If we could see both directions, we could answer that question. There is, of course, another possibility, bro."

"What are you thinking?"

Roberto pulled my flashlight from the skeletal hand, climbed out of the pit, and handed it to me. "Well, what if the bagsu was placed in the hand with the point down, not up?"

Spinning around, I looked south. "That would mean it was pointing to something out in the depths of the desert. Something out near Samael's—"

"Or it could have been pointing in both directions. Or maybe it was pointing at nothing. Maybe the dagger isn't the clue. Maybe it's the skeletons that are the clue. Or the stela."

Blinking rain from my eyes, I said, "I wish I knew."

Roberto pulled his soaked shirt loose where it conformed to the outline of the pistol butt. "Speaking of the stela, has it occurred to you that the person who dropped the stela on the skeletons may have seen you out here with Samael and assumed this is where—"

"He was looking for the dagger?" I cut him off. My God, that made perfect sense. "Roberto? I need to go back to the sterile pit."

I broke into a trot, making time across the wet sand. Roberto's steps pounded behind me.

When I reached the pit, I stepped down into the excavation, picked up the trowel, and said, "I want us to switch imaginary rolls. I want you to be the murderer this time."

"Okay, what do you want me to do?"

Pointing with the trowel, I said, "Can you hide behind the fortress wall, watch me for a while, then come toward me."

"Got it."

While Roberto trotted for the fortress wall, I pulled out my flashlight and buried it in the hole where I'd hidden the dagger, covered it with sand, then started carefully excavating it. Trying to place myself in Samael's head, I sat down. *I am old, frail, and mostly blind, but I've been a great archaeologist for most of my life. I have to do this by feel alone. Feel the dirt. I don't want to destroy any fragile artifacts that might be buried here, including the bagsu. So I must go slowly, very slowly. When the pile of dirt beside me starts mounting up, interfering with my ability to dig, I scoop it up with both hands and add it to the back dirt pile. Five seconds later, my trowel "tinks" on something buried about thirty centimeters deep. Laying my precious trowel aside, I reach down into the hole and pull the object out with my fingers.*

Behind me, I hear footsteps.

Panic seizes me. I have to hide it! Not on me. Not in the hole I just dug. Where? Without thinking, I do the only thing I can. I blindly shove the dagger into the back dirt pile to my left.

The footsteps came closer.

Roberto said, "Hey, Samael, what are you doing out here?"

Frantically, I dove into the back dirt pile, throwing sand out with both hands. "Roberto, get over here and help me!"

"You think he hid it in the back dirt pile?"

"Yeah, come on! I think he shoved it in the dirt, then when he was attacked, he fell into the pile, probably pushing the dagger deeper."

Roberto charged over and started throwing dirt aside as fast as he could.

The clouds moved back in, turning the world a velvet black, punctured now and then by flashes. We'd been throwing dirt out for about five minutes when the sky opened up and poured rain on us, soaking us to the bone, but we kept digging.

When my hand touched warm metal, my fingers went tight around it. I pulled the dagger out and held it up to the flashes of lightning. The golden blade flickered as though catching fire.

Laughter. From the other side of the fortress. "I should have guess—"

"Hal, get down!"

Roberto shoved me so hard I tumbled sideways.

From the corner of my vision, I saw him draw the pistol from his shirt, aim it, and cry, "Stop! Who are you?"

Ten feet away, right where the fortress wall ended, a white light burst through the storm. Like a blossom opening. A white carnation. Then again. My body jerked with each blast. But I saw Roberto stagger and fall. He didn't drop the pistol until he hit the ground, then it bounced a few feet away.

Dragging himself toward it, he shouted, "KARNAK! KARNAK! Hal, *run!*"

Instead of running away, I ran to help Roberto.

Blood poured down the side of his face, and gushed from his leg. I willed the world to freeze, the blood to stop seeping out of the wounds.

Please, God. Not like Cleo. Not again.

Steps approached, heavy steps.

The darkness withered, going from velvet blackness to lunging flashes of white faces. Three faces. Big men in uniforms. That was the greatest shock. I was staring at the end. Even on my worst days, I had always felt hope. My brain was frantically trying to figure a way out. *Tackle the lead man. Grab his gun. Kill the others.*

I felt Roberto's fingers slide over my hand, weakly grip it, and drag it across the sand until it touched wet metal.

Abruptly, I was weightless.

My fist closed around the pistol.

CHAPTER FORTY-THREE

Wildly, I fired at the lead man, then I rolled to my feet and sprinted away. When I stole a glance over my shoulder, I saw one of the men on the ground, but the other two were after me and catching up fast.

The big man yelled, "Drop it!"

That deep voice . . . he was the man who'd attacked me last night.

I charged blindly out into the storm, heading westward. The chunks of wet glass that scattered the ground flickered in the storm. It was like running across a field of winking sparks.

"Stevens, stop! Don't make me shoot you!"

My mind was on overdrive, calculating how long it would be before they overtook me, fifteen or twenty seconds? I ran as hard as I could. Breath was sucking at the bottom of my lungs, trying to find air.

"Goddamn it!" someone shouted.

A shot rang out to my right and I saw sand fly up. A miss.

"Don't be a fool, boy! We don't want you dead."

"You shot my friend!" I screamed back.

"He had a gun!"

In the distance, a yellow halo glittered, like a bonfire's gleam filtered through the falling rain. Fire meant people. I charged toward it, wondering who had stayed behind to build a fire.

"You're giving me no choice, you young idiot!"

I glanced over my shoulder and saw the big man steady his pistol and draw a bead on me. From this range, even with the downpour, he couldn't miss.

A shot rang out, followed by two more, but I felt no bullets impact my body, and I couldn't figure out why. They were almost on top of me. I could hear their boots slamming the ground right behind me.

When I turned back, I saw Tashir appear out of the storm ahead of me, his gun in his hand, planning to finish me off. But less than two paces away, he yelled, "Hal, get down!"

I dove headfirst for the sand, listening to the gunfire echo from the fortress wall and ruins.

Tashir whirled around, stumbled, and toppled in front of me, less than a pace away.

I lay there, rigid, staring into his wide eyes. He clutched his chest as though to stanch the blood gushing between his fingers.

"Tashir?" I scrambled toward him on all fours.

When I huddled over him, looking down, I heard a sound I'd heard before while deer hunting. A watery sputter. Blood was filling up his lungs. He wheezed, "Tell . . . Moriarity . . . didn't know it was her . . . until too late . . ."

The relentless rain washed over his face and body as his muscles relaxed, and he went limp.

I lunged for his gun.

Before I could reach it, two men grabbed me by the arms, ripped the dagger from my hand, and roughly dragged me toward the yellow gleam.

"You have what you want, let me go! I have to go take care of my friend!"

The big soldier replied, "Dally's dead."

I felt like my guts had been kicked out.

Though I roared and fought like a wildcat against their iron hands, they dragged me toward the temple. The worst part was their eyes. Cold and hard, they resembled black stones set in their faces. These were not men, but machines following orders. Obviously, they'd been told to capture, not kill, me. Why? They had the dagger. Why did they still need me?

When we reached the rim of the temple, I gaped at the light flooding from the tunnel. My tunnel. The temple bricks turned to glass in the lightning flashes.

"Get down there. He wants to see you."

"Who?" I cried. "Who wants to see me?"

The big man shoved me toward the wet steps. "Move."

Holding my hands over my head, I felt my way down the steps one at a time. Running with water, it was like skating on black ice. My feet kept slipping, but I knew I had to stay on my feet. The big soldier was two steps behind me with a gun in his hand. All around, tiny waterfalls poured down the temple walls. How deep was the water on the floor? Had the newly excavated tunnel and corridor flooded?

When I hit bottom, I heaved a shaky breath. The other soldier remained at the top of the stairs with his rifle. Whatever their reason for keeping me alive so far, it would end.

"Walk to the tunnel."

I walked.

As we got closer, the soldier said, "Stop," and shoved the dagger into my hand. "Go now."

I blinked at the dagger, then up at him, not understanding at all.

"Move, boy. Into the tunnel."

When I entered, I heard voices.

Bracing myself, I started my journey down into the mythical Kingdom of Osiris. Maybe that's why Cleo had been down here? She had just walked up a few steps from the land of the dead to meet me. *Where are you, Cleo? When the time arrives, please come for me?*

The tunnel was sweltering, much hotter than the cool rainy air above. An exotic fragrance wafted around me, and I wondered if it were incense rising up from a long-vanished world. The deeper I went, the stronger it became. Strange. Like a blend of cedar oil and cinnamon.

I hit the last step and stood looking down the corridor at the square of orange, like candlelight slipping around the edges of a door. The dagger in my hand warmed up. Probably just picking up the heat of the air, but it knew something I did not. I forced my shaking legs to continue. Thirty feet.

The faint outline of the door came clear. It was unadorned, rough-hewn, heavy, but surely not the entry to the tomb of a royal member of the Ptolemaic dynasty. A pile of crumbling plaster lay mounded on the floor to the left of the door, refuse left by hasty workers trying to see what lay behind the dead-end wall.

I glanced back at the junction with the tunnel. The curious cartouches were little more than oval patches of gray that seemed to float disconnected from the wall, suspended on the pale light.

Why had no one followed me down here?

They want me to see something.

Marching forward, I shoved the heavy door. It creaked open on its hinges. The sudden glare made me squint. The radiance came from the combined glow of dozens of small oil lamps situated in niches around the walls of the chamber.

My mouth fell open.

Dust shrouded everything, but not even millennia could tarnish the glory.

The octagonal room spread around one hundred feet across, and the ceiling soared at least thirty feet over my head. I could see other chambers receding into the darkness beyond the lamplight. Every square inch of the walls was brilliantly painted with red, white, green, and black hieroglyphics. To my left, a line of figures in white robes, accompanied by animal-headed gods, carried offering bowls toward a seated pharaoh . . . Cleopatra in the guise of Isis.

My gaze scanned the life-size marble statues that stood on each wall of the octagon. They cast fluttering shadows across the walls and ceiling. I recognized Osiris, Set, and Isis. And Ammut. Standing on her hippopotamus' hindquarters, she was the largest statue. She loomed over the others, as though in charge of this affair. The other statues, of gods I did not recognize, wore coiled cobra headdresses. The serpents' heads were up, their jeweled eyes flashing at me as though curious about my identity. Everywhere, gold and silver blazed. Despite the dust, it was almost blinding. The gilded masks, heavy shields and necklaces, armbands, were all made of gold, inlaid with silver and gaudy jewels. King Tut's stunning tomb was shabby in comparison. I couldn't believe I was standing . . .

My breath caught.

I've seen this before. At Actium . . . just before I walked up to speak with Cleopatra . . . the marble statues, the aching loneliness . . .

My gaze drifted to the figure lying flat on its back on the table in the center of the chamber. It was a mummy, but it had not been prepared as such. There were no wrappings. The mummification had been accomplished by Egypt's climate. He was a big man. Tall and broad-shouldered. His skin had dried and shrunken over the bones, leaving a gaping mouth and dark empty eye sockets.

With the high water table in Pelusium, how could this chamber still be intact? The entire place should be filled with water and mildew, the corpse nothing but a mound of mold. Then I remembered what Moriarity had said about the ancient priests and their great magic. Had they sealed this chamber with magical spells to protect it?

Muffled sounds.

Somewhere in the temple above.

Walking closer, I stood at the mummy's side. A ceramic cartouche, matching those in the corridor outside, hung around the neck, as though announcing his identity to everyone who entered this chamber. As though waking from a dream, I finally understood: Dionysus. The ecstasy-inducing god of wine and revelry.

On his way to Tarsus in 41 BC, Antonius had been hailed as the New Dionysus.

The man's hands had been folded over the chest and covered with a rectangular shield about a meter long. Called a *scutum*, it curved to protect the soldier's body during battle. The clothing could not have been plainer. As though hastily dressed, the mummy wore a simple royal purple sheath and sandals. A rip zigzagged down the left side of the sheath. To my uninformed eyes, it looked freshly done. But what did I know? Ancient fabric was fragile. A spot of oil, a ray of sunlight, or the feet of a beetle could contaminate the weave and, over time, it would unravel and crumble to dust.

Awe swelled my chest until I thought it would burst wide open. That day on the bench outside of Starbucks, Cleo said she'd betrayed Antonius before Actium. The only thing that made sense was that Cleopatra had ordered this tomb built in secret long before his death, perhaps a year or more in advance. She knew what she had to do to save her nation, and it broke her heart, but she had built an extraordinary monument for the man she loved . . . the man she had already betrayed to his enemies, and would betray again, at the bitter end. Perhaps she'd hoped to join him here, but Octavian had left her no . . .

Voices. Closer this time.

I didn't have long.

Walking around the table, I noticed metallic flickers at the mummy's right side. Reverently, I lifted the edge of the sheath to look at the source. A *gladius,* the Roman short sword of choice, lay next to the desiccated body. About twenty inches long, it had a double-edged blade. The handle was bronze, inlaid with silver geometric shapes that had tarnished over the centuries. Nonetheless, it was beautiful.

Boots in the corridor . . .

Sweating profusely, my hand was slippery. I took a new grip on the sacred dagger that I believed had belonged to Cleopatra; it was the dagger she had carried at her waist when I'd seen her standing on the hill overlooking Actium. "Help me, Cleo."

The door creaked open, and a tall man stepped through. He let the door fall closed behind him. He'd changed clothes. Now he wore a crisply ironed white shirt and cream-colored slacks. Not the attire of a police officer. This was a businessman. I suspected his gold watch would pay my college tuition at Harvard for four years.

Stunned, I opened my mouth to say something, but no words came out.

"Are you well, Halloran?"

He slowly walked forward to stand on the opposite side of the mummy's table. Black hair fell over his forehead in damp wisps.

"Wh--what do you want, Sattin?"

"Your help."

"What?"

There was no movement in his eyes, no soul, only glacial silence eons deep. Inhuman eyes that saw, but didn't really see. That's what scared me. To this ghost of a man, I was simply a momentary illusion like a trick of the mind to be soon ignored.

As though trying not to frighten me, he lifted his hands and held them, palms open, in front of him. "I want you to know it wasn't my idea to kill Cleopatra Mallawi."

"You killed her? You? She hadn't done anything to anyone!"

His frozen eyes reflected the flickering lamplight like mirrors.

Slowly, he lowered his hands and reached over to pull open the mummy's sheath where it had been ripped. He stared unmoving, his immobility so complete I wondered if he'd been trained to do that. To go still and silent, to blend with the desert, maybe while enemy soldiers passed by only yards away. "Did you look?"

I shook my head. It was a spastic motion. Except for when he spoke, he didn't seem to be breathing.

"You should look. You will understand, I think." Lifting the ancient fabric more, he gestured for me to peer beneath.

The light was wrong. I had to shift positions to see. Walking down the table with the dagger clutched tightly in my fist, my breathing sounded like a freight train chuffing up a steep mountain pass. When I had the angle right, I risked taking my eyes off him to stare at the mummy's body. A gash slit the left side just below the ribs, as though the man had been stabbed.

"You think that . . . that's where he thrust the gladius into his body?" I asked in a shaking voice.

He dropped the fabric and leisurely smoothed it back into place. "I think it was a final act of love. She knew Octavian would parade his corpse through the streets of Rome, so she staged a burial in Alexandria, then had her servants sneak his body out and bring him here where he would be safe." The words never disturbed the absolute stillness of his body. His hands remained on the mummy as though part of the weave. "It must be Antonius."

"Why am I alive?"

"I told you. I need your help. That's why I returned the dagger to you. As a sign of good faith."

The chamber wavered around me. Several of the lamps spluttered out, plunging the corners into shadow. As the marble statues went dim, they seemed to grow smaller and smaller, receding into another darker world.

"Help how?"

Sattin blinked once. "You know where her grave is, don't you?"

"Cleopatra's grave?"

"Of course."

"No."

That dreadful lack of motion returned. His manicured hands resting on the mummy were dead white against the ancient purple linen. It was like being stared at by an alien lizard.

He removed one hand from the mummy and extended it to me. "Then give me the queen's dagger. You won't be needing it."

"So, if I don't know where her grave is, you're going to kill me?"

He just kept his hand out, waiting.

For several moments, I clutched it to my heart, while I tried to count the number of voices in the corridor outside. Two? Three? More than enough to take care of me.

When I reached beneath the shield and tucked the dagger into Antonius' mummified fingers, Sattin didn't even blink. He just withdrew his hand. Now, if they wanted the bagsu, they would have to take it from the hands of the man who had loved her more than life itself.

Picking up the ancient gladius, I backed across the room. Which was totally insane. I should just go with them. But I figured I was dead either way, so I might as well die on my feet fighting like a man. Somehow, I knew that would matter to Antonius.

"An old sword will do you no good," Sattin said.

Gripping the gladius in both hands, I spread my feet, preparing myself. "Why do you want to find her grave?"

Amusement glittered far back in his eyes. "I have heard that you're trying to release her, to free her from this world so she can go to the afterlife. Is that correct?"

"Says who?"

Sattin casually dragged the fingers of his left hand along the table as he walked around it and took a step toward me. "Why would you throw away your life to save someone who has been dead for over two thousand years? It's beyond foolish."

Faint cries penetrated the chamber. Sattin stopped and cocked his head, as though trying to identify where they'd come from.

"Give me the gladius, Halloran. You don't even know how to use it." He took another step toward me.

The cries rose and fell as though riding the storm winds like falcons, soaring closer.

The voices in the corridor stopped.

Sattin heaved an annoyed breath. "All right. I'll do this the hard way." Over his shoulder, he called. "Come in."

The heavy door swung open and LaSalle entered, flanked by two soldiers.

Seeing her was like being bludgeoned.

I shouted, "Did you kill Cleo? The police said she fought with a woman."

She took a step toward me. "Hal, it wasn't supposed to go down like that. She fought, and then she ran."

"You . . . You killed her? You killed my Cleo?"

"Not me, personally. We were struggling and when she got the upper hand and my guard Malik . . . Well, it was accident. The simple truth is that we couldn't scare her into giving us the medallion, and she was stronger than she looked."

This had to be an inhuman nightmare. I leaned my shoulder against the statue of Isis and locked my shaking knees. "Why are you doing this? Just tell me why."

Sattin quietly took another step forward. As did the soldier. They were boxing me in between Isis and Set. "That dagger is worth a fortune, Halloran. And more than a fortune if we can offer it along with the documented mummy of Cleopatra VII. We're talking maybe five hundred million dollars."

Gunshot . . .

Sattin glanced toward the sound but didn't seem upset.

I swear, the statue of Set to my right moved. Like molten gold in the fluttering lamplight, the god's hand twitched.

"You're involved in an antiquities looting ring? This was all about money? You killed Cleo for money?"

"Everything is about money," Sattin said. "And looting Egypt is very, very lucrative."

"LaSalle, I can't believe that you would sell off a nation's heritage."

"Well, Hal," she said with a small smile. "A museum administrator's salary is pretty paltry. Now, don't make us hurt you. I don't want the same thing to happen to you that happened to Cleo."

To make the point, the big soldier fingered his gun. "Let's be done with this. He killed Malik. Let me shoot him."

LaSalle shook her head. "He knows the location. I'm telling you. I don't know how, but he has the same gift that Samael had. The dead speak to him."

"Did you kill Samael?" My voice was shaking.

"The old man died of a heart attack," the soldier said. "He wouldn't talk, and when I aimed my rifle at his head, he grabbed his chest and fell over." To make the point, the soldier lifted his rifle and aimed it at my head.

Carefully, so as not to force me into doing something stupid—which I was about to do—Sattin ambled forward as though he hadn't a care in the world. When he stood less than a pace in front of me, he said, "Go ahead. Strike me down with the sword. You don't have the guts. You're a soft American child."

I positioned myself to thrust with the gladius and extended the weapon, prepared to do battle. The big soldier edged another step closer, his finger on the trigger of the rifle. "Don't push me! I— "

Swift as lightning, Sattin leaped forward and knocked the gladius from my hands, sending it cartwheeling across the floor. Which I was pretty sure would not have impressed Antonius.

An unearthly far-off roar shook the chamber. As people looked around anxiously, I grabbed for the statue of Set to stay on my feet. It felt strangely warm, lifelike. Mutters broke out when my enemies started asking one another questions.

"It's the demon," I said.

Sattin laughed, but it was an uneasy sound. "This isn't Halloween, boy. Just a bad storm."

"Then why are you so afraid?"

"It is you, I think, who are afraid, and you should be."

"I'm telling you, it's Ammut. She's coming."

Sattin stepped forward and knocked my forehead with his fist. "I've heard you're a crazy kid. I think your demons are up here, Halloran Stevens."

That struck home a little too hard. My head pounded. "We're all on the same side now. We have to get out before she gets here."

"No one is on your side."

The roar became a harmonic shriek, like a thousand voices crying out at once as they rushed toward us.

"I'm telling you—"

"Enough," Sattin said. "No more stalling. No more ghost stories. Shut up, and take me to her grave."

He gripped my arm and hurled me toward the corridor.

"Corbelle, don't forget the bagsu. It's under the shield, in the mummy's hands."

Her head turned to look. "In his hands?"

"Yes. The boy put it there."

Licking her lips, she sucked in a breath, as though worried about that task. "All right."

"Get the door," Sattin ordered the big soldier.

The man trotted forward and swung open the heavy door as La-Salle walked toward the mummy.

"Can't you feel her presence?" I cried as Sattin shoved me into the wind-swept corridor. Rivulets of rain trickled down the floor.

"Move, child. I have no patience for weakness."

My stomach cramped. I walked, staying close to the wall in case my feet slipped in the water. When a gust of wind swept around the corner and blasted us, I flattened against the wall, but Sattin staggered.

Which gave me the chance I'd been waiting for: I ran.

With every ounce of strength in my body, I fled up that corridor like a hunted animal, gasping in terror, waiting for the impact of the bullet.

When I hit the tunnel, I leaped up the stairs two at a time, my teeth chattering so hard I was sure my jaw was going to . . .

The scream from the chamber below was inhuman, wavering up and down the scale as though being torn from the throat by a rusty hook. My spine stiffened as adrenaline surged through me.

Sattin and the soldier hit the bottom stair just as I charged out into the storm lashing the temple. Rain fell so hard I couldn't see my hand in front of my face. I had no idea where I was. *Run straight across. Keep moving!*

Bulling forward was like drowning. I was sinking away from my own mind, floundering in the wind. My thoughts unraveled into disconnected strings around me.

Stray words, five paces away.

And then different sounds pierced the horror. Like clothes flapping. Something was struggling out there. Close by.

Grunts and whimpers. I couldn't tell where they came from.

Move. Keep staggering forward.

The flapping stopped. I heard a zipper unzipping. Fingernails clawed against nylon.

Pressure mounted behind my eyes as wind sucked the air from my lungs.

Hurricane. Had to be.

I felt fingers rake my leg and graze down the side of my pants.

Without warning, something grabbed my ankle. That quickly, it had me. Talons closed around my leg, and the terrifying weight crawled higher, and clung to my thigh. It hung from me, pulling itself up until it could grab my shirt and hiss in my ear. *"Get down! Be still!"*

I threw myself to the temple floor.

We lay side-by-side in water that almost covered our prone bodies.

Sobbing without making a sound, I could only think the words, *Roberto, they told me you were dead.*

CHAPTER FORTY-FOUR

R oberto grabbed my arm, as though signaling me to be quiet.
I couldn't have spoken if I'd wanted to. Symphonic calls
flowed and ebbed on the wind, powerful, hushed, as though the long-
dead gods of ancient Egypt had risen and were riding on the flashes
of lightning just visible through the downpour. The thunder of their
ghostly chariots rolled through my chest.

A gun boomed!

Someone shouted. Sattin?

My whole body became a mass of quaking muscles.

Then. Movement . . . to my left.

It glowed turquoise through the wall of water, coming out of the
tunnel as though emerging from the primordial waters of chaos that
had existed before the world was born. Once again, Set lived. Red-
haired. Vastly taller than the being I'd seen in Colorado, pointed
teeth shone in the crocodile head. One of the most ancient of Egypt's
gods, the brother of Isis, Set took great monstrous strides across the
temple.

Roberto's hand clamped around my wrist so hard I feared he
might break my arm.

"*Hal?* What—"

"Keep your head down!" I yelled.

The temple shuddered as the constant roll of thunder grew deaf-
ening.

Sattin let out a hoarse scream and backed up against the hieroglyphic panel as Set reached for his throat.

The big soldier fired his pistol at Set, and cried, "Get out of there!
Colonel, run!"

Set ripped Sattin's head from his body and tossed it on the ground, then swung around to face the soldier. The man appeared to be in shock. His gun fell from his hand, and one long cry escaped from him before Set tore out his throat.

Then he vanished. Just vanished.

An eerie hush descended.

"We have to get out of here!" Roberto said.

"Not yet. Wait!"

It was as though the tornado had twisted away, or the eye of the hurricane was passing over the top of us. Sattin and the body of the big soldier lay crumpled like paper dolls at the base of the hiero-glyphic panel. Their disembodied heads still rocked where they lay beneath the figure of Cleopatra dressed as Isis. Overhead, black clouds rumbled and flashed as they moved on, sailing south out into the desert. The air reeked of ozone.

For five minutes, both of us lay there quaking in the pool of shallow water.

"Hal?" Roberto finally said, struggling to sit up. "I'm hurt. Can you help me?"

Around his right thigh, a widening pool of blood spread out through the six inches of water that covered the floor of the temple. And the bullet graze on his head was still pouring blood down his face.

"Oh, my God."

Lunging for his arm, I helped him sit up, then I frantically scrambled around through the water to get to his right side where I could see his leg wound better. The bullet had gone clean through the outside of his thigh, high up near the hip. "Thank God, it didn't hit the femoral artery, but you need a hospital, Roberto. How on earth did you walk over here?"

Roberto shifted a pistol to his left hand, and I realized it had belonged to Corporal Bektash. "Had to. You were in trouble. Get me out of this swimming pool, okay?"

Pulling him to his feet as gently as I could, I wrapped his arm over my shoulder and headed for the stairs.

Each step was a waterfall. I had to be careful, take it slow, which was agonizing for Roberto. At the top, I saw the dead soldier who'd stood guard up here.

"That's the gunshot I heard when I was in the chamber?"

Wincing against the pain, Roberto nodded. "Yeah." He squinted at the dead man and seemed stunned. Guilt tortured his expression.

"Thanks, buddy."

Through gritted teeth, he said, "Let me sit down now, Hal, okay? I can't walk anymore."

I eased him to the wet ground and knelt beside him. The first veils of morning sunlight poured through the clouds, falling across Pelusium in bars and streaks of fallow gold. The entire site was a glittering shallow lake.

Reaching down, I ripped open his blood-soaked jeans where the bullet had torn them. Thank God, it had not struck the bone. "I'm going to make a bandage, then carry you to the emergency phone and call an ambulance. Hold on."

Removing my shirt, I tore it into strips and wrapped the wound. The entire time, my eyes kept returning to the temple, waiting for Corbelle to step out of the tunnel.

"Who are you looking for, Hal?"

"Corbelle. She was in the temple." I had to bite back a sob before I could say, "One of her guards, Malik, killed Cleo."

"She told you that?"

I nodded. As I tied off the ends of the bandage, Roberto lost his balance and fell sideways onto one elbow.

"Not . . . doing so well." He swayed, clearly on the verge of passing out.

"You've lost a lot of blood. Just hold on. I'm going to get help."

I grabbed my best friend, lifted him over my shoulder, and staggered to my feet.

CHAPTER FORTY-FIVE

O nce they'd loaded Roberto into the ambulance, I tried to get
into the rear with him, but the emergency tech said, "No, no
room," and pulled the door closed in my face.

Watching the ambulance drive away with the tires flinging mud,
I felt even more alone than I usually did. My blood beat a dull rhythm
in my ears. For a few seconds, I just stood there.

The police would be here soon. I could hear their *ooo-ah* sirens
blaring in the distance. I'd also called Moriarity, but it would take
him at least another hour to get here. He'd taken Sophia to the Alexandria Hilton for the night.

Turning, my feet hewed a dark swath across the mud as I walked
back to the temple and trotted down the steps. Most of the water had
soaked in, but about an inch remained on the floor. Splashing through
it, I cast only a glance at the dead bodies beneath the hieroglyphs.

When I reached the tunnel, I hesitated, frightened to enter, but
only for a second. If the old gods hadn't killed me when I was lying on
the floor of the temple, I figured they weren't going to kill me now.

At the corridor, I sucked in a deep breath and reached for my
flashlight. Switching it on was an event. Shreds of mist crawled
along the wet floor, probably born of the cold rain colliding with the
hot corridor, but they seemed alive, creeping toward the ajar door at
the end where lamplight still flickered.

"Dr. Corbelle? Can you hear me?"

Water sparkled as it ran in braided streams toward the chamber.

"LaSalle?"

When I eased open the door and peered into the chamber, I saw
that about two inches of water had accumulated on the floor. In the

gleam of the three oil lamps that still burned, the pool rippled, casting luminous reflections over the chamber.

Wading forward, I saw the dead body beside the mummy's table.

The sight stunned me. I wasn't sure it was her. The body had
swollen hideously. Her neck looked like it had been wrenched back,
and her jaws pried open. In places, her skin had ruptured and the
flesh burst out. The gladius rested nearby, and I wondered if she'd
sliced open the skin herself.

"What happened?" I whispered as I slogged forward and picked
up the ancient weapon.

Tearing my gaze away, I shone my flashlight around the rest of
the room. Everything was exactly as it had been, except the shield
over the mummy's chest was resting at an angle. She must have
knocked it sideways when she'd reached for the dagger.

I approached him reverently and placed the gladius at his side on
the table. "I'm sorry, Antonius. You won't understand this for a while,
but please trust me."

When I lifted the beautifully painted red shield to look for the
bagsu, something slithered.

"What. . . !"

Dropping the shield, I shuffled away until my back hit the wall.
Right in front of me, an Egyptian cobra lifted its head to stare at me
with bizarre shining eyes. It flicked its tongue.

Petrified, I couldn't move. The snake was absolutely lethal. It
must have crawled in during the storm and . . .

As I watched, the cobra slithered across the shield and down the
table into the water. It swam across the floor, and headed for the
statue of Set, where it lovingly coiled around the god's feet, like a pet
or a supernatural companion.

Carefully, I lifted the shield to look beneath it, then grabbed the
dagger and tucked it in my pocket. Convinced that my next act was
insane, I nonetheless ran the gladius through my belt and lifted the
mummy into my arms—it was feather light.

I carried him up the corridor as quickly as possible, then slogged
across the wet temple outside, and climbed the stairs to look out at

the wet site of Pelusium. The amphitheater and the standing marble columns literally shimmered.

The police were close. I could see three cars headed toward the field camp, less than ten minutes away.

It took five minutes to reach our tent and wrap the mummy in my sleeping bag.

By the time the police arrived, I was waiting for them in the parking lot. Most of the lake had evaporated or soaked in, leaving behind a delicate embroidery, as if the ground and ruins were netted all over with liquid silver spiderwebs.

So far as I knew, I was the only living person who had seen the mummy. . . .

CHAPTER FORTY-SIX

S itting in the white hospital room, watching Egyptian soap operas on the TV was about as interesting as watching Roberto's mother rearrange his bedcovers for the thousandth time. They'd flown in that morning, along with my parents, and had been hovering ever since.

"Doctor says he's going to be okay, Martha," Roberto's father, a tall brown-haired man, said. "Stop fussing with his blankets. You'll wake him. He needs his sleep."

Mrs. Dally straightened with tears in her eyes. "Are they sure he'll be able to walk again?"

"You heard the doctor, same as I did. Yes, he'll walk. Now, come on. Let's go find a cup of coffee and something to eat."

Mrs. Dally turned to me. "Will you stay with him, Hal? Till we get back?"

"Sure, Mrs. Dally."

"All right." She reluctantly turned toward the door. Mr. Dally put his arm around her and guided her down the hall, speaking softly to her.

The soap opera stars spoke way too fast for my limited Egyptian. Sometimes I caught a word or a phrase, but mostly I couldn't understand much. I reached for the remote to turn off the sound, and idly listened to people hurrying by in the corridor outside, while I thought about the past few days.

By the time Moriarity arrived back at the site, the police had been all over the tomb and temple. They'd kept asking me about the mutilated bodies. How had they been decapitated and ripped in half? Obviously, they didn't believe me and Roberto when we said the rain had been so heavy we hadn't seen a thing. But what were we supposed to tell them? Not the truth, that was for sure.

"Hey, Hal?" Roberto said without opening his eyes. "You still here?"

"I'm not the only one who's here. Your hospital room has been Grand Central. Your parents, my parents, Moriarity, Sarah. Half the field crew has been here to stare at you."

"Yeah? Am I a hero?"

"More like a reality show star. Nobody really likes you, but they can't take their eyes off you."

He smiled.

After three days, one surgery, and enough antibiotics to heal a horse, he was doing better. An IV slowly dripped into his arm while he dozed. He was going to have a great scar over his right ear from the bullet graze, but the doctors said his leg would heal up nicely.

"How you doing?" I asked. "You hungry?"

"I could eat a dead cat."

"Nurse was by a little while ago. Said your lunch is coming."

"Good to kn . . ." His eyes widened. "Hey, turn up the TV. Your favorite person is on the news."

I turned to see Moriarity talking to a woman reporter.

Grabbing the remote, I turned up the sound. It was in English.

"Dr. Moriarity, the police are lauding you as the hero of the day for breaking up a major illegal antiquities ring. What was your first clue that your colleague, Dr. LaSalle Corbelle, was an antiquities smuggler?"

Moriarity was in his element. The limelight. In his dusty fedora, he looked very much like an older version of Indiana Jones.

"Well, Miss Ragab, it was the missing artifacts that first tipped me off. Some of our best finds went missing and ended up being sold on the open market. The only person that made sense was my colleague from the Royal Ontario Museum. So I planted my students on her crews to watch her and report back to me if they saw anything—"

Like Tashir.

"I guess he's as famous as Lord Carnivore now, huh?" Roberto asked.

Turning down the sound, I set the remote on the bedside table. "Carnarvon. Yeah, for the moment."

Roberto looked out the door, and lowered his voice. "Speaking of spectacular finds . . ."

He let the sentence dangle, because it wasn't necessary to finish it.

"In a safe place," I answered.

Roberto shoved the sheet off his chest, and straightened his blue hospital gown. He just stared at the quiet TV for a while.

"Then what, Hal?"

I took a breath and let it out slowly. "When you're better, we take a trip. Sarah's been great. Without her, I don't know where I'd have stowed the mummy."

"She hid the mummy for you?"

"Yeah. In one of the big storage boxes on the site. I didn't have anyone else to turn to. She's okay, Roberto. Didn't even hesitate."

A broad grin brightened his face. "Yeah? Knew I liked her."

As though another thought had occurred to him, his smile faded. After a few deep breaths, he turned away to look hollowly at the corridor outside where people hustled by. "I keep reliving it, do you?"

"Yeah. Sure, I do."

"God, Hal, I keep trying to figure out if I could have saved you without killing someone, but I don't see how."

The guilt must be smothering him, just as it was me. In my dreams, I went over it again and again, struggling not to kill Malik. "If you hadn't fired when you did, I'd be dead, Roberto. And probably so would you."

"Guess so. I just wish . . ."

"*You're awake!*" Mrs. Dally cried and rushed back into the room. Mr. Dally and my parents hurried in behind her. As she leaned over the bed to kiss Roberto's forehead, Mrs. Dally said, "My God, I'm never letting you out of my sight again. Do you hear me?"

"I thought you wanted me to go away to college. Far away."

"Not anymore." She was crying when she carefully slipped her arms around Roberto and hugged him. "I've decided I'm going to tie a rope around your neck and drag you with me everywhere I go for the rest of your life."

Roberto gave her a big hug. "Oh, that sounds like fun, Mom."

My father walked over and stood beside my chair. Resting a hand on my shoulder, he gave it a squeeze. "You all right, Hal?"

"Yeah, Dad. Did you get your plane tickets rebooked?"

He nodded. "All taken care of. We're leaving day after tomorrow. And we'll see you in ten days, right?"

"Right. How did Mom take the news that I wouldn't be flying home with you?"

Dad turned his head to look at Mom where she stood near the door speaking with Mr. Dally. "I told her you're a man now, and we have to treat you like one. She didn't even argue."

I stared at my mom. Mr. Dally was apparently having a serious conversation with her about Roberto's psychology, because he kept glancing in at his son, then whispering to Mom.

I reached up to grip my father's hand where it rested on my shoulder. "Thanks, Dad."

CHAPTER FORTY-SEVEN

Three weeks later . . .

I dreamed of sunlight.

And then I woke, and the sunlight was real. I could feel it warming the nylon of my windbreaker. For a while, I drifted, listening to the wind rustle through the palm fronds. Dawn had just touched the desert. Far out in the distance, luminous veils of sand blew across the dunes.

"You awake?"

"Just."

Roberto stood ten feet away with his shoulder leaned against the trunk of an ancient olive tree. The blossoms were gone now, though shriveled petals created a ring around the green pond at the oasis Samael had loved so much. Roberto was doing well. His leg had healed, and he was getting stronger by the day, but yesterday's hike had been the first real test of his endurance. When we'd arrived at dusk, he'd been exhausted, limping. The stars had been so magnificent we'd slept outside and talked long into the night while we'd stared at them.

"How you feeling this morning?"

"Sore. Nothing major."

His brown beard had grown out, but he'd cut his hair short after he got out of the hospital. He seemed older. Of course, part of that was the new look in his blue eyes. Some of the old fun was gone, replaced by a harder edge.

"You said you wanted to start at dawn."

"I do." I got to my feet.

The mummy rested inside the mouth of Samael's cave, shrouded with sunlit glitters. It had been over two thousand years since he'd awakened in the morning sunlight, feeling the wind on his face. I wondered how he felt. Did he understand why we'd brought him here?

"I have the dagger. Can you get the gladius and the tools?"

"On it," Roberto said.

While he gathered the things we'd need, I walked over and lifted the mummy into my arms. The purple sheath was so fragile now. Threads crumbled beneath my fingertips as I carried him outside.

The walk along the cliff face was mostly silent. Roberto's steps padded behind me. Hawks circled overhead. I daydreamed of cobras.

When we reached the "demon" cave, I thought about Samael. No wonder he'd told everyone there was a demon locked in this cave. People out here believed such things. How many lifetimes had he spent protecting this place?

I gently lowered the mummy to the sand. "Let's dig out as much dirt as we can. That should give us enough space."

With both of us digging, it didn't take long to expose the bedrock and the hole beneath the board.

"Okay, Hal, this is big enough. Why don't you go first, and I'll slide the mummy through to you."

Warm darkness cocooned me when I crawled through. Digging into my pocket, I grabbed my flashlight and panned the beam across the gigantic hieroglyphic panel. My throat tightened with emotion. The huge ships, the countless rows of soldiers standing with lances in their hands . . . Why hadn't I made the connection when I'd first seen this panel? It was the Battle of Actium. My beam drifted to Ammut where she sat on her hippopotamus hindquarters with her crocodile jaws gaping wide at the figure of Cleopatra carrying a platter of food and a cup of wine to a kneeling man. Antonius, of course. They had clearly already been judged and their souls found too heavy to travel to the afterlife. Ammut was merely carrying out her duty to the gods. She was not evil. Just obedient.

"Here he comes, Hal."

I got on my knees and carefully pulled the mummy into the cave.

Lifting him in my arms, I stood up, leaving room for Roberto to crawl through.

"There's a breeze in here, Hal. Where's it coming from? Is there another entrance in the back of this cave?"

"Never made it all the way back. Let's find out."

"Wait a minute," he said frowning at the rows of ships painted on the wall. "What is that?"

"Battle of Actium, I think."

"Where Antonius abandoned his troops and chased after Cleopatra's flagship."

I nodded, and remembered his utter despair as he'd looked out over the giant encampment spreading across the Greek lowlands, his fear that Cleopatra was poisoning him. And his desperate love for her, even in the final moments of his life.

Gently holding his body against my chest, I started walking.

Within thirty paces, faint whispers eddied around us, and my skin started to tingle. Roberto didn't see the pyramid until his penlight beam flashed across it.

"My God," he whispered in awe.

I let my gaze climb upward through the thousands of lances, spears, swords, and daggers, encircled by the ring of dark oil lamps. With the beams of our two flashlights bouncing around the spectacular structure, it became an inferno of gold and flickering jewels.

"I need you to wait here with the gladius. Is that okay?"

"Sure." He spread his feet and cradled the Roman sword across his chest as though standing guard.

I walked deeper into the cave, past the throne where I'd found the dagger, and kept going until tongues of darkness licked at the boundary to the dark underworld of Osiris.

Roberto quietly watched me and waited.

When the hair on my arms began to rise, I heard the soft footsteps coming toward me.

"Hal?" Roberto whispered.

"It's all right. I understand now."

The steps halted right in front of me, and I smelled Cleopatra's perfume, as sweet and exotic in this enclosed cave as it had been in my bedroom two months ago. The urge to weep was so powerful I had to squeeze my eyes closed for a couple of seconds to compose myself. My voice sounded hoarse: "I brought him to you."

As I carried the mummy deeper into the cave, the darkness became crushing, swallowing my flashlight beam as though the battery was almost gone.

Then I saw her.

In a small chamber in the deepest part of the cave. By the time they'd brought her here, she'd been dead for days. They must have wanted to get it over with and get back to Alexandria and their rewards. Though, if I knew Gaius Julius, their rewards had been swift beheadings. A shrewd politician, he'd have left no witnesses.

"Did you find her?" Roberto called.

"Yeah . . . Yeah, I did."

"How do you know? Is she talking to you?"

"No. But I know it's her."

The small skeleton rested on its side. Her purple robes had faded to blue over time. She had begged to be buried with Antonius. Cleo had told me she couldn't bear to enter the afterlife without him.

Inhaling a deep breath, I knelt and eased the mummy to the floor, laying him beside her.

From where he stood by the pyramid, Roberto studied me with a curious expression. "Now what?"

"Now, I keep a promise."

As gently as I could, I eased the jeweled dagger into the tangle of her finger bones. My throat had constricted. It was hard to speak. "I'll always love you. You'll find your way now. Both of you. I know you will."

There was no tunnel of light, no appearance of ancient scary gods, no trumpets or fanfare. Which, I had to believe, was just as they would have wanted it.

Lonely, frightened, emptier than I had ever been, I rose to my feet and walked back toward Roberto.

As I curved around the shimmering pyramid of weapons, I felt like an angel tumbling from heaven with broken wings, spiraling down, the ground getting closer by the second, like I was fighting gravity.

I couldn't explain it.

"You're breathing weird, Hal. Everything okay?"

"Leaving her is harder than I thought." I didn't look back as I said, "Okay, your turn, Roberto. Samael's last request was that we add a weapon to this pyramid. Ready?"

"Yeah."

Carrying the gladius in both hands, Roberto stepped inside the ring of dark oil lamps, knelt, and carefully placed it across two lances.

As he rose and backed out of the ring, wind breathed through the pyramid like a thousand hushed voices sighing in unison.

Roberto's gaze darted around. "Hear that? What. . . ?"

Light exploded in the cave.

Roberto cried out and threw up an arm as he leaped backward away from the spinning whirlwind of sparks that whipped through the pyramid. When it reached the very peak, the whole structure roared up in flames, the heat unbearable, rubies, emeralds, gold, and silver blazing.

I thought Roberto might be yelling at me, but I couldn't hear him now.

In front of me, a blinding passageway extended into the sunlit distance, where a palm-covered island floated upon the Nile. A boat rested on the shore, bobbing as though waiting for the last passenger to arrive.

Barely audible, I said, "My God, it's been here all along. Samael guarded the entry, and her, his entire life. If only I'd walked deeper that day—"

Halloran?

Twenty feet away, she formed out of the sunlight, as though pulling golden threads together to weave her image. Wearing a white T-shirt and jeans, she had her hair tucked behind her ears.

"Cleo?"

As she walked toward me, tears blurred my eyes. Was this my

imagination, or was she truly there? For the moment, I didn't care. Happiness filled me.

She stopped in front of me. *I had to see you one last time. I love you, Halloran.*

I stepped forward and pulled her into my arms, holding her as though I'd never let her go. She felt real, warm and soft in my arms. Against her hair, I said, "I'll always love you, Cleo. Now, you'd better hurry. I don't know how long the passageway stays open."

When she backed away, it broke my heart.

Someday you will cross over the threshold and step on to the island alive and well, and I'll be waiting for you.

She turned and started walking toward the boat on the shore. I kept my eyes on her. I wanted to see her for as long as I could. At the far end of the tunnel, a big man stood beside the boat, waiting for her. He was dressed as a soldier now, in full regalia, with his helmet and shield, and his short sword glinting where it hung from his belt. Antonius.

Cleo turned one last time and gave me the same loving smile she had that day on the bench in front of Starbucks. *I'll see you before you know it. It'll be less than a moment.*

As they stepped into the boat that would take them across the gulf that separated this world and the next, I whispered, "Less than a moment."

Like a candle flame dying, the light fluttered and went out.

But a glow remained, and I realized my flashlight was still on.

I turned to look at Roberto standing beside the dark pyramid, and called, "Did you see any of that?"

"I saw the pyramid become a torch. Is that what you mean?"

I bowed my head for a long time.

At last, Roberto said, "I'm tired, Hal. Let's go home."

"*Ginest-hoi, bro.*"

CHAPTER FORTY-EIGHT

Passing the magnificent hieroglyphic story of the Battle of Actium without a second glance, I got down on my hands and knees and crawled out into the brilliant water-scented sunlight.

Roberto slid through on his belly and sat on the sand beside me for a while. "I'm nailing the board back in place. You fill the hole."

When we'd finished, we picked up the few belongings we'd brought with us, and started hiking across the desert to the Jeep Sarah had left for us when she'd flown home a few days ago. The rental was up tomorrow night, a couple of hours before we were scheduled to board our plane to Colorado.

By the time the Jeep came into sight, the sand was dragging at my feet. I turned around to see how Roberto was faring.

"You okay?"

"Yeah. Thinking, that's all." I suspected he'd suffer some pain-filled nights for helping me carry out this one last duty to the dead.

"'Bout what?"

"Well." He shrugged. "You remember when Samael said I was a shabti and I'd know what to do when the time came?"

"Yeah."

"I did, Hal. I knew just what to do."

I blinked, kept walking. The Jeep was just ahead, sitting off the side of the road covered with dust. I pulled the keys from my pocket. After we'd thrown our stuff in the back, Roberto tugged on the leather cord around his neck to draw out the fabulous medallion. He'd started wearing it as a pendant in the hospital.

I said, "So do you think you're Cleopatra's servant in this world or Antonius'?"

"I'm not saying I believe this stuff," he acted embarrassed that he'd mentioned it. "Just . . . What happens when a shabti's duties are fulfilled in this world?"

"No idea."

"Well, what if I vanish into thin air and return to the Island of the Two Flames to continue being a servant in the afterlife?"

"There's nothing you can do about it, so why worry?"

He shoved the medallion back inside his shirt, and we both got into the Jeep. Dust boiled up behind us as we headed to the airport in Port Said.

Roberto rode with one elbow hanging out the window while he watched the passing desert.

Seven hours later, the glow of Port Said rose into the vast bowl of Egyptian stars.

"Hal? Tell me the truth. What was that in the temple? You saw it, too. I know you did. We haven't talked about it, but—"

"'Course, I saw it."

"What was it?"

Matter-of-factly, I answered, "Set, ancient god of war, brother of Isis."

Roberto slouched in his seat and folded his arms across his chest. "It was kind of like he was protecting us. I mean, that's what it looked like to me."

I didn't answer. Didn't know what to say.

Roberto made an airy gesture with his hand. "Do you think he wanted to help us free Cleopatra and Antonius from this world? Is that why he killed our enemies? Did he talk to you?"

"Didn't say a word to me. But he was definitely protecting us."

For the next thirty minutes, Roberto drummed his fingers on his arms and shifted in his seat.

Finally, he said, "What do you plan to do for the rest of the summer?"

"Don't know. You?"

"Probably spend a month hiding under my covers, while I wallow in a sea of shallow thoughts."

"Let me know if you need toilet paper."

"Okay."

The one thing I did not want to do—could not do—was go back to my old life. I'd gazed into the sunlit afterlife with my own eyes. I knew, someday, I would step onto the Island of the Two Flames alive, as Samael had done, and find Cleo waiting for me. The longing to be there, with her, was a constant ache inside me. I just had to find an Egyptian magician to teach me how to cross over.

We pulled into the stream of airport traffic, parked the Jeep in the lot, and turned in the keys.

As we grabbed our backpacks from the rear, and headed for the door, Roberto heaved a breath. "Homeward bound, dude."

"Guess so."

After we'd checked in, we stopped to buy canned soft drinks and swerved through the crowds to find our gate.

"Can't be." Roberto craned his neck to look at something. "What's he doing here?"

"Who?"

When a gap opened in the crush of people, I saw Moriarity sitting at our gate, reading something on his phone. His fedora was shoved back on his head.

Moriarity jumped when Roberto dumped his backpack onto the floor two feet away. "Oh, sorry, I didn't see you boys coming."

Roberto took the chair to Moriarity's left, and I took the chair to his right. Most of the seats at our gate were still open, but it was a couple hours until our flight.

I said, "What are you doing here?"

Moriarity rearranged his glasses. "Just thought I'd see you off. My flight is actually leaving from another gate in four hours."

"Nice," Roberto said. "Thanks. Bye."

"Now, wait a second. I have a proposition for you."

Neither of us asked what it was.

Moriarity continued, "Listen, I know you found it. You found the way to the Island of the Two Flames, didn't you? Did you go there?"

Popping the top on my can of Coke, I let the question hang in the air for ten seconds, before I replied, "No."

Moriarity leaned toward me to whisper, "Come on, Hal. Tell me. How'd you get there? What was it like?"

I watched people passing by.

Moriarity said, "Okay, never mind. Forget I asked. The reason I'm here is because I have an excavation starting in the legendary temple city of Karnak in a month, and I need crew members who aren't afraid of visiting the land of the dead."

Roberto and I exchanged glances.

Roberto said, "You know we almost died on your last excavation, right?"

"Adversity builds character, and you are sorely in need of that, Robert. Besides, I think Hal wants to walk the halls of the dead as much as I do. That's what Karnak is all about. It's filled with secrets and hidden tunnels to other worlds."

Moriarity must have seen the gleam in my eyes. A knowing smile came to his lips. The professor slapped me on the shoulder. "Gotta go. I'll need your answer within the week."

He rose and walked away through the jostling crowd.

When he'd vanished, I moved into his chair.

Roberto gave me a bland look. "He's plotting to murder you after you show him how to find the Island of the Two Flames. You know that, right?"

"Oh, yeah." I took a long drink of my Coke and thought about it for a couple of seconds, before I said, "I'm in. You?"

"Absolutely."